HOLLOW

STRENGTH

Art Keller

Veritatem Cognoscere Press

Dedication

To the people of Iran, who await the arrival of a better day, the officers of the Central Intelligence Agency who, unknown and unthanked, toil ceaselessly in the second oldest profession, and finally, to the US Navy Fifth Fleet, which makes maintaining one of the highest operational tempos in the world look deceptively easy.

PROLOGUE

His wife summed it up almost twenty years ago, at the first work picnic he took her to. With a whisper that managed to convey amusement, Claire leaned into his ear and said, "You all look so ordinary."

Joe riposted with the gentle sarcasm he reserved for his wife alone.

"Gee, Honey, thanks. I'll be sure to mention that ringing endorsement to my boss. It'll help come promotion time."

Still, looking around the picnic, it was hard to argue her point. There was no shortage of balding, paunchy men, accompanied by women whose figures never came back after the last kid. Certainly there was nobody who, in the shorts and T-shirts appropriate for a picnic in the painfully muggy northern Virginia summer, gave the impression of being particularly menacing, debonair, or even smarter than the average plumber.

"You forget," Joe added, "The world is run by a cabal of mediocrity, of faceless gray men. We fit right in."

Claire lobbed back, "You mean appearing 'ordinary' is part of your 'cover'?"

Joe said, "Who said anything about cover?"

CHAPTER ONE-THE SUPREME LEADER

June 04 2014, Tehran, Iran

Captain Ali Reza Akhlagi of the Iranian Revolutionary Guard Corps Navy Destroyer "Shaheed" paced nervously in the Supreme Leader's anteroom. He was a tall, spare man in his late 40s, with iron gray hair and penetrating brown eyes. As with many Iranians in government service, Akhlagi felt compelled to cultivate a beard, but used the excuse of military necessity to keep the beard short and closely trimmed. Akhlagi hated beards, finding them itchy, but growing a beard was one of the lesser sacrifices he had made to attain his current position.

Akhlagi barely noticed the wonderful aroma wafting from a tea set containing a rare saffron-scented tea; a special blend reserved for those exalted few privileged to personally visit the reclusive Supreme Leader. The waiting room in which the Captain paced was strewn with a Shah's ransom of ancient hand-knotted silk rugs with the trademark muted red dyes and elaborate floral patterns that subtly proclaimed Isfahan origin. Eager to meet the Leader, but also a bit jumpy with tension, Akhlagi ignored the beauty of the luxurious appointments.

Even wealthy Iranians usually considered such rare antique rugs too fine to tread upon; the liberal use of museum-quality pieces proclaimed to visitors that the Supreme Leader had both access to staggering wealth and complete disregard for such "earthly concerns" as abuse of masterpieces of the Persian weaver's art. In anyone else's home, Akhlagi, with his Persian pride, would have considered the casual use of such national treasures a sign of excess. In the Supreme Leader's home, such a thought would never have crossed Akhlagi's mind.

Akhlagi was, by carefully cultivated reputation, one of the most loyal and dedicated officers of the post-1979 Revolution generation. Ongoing loyalty to the Islamic Revolution and the

Supreme Leader, increasingly rare in Iran, naturally played no small role in Akhlagi's recent selection as Captain of the Shaheed.

The Shaheed was the best ship to join the Iranian armed forces in decades. The fact that the ship was added to the ranks of the Revolutionary Guard Corps Navy rather than the rival Regular Navy had created bitter envy in the Regular Navy. One quid-pro-quo of winning command of the Shaheed was a transfer by Akhlagi from the Regular Navy to the more "theologically pure" Revolutionary Guard Corps Navy. The IRGC Navy, which usually used small attack boats, had no officers experienced at handling larger warships. To handle the Shaheed, the IRGC Navy had cherry-picked many of the best Iranian Navy officers and crewmen away, Akhlagi among them, with the enticing lure of serving on the most powerful warship in Iran.

Akhlagi's willingness to jump to the IRGC Navy, while it won him a certain grudging admiration for having deftly outmaneuvered potential rivals, also greatly increased the ranks of Akhlagi's detractors in the Iranian Navy. There were bushels of sour grapes over his move to the IRGC Navy, including entirely predictable but baseless rumors that Akhlagi's choice as Captain was entirely based on his ideological purity, rather than his allegedly "barely-adequate" ship-handling skills.

As he continued to pace nervously, all thoughts of the deal-making it took to land the Shaheed were now a million miles from Akhlagi's mind.

Strip away the loose-fitting, forest-green IRGC uniform, with its red collar tabs and black shoulder boards displaying the rank of Captain in gold thread, and any observer would have thought the Captain had just been given a long-hoped for son from a wife the doctors had proclaimed barren. Akhlagi was trying for an expression of quiet, dignified pride and failing miserably; a grin kept creeping onto his face.

This was an honor he couldn't wait to share with his family, friends, and fellow officers. In a society where prestige and connections to power can be worth more than any amount of money, a meeting with the Supreme Leader, especially coming on the heels of winning command of the Shaheed, could only be perceived by all as proof that his star was rapidly ascending.

In his excitement, it never occurred to Akhlagi to wonder why this secondary residence of the Supreme Leader seemed a virtual tomb, without the ring of sycophants and security personnel that would usually surround such an august personage.

Nor did he ask himself why the meeting was taking place at 11 p.m., or why it was taking place at this plush compound in Northern Tehran, instead of at the Supreme Leader's official residence in central Tehran.

Akhlagi's excited reverie was interrupted by the entrance into the anteroom of a middle-aged man impeccably dressed in the finest charcoal Italian-cut summer-weight silk suit. The man's suit, mirror-gloss shoes, manicured hands, and carefully coiffed hair largely obscured the assistant's paunch and other signs of high living. The exquisite outfit of the assistant, as well as his ultra-confident demeanor, spoke louder than words: the Leader's assistant knew proximity to the Supreme Leader conveyed immense influence.

"Captain Akhlagi, the Supreme Leader will see you now."

Now that the moment of the meeting was upon him, Akhlagi was gripped with a mild fear that finally helped him banish the grin. Smiling was for *after* the meeting with the great man; only a serious and reverent demeanor was suitable for meeting with the spiritual leader and temporal ruler of the Islamic Republic of Iran.

Suddenly Akhlagi found himself standing in front of the Supreme Leader as the assistant, who had not introduced himself, slipped unobtrusively through a door into an adjoining room. The Supreme Leader was reclining on a wide, low couch. This man's face had stared out at Akhlagi from a million posters across Iran, and now Akhlagi was seeing him in person. Akhlagi spoke the ritual greeting, "Salaam Alekum," and then stood mute, waiting for the Supreme Leader to respond. Akhlagi knew not to meet the eyes of his Supreme Leader, and so instead he looked at the lower part of the Supreme Leader's face.

What he saw there shocked him.

The Supreme Leader had the puffy, blackened lips of a habitual opium smoker. The Captain had heard rumors for years that the Supreme Leader and other senior Ayatollahs were regular users of opium, a practice strictly forbidden by Sharia, but one with a strong cultural tradition in Iran. Akhlagi had always assumed those rumors were lies spread by the Leader's detractors.

Now he was stunned to notice a vafour, a Persian opium pipe, next to the Supreme Leader's low couch. In keeping with the traditional elegance of the surroundings, the vafour boasted a gold-inlaid rosewood stem culminating in a bulbous bowl decorated with hair-thin platinum filigree. A glowing piece of charcoal sat on a brass plate near the pipe. Next to the charcoal were narrow metal tongs used to hold the charcoal on top of the bowl of the vafour; the charcoal's heat would literally vaporize the opium in the pipe bowl when a user inhaled.

Akhlagi kept respectfully silent to allow the Supreme Leader to speak when he so chose, but as he stood quietly, he could not help but notice the unmistakable scent of opium fumes hung in the air. He fervently hoped his shock at the Leader's behavior, particularly in view of Iran's rampant drug problems, did not show on his face.

Akhlagi risked a quick look at the Supreme Leader's eyes, and saw something he never expected to see: the Supreme Leader's gaze transforming in an instant from a stern glare to one of querulous confusion. With a look of sudden desperation, the Leader reached out for a bell sitting next to the vafour. The bell was a miracle of gold and silver, and inlaid with jade. The Leader began shaking it furiously and discordantly, while loudly calling, "Hamid, Hamid, where are you?"

The well-dressed assistant quickly reappeared and was at the side of the Supreme Leader in less than five seconds. The Supreme Leader said in theatrically hushed vocal tones that were probably meant to be a whisper, but which exceeded that mark by about 20 decibels: "Hamid, who is this man, and why is he here?"

Akhlagi saw an expression of worry flash over Hamid's face before the assistant was able to suppress it. Hamid replied with a real whisper into the Supreme Leader's ear, "Oh Wise One, this is Captain Akhlagi, who you appointed to command our glorious new ship, the Shaheed. You wanted to speak to him about plans for the maiden voyage of the Shaheed next week."

The Supreme Leader nodded as Hamid's explanation flowed into his ear, but Akhlagi noted that the stark confusion in the Supreme Leader's eyes only ebbed to a mild befuddlement, as if the Leader was now trying to remember a famous Sura of the Koran whose exact wording remained tantalizingly out of reach.

The Supreme Leader commanded Hamid in another not-whisper, "Tell him what is needed."

Hamid stood and assumed a grave demeanor. "Captain Akhlagi," Hamid began, "you have been given a singular honor, command of our finest ship, the Shaheed. Your service to date in the Regular Navy has been exemplary; you would not have been chosen to receive this high honor if it had not been. You were also chosen for another reason: as the son and brother of true Shaheeds, martyrs who defended the Islamic Republic against the cursed Hussein and his Babylonian thugs, you know that sometimes absolute obedience and supreme sacrifice are necessary to protect the strength and piety of the Revolution. The Glorious Revolution freed us from the chains of the Pahlavi dogs and began to prepare the way for the return of the most holy 12th Imam. Such glorious Shaheeds as your father and brother worked the will of Allah directly and are greatly rewarded in Paradise."

Hamid, gazing steadily at Akhlagi while giving this speech, noted an infinitesimal tremor of nervous fear in Akhlagi's eyes at Hamid's implication of the possibility of becoming a shaheed, a martyr.

While Akhlagi honored the memory of his father and brother, like professional military officers the world over, Akhlagi felt "martyrdom" was too often used to compensate for poor strategy and shoddy armament: "precision-guided" bombs *were* cheap, when the guidance system was a human brain. While Iran's swollen population presented no shortage of such raw material, Akhlagi did not transfer to the IRGC Navy to "win the opportunity" for martyrdom, but rather to advance his career. If that advancement required a consistent and fervent will to do anything for the Revolution and the Supreme Leader, so be it, such was the cost of advancement in a theocracy. How else was Akhlagi to assure his wife and children a comfortable life, and win his sons coveted slots to attend university? But *actual* martyrdom of a skilled senior officer would be a waste. Akhlagi was honest enough to admit to himself that he had no desire to prematurely attain Paradise.

Hamid was long used to judging the wheels-within-wheels-within wheels of Persian thought processes. He saw immediately that he had judged Akhlagi correctly: like most professional Iranian military officers, Akhlagi did what was necessary to advance himself and no more. If Akhlagi's advancement was more rapid because his paeans to the glory of the Islamic Revolution and the Supreme Leader were marginally more sincere-sounding than that of Akhlagi's rivals, at the end of the day, mouthing such phrases did not truly say anything about Akhlagi's character beyond highlighting a driving ambition, and such ambition was de rigueur in Iran.

Hamid let Akhlagi off the hook just a bit.

"Unfortunately, you may not have the opportunity to serve as a shaheed anytime soon. As a skilled officer, we cannot allow you the luxury of Paradise. Instead, you must continue to serve *Khoda* with the naval skills the Islamic Republic has fostered in you."

Hamid noticed that Akhlagi managed to conjure a look of sadness as the "luxury" of martyrdom was withdrawn. Hamid smiled an internal smile that did not reach his eyes or face, and thought to himself, "This Akhlagi is a clever one. He could have gone far."

"Captain, during this crucial maiden voyage, the eyes of the world will be on our great Islamic Republic, on our noble protectors in the Revolutionary Guard Corps Navy, and most especially, on you and the crew of the Shaheed. You must give your utmost efforts to ensure this voyage experiences no problems and *absolutely no delays*, not by so much as an hour. In addition to the many members of the press, you will have many senior clerics onboard, honored Ayatollahs whose names you would recognize instantly, but which I cannot disclose for security reasons.

"The Supreme Leader summoned you here tonight to inform you of the arrival of these guests. They will arrive at the dock less than an hour before you set sail next week. See that they are treated with the same reverence and respect you would display for our holy Supreme Leader. Also, another matter: a software technician will arrive at the same time as your honored guests, to perform a software update on your shipboard systems. It is your job to deal with your honored guests, not to delay the technician in the performance of his tasks.

"For security reasons, you will not tell anyone of this meeting here tonight, not your crewmembers, not your family, not one living person. Your obedience in these tasks is required by the Supreme Leader. Nothing less will be tolerated. If these orders are not followed, removal from command of the Shaheed will be the least of your worries. Is that clear?" Hamid finished with a stern, almost menacing tone.

Akhlagi gave the only answer possible to one who had ascended to senior rank by pretence of absolute obedience. He replied crisply, "Of course, Sir. It is my duty and my pleasure to fulfill the just orders of the Supreme Leader to the utmost of my ability. I have but two questions, only asked that I may faithfully execute my orders. In order to prepare suitable accommodations, how many senior clerics will be arriving?"

"Second, in my experience, Sir, computer upgrades and ship repairs often create flaws and problems that need to be fixed before normal shipboard operations can resume. Perhaps it would be possible to delay the computer upgrades until after the maiden voyage, when neither the honored guests, nor the many members of the press will be inconvenienced by any unanticipated delays?"

The Supreme Leader's aide smiled thinly, pleased that he had struck fear into Akhlagi's heart with his threat of removal from command. Hamid chuckled once more internally, while noting Akhlagi's cleverness in characterizing the problems a software upgrade might cause as only a possible inconvenience to honored guests, not as a problem the Captain did not want to deal with while he had so many other duties to perform. Iranians had a phrase for such a ploy, "removing responsibility from oneself,' but Hamid found he preferred the more direct version he had learned in America: "covering your ass."

As a cat toying with a mouse, Hamid replied, "Come, come, Captain, have you so little faith in our computer technicians? More importantly, have you no faith that, Inshallah, all will go according to the divinely inspired plans of the Supreme Leader, earthly representative of the Hidden Imam? It pains me to hear such a lack of faith, and from a man the Supreme Leader believed was worthy of command of the Shaheed! "

Akhlagi, knowing there was no possible defense when the Supreme Leader's aide held all the rhetorical ammunition, remained mute, but at attention. His face was expressionless.

Hamid continued, after a deliberate delay to make Akhlagi sweat just a touch more. "Very well, Captain. You may plan for twenty senior clerical visitors. It is possible less may arrive, but planning for twenty will allow you a margin for error. I have been assured by highly competent computer programmers that this software upgrade is vital to your ship and will cause no delays in the launch of the Shaheed. If by some minor chance there is a problem *and* you can prove that the problem is attributable to the upgrade, you and your crew will not be held responsible. If the launch of the Shaheed is delayed for any other reason, you will not fare so well."

The meeting had not gone as the Captain had hoped, but Akhlagi could see the audience was at an end. He wanted to make a hasty retreat from a meeting that had unexpectedly devolved into a blatant browbeating. He responded to Hamid as if Hamid were the Supreme Leader, instead of the wizened, perplexed, and silent old man reclining beside Hamid. "Very good, honored sir. I am truly blessed by *Khoda* to be given the opportunity to perform my duty for the Islamic Republic and carry out the wishes of the revered Supreme Leader exactly as ordered."

The Supreme Leader remained entirely silent, while Hamid gave an abrupt nod of dismissal more appropriate to the ever-hasty Americans than a society where elaborate social niceties were as commonplace and necessary as air. Akhlagi backed out of the room as quickly as was possible without actually breaking into a jog.

If Akhlagi had chosen to return to the Supreme Leader's chamber in that instant, he would have seen the Leader reaching for the porcelain bowl of the vafour to load it with a large chunk of opium.

Once back in the anteroom, Akhlagi relaxed his rigid control over his facial expression. He was deeply disturbed. He now had firsthand knowledge of the Supreme Leader's rumored opium use. This was dangerous knowledge to have. Drug users were often punished by hanging, but Akhlagi was not foolish enough to think the Supreme Leader would ever face such punishment…but anyone who dared accuse the Supreme Leader of opium use might. While departing, Akhlagi finally noticed the strange emptiness of the Supreme Leader's residence, and the deliberate attempt at utmost secrecy that it implied. Perhaps most disturbing was the Supreme Leader's confusion, one that obviously went beyond the dreamy detachment of the opium user.

Hamid's order for absolute silence about the meeting meant Akhlagi would not be able to trade on the prestige of meeting with the Supreme Leader, something he had dearly looked forward to. Also, there was nothing normal or logical about attempting a software upgrade to the ship's systems in the midst of media frenzy. And Akhlagi could think of no good reason why the Supreme Leader's office would possibly concern itself with such a minor detail of shipboard operations.

An outside observer looking at Akhlagi as he hurried away from the Supreme Leader's compound, shoulders now slumped, would no longer have seen Akhlagi trying to suppress a proud grin. The Captain knew enough about the ways of Iranian politics to have the faint yet unmistakable feeling that he and the Shaheed had just become pawns in a game of Shah. He hoped both would be left standing when Shah Mat, checkmate, was declared.

* * *

Though the Captain would never have guessed, Hamid Ansari, whose full name the Captain would never learn, as Ansari had not introduced himself, actually admired the intelligence and ambition of Akhlagi. The heavy-handed browbeating of Akhlagi during the meeting was regrettable, but absolutely necessary. Ansari could think of no other way to distract Akhlagi from the condition of the Supreme Leader, except by making Akhlagi worry about his job and future. Hamid had needed to snap Akhlagi into a state of obedient, silent attention. Ansari also had to avoid extensive questioning on the wisdom of a mysterious last minute software upgrade just prior to a highly publicized maiden voyage. The aide hoped that his injunction to Akhlagi to speak to no one of this meeting would be sufficient to stifle any dangerous opinions the Captain might have formed.

Hamid Ansari's MBA from Harvard stood him in good stead as one of the primary assistants and advisors to the Supreme Leader. The Supreme Leader's clerical background was long on the Islamic jurisprudence known as Sharia, but short on the intricacies of geo-politics and the global marketplace. The Supreme Leader's comprehension was further limited by his opium use. All this was normal, beneficial, in fact. It made the Supreme Leader more dependent on Ansari. Many of the Supreme Leader's advisors offered little beside theological platitudes; Hamid's experience in the West allowed him to advise the Supreme Leader how best to work with *ajnabi*, untrustworthy foreigners like the Chinese or Russians, and do so in a way that frustrated American designs on Iran.

Over the last few months, Ansari had noticed "The Leader" suffering unmistakable moments of irrational suspicion and confusion. Unfortunately, instead of seeing a doctor, the Supreme Leader had started treating this problem by increasing his intake of opium.

The Supreme Leader remained lucid (or as lucid as one might expect of a habitual opium smoker) much of the time. Few but Ansari and other close aides knew the Leader was slipping. In fact, the meeting with Akhlagi was the first time that the Leader had suffered one of his lapses during an official meeting…a lapse which had occurred despite Hamid's best efforts to avert it. Hamid had reminded the "Old Man," as Hamid often thought of the Leader, of Akhlagi's name and the purpose of Akhlagi's visit immediately before fetching him in from the anteroom. The Old Man had managed to forget all of this during the ten seconds it took to escort Akhlagi in. Hamid consoled himself that Akhlagi was the only one at the meeting and that, *Khoda* be praised, the doddering old fool at least had the wit not to use the opium pipe while Akhlagi was in the room.

Ansari had been around the Old Man too long to have any illusions about the man's claim to divine guidance or wisdom. He considered the Old Man's view of the world provincial, narrow, and bigoted. When Hamid spent time with his friends, ultra-wealthy merchants of Tehran's *Bazaarii* families, Hamid privately mocked the Supreme Leader, who wore the traditional *abba* clerical robes, as a "robe-wearing *ahmagh*, an idiot."

Of course, Hamid had no objection to serving an idiot, if he could thereby procure himself a highly prosperous and stable existence. Hamid's commitment to the Islamic Revolution did not extend beyond his own self-interest in supporting a system that offered him and his associates fantastic opportunities for self-enrichment and prestige.

Hamid had long enjoyed the challenges and unprecedented level of perquisites that came with the position. Yet ever since the Supreme Leader's "episodes" had started, Ansari's delight in the secret power of his job had begun to wane. Instead, he was gnawed by the fear that the Old Man's lapses might grow worse, and that the side effect of those lapses would be further irrational decisions, like the Leader's foolhardy plan set in motion by Captain Akhlagi's visit tonight. Because the Old Man's condition was unknown, he still wielded the full measure of his power, for good or ill. He still directly commanded many men who believed an order from the Supreme Leader was akin to a command from the Prophet, praise be his name. The wisdom of those orders would not be questioned.

In many cases, the Old Man made unrealistic demands, and Ansari, as the defacto chief of staff, had to figure out some way to accomplish what the Leader wanted. In this case, the Old Man had circumvented Ansari and had gone directly to "The General," but the Leader, as ever, still relied upon Ansari to help execute "The General's" plan.

Ansari disapproved, but going along was the path of least resistance, and thus continued privilege.

While Akhlagi retreated from the meeting with new worries furrowing his brow, Ansari also felt unsettled by the meeting. He feared that an ill-omened wind had just started blowing, one that might sweep away the Revolution if things went wrong.

CHAPTER TWO-THE LAUNCH OF THE SHAHEED

June 11, 2014, Bandar Abbas, Iran

His whipcord lean frame, erect posture, and general aura of competence aside, the Shaheed's executive officer, Commander Mohsen Saeed, could not hide the fact that he was baffled. On what should have been a day of triumph, Captain Akhlagi was acting irritable and moody. Three times during the week, Saeed had had to intervene to keep the Captain from lashing out at the sailors who had failed to meet perfection in some intangible way. Akhlagi usually had a light touch as a captain, most of the crew of the Shaheed felt lucky to serve aboard her, at least they *had,* until Akhlagi's mood took a turn for the worse. Just ten days ago, Akhlagi had confided his excitement to Saeed about the impending christening, an event which would formalize Captain Akhlagi's assignment as the Shaheed's first commanding officer. As commander of the newest and finest warship in the Iranian military, most of Akhlagi's peers and contemporaries looked on the assignment with undisguised envy.

Before heading to Tehran last week, Akhlagi had confided to Saeed that he was off to a meeting at the Supreme Leader's residence. When he returned the following day, Akhlagi was a changed man. Saeed tried to gently probe his commander; had something gone wrong at the meeting? Akhlagi had only whispered tersely that he should never have told Saeed about his appointment to meet the Supreme Leader, and that under no circumstances was Saeed to mention the meeting again, or discuss the meeting with anyone else.

Then just two days ago, Akhlagi ordered the Shaheed's anti-submarine helicopter, along with the helicopter crew, put ashore so that a lavish tent could be lashed to the helicopter pad amidships, sheltered from wind by the superstructure of the very large, boxy exhaust stack. Akhlagi ordered Saeed to find a way to furnish the interior of the tent by begging, borrowing, or stealing comfortable rugs, cushions, couches, and a tea samovar. The Shaheed's cook was ordered to provide a meal fit for the 12th Imam, or face being transferred to a ditch-digging crew in the middle of Baluchistan.

Rumor had it that the cook had smuggled his mother aboard to assist in the preparations and make sure the cuisine was up to the exacting standards of a traditional Persian mother. Saeed knew if he saw a chador-clad figure ghosting through the areas near the mess deck he would exercise the willful blindness of good naval officers, who understand the difference between what regulations allow (bringing your mother on-board as an auxiliary cook was most definitely *not* within regulations), and what it takes to get the job done right. Saeed would fail to notice any mother-shaped objects aboard as long as she removed herself before the actual launch.

Who these grand arrangements were for, Akhlagi refused to say. Certainly it was not for the press observers, who had already been given simple chairs on the bow beneath the imposing and deadly twin tubes of the forward cannon. The only information Akhlagi would share was that the special visitors were high-ranking clerics who would be showing up one hour before the christening ceremony.

The mysterious tent was strange, but then suddenly at 2300 hours last night, things became even stranger. Akhlagi had ordered the Shaheed's underwater welder and combat diver to suit up in scuba gear and make a thorough underwater examination of the entire length of the Shaheed's hull, even though it sat in the protected harbor of the Iranian Naval Shipyards at Bandar Abbas. The puzzled diver, Explosive Ordinance Disposal Technician 1st Class Izad Vahdat, asked Akhlagi if there was anything in particular he should be looking for.

Akhlagi looked incensed at the question and sputtered vaguely, "Navigational obstructions of any sort! Now stop questioning my orders and do your duty."

When Vahdat returned an hour later and reported no problems, Akhlagi accepted the report with a simple "Dismissed," but continued to pace the bridge with a tenseness that suggested he was heading into combat. The Captain certainly was *not* behaving as if tomorrow were a leisurely cruise of a few hours length accompanied by a tame press contingent, one sure to describe Akhlagi as the best Persian military commander since Cyrus the Great.

Saeed wondered quietly to himself, "What could be agitating the Captain so badly?"

Like a rampant contagion, Akhlagi's unease was infecting Saeed, although Saeed had no concrete reason, beyond the Captain's foul mood, to believe anything was amiss with the Shaheed or the preparations for the launch.

Two hours before the scheduled launch, the Iranian media began to arrive and congregate in their designated areas underneath the looming guns on the bow. First was a film crew from Irinn TV. Next came separate film and radio crews from Sedah-va-Seemah. Two newspapers beloved by religious conservatives, *Kayhan-Tehran* and *Inghelab Eslammi*, both sent a reporter and photographer each. Amazing the entire crew of the Shaheed, the Ministry of Islamic Guidance had also allowed on board a camera crew from the mouthpiece of the Great Satan, CNN. Saeed presumed the Ministry and the Supreme Leader were sending a not-so-subtle signal to the American Navy, who treated the Persian Gulf like it was an American lake. With the acquisition of the Shaheed, Iran was becoming a naval power to reckon with in the Persian Gulf, not just in terms of small attack craft, but also in terms of "capital" ships.

While the reporters waited for the christening ceremony to begin, junior lieutenants escorted the press around the ship in groups of three, reciting to the escortees diligently memorized scripts about the might of the Shaheed. Even though the reporters were only allowed brief glimpses into the bridge and Combat Information Center, Saeed noticed that Captain Akhlagi tolerated their appearance with ill grace, despite the fawning plaudits all the Iranian reporters were lavishing on Akhlagi about the trim condition of the ship. Saeed knew that whatever was bothering Akhlagi, it had little to do with the coverage the Shaheed would receive in the Iranian press.

The white-painted steel bulkheads of the bridge were lined with Russian-built, boxy, mustard-yellow command and weapons consoles with prominent black plastic dials and switches and large cathode ray tube displays. The consoles wrapped around the bridge and extended back into the Combat Information Center connected to the bridge. Despite the bulky and seemingly antiquated consoles, the electronic guts of the command and control systems had all been modernized; they were the best systems Iranian petro dollars could buy…but none of the fawning reporters even bothered to ask about the ships' controls.

Just an hour before the scheduled start of the christening, Saeed saw several Mercedes limousines and Range Rovers pulling up to the dock where the Shaheed was moored. These were obviously conveying the important visitors for whom the tent had been erected. Saeed, intensely curious, moved rapidly to the gangplank and down to the dock, accompanied by a petty officer and five common sailors to act as escorts. Saeed knew that visitors of such rank would not like to be kept waiting.

Slowly, the limousines' rear doors were opened by the drivers, whose size and serious demeanor suggested they were both drivers and bodyguards. Emerging from each limousine were two to three old men in spotless *abba* robes and the white *am-amm'eh* turbans of Shia clerics. Although anticipating visitors of high rank, Saeed was almost speechless: these men he recognized. All of them. He counted the numbers, and could not believe his eyes, which had widened involuntarily in astonishment at the sight. Twelve men in robes.

It was the entire membership of the Council of Guardians. Barring the Supreme Leader himself, nobody in Iran, and few in this entire region of the world, held more power than these men.

The Council was currently made up of twelve Ayatollahs, senior clerics, each with large personal followings, all revered by Shia of conservative religious bent. The Council was one of the ultimate power centers in the Islamic Republic, a sort of reverse of the American "check and balance" system of democracy. The Council's sole purpose was to make sure Iran did not suffer a slide into that most disreputable of conditions: unrestrained democracy.

The Council of Guardians "guarded" the 1979 Iranian Revolution by making sure that all candidates for the Iranian parliament, the Majlis, met the standards of theological purity set by the Guardians. Those candidates deemed insufficiently fervent, which was usually over 90 percent of those who tried to run for the Majlis, were barred from the elections. Of course, accidents can happen, even in a rubber-stamp deliberative body like the Majlis. To counter any other potential problems, the Council of Guardians also held the power to simply declare any legislation passed by the Majlis that did not mesh with the theological (or financial, political, or familial) wishes of the Council of Guardians null and void.

Only by force of will was Saeed able to keep his mouth from gaping in astonishment. To have all the members of the Council attend a ship-christening and maiden voyage was unprecedented. In many ways, it was bigger news than the launch of the ship itself.

Saeed made the ritual "Salaam Alekum" to each individual Council member as he approached the gangplank, and sent each cleric onto the ship with an escort as soon as he arrived. There would be no "permission to come aboard" nonsense with men of such rank and power as these. The Guardians were men who occasionally gave permission, but *never* asked it.

Commander Saeed would have been surprised to know that most of the members of the Council were not happy to be there. Their presence had been requested vehemently by the Supreme Leader's office in the deceptively polite tones of official Iran. The Leader's office proclaimed that the Iranian faithful needed a reminder of the triumph of the Iranian Revolution. The Council of Guardians, chief protectors of that revolution, should therefore attend the christening to be photographed on Iran's newest and most powerful vessel. The juxtaposition would serve to remind Iran's Shia faithful of the service of those who protected Iran from the wiles of the Great Satan.

Such senior and "godly" men rarely indulged in activities as plebian as trying to bolster the domestic image of the Islamic Republic. Typical of any group of men whose great power conveyed a sense of boundless entitlement; most of the Guardians resented even the smallest infringement on their prerogatives. But the Supreme Leader had been insistent that it was the godly duty of each Guardian to help bolster the Iranian people's flagging faith in the Revolution and the Supreme Leader's office had offered each Guardian a nice package of financial favors to sweeten the deal. So persuasive was the bait that the senior Ayatollahs had all grudgingly agreed to attend the christening and maiden cruise of the Shaheed.

Even in a theocratic society, where the eyes of the leaders were alleged to be focused more on earning Paradise than the bottom line, money talked very loudly.

Saeed left three sailors outside the tent to make sure the Guardians were not disturbed. Once he had them safely ensconced, drinking tea and eating fresh pistachio pastries and baghlava, the executive officer retreated at full speed to the bridge to share with Captain Akhlagi his astonishment at the rank of the visitors. As soon as Saeed entered the bridge, he walked over to the Captain's chair in which Akhlagi sat, still wrapped in a brooding air. Saeed leaned over and whispered so that he did not show his surprise at the identity of the visitors in front of the bridge crew. "Captain. It is the Council of Guardians. All of them. All twelve are aboard the Shaheed in the special tent. You should go welcome them."

Saeed had assumed until that moment that Akhlagi knew the identity of the special visitors and simply had not shared it for security reasons. Akhlagi's reaction changed Saeed's mind; the Captain became so pale he was almost gray. Then his face was swept by a look of resignation.

He told Saeed, "Mohsen, I am going to retire to my cabin for the next 15 minutes. After that, I will have some orders for you and our crew that must be executed immediately and without fail. While you are executing those orders, I will go greet the Guardians."

The Captain gestured to a man neatly dressed in civilian clothes standing near the Combat Information Computer array, fiddling with the computer that processed the incoming radar/sonar signals. In his excitement, Saeed had overlooked the stranger on the bridge.

"While you were busy with the Guardians, a technician from IRGC Naval Command arrived with a software update for our radar and sonar systems. His work will be done shortly. See that he is not interfered with. You have the bridge."

Akhlagi strode off towards his cabin in a rush. Akhlagi's strange reactions over the past week, the arrival of visitors of such senior rank, and now a poorly-timed computer upgrade all combined to leave Saeed feeling off balance.

*　　　*　　　*

The Captain immediately turned on his personal laptop when he reached his cabin. While waiting for it to boot-up, he took a seat and gently lifted a picture of his wife and child off the bulkhead and stared at it. The disease of rampant individualism had not yet completely corrupted Iran. Like most Iranians, Akhlagi's actions were more often than not dedicated to assuring that his wife and children were well cared for and protected. This led Akhlagi to compromises with his conscience that he would not have made if he had cared for only himself. But the Captain also had a crew and a ship to look after, a duty to his men and the families of his men.

The Captain put the picture back on the wall, and reopened a letter he had started late last night, after the sweep of the hull by EOD Diver Vahdat. Typing away at his desk at 12:45 a.m. he had felt foolish even starting to write this letter; it had seemed a product of runaway doubts and worries. Now he was glad he had. There was no way he could have started from scratch and written everything he needed to say in the time he had before duty compelled him to go greet the Council of Guardians.

He reviewed what he had already written, then added several extra sentences. Ten minutes after powering on the computer, the Captain printed what he had written on stationary embossed in gold with, "Ali Reza Akhlagi, Captain of the Shaheed." The stationary had been a gift from his wife, the joy he had derived from her gift now metastasized into a bitter sense of foreboding. Akhlagi signed his name to the document and then sealed the letter into a plain envelope which he tucked into his crisp uniform blouse.

Commander Saeed was seething with apprehension as he waited for Akhlagi to return to the bridge. He didn't know whether to be relieved or even more anxious when he saw the carefully neutral expression on the Captain's face when Akhlagi strode back in.

Saeed stood up from the command chair as Akhlagi leaned close and whispered intensely, "Mohsen, my friend, I know I have been acting strangely. Probably I have seemed like a crazy old woman, temperamental and fussy. Inshallah, my fears are simply the result of an overactive imagination. Perhaps we will have a good laugh about all this before nightfall. But for right now, I cannot afford to act as if my suspicions were incorrect."

The Captain handed his executive officer the envelope with the letter he had just finished writing. "Hold this envelope for the present, and listen closely. You are to follow my orders now, and follow them immediately and exactly, without question. Quietly and quickly visit the junior officers and petty officers. I need you to send every sailor, petty officer and officer who is not urgently needed for the christening cruise ashore. You will also be going ashore. None of you will be accompanying the Shaheed on the maiden cruise."

Akhlagi saw questions and protests forming in Saeed's eyes. The Captain raised his hand to forestall questions and commanded, "If asked, say it is a nice break, a reward for the hard work in preparing the Shaheed for today. Say that the Captain wanted to prove how efficiently he could run the Shaheed by using only a skeleton crew. I don't care what you say, just come up with something to say, and do it now. After the Shaheed launches, go to the command center in the shipyard. I want you to closely monitor all communications with the Shaheed. If there are any problems during the cruise, you are to open that envelope and read what it contains. Under *no circumstances* are you to open that envelope unless there are problems during this cruise. Clear?"

Akhlagi was no martinet. He tended towards a more easygoing command style than was the norm in Iran. All the more startling, then, was the Captain's intensity. His gaze looked like he was trying to bore holes into Saeed's soul as he gave the orders.

Saeed was straining to imagine what reason Akhlagi might have for issuing such bizarre orders in the midst of the christening ceremonies, but it was clearly something Akhlagi took seriously. Saeed had a million questions, but no time to ask them. In the end, he was forced to simply fall back on his training. He would follow the Captain's orders. He nodded his head and started to turn to go. Akhlagi stopped Saeed by grabbing his arm.

The Captain quickly and unobtrusively shook Saeed's hand, and whispered, "May *Khoda* preserve you, my friend."

The phrase chilled Saeed's heart. The strange orders were upsetting, but Akhlagi's farewell sounded more like a funeral dirge than a casual parting. For the first time, Saeed was truly afraid for his ship and his Captain.

Saeed was so distracted he forgot to pass along to the Captain that the IRGC computer technician had already finished his software installation and departed. Miracle of miracles, no systems seemed to have crashed yet as a result of the software upgrade, but then again, such failures only happened when they were least expected and most inconvenient.

Akhlagi called a senior lieutenant to take over the bridge. As Captain Akhlagi made his way to the Guardians' tent, he could see Saeed moving rapidly all over the Shaheed. Akhlagi could also see bewildered-looking sailors in clumps of one and two starting to disembark from the Shaheed. Akhlagi thought to himself, "Praise *Khoda* for Mohsen's efficiency; he is a better executive officer than I deserve."

Akhlagi approached the special tent where the Guardians were taking their ease. He noted with fleeting satisfaction and pride that the tent walls were drawn as taught as a violin string. Even while underway, there should be minimal flapping or noise from the tent fabric to inconvenience the Guardians. He nodded at one of the Guardian's bodyguards, and gave the man a post-Islamic Revolution greeting, saying, "I hope you are not tired. I am Ali Reza Akhlagi, Captain of the Shaheed. I would like to bid the revered Ayatollahs of the Council of Guardians welcome. Can you announce me?"

The bodyguard, used to being treated like furniture by his protectees, appreciated Akhlagi's politeness and showed the

Captain a quick smile. "I hope you are not tired" had emerged as a greeting after the Revolution, to imply that loyal Iranians were working so hard to maintain the "Glorious Revolution" that they would always be tired from their virtuous labor. In the case of the bodyguard, Akhlagi had no doubt that his demanding charges probably *did* run him ragged. The bodyguard quickly entered the tent, and returned seconds later, holding the entrance flap aside for the Captain.

As soon as he stepped inside the tent, he noticed the heavenly scents of traditional Persian cuisine, including succulent lamb and saffron rice, which masked the ever-present smells of a warship: a mélange of machine oil, rust, fresh paint, sea-air, and male sweat. Judging by the plates that were three quarters full of various delicacies (which were rapidly disappearing into their gullets with near-unseemly haste), the gang of senior clerics probably had no inclination to tear themselves away from the stunning repast. Nevertheless, Akhlagi extended his abject apologies to the Guardians for not greeting the Council members immediately upon arrival, and offered to personally escort them about the ship on a tour before the christening and launch. The chief cook and his "helper" had apparently outdone themselves. Akhlagi made a mental note to promote the man.

The clerics were partially mollified by the food, but they still felt the need to impress upon the Captain the honor and privilege that their attendance represented. As learned Ayatollahs, they generally found the best way to convey this message was to relentlessly grill a person of lesser status (i.e. everybody) on matters in which they considered themselves expert (i.e. everything).

One of the Council members who had stopped eating long enough to catch his breath asked, "Tell me, Captain, why was it necessary to buy this ship from the Chinese? Do our shipyards not produce fine vessels? We produce countless mini-subs and other craft. Has not the Islamic Republic-built destroyer, the blessed Jamaran, proved that our shipyards can produce a destroyer as fine as this one? Why spend 400 million dollars purchasing a ship from the Chinese?"

Clearly, Akhlagi knew that the truth would never do. Odds were at least one of the Guardians had some sort of financial or personal stake in the shipyards. The mini-subs and coastal patrol boats the shipyards constructed were very serviceable. But the difference between building a relatively simple twelve-meter mini-sub and 156 meter destroyer and integrating multiple weapons, sonar, radar, and communications systems was the difference between being a casual jogger running five kilometers and winning the gold medal for the Olympic marathon. Yes, both involved running, but…

Akhlagi could *also* never say, as might have been expected when attempting to build a vessel more than twice the size of anything previously attempted by the Iranian shipyards, that the Destroyer Jamaran had undergone numerous major mishaps during acceptance trials. The Jamaran had suffered everything from engine breakdowns, to near-disastrous drive-shaft seal leaks, to the accidental electrocution of several sailors due to misrouting of the main power conduits on the Jamaran's bridge. Only now, after six years of working the "bugs" out, did the Jamaran seem to operate somewhat reliably.

The Iranian Revolutionary Guard Corps Navy had apparently decided they did not have six years to wait for the shipyards to work the bugs out of the Jamaran's design and systems integration, plus however long it took to build an improved successor to the Jamaran.

Also, there were the politics of it. The Iranian Navy controlled the shipyards at Bandar Abbas, and the Iranian Navy had no desire to see the IRGC Navy compete with them. Likely the Iranian Navy would have done everything possible to make sure any ship built for the rival IRGC Navy experienced numerous "unexpected" production delays.

It was simpler, faster, and in the long run, probably cheaper, to buy the improved *Sovremenny* class destroyer from the Chinese, which was extremely modern, as the Chinese had themselves taken delivery of it from Russia in 2006, and had upgraded it since.

"Honorable Ayatollah, such decisions are made above my level. I can only speculate that the shipyards were fully booked with other vital projects, and thus were not able to devote the lion's share of their skilled labor to the project for several years, which is what it would take to construct a destroyer from scratch. As it was, we monopolized much of the skilled labor of the shipyards for the last two months merely assuring that the Shaheed, which was already in excellent condition when received from the Chinese, passed our acceptance trials. Presumably our Admirals felt that such shipyard resources could not be spared for several years."

Akhlagi's answer was a half-truth at best, but it seemed to satisfy the Ayatollah. From the positive response, Akhlagi presumed that the Ayatollah would somehow use the answer to justify expanding the Iranian shipyards, further lining the pockets of the Ayatollah's friends and associates in the process. Such was the way of military procurement all across the globe: militaries were given what it was most profitable for their leaders to produce, not necessarily what they needed.

The Captain continued answering a series of questions from various Guardians on every topic under the sun until, blessedly, he was interrupted by an ensign scratching at the fabric of the tent flap to signal his presence. The ensign notified Akhlagi that the dedication ceremony was to begin in ten minutes. The Captain urged the members of the Council of Guardians towards the small reviewing stands assembled on the bow for press observers and VIPs.

*   *   *

Commander Saeed watched from dockside as a tug nudged the Shaheed slowly away from the dock. The warm June sun gleamed on the freshly painted gray decks of the ship as a gentle breeze flapped the IRGC battle pennon flying near the radome above the bridge. To Saeed's mind, the receding ship possessed a deadly grace, her long, lean silhouette making him think of a vast steel killer-shark roaming the Gulf.

The dedication ceremony had gone well, meaning there were no noteworthy events that might have made it worth remembering. Instead, it was an hour of mind-numbingly boring blather, filled with hot air produced by a variety of self-aggrandizing senior IRGC Navy and Iranian Navy officers. Commander Saeed was not sorry to have missed that, but did feel a pang watching his ship set sail without him, even if it was only a short "out and back" cruise for the benefit of the press and the VIPs.

Saeed turned to the senior lieutenant and chief bosun's mate standing next to him, and instructed them, saying, "Find a place for the disembarked crew to relax, have some tea, and watch the Iran-Turkey football match. There is a lounge in the yards for shipwrights and pipefitters that I think you may use. Are your cell-phones charged?" Both drew their duty cell phones from small holsters on their belts and confirmed to the Commander that their phones were charged.

"Very well. Make sure you and the crew stays available for quick recall. Get a car and driver to take me over to the communications center. After that, you may relax until I call you."

The chief bosun's mate replied, "I will have the driver to you in five minutes, Commander, Inshallah," and walked off while dialing his cell phone to relay the orders.

The lieutenant, Kamyar Khani, one of the Commander's favorites, asked Saeed quietly, "Sir, why have we disembarked? Is something wrong?"

Saeed liked Lieutenant Khani, but he also wanted to avoid spooking the Lieutenant, and by extension, the rest of the crew, who already had to be muttering about the strangeness of disembarking before the ceremonial cruise began. "Nothing is wrong, Inshallah, Lieutenant. Just politics. You know as well as I, nothing is free of such considerations."

Lieutenant Khani nodded acknowledgement of this basic truth of life in Iran and walked away to insure the chief boson's mate had no problem finding a place to stash all the disembarked sailors.

*   *   *

Commander Saeed was not the only person intently watching the departure of the Shaheed from the docks. If questioned by shipyard security on his loitering, Farid Nouri would have produced impressive-looking credentials embossed with the seal of the office of the Supreme Leader. In fact, Nouri was in the personal employ Hamid Ansari. Ansari assured him he would have no shortage of opportunities for personal enrichment as one of the unofficial "eyes and ears" of the office of the Supreme Leader, and thus had won Nouri's undying loyalty.

Ansari's command to Nouri in this case had been simple: confirm that the Council of Guardians arrived as planned, that the dedication ceremony went as planned, and that the Guardians were still aboard when the Shaheed departed on the short cruise. Nouri pulled out an encrypted phone and left a short message for Ansari. "No problems. The Shaheed was towed out past the breakwater five minutes ago, and was heading southeast under its own power."

Nouri closed the phone and walked 300 meters to his nondescript Samand car for the long return trip to Tehran. Ansari had instructed Nouri not to linger after the Shaheed had departed. Nouri was a smart, efficient man; Ansari would have tolerated nothing less. Therefore, the report Nouri left Ansari was correct, insofar as it went. However, Nouri knew nothing of naval procedure or ships. When Nouri saw sailors from the Shaheed offloading, he assumed those sailors were simply extra hands from other ships helping the Shaheed's crew bring the ship to spotless condition for the launch. He didn't realize that more than half of the crew of the Shaheed had offloaded before it departed, which definitely was *not* according to the Supreme Leader's plan.

*　　*　　*

The duty officer in the communications center recognized Commander Saeed on sight, and thus was very surprised to see him walk in the door. The duty officer had heard from the Shaheed's radio operator thirty seconds ago that the Shaheed had just opened up her twin turbine engines to full power, to give the VIPs the feel of a powerful warship steaming at full speed.

"Is there a problem with the Shaheed, Commander Saeed? Why are you not aboard?"

Saeed was under no obligation to answer the watch officer, IRGC Navy Lieutenant Junior Grade Assad Mumtaz, who was far junior to Saeed. Nevertheless, the Commander felt it wise to stop any sort of rumor about irregularities with the Shaheed before they started. A few members of the Iranian press, as well as a CNN translator, were in the command center getting further background on the Shaheed. None of the reporters appeared to be close enough to hear the watch officer's question or Saeed's response, but just to be on the safe side, Saeed whispered, "Captain Akhlagi wanted to demonstrate to the dignitaries aboard that the Shaheed was so modern and the crew so well trained, that it could easily be run by a skeleton crew. He also wanted to reward as many of the men as he could with a chance to watch the Iran-Turkey football match. So he sent many of us ashore."

While unloading part of the crew was certainly an unusual choice for a maiden voyage, junior lieutenants who publicly question the wisdom of senior commanders and captains in front of the press tend to have a hard time getting promoted.

Lieutenant Mumtaz therefore responded, "Excellent idea. How fortunate you are, to serve under a Captain who takes such good care of his men."

Saeed asked for a position update on the Shaheed.

* * *

The Shaheed's senior combat diver, Izad Vahdat, was bored out of his skull. As his duty station was below decks and everyone else who worked in his compartment had been offloaded without explanation, he had nobody to talk to, and little to do. He was on board simply because regulations dictated there must always be at least one trained underwater welder aboard every time the Shaheed sailed.

He could tell from the vibrations through the hull that the Shaheed was picking up speed. As Vahdat had a rough idea of the course of the cruise, he surmised that the ship must finally be passing to the southeast of Qeshm Island and heading into the Western reaches of the Persian Gulf. Although he had been ordered to stay below during this cruise, Vahdat was aware that the ensign who gave that order was among those offloaded. Vahdat was sure that he could quickly slip topside, find a niche to have a quick smoke, and maybe even send a text message or two to one of his friends while he was still within range of Qeshm's cell phone towers.

Vahdat worked his way to the deck access hatch near the rear of the ship at the tail end of the helicopter pad. He stepped out onto the deck, looked around for any superiors, and, seeing none, quickly cupped his hand around a counterfeit Marlboro Red cigarette and ducked into the lee area of the helicopter deck to get out of the wind of the ship's passage.

The deck was now thrumming at what Vahdat estimated had to be close to full power. The ship beneath him was knifing cleanly through the shallow waters of the Gulf, which in the vicinity of Qeshm took on a startling shade of turquoise blue reminiscent of picture postcards of the Bahamas.

Once he had taken the first few anxiety-relieving puffs, he pulled out his cell phone and was pleased to see that he had four bars of reception. The Shaheed must indeed be near Qeshm to have so strong a signal. He decided to call his best friend and fellow combat diver, Javid Ziyaii, who served aboard the destroyer Jamaran. He hit the speed dial button for Ziyaii.

*   *   *

Passing just to the south of Qeshm city, Akhlagi had decided to give his guests a thrill and ordered, "Full speed ahead." The Shaheed accelerated smoothly and had been cruising at 25 knots for two minutes. Akhlagi was starting to hope that his fears about the cruise of the Shaheed were "womanish vapors." The sun was sparkling across the waves, all systems were green, and the sonar combat information computer appeared to have swallowed the software upgrade without so much as a burp. Akhlagi had ordered the sonar operator to run a full diagnostic on system. The sonar appeared to be performing well, and was now processing incoming sensor data faster, to boot. *Khoda* be praised.

Fortunately, three of the Ayatollahs on the Council of Guardians had unbent enough to accept Akhlagi's invitation to join him on the bridge. Though they were always called "peaceful holy men" by their followers, the Ayatollahs seemed to be having the typical male response to being on a new warship—reacting as though the Shaheed were a very large, sophisticated, and enjoyable toy. Captain Akhlagi, as steward of this most elaborate toy, was now a splendid fellow in their minds.

It fleetingly crossed Akhlagi's mind that while he was not allowed to say he met with the Supreme Leader, he could now claim to be personally known to and friendly with three members of the Council of Guardians, which was nearly as good. Akhlagi wasted no time extending invitations to all the relatives of the Guardians to tour the Shaheed when it was in port, and to take similar short cruises as the ship's schedule allowed. One of the Guardians stroked his beard thoughtfully, then grinned slightly and allowed as how he and his grandson might take Akhlagi up on that generous offer soon.

Akhlagi felt a blush of pleasure at the Guardian's reaction an instant before he noticed the Shaheed's sonar operator, Warrant Officer Najafi, shoot to his feet with an alarmed look on his face. Najafi shouted, "Captain, we have launch signatures. Passive sensors suggest multiple inbound torpedoes."

For the second time that day, Akhlagi's face lost all its color. As soon as Najafi shot to his feet, the Captain knew in his heart that something was very wrong. Nonetheless, Akhlagi reacted instantly. "Go active on sonar. Helm, flank speed! Come about starboard, 180 degrees from our current heading. Notify the Naval Command Center that we are under torpedo attack from an unknown source."

Booms of acoustic energy started blasting from the Shaheed's sonar systems into the surrounding water.

"Sonar, what have we got?"

"Captain, I am showing eight inbound torpedoes, the closest is 600 meters and closing. I show two large submarines, hovering near the bottom of the Gulf about 1000 meters due west. We cannot identify their propulsion systems clearly, but they appear large enough to be American Sea-Wolf class attack submarines."

Akhlagi cursed the fact that IRGC Naval logistics, never efficient at the best of times, had not provided ammunition for the Shaheed's weapons systems, despite Akhlagi's constant demands. Sovremenny-class destroyers were *normally* highly dangerous fighting ships. Right now, though, the Shaheed was a toothless tiger. The Shaheed hadn't even had a chance to load countermeasures canisters that might confuse enemy torpedoes.

*   *   *

The reek of fear and adrenaline was flooding the bridge of the Shaheed. Everyone was clutching at the nearest fixture to stay upright as the ship heeled over in the emergency turn. The Ayatollahs on the bridge started loudly praying until the Captain, maintaining an inhuman calm, said, "Quieter, please, your Excellencies. I need to be able to clearly hear my men."

Captain Akhlagi was racing the Shaheed back towards Qeshm, hoping to bring the ship close enough to shore before impact that any survivors would have a chance to swim to land.

Since the sonar system had appeared to be operating normally after the diagnostic, in the stress of the moment, Captain Akhlagi had temporarily forgotten about the upgrade.

Warrant Officer Najafi was shouting, "Captain, torpedo impact in 10 seconds."

Akhlagi ordered, "All hands, prepare to abandon ship! Radio our position to the command center and send out an open call on all marine distress channels with our position and a request for immediate rescue."

Nobody would have been more surprised than Akhlagi to know that there were no torpedoes, nor enemy subs, only clever combat simulations that the software upgrade had uploaded into the sonar computer. The torpedoes were phantoms.

However, the fifty American-made Mark I Mod III limpet mines which had been affixed a meter below the waterline of the Shaheed early that morning, just two hours before dawn, were very real.

*   *   *

Standing below the overhang of the helicopter deck, the Shaheed's combat diver was glum that he hadn't been able to get through to his fellow combat diver, Javid Ziyaii, who seemed to have his cell phone turned off. Vahdat did have a voice-mail from Ziyaii waiting for him in his own mailbox, though.

With barely suppressed glee, Ziyaii's message said, "We have tricked you, my friend! There will be much embarrassment aboard the Shaheed come sundown!"

Vahdat had no idea what Ziyaii was talking about. He called Ziyaii's phone again and started to leave a message. The ship started making a sharp turn to port, which caused the decks to heel steeply to starboard. Then "battle stations" klaxon started hooting. Vahdat assumed Captain Akhlagi was putting on a good show for the VIPs.

Screaming into his phone to be heard over the klaxon, Vahdat said, "I don't know what your 'surprise' is, my friend, but you should be here now! The Captain is playing war games for our visitors. And he had me out checking the hull last night until midnight. What did he expect me to find? Ha! See you soon, Inshallah."

Vahdat was reaching up to terminate his call when the limpet mines detonated. By a strange trick of the physics of shock waves and flying shrapnel, Vahdat's cell phone, as well as the hand that had been gripping it, was blown free of the Shaheed and deposited by a blast wave into the blue-green waters of the Gulf. The synchronized crump of multiple mine detonations were clearly transmitted over the airwaves into Ziyaii's voicemail box before the saltwater of the Persian Gulf shorted out Vahdat's phone.

*   *   *

Within five seconds, catastrophic explosive flooding took the Shaheed from floating *on* the Persian Gulf to being *in* the Persian Gulf. The pressure and shock waves, the flying molten metal, superheated gases, and scalding flash-steamed water vapor created conditions as hostile to life as the cosmic furnace at the heart of the sun. The explosions left nothing that even the most hardened trauma surgeon, accustomed as they were to gruesome injuries, could have gazed upon without horror or pity. On a sunny June day, at 11:43 a.m. local time, the Iranian Revolutionary Guard Corp Navy Destroyer Shaheed, carrying a load of VIPs and press on its maiden voyage, was lost with all hands.

CHAPTER 3-THE PHONE CALL

In Joe Cerrato's experience, most operations of the cluster-fuck variety start with a phone call in the middle of the night. Something, somewhere happened, absolutely requiring an IMMEDIATE response. And for some reason, that response was never, "Hey, we should catch our breath, think about what this means, get information from our assets, and then make a measured response consistent with our foreign policy for the region."

Oh no.

It was always, "Something has happened and we have to react NOW, NOW, NOW. The President or the Vice President, or Secretary of Defense or (insert assorted high-ranking, jerk-off, why-can't-the CIA-do-what-Jack-Bauer-does-in-'24'-reruns asshole) demands action! Find out what is going on. Oh, and by the way, since you are the CIA, it is your job to have perfect knowledge of all events everywhere, *before* they happen. Anything less is an intelligence failure. And although you repeatedly warned that something like this was going to happen, since the high ranking political assholes *didn't pay attention* to your warnings, you are going to be investigated by Congress while trying to respond to the crisis. You might want to get a good lawyer."

Ring, ring. He looked at the clock. Not quite 6 a.m. Coulda been worse, he usually got up at 6:30 in any case.

"Yah, Joe here."

"Mr. Cerrato, this is the Ops Center watch officer. You're 'On the list' for this one. You need to come on in."

"What's this about?"

"Turn on CNN while you're getting dressed, you'll figure it out." Click.

Joe groaned, levered himself out of bed, and said to his wife, Claire, "Sorry, honey, gotta go in early. Sorry 'bout the noise, but I need CNN."

Joe clicked on the bedroom TV, and then pushed a button on the wireless clicker on his bedside. While no big fan of whizzbang technology, he had to admit that having a wireless clicker that started your coffee brewing remotely was pretty handy in coping with these off-hour summons.

A CNN reporter was doing a standup shot outside a drab building flying the flag of the Islamic Republic of Iran, saying, "...officials of the Iranian Revolutionary Guard Corp Navy are confirming the loss, with all hands, of the newly christened IRGC Navy Destroyer Shaheed. Among the dead was a large contingent of Iranian press. Also aboard was a CNN camera crew present to cover the christening. Most sensationally, we are getting unconfirmed reports that the senior Ayatollahs aboard were actually members of the Iranian Council of Guardians. Nobody from the IRGC Navy or Iranian Navy is willing to go on the record, but I have seen a lot angry faces in the command center behind me."

"On background, I have been told they have preliminary information to suggest that the loss of the Shaheed was due to an unprovoked torpedo attack by American or Israeli sources on the Shaheed. Accusations are flying that killing the Council of Guardian members was a deliberate mass assassination aimed at destabilizing the government of Iran. The atmosphere here is very tense, Tom."

Joe clicked off the TV and mumbled, "Shit. This is gonna be a real, real bad one. Gotta go, honey."

"Will I see you tonight?" Claire asked drowsily.

"Maybe. I might have to be in so late that it makes more sense to sleep at the office."

After taking a two minute shower to wash the sleep out of his eyes, Joe threw on a navy blue dress shirt, some khaki dress slacks, and some hand-made Italian loafers. It was ironic to Joe that he often received compliments on his shoes. He only wore custom-made shoes because case officers spend a lot of time walking during surveillance detection routes or standing at diplomatic functions, and he couldn't get away with wearing sneakers, his natural preference, on such occasions. Having your shoes custom-made was the next best way to insure comfort.

Truthfully, he hated coats, ties, and all manner of fancy dress, particularly in the god-awful soupy heat of a Northern Virginia summer.

In the kitchen, he filled an insulated travel mug with fresh coffee and grabbed a pristinely shiny silver pack of Pop-Tarts for breakfast while heading out the door. Fucking Pop Tarts. He hated them, had no idea why Claire kept buying them, but had no time for anything else.

Joe headed north on the 495 Beltway in his perfectly anonymous, off-white, slightly shabby Toyota Camry, thankful that heading in early meant less traffic. He reached into his glove box for the electric razor he kept there for just such occasions, plugged it into his car's cigarette lighter, and started mowing the stubble off his face. He hated doing it because using an electric razor after a shower tore his face and neck to pieces. He could already feel the razor burn starting.

Joe drove mechanically, running over probabilities in his mind. Would we have sunk an Iranian ship? Without already being in the midst of a shooting conflict? Joe was 95 percent certain the answer was no. The other five percent was still open because it was impossible to tell what the Department of Defense was up to. Still, firing on a ship outside of an armed conflict? That would require Presidential approval to exceed the standard Navy peacetime rules of engagement, and if CNN was right and senior Iranian leaders were aboard, such firing would be considered assassination, which is loosely defined under US regulations as the targeted killing of an individual for political reasons. Assassination had been barred for decades by Executive Order 12333. By the time Joe merged onto the George Washington Parkway headed east towards the back entrance to the CIA, he largely ruled out US involvement, based on political realities and US laws. Not that half the Middle East wouldn't already be *certain* the sinking of the Shaheed could only have been at the hands of the US Navy, but it didn't ring true.

The other half of the Middle East would assume it was the Israelis "whodunit," and that was Joe's working assumption, too, at least until he arrived in the ops center, was briefed, then headed to his own desk in the revived Iran Task Force to start sending out cables to start the information flowing.

Israel had no compunction against assassination. The fact that members of the Council of Guardians had been on the ship would only have made the Shaheed a more attractive target. Israel and Iran were not in a state of war, but then again, most of Israel had a bunker mentality, and Israelis more or less *always* saw themselves as being in a state of war. In their eyes, they were the righteous "Chosen People," surrounded by a sea of enemies. Israel had always been very willing to undertake military strikes on the basis of a neighbor's *capability* to harm Israel, quite apart from proved intent to do so. Hell, only American refusal to permit Israel overflight rights over Iraq had prevented the Israelis from bombing the shit out of Iran's nuclear facilities in the closing days of the Bush administration six years back.

Of course, given Iranian rhetoric in the past decade about "incinerating the Jews" and "driving the Jews into the sea," it was not really a stretch for the Israelis to imagine a ship like the Shaheed could pose a major threat to Israel. Many on the Israeli General Staff would consider the sinking of the Shaheed a good day's work, removing threats to the Israeli state with little attention paid to the repercussions of such an attack.

"Shit, shit," Joe said aloud, "if this goes bad, it could be war. At a minimum, it probably *is* going to lead to reprisal attacks in response, on the assumption that the US or Israel did it."

Joe pulled into one of the open parking spaces in the North Lot and headed inside. For a second during the walk in towards the Old Headquarters Building, he became aware of the glutinous, disgusting mass of Pop Tarts he was mechanically chewing and washing down with coffee.

Claire once told him that his initial response to stress, on rare occasions, at least, was comically misdirected flashes of anger over trivial annoyances. His instinct for bad situations having been honed by years of experience, Joe knew his stress level was about to go off the charts as soon as he got inside, but he wasn't thinking about that right now. He was thinking how much he hated these fucking tasteless, paste-like, life-sucking Pop Tarts.

CHAPTER 4-FLIGHT

Sitting in the IRGC communication center when the radio started squawking frantic reports of torpedoes closing on the Shaheed, Commander Saeed felt as if his heart had been dipped in liquid nitrogen. Captain Akhlagi's unstated but unmistakable fear that something bad was going to happen to the Shaheed suddenly took on a dreadful weight. Reports from the Shaheed kept coming in, the voice of the Shaheed's radio operator more agitated with each burst of words. After four minutes, the frantic radio calls suddenly ceased in mid-sentence. Simultaneously, the GPS beacon signal that tracked the Shaheed's location winked out. A shocked silence rolled through the communication center, muffling all sounds. Conversation stopped.

Someone could be heard quietly uttering one word in Farsi, over and over again, *"Fajeh'eh, Fajeh'eh*: Disaster."

The room abruptly came back to life when Saeed broke the spell with a command barked at the watch officer as sharply as a whip-crack. "Lieutenant, I am going to the Shaheed's ASW helicopter right now. We will fly to the Shaheed's last position and relay what we find. Stand by to form rescue parties on my command." In a harsh whisper, Saeed leaned over to the watch officer and added, "You are to tell *nobody* that any of the crew of the Shaheed, besides myself, were offloaded before the voyage, unless I give you permission to do so. Get Security to lock-down all these reporters for the next hour, at least until I can get to the site of the Shaheed and report back."

Commander Saeed knew his order not to reveal that most of the Shaheed's crew was ashore would only hold until someone of higher rank got around to directly asking the watch officer about the matter. Saeed did not even know why he gave the order, besides a feeling in his gut that Akhlagi's move to offload the crew had been an attempt to save as many as possible from whatever fate he foresaw for the Shaheed. He guessed that Akhlagi's last-minute order would prove to be a surprise move, not just to Saeed, but to everyone.

Until he learned the fate of the Shaheed, Saeed's instincts told him to keep that particular surprise under wraps.

The letter Akhlagi had given Saeed was like a red-hot iron bar in his uniform jacket. Still, as Saeed and his driver raced for the pad where the Shaheed's anti-submarine helicopter had been temporarily stored, Saeed's instinct for self-preservation told him he needed privacy to read whatever Akhlagi had written. Instead of giving into his need to tear open the letter, Commander Saeed was on his cell phone calling the crew of the beached helicopter, telling them to report to the helicopter immediately, and bring a rescue diver for a highest priority emergency flight.

Five minutes later, Saeed pulled up to the Ababeel. The Ababeel was a Kamov-27 "Helix" helicopter with a peculiar-looking coaxial rotor that was starting to slowly spool up. Saeed ran to get onboard, put on a headset, and got a status check from the helicopter's Chief Pilot, Lieutenant Commander Saboori.

"Commander Saeed, the rescue swimmer is enroute, but will not be here for another five minutes. I am spooling up now; we will be able to lift off the second he is aboard. Sir, what is this about? Where are we going? Is there a problem with the Shaheed?"

Commander Saeed handed the pilot a scrap of paper with the Shaheed's last known coordinates scrawled on them so the copilot could plug them into the helicopter's navigational computer.

"Saboori, this is where we are going, the Shaheed's last reported position. They radioed that they were under torpedo attack from an unknown source, then all radio transmissions stopped, as did their GPS beacon. We need find out immediately what is going on, and lead a rescue effort if necessary. Fly us there at flank speed, using full emergency power."

The pilot Saboori was stunned into silence. Realizing Saeed had little more to say, and the fastest way to learn more was to get to the Shaheed, Saboori nodded and turned back to make sure the copilot was programming the navigation computer correctly and that pre-flight checklist was complete.

Commander Saeed saw that the flight crew was engrossed in the flight preparations and estimated that he had a short window of private time before the rescue diver arrived. He moved towards the rear bench of the helicopter, reached into his uniform jacket, tore open the envelope with the letter from Akhlagi, and hurriedly began reading, keeping an eye open to make sure none of the helicopter crew could see what he was reading.

"Saeed, time is short. If you are reading this, that means my fears were somehow justified. I don't know what may have happened; all I can tell you is what worried me so: When I went to see the Supreme Leader a week ago, I received a great shock. The meeting was not at his home in Central Tehran; it was at some posh place in Northern Tehran, the area where all the rich *Bazaarii* bastards live. It was late at night, and there was only one other person there, his aide. No other attendants. No security. And I was ordered not to discuss the fact that I had attended a meeting with anyone, even you. The whole situation felt dubious at best.

The rumors *are* true: the Supreme Leader smokes opium. He had a vafour by his side and the smell of it was heavy in the air when I walked into his room. Also, the Supreme Leader was very confused, and it was more than just opium haze. His aide, Hamid, did all the talking. He warned me of senior clerics coming to the launch, but not who. And he told me to be ready to receive a sonar software upgrade on the day of the launch. He would not explain why the upgrade could not be postponed to any other day; he only threatened me to keep silent or face dismissal.

When I started writing this letter last night, I was convinced that I was being a paranoid fool for writing it. The arrival of the Guardians changed that. Never did I expect visitors of such eminence. Their rank makes me more certain that something peculiar is going on. But I have no answers for you, my friend, only questions. Why the secrecy? Why is the entire Council of Guardians on the Shaheed? Why would the Supreme Leader's office involve itself in something as trivial as preparations for a software upgrade? How could the Supreme Leader be so foolish to have a smoldering vafour next to him? Did he not care that I saw, that I left the meeting with such dangerous knowledge?

And there is something else. You know I have nagged IRGC Navy logistics to get the Shaheed's munitions loaded every day for the last three weeks. Four days ago, just to placate me, I think, I got a call from the junior clerk at the munitions office that I had been hounding mercilessly. He told me a black market shipment of some advanced American limpet mines had arrived, and asked did I want some for our combat divers to train with, and for special ops use? I said yes, and that I would come immediately to pick them up, before crews from the special ops mini-subs could snatch them all away. When I got there, the clerk had disappeared. The only person at the supply office was that *rubah'* Lieutenant Jafari. You know as well as I, that man's corruption is boundless. No man can lie so well, even while telling the exact truth.

Jafari told me the clerk had called in error, as the mines were not ready yet for distribution. They were being unpacked and certified, and would be ready in a few days, perhaps on the day of the launch. He said not to worry, the entire shipment was reserved for the Shaheed, and he would personally see they were aboard the Shaheed in a week or less. Here was this lying dog, suddenly being helpful, when he would not help his own mother if she were on fire.

I did not know what else to do, so I went to see Captain Rahimi of the Jamaran. He is no longer my friend as he once was. I think he feels he should have commanded the Shaheed, but at least he does not openly hate me now, like so many others who were passed over when I won command. I asked him if he knew anything about shipments of limpet mines, or any training exercises using mines, as no such training exercises have been announced. Rahimi looked startled at the question, but he said he knew nothing of any mines or training. He was lying, but I do not know why. I thought my enemies might try to embarrass me by sneaking dummy training mines onto the ship before the launch, but as you know, Vahdat found nothing. Intuition tells me something political is going on here, something far beyond the usual disagreements between the IRGC and the Regular Navy. I fear for our ship; few things are more dangerous these days than getting mixed up in political infighting.

I do not know what is going on, but something feels wrong. I have no proof, only suspicions, and I dare not stop the christening ceremony and cruise with the Guardians and media aboard. But if the Shaheed is damaged during the cruise, I know in my heart that it was not an accident. It was planned, and *Khoda* alone, and perhaps the Supreme Leader's office, knows why. Talk to Captain Rahimi. He knows something he is not telling. And take care of yourself, and the crew. Goodbye, my friend."

(signed)

Akhlagi

Saeed, so absorbed in the letter, did not stop staring at the sheet of paper until the wind of the rotors shot through the cabin as the crew chief opened a hatch to let the rescue swimmer clamber aboard with his diving gear. Saeed hastily tucked the letter back into the envelope and hid it inside his uniform once again. Good as his word, Pilot Saboori had the Ababeel airborne less than ten seconds after the crew chief swung the hatch closed behind the diver. In two minutes, the Ababeel was racing at 270 kilometers per hour towards its parent ship.

All aboard were fervently hoping the last frantic seconds of the Shaheed's radio broadcast, about imminent torpedo impact, was a hoax, a lie, a deception, or an unannounced war-game. All feared that was a faint hope.

The Ababeel did not have far to go. Fifteen minutes after liftoff, cutting directly over the Eastern tip of Qeshm Island, they found what was left of the Shaheed: floating oil slicks, bobbing pieces of wreckage and flesh. The Ababeel made repeated passes over the area, but located no survivors. For the sake of thoroughness, Saeed ordered the Ababeel to drop active sonar buoys and lower their dipping sonar to see if there were any ships or submarines in the area. Nothing was found. The helicopter radioed their findings back to the communications center ashore.

Saeed got on the intercom and said, "Attention Pilot and crew: We will return to Bandar Abbas in ten minutes. You are all ordered, on pain of court martial, not to transmit news of what we going to do next. Nor shall you discuss it with ANYONE. Not with an admiral, not with a family member, and not even with each other after we return to Bandar Abbas."

Saeed turned to face the rescue swimmer. "Erfan, the Shaheed appears to be in 40-50 meters of water. That depth can be dangerous with just standard scuba gear, but I only need you down there for 30 seconds. Look at the hull of the Shaheed, and see if you can learn what sunk her. Do not linger. No more than 30 seconds at that depth, then return immediately to the surface, as fast as you can without risking the bends. We will tell NOBODY that we have looked at the hull. I and I *alone* will report on what you learn to the IRGC leadership. Is that clear?"

A chorus of "Clear, sir" came over the intercom. Ten seconds later, the rescue swimmer Erfan was winching down to the water above the Shaheed, trying to dodge the bobbing wreckage, some of which was once shipmates. Saeed did not envy Erfan the grisly task, but had no choice but to send him. Saeed *had* to know what really sunk the Shaheed. If a rescue swimmer had not been available, he would have grabbed scuba gear before takeoff and attempted the dive himself.

It was a sunny day, so even at 40 meters depth, there was a diffuse, gloomy light on the hull of the Shaheed. Erfan gave thanks to *Khoda* that he had been issued an electrical device that repelled sharks. With so much blood in the water, they were being drawn from far away to feast on the remains of his shipmates. His powerful hand lamp illuminated pieces of bodies suspended in the water above the Shaheed. Erfan fought to keep his lunch down; he knew that if he started vomiting underwater, he might foul his mask and then drown.

He also knew this dive would haunt him as long as he lived.

It was not necessary for Erfan to get more than 30 meters down, close enough to see clearly a 50 meter stretch of the Shaheed's hull. About every seven meters, regularly spaced, were a series of holes in the Shaheed, each about a meter in diameter. Erfan only looked for five long seconds before starting back up. As he had not lingered at depth, Erfan only needed to halt at five meter's depth for a brief decompression pause before continuing to the surface. Less than ten minutes after exiting the Ababeel, he was being winched back aboard.

The nose of the Ababeel dipped as it began racing back towards Bandar Abbas.

Erfan pulled off his mask and the hood of his wetsuit, hoping against hope no human remains from the wreckage clung to him or his gear. Erfan started to put on an intercom headset to make a report, but Commander Saeed shook his head no and pointed to his own ear. Erfan moved to Saeed, cupped his hands around Saeed's ear to help block out the thunderous noise of the helicopter engines, and said, "Limpet mines. I have seen holes like that before on training exercises. Torpedoes, or even floating mines, would have made larger, more ragged holes."

Saeed cupped his hands around Erfan's ear in turn. "You are sure of this? Would you swear to such before *Khoda*? Would you be willing to risk your soul, your chance at Paradise, that what you saw was caused by limpet mines and nothing else?"

Erfan replied simply, "Swearing before *Khoda* on this would not place my soul in jeopardy. On my honor, my skill, and the souls of my family, only one thing could have caused holes such as these: limpet mines."

Erfan was shocked to see that Commander Saeed was *not* surprised at the news that mines had sunk the Shaheed. Erfan did not need Saeed to tell him that if Akhlagi had not unloaded the Shaheed's crew, both Erfan and Saeed would have been part of the wreckage below, a wreck caused by mines, *not* torpedoes, as the radio calls from the Shaheed had said.

Erfan wished with all his heart that Commander Saeed had chosen someone else to dive to the wreck of the Shaheed. Not only did Erfan wish he had not witnessed the grisly remains of the wreck, but he instinctively understood, as most Iranians do, that nothing is more dangerous to a person living in a country ruled by lies than knowledge of the truth.

CHAPTER 5-RAHIMI

The short flight back from the wreck of the Shaheed gave Saeed a chance to think over his next step. He knew that he did not yet have all the information he needed, and that he had to get that information immediately. In the meantime, he had to keep moving. If luck was with him, it was still unknown that much of the crew of the Shaheed was safely ashore when it sank.

As the Ababeel was spooling down back at Bandar Abbas, Commander Saeed began cracking out orders. "Saboori, I will be back in an hour. At that time, I expect you to be ready to fly. Strip all the surplus gear, sonobuoys. I want everything out of the Ababeel. We won't need the sonar operator for this flight, either. Get a fuel bladder in the cargo space. Get as much fuel onboard as we can. We will be flying straight through to Tehran to report to senior IRGC officers on the Shaheed. Discuss this flight with nobody but your flight crew. If anybody asks, you don't know where I am. Make the flight preparations, and standby for my return."

The pilot looked a little surprised at the orders, as there were plenty of faster ways to get to Tehran than helicopter. Still, Saboori would raise no objections. He was incredibly grateful to have a mission right now. Having a mission to prepare for meant he did *not* have to think about the loss of his ship and shipmates.

Taciturn by nature, Saboori only nodded his acknowledgement to Saeed, then started barking orders at the Ababeel's crew chief.

"You heard the Commander, move your pox-riddled buttocks! Get the sonobouys off-loaded! Get a fuel bladder and tanker truck over here! If I don't have the fuel in under an hour, I will put a saddle on your back and strap a rocket to your ass so you can fly Commander Saeed there yourself by flapping your arms. Move!"

Saeed stalked away from the Ababeel towards his waiting car and driver, then turned around and started walking back. He stopped before Erfan, who was slowly moving away from the Ababeel loaded down with his scuba gear.

"Erfan, you are a good diver, a good crewman. I thank you for making that dive; I can see it troubles you. What I have to say to you now, you need to listen to very closely. Return to your quarters. Dump your gear. Are you married?"

"No, Commander."

"Do you have access to a car?"

"Commander, several of the Shaheed's divers chipped in to buy one. EOD Tech Vahdat, EOD Tech Kazimi and I own a Pride together."

"Erfan, if asked, you did not dive today. There was no point, as the Shaheed obviously had no survivors. Go and get Kazimi. Beg, borrow or steal some camping gear. You two are officially given two weeks leave as of this moment, but for your own safety, you MUST do the following: Go somewhere with Kazimi where neither of you are known. Do not contact your family. Do not use your cell phones. Do not send any emails to anyone you know. Disappear for the next two weeks. What you just saw is dangerous. If I guess right, in two weeks, the danger will have passed. If not, I can only suggest you try to get out of Iran. The entire Council of Guardians was aboard the Shaheed when she was sunk. That means this is politics. You do not want to see the inside of Evin."

Erfan's eyes grew wide at the mention of Evin, and he cried, "*Khoda* preserve me, he is the most merciful! I curse this dark day! But I will heed your orders. An hour from now, I will be a ghost. I know just where to go."

Evin was notorious in all of Iran as a place where political prisoners were sent to be broken. Those sent to Evin for being foolish enough to cross the Ayatollahs, and foolish enough to remain defiant in the face of the "persuasions" of Evin's staff of professional sadists, were often simply shot or beaten to death. Innocent or not, one cannot appeal a sentence administered by bullet. Erfan took the Commander's warning seriously and began to jog quickly in the direction of his barracks, despite being burdened by scuba gear.

Saeed entered his waiting staff car.

"Do you know the location of the home of Captain Rahimi of the Destroyer Jamaran?"

"Yes, sir. I have driven Captain Akhlagi there several times."

"Take me there now, as quickly as possible."

Saeed's mind was racing. If Rahimi knew something he was not telling, the Commander would know. Rahimi was a terrible liar; he was too stiff necked, pious, and proper to carry it off. The streets of Bandar Abbas whizzed by, punctuated by the screams, curses, and horn blasts of Saeed's driver, who was obviously a man with frustrated dreams of being a Formula One racer. The driver was doing his level best to get Saeed to Rahimi's as fast as humanly possible or kill them both in the attempt. Under other circumstances, Saeed would have cursed the driver as a reckless, dangerous fool.

As it was, Saeed's mind kept being drawn back to the image of the smoldering wreckage of the Shaheed, bobbing within sight of the southern tip of the city of Qeshm.

Whoever had destroyed the Shaheed would pay, politics or not, conspiracy or not. Saeed vowed his life on it. Akhlagi had saved him and many of the crew. To Saeed, this was no accident: it was the hand of *Khoda* working through Akhlagi. Saeed felt his will hardening into diamond purity. *Khoda* was merciful, but his retribution was also swift and sure. The car lurched to a stop in front of a large waterfront building subdivided into luxury apartments facing south, each with a view of the Persian Gulf. Saeed moved to the entrance and pressed the button for Rahimi's apartment.

Rahimi's voice warbled over the tinny speaker in response, sounding far more feeble and unsure than his normal gruff, blustering tones.

"Yes, what is it? Who is there?"

"Captain Rahimi, it is Commander Saeed of the Shaheed. I need to speak to you, immediately."

"Go away. I am very ill," was Rahimi's transparently false response.

Saeed was not about to let Rahimi evade responsibility if he was somehow connected to the loss of the Shaheed. He pressed the button for one of Rahimi's neighbors, who Saeed dimly recalled meeting at a dinner party hosted by Rahimi three months ago for senior IRGC Navy and Iranian Navy officers and other local elites.

"Yes?"

"Mr. Amir, this is Commander Saeed. I believe we met some months back at a dinner party at Captain Rahimi's apartment. I need to get in to see Captain Rahimi, and the buzzer to his apartment seems to be broken. I cannot get through to him. Could you be so kind as to let me in? This is an urgent naval matter."

Amir's response was fortunately swift.

"I do remember you, Commander, Inshallah, you are well? Please pass my dear neighbor, Captain Rahimi, my regards when you see him."

The door buzzed open. Saeed moved to the stairs, not having the patience to wait for the elevator to take him to the fourth floor. Once in the fourth floor hallway, Saeed stopped and paced the length of the hall, examining what he had to work with. This was a posh building indeed; most buildings in Iran don't bother with such safety appurtenances as fire extinguishers and a fire ax. Yet here, both were mounted in the far corner of the hallway, behind glass.

Protected by his thick, starched uniform jacket, Commander Saeed swung his elbow into the thin glass, breaking it easily. He took care not to slice himself open on jagged glass shards while removing the ax. When he reached Rahimi's door, the Commander rapped on it sharply with his fist. He heard footsteps approach the door from the other side. Saeed could see the light from the fisheye lens set in the door go dark; he knew Rahimi was standing on the other side of the door, peering out through the lens, looking into the hallway.

Behind the fisheye lens, Rahimi murmured to himself, "May *Khoda* have mercy upon me," then spoke loudly enough to be heard by Saeed on the other side. "Go away, Commander. I am very ill."

Saeed held the axe up where it could be seen through the fisheye lens and rapped the flat of the axe head sharply against the door, shivering the door in its frame.

"I do not give a fig for your wants, Captain. You open this door, or I will be coming through your door with the help of this axe in five seconds. Your choice!"

Saeed began to count down: "Four. Three. Two. One."

Rahimi saw Saeed back-up, square his shoulders, heft the axe, and prepare to swing.

"Wait" Rahimi cried, quickly pulling open the door, "Come inside, quickly!"

When Saeed entered, he was surprised to see that a young, fit Iranian Navy sailor was also standing in the foyer with Rahimi, looking highly distressed. It took Saeed only a millisecond to look at the rank, ship, and specialty patches on the sailor's uniform: Explosive Ordinance Disposal Technician 2nd Class Javid Ziyaii, of the Iranian Navy Destroyer Jamaran.

Saeed dropped all pretense of military courtesy.

"Rahimi," said Saeed in a carefully controlled monotone, which suggested to Rahimi, quite rightly, "The Shaheed lies at the bottom of the Persian Gulf. All aboard are dead. I just returned from visiting the site on the Ababeel, the Shaheed's ASW helicopter. My rescue swimmer was looking at the wreckage of the Shaheed on the floor of the Gulf not an hour ago. And do you know what he saw? There were no torpedo holes. Captain Akhlagi, the crew of the Shaheed, and the entire Council of Guardians are dead. There is no escaping these facts. And why are they dead? My diver assured me, beyond a shadow of a doubt, that my crewmates have gone to Paradise because the Shaheed was sunk with limpet mines."

At the word, "limpet mines," the sailor Ziyaii dropped to his knees with a wail, crying,

"*Khoda* forgive us. Commander Saeed, we killed them, we killed them, we killed them!"

Rahimi started shaking, then turned and fled to the bathroom. Saeed could hear Rahimi being violently ill.

Although it was standard practice in Iran for officers to strike sailors to discipline them, Saeed had never done so until now. Switching the axe to his left hand, he strode forward, raised his right hand, and with a rocketing, openhanded slap, hit Ziyaii across the face so hard the explosives expert was knocked sprawling on the plush Tabriz carpet of Rahimi's living room.

"What do you mean, you killed them, *Maadder Ghahbeh, Son of a Whore ?!*"

Ziyaii struggled to his knees, crying and clearly grief-struck. "Commander, you must believe me, it was to be nothing put a prank. Your own EOD tech, Izad Vahdat, was my best friend, dearer to me than a brother! I would never have hurt him! Never! I would sooner have killed myself, as *Khoda* is my witness!"

"Last week, Captain Rahimi came to me and said we were to play a prank on the Shaheed. He said he had limpet mine simulators used by America for war-game training. He said they did nothing but release a large quantity of liquid dye with a small bursting charge of a few grams of explosive. Not enough to even scratch a ship hull, he said! Just enough to make a clang, so those onboard would know a simulator mine had gone off. He said later this afternoon, after your cruise was over and you were back at the dock, the simulator mines were to go off. A shipyard prank, nothing more."

Saeed shouted, "If it was a prank, why is my ship on the floor of the Persian Gulf, my crew dead? If the mines were to go off this afternoon, why did they go off 90 minutes ago?"

Ziyaii's responses were becoming increasingly drained and lifeless. "I had never seen these types of munitions before, Commander. They were American made. When I asked to see the manual to see how they worked and set the timing on the fuzes, the officer who delivered the mines to me said they had all been certified in working condition, and the timers were already preset.

He said I had nothing to do but load them on an underwater diving sled, go to the Shaheed, and hold each mine to the hull, and switch on the magnetic clamps. I starting at two a.m. this morning and finished an hour before dawn. When the Shaheed sailed as scheduled, I knew they had not been discovered. I called Vahdat and left a message two hours ago, poking fun at him about the prank."

"How many mines, Ziyaii?"

"Fifty, sir."

"Did they have any markings you could read?"

"I read English well, sir, but all it said was Mark I, Mod III."

Saeed was revolted. He made it his business to know the weapons systems of his foes. He knew exactly the lethal capability of that mine. Weighing over 10 lbs, the American-made Mark I Mod III limpet mine was a particularly nasty mine, packing enough explosive power to rip through more than a foot of steel plate, creating a hole several feet in diameter and transforming the blasted metal of the ship's hull into lethal shrapnel in the process. It also had an electronic timer which made it easier to reliably synchronize groups of mines to detonate with maximum effect.

Most any modern warship, built as they are with water-tight compartments that could be sealed off to prevent the spread of flooding, could survive the detonation of several limpet mines. However, no vessel afloat, not even the mighty Shaheed, could survive the simultaneous detonation of a large quantity of limpet mines.

Ziyaii, although clearly in peak condition, weakly pawed at his own uniform tunic as if he had less strength than a bed-ridden 90-year-old man. He finally managed to extract a cell phone and hit a speed dial button, and held the phone up to Saeed.

"You need to hear this, Sir. It is your EOD Diver, Izad Vahdat. He left me a voicemail. He called from the Shaheed, Sir. When I got it, I rushed over to talk to Captain Rahimi. To find out what was going on. That was just before you arrived."

Saeed listened to Vahdat's message, a voice from beyond the grave being reproduced with chilling digital accuracy. He heard the battle station klaxon Vahdat ignored. The loud bangs at the end, clearly the sound of the mines detonating, struck Saeed like a blow to the stomach. His anger exploded suddenly and evaporated, like a balloon popped by a pin.

"May *Khoda* have mercy on us! Ziyaii, who brought the mines to you? Who delivered them and said they were ready to go?"

"The IRGC Navy logistics officer, Lieutenant Jafari. Do you know him, sir? He was very kind to me, chuckling about what a good joke we would play. I had never met him before."

Saeed knew Jafari, most every senior officer at Bandar Abbas did. Jafari was a wretched dog of a man, even worse than Captain Akhlagi had described him in the letter. Jafari was the worst sort of *shayyad*, hypocritical cheater. It was common knowledge that at least ten percent of the budget allotted for shipyard supplies wound up in his pocket. On the salary of a lieutenant, he drove a new Mercedes, wore a Rolex, had his uniforms custom made, and lived like a pasha. He was married, with a wife and children, but was known to regularly fly to Dubai to use prostitutes. One of the Navy doctors Saeed was friendly with confided that he had treated Jafari for syphilis on three separate occasions in the past four years. Jafari drank alcohol, yet he loudly proclaimed his purity from the temptations of alcohol. Lastly, he was a terrible officer, often blaming missing equipment or funds on his subordinates, with the result that two of them had already been sent to prison.

All these abuses rankled the officers who served honorably, but he was untouchable: his cousin was Major General Mohammed Ali Jafari, Commanding General of the IRGC.

Saeed moved slowly toward the bathroom and looked in to see a wretched-looking Rahimi hunched over the toilet, his shirt flecked with vomit, a rope of saliva dangling from the corner of his mouth.

He started to speak. "Saeed, Jafari came to me and said the mines were just a joke to embarrass Akhlagi, to take him down a peg after getting command of the Shaheed. It made sense. A lot of people were jealous of Akhlagi, including me. Akhlagi had no friends left in the Regular Navy after he switched over to the IRGC to win command of the Shaheed. I never intended to kill him, and, as *Khoda* is my witness, I had no idea the Council of Guardians was going to be aboard! It was just to embarrass Akhlagi, nothing else, I swear on my soul!"

"Jafari and I went down to the berth where the Jamaran was moored last week. He said he had arranged a demonstration of the mines in action. Jafari pointed to a spot on the hull of the Jamaran, underneath the waterline. There was a thump and a clang, and then a few bubbles rose to the surface, along with a great quantity of yellow dye. But it did not harm the Jamaran. Jafari said that was all the mines would do."

Saeed responded to Rahimi's idiocy with a cold fury.

"Rahimi, you are a *Captain*. You are responsible for *all* that is done by your crew, in your name, or on your behalf. You KNEW Jafari was a lying dog, he has sent men to prison to hide his thievery, and yet you trusted him? Did you even look at the mines you asked Ziyaii to attach to my ship? You didn't check the mines, did you? Jafari gave you what you hungered for, a chance to embarrass Captain Akhlagi. You didn't look at the gift, or wonder why a viper had suddenly become your friend? You weak, vain fool! I tell you truly, Rahimi: Shaitan is preparing a place for you in hell."

"Your incompetence just killed more Iranians than anybody since that madman Saddam! Word of this will get out. You will be the Captain who sank the newest destroyer of his own country. They will say you are an agent of the Jews. Or do you think Jafari will take the blame, you murdering dog, you coward, you idiot?"

Saeed paused in his rant, but continued more slowly, his last pronouncement to Rahimi carrying the finality of the grave.

"Suicide is the blackest of sins, Rahimi, but you can only be damned once. Have mercy on your wife and family. Spare them the shame."

Rahimi started shuddering again and quietly weeping. Saeed turned his back on him.

Saeed returned to Ziyaii who was still sitting on the carpet and crying, his eyes haunted with the distant stare of a combat veteran who has seen and done terrible things. He was whispering a litany to himself, oblivious of Saeed's return.

"Izad, my brother, forgive me. Forgive me. Forgive me."

Although Ziyaii's were the hands that affixed the mines which had killed the Shaheed, Saeed, knowing that Ziyaii was little more than a dupe of his officers, no longer had it in his heart to be angry with him.

Saeed knelt down by Ziyaii, and gently shook him to gain his attention.

"Ziyaii, Ziyaii, listen to me, foolish boy. You did not know what you were doing, but that does not change the fact that you did it. You will have to live with that the rest of your life. But do not fear. *Khoda* is merciful. Izad Vahdat is now in Paradise. If he was truly a brother of your heart, he will beg *Khoda* for forgiveness for you."

Ziyaii began to focus more clearly on words of the Commander.

"I don't know why this happened, but it was no simple mistake. Captain Akhlagi warned me that something was not right. The office of the Supreme Leader is somehow involved. Do you understand what I am saying? I think you just helped the Supreme Leader kill the Council of Guardians."

"You will find no rest anywhere in Iran, no safe haven. From this moment on, you will be hunted. After Vahdat's phone call, you rushed over here to see Captain Rahimi. That is probably the only reason you are still alive. As *Khoda* is my witness, there will be a team waiting somewhere nearby to either kill you the next time you show your face, or arrest you and take you to Evin. That is a trip you will not survive. They will say you conspired with your idiot Captain, Rahimi."

"You have to pick yourself up. You have to flee, right NOW, with the clothes on your back! Do not return to base. You must leave Iran immediately! And turn that cell phone off, they will be tracking you by it! If you can, save that voicemail from Vahdat; it may one day be your salvation. Make a copy of it as soon as you get a chance, and keep that copy safe. I must go, and so must you."

Saeed patted the foolish young sailor gently on the head. The Commander had been moving constantly since the Shaheed went down. Whoever originally set in motion the sinking of the Shaheed probably still had no idea that he was alive. If he could keep it that way for just a few more hours, he might survive to fulfill his vow: to punish those who had ordered the Shaheed sunk.

In the meantime, he had a helicopter to catch.

*   *   *

Ziyaii pulled himself together, stood up, and shakily walked out of Rahimi's apartment. He did not bother to take his leave of his Captain; he left Rahimi's front door wide open.

*   *   *

Captain Rahimi, still weeping desolately, heard the wail of an approaching siren. Even from the fourth floor, he could hear the sound of crashing glass, of men forcing their way into his building. He knew they were coming to get him. He knew there could be no defense. Bolts of fear galvanized him. He pushed himself to his feet. He ran for his bedroom, jerked open the wardrobe, fumbled for a box in the back.

He pulled out his dress pistol, a blocky PC-9 combat pistol that had been chromed and had its black checkered-plastic handgrips replaced by carved ivory. Despite the cosmetic ceremonial refinements, the gun's deadly function remained unaffected. He fumbled one round into the chamber before walking back to his bedroom door and pushing it closed. He sat down on the edge of his bed, and was raising the gun to his temple just as he heard the sound of running boots echoing from the fourth floor hallway.

The men who came for Rahimi started moving more cautiously when they found the door to Rahimi's apartment hanging open. Two men entered slowly, guns drawn.

From behind Rahimi's bedroom door, a shot rang out.

CHAPTER 6- TEHRAN

As his driver sped Commander Saeed away from Rahimi's apartment and towards the waiting Ababeel, Saeed had to force himself to stop examining the larger implications of what he had learned from Ziyaii and Rahimi long enough to give a few crucial orders. Traveling at breakneck speed once again, they were already halfway back to the helicopter pad when Saeed picked up his cell phone and called Lieutenant Kamyar Khani.

"Lieutenant, this is Commander Saeed. I want you to…"

His voice full of anguish, Khani interjected, "Sir, what has happened to the Shaheed? Is it true? Is she lost?"

Saeed had been so wrapped up in determining the fate of the Shaheed, he had forgotten that most of the Shaheed's disembarked crew would be in the dark, but hearing rumors of the loss of the Shaheed. They would just be starting to experience a mixture of bewilderment, grief, anxiety, and survivor's guilt.

"Khani, Khani, yes, it's true. Sadly, the Shaheed was more aptly named than we knew: all aboard are now martyrs. I have no time to explain further, but I and the crew of the Ababeel saw with our own eyes that nothing was left of the Shaheed. Put aside your grief for now. Your duty calls. We must take care of our crewmembers that remain. I need you to relay this order to all crewmembers as soon as possible. Effective immediately, all crew members are given two weeks emergency leave to grieve for their shipmates. Crewmembers are encouraged to leave the area as soon as possible, go visit family, go on vacation somewhere. Tell them to stay away from phones and email. The press will want to talk to the crewmembers, but that must be avoided for now. I am sure there will be an investigation into the fate of the Shaheed and nobody should talk to the press until that investigation concludes. Tell the men to get out of town if they can, and maintain their silence. Do you understand your orders?"

"Aye, aye, Commander, I understand, but Sir, what about..."

"Khani, I have no time to discuss this with you further."

"Aye, aye, Commander."

"One other thing: Half an hour from now, I want you to visit the IRGC communications center and tell the watch officer that I have taken the Ababeel to Tehran to report to IRGC headquarters. Do NOT go now; you are to wait exactly one half hour before letting them know. We will be putting down at Mehrabad Airbase. Relay that to the watch officer, and then head off on your own leave. Do you understand these orders, Khani?"

"Aye, aye, Commander."

"Then carry them out." Saeed ended the call and turned off his cell phone.

Saeed didn't care one whit about crew-members talking to members of the press, or about "impairing the investigation." He knew there could be no *real* investigation. He had ordered the remaining crew members to disperse and go silent for one reason: to sow confusion. Before long, news that much of the crew of the Shaheed had survived would spread through the IRGC Navy and Regular Navy chain of command. As soon as that happened, the news would leak to the press. Everyone involved in the plot to sink the Shaheed would want to get hold of the crew members, find out why they were not aboard the Shaheed, and what they knew about the sinking. Saeed had sent almost 200 crewmen ashore before the Shaheed had sailed; that would be 200 people for the plotters to attempt to quietly track down.

Of course, Saeed had no illusions. As the surviving ranking officer, and the first person on the scene after the sinking, he would be very first person on the list of those to be questioned by IRGC interrogators, or perhaps those of the Ministry of Intelligence and Security, the MOIS.

Commander Saeed drew a sigh of relief five minutes later as he and his driver drew up to the Ababeel. Saeed ordered the driver to leave the vehicle behind and accompany him on-board the helicopter. The driver, whose name-tag declared he had the same last name as a past Iranian president, Khatami, was startled enough to blurt out to Commander Saeed, "But why, sir? I am a staff driver."

"Are you questioning my orders, Khatami? Do you believe your curiosity gives you the right to refuse orders from senior officers?"

The sailor snapped to attention and saluted.

"Sir, no sir! Please forgive my curiosity sir. I was merely surprised."

"Very well. See that your curiosity does not lead you down the path to insubordination again. If you have anything to read or any personal items in this car, bring them with you. Also, hand me your cell phone." Khatami looked puzzled again, but after the tongue lashing, was not about to start asking questions. He handed over his cell phone to Commander Saeed, who took the phone and turned it off.

Saeed, of course, couldn't explain to the driver that he was coming on the trip to Tehran for two simple reasons: Khatami had driven Saeed to Rahimi's apartment and had heard Commander Saeed order Lieutenant Khani to disperse the crew of the Shaheed. Saeed did not want either of these facts to become known as of yet. Khatami was an ordinary Regular Navy sailor who did not serve aboard the Shaheed, but was assigned to the Bandar Abbas naval staff pool of drivers. He would be less inclined to obey unusual orders from Commander Saeed if Saeed wasn't present to enforce them. If a senior official started asking the driver questions about where Saeed went today, or what orders Saeed had given, Khatami would answer. Saeed had no choice but to take the driver to Tehran to limit the spread of that information until most of the surviving crew of the Shaheed had left Bandar Abbas.

"Khatami, remind me to give you your phone back when we arrive at our destination. Now get your belongings and get in the helicopter immediately. Seat yourself at the bench at the rear of the cabin."

The sailor grabbed a brightly woven sack from the back seat of his staff car. From the lumpy shape and size, Saeed guessed it carried food, and reading material to while away the long hours spent waiting. Waiting on the peculiar whims of the officers they ferried about was the real occupation of all military staff drivers; the smarter drivers anticipated this and carried food and other supplies for the times when their driving duties demanded long hours.

As the driver boarded the helicopter, Saeed approached the pilot who was waiting outside the Ababeel with an expectant look on his face.

"Is everything ready, Saboori?"

"Yes, sir. Khoda be praised, my crew chief has worked some miracles. We are fully refueled, and have a fuel bladder aboard with an additional 600 liters."

"Excellent, Saboori. You serve your country well. Let us depart immediately."

Saboori climbed aboard through the main hatch, followed by Saeed. After both were seated, Saboori pushed the engine ignitors. The sound of the two Isotov turboshaft engines started as a low rumble and began to spool up to a high-pitched whine. Ponderously at first, then increasingly faster, the Ababeel's two counter-rotating helicopter rotors began whirling in opposite directions. The sight of two giant rotors, one set atop the other and separated by less than two meters, never fails to astonish anyone who sees it. That sight also instinctively raises the question of what would happen if the two rotors, so close and yet spinning in the opposite direction, were to touch? The strange rotor arrangement made the Russian-built Helix-class helicopter *appear* to be a flying deathtrap. In fact, the unusual arrangement brought one major advantage: having two counter-rotating main rotors meant the helicopter didn't need a tail rotor, and tail rotors are quite finicky. The design may have looked precarious, but it worked well enough, and that was all Saeed cared about at this moment.

Commander Saeed put on a headset and asked, "Saboori, can we get a private channel on this intercom? I need to discuss some classified matters with you."

"Yes, Commander Saeed. You will see a channel selector on the wire connecting the headset to the bulkhead. Set it to channel four. That is a direct line to the pilot's headset."

After switching to channel four, Saeed continued,

"We have a grave and extraordinary situation, one that requires extraordinary responses. We need to get to Tehran as quickly as possible. How fast can we get there?"

"Commander, Tehran would normally be just outside the range of the Ababeel. With the extra fuel on board, we can easily reach it, though."

"But how fast can we get there?"

"That depends, Commander." Saboori launched into a convoluted explanation of the tradeoffs between range and speed. He wrapped up the monologue, saying, "Which would you prefer, Commander, top speed and a refueling stop, or flying straight through at the slower but fuel-efficient cruising speed?"

Saeed didn't even have to think about the answer. Setting down to refuel would be a point of vulnerability, a chance for local authorities to deny him fuel, or even take him into custody. Saeed had no intention of stepping off the Ababeel until he arrived in Tehran. If simple speed had been his goal, the fastest way to get to Tehran would have been a commuter jet flight from Bandar Abbas Airport to Tehran's Mehrabad International. He would have arrived in less than two hours, but would have been relegated to mere passenger status. Slower though the Ababeel might be, it was the helicopter from *his* ship, and directly under his orders. He could decide where the Ababeel flew, the route taken to reach the destination, and, most importantly when, where, and how it landed. The Commander was hoping that flexibility would keep him out of Evin Prison.

"Saboori, do the fuel efficient cruise. How long will that take?

"Commander, it is about 1075 kilometers to Mehrabad Airbase in Tehran using the most direct route. With the extra fuel on-board, I can bump up speed to 220 kilometers per hour, slightly above the most fuel efficient cruising speed. We can be touching down in a little less than five hours."

"Excellent, Saboori. That is exactly what we shall do. Get us airborne as quickly as possible. You must know, Saboori, that enemies of the people of Iran would be happy if this helicopter, and the information I bear, did not reach Tehran. I am flying with you because you will do what it takes to see that this flight to Tehran, which may be the most important mission you have ever flown, arrives safely. To ensure this, we are going to have to deviate from standard procedures on several points, the first being the use of the radio. You will not use the radio to request clearance from the control tower, or file a flight plan. Radio traffic is routinely monitored, but we cannot afford to let our enemies know what we are doing. Therefore, this entire flight will be conducted under conditions of radio silence. In fact, I want you to shut the radios down until we reach the vicinity of Tehran."

While everything Saeed was telling Saboori was true, it was an incomplete truth. What Saeed did not say was that the "enemy of the people of Iran" that Saeed had alluded to was the Supreme Leader of Iran. The less Saboori knew, the safer he would be.

"Commander, regulations require that we get clearance and an assigned flight path and altitude for this airspace. Failure to do so could get me court-martialed or lead to a mid-air collision."

Saeed responded forcefully, "Saboori, I am well aware of the flight regulations. There are times when rules must be broken for the greater good, and this is one of them. If you are questioned about the lack of flight plan or other violations, say that I ordered you to break regulations. I will take any blame for that. Have no fear; as the ranking officer and your commander, the responsibility is mine. As for the risk of mid-air collision, yes, there is risk, but you flew far riskier missions as a junior Lieutenant during the war with Saddam. I do not think *Khoda* spared us the fate of the Shaheed, only to have us crash on the way to Tehran. Have faith, Saboori, Inshallah, we will be fine."

"Very well, Commander, radio silence until Tehran. We lift off in one minute."

Five minutes after the Ababeel roared off the helipad and pointed its nose north-west towards Tehran, Saeed finally leaned back against the helicopter bulkhead and allowed himself a moment of rest. Of course, right now, true rest was impossible. The Commander's mind was seething with the implications of what Rahimi and Ziyaii had told him. It strained belief to think that Lieutenant Jafari had decided to mine the Shaheed by himself. Far more likely that he had approached Rahimi to co-opt him for the "prank" on behalf of his cousin, Major General Jafari. The sonar blips reported by the Shaheed deliberately, but falsely, suggested torpedo attack. Phantom sonar readings, coming on the heels of a sonar software upgrade arranged secretly by the Supreme Leader's office, meant only one thing: the Supreme Leader, with the direct connivance of the most senior IRGC officer, arranged the sinking of the Shaheed. He wanted to kill the Council of Guardians, and do so in a way that could be attributed to Iran's enemies.

Saeed knew the torpedo attack was a lie. That knowledge placed him, and all those closest to him, in grave danger. If he reported to IRGC headquarters, he would be questioned. If he told the truth of what he knew, he would be executed. If he lied, the IRGC would eventually discover, within days or weeks, that Saeed had ordered a rescue diver to examine the wreck of the Shaheed, and then had personally gone to talk to Captain Rahimi. They would strongly suspect Saeed knew the Shaheed sank from mines set in place by Iranians, not torpedoes from America or Israel. That suspicion would be enough to doom Saeed and all his close relatives, as the plotters would fear he had shared the dangerous knowledge. That left Saeed with only one option: as soon as he touched down in Tehran, he had to become a ghost.

CHAPTER SEVEN- *RUBAH'* -THE FOX

Lieutenant Jafari terminated the phone call from the Qods Force team with a sense of great satisfaction. The Qods Force team sent to Captain Rahimi's apartment had found Rahimi dead, just seconds after he had committed suicide. Rahimi was a fool and deserved no better, but at least he was a fool whose suicide might prove extremely convenient for Jafari. If the story of the phantom torpedo attack came to light, IRGC investigators would "discover" that Rahimi had been a paid agent of Israel. The mines and the phantom torpedo signals from the bogus sonar upgrade would simply be a plot concocted by Rahimi. Discovery of this damning evidence, should it be needed, would be so much easier now that Rahimi was no longer alive to gainsay it.

Rahimi had spared the Qods Force the cost of a bullet.

Jafari always felt happiest when his schemes had a solid backup plan to deflect blame. Rahimi's death made the back-up plan seem completely secure. Most of the tracks leading to Jafari had been covered. All that remained was for the Qods Force team to locate that naïve donkey, Ziyaii, who had been tricked into planting the mines. The Qods Force tracking team had just informed Jafari that Ziyaii's cell phone was off, which would make finding him more of a challenge. Still, Jafari was confident that sooner or later, they would get him. Nowhere in Iran was safe when you were hunted by the IRGC's elite Qods Force commandos.

Jafari looked back at the muted TV in his office. It was still broadcasting a show on gardening. When news of the sinking of the Shaheed got out, it would preempt all TV shows in Iran. Gardening meant the news had not yet spread.

Jafari could not go to the IRGC Naval communications center at Bandar Abbas yet. He had no plausible reason, as a logistics officer, to know anything about the sinking of the Shaheed until the news became general knowledge. As soon as it did, Jafari would be able to bully his way inside the communications center and determine whether the rumors and speculations in the IRGC Navy and Regular Navy were flowing in the direction he needed them to go. Jafari had few doubts that all would be well on that account; Inshallah, nobody but Ziyaii had any reason to believe the Shaheed had not been sunk by torpedoes, and nobody (or more precisely, nobody in a position to gainsay Jafari and live) ever would.

Less than an hour after the sinking of the Shaheed became public, Lieutenant Jafari would start to play more of a starring role in this great drama. As had already been planned, Major General Jafari would appoint Lieutenant Jafari to head the investigation into the sinking of the Shaheed.

Lieutenant Jafari was far from the most logical choice to head an investigation. He was a supply officer, not a detective. Nevertheless, blood connections to power trumped all else in Iran. As the Iranian people absorbed the shocking loss of the Shaheed, few would find it strange that General Jafari had appointed a relative to head the sensitive investigation, if that relative was conveniently on the scene in Bandar Abbas and also happened to be an IRGC Navy officer. The investigation would find precisely what the Lieutenant, his cousin the Major General, and the Supreme Leader wanted it to find: this gross infamy, the sinking of the Shaheed, was the work of the Great Satan.

The TV picture abruptly changed to a reporter from IRIB TV doing a live feed by IRNA, Iranian national news broadcasting, from outside the IRGC Naval communications center at Bandar Abbas. Jafari turned up the sound.

"…was apparently lost with all hands, including, most sorrowfully, those twelve good and holy protectors of our beloved Revolution, the entire Council of Guardians. Great is our anguish on this tragic day. Dear viewers, details are still preliminary, but from what we know, The Shaheed's own anti-submarine helicopter, which had been put ashore before the maiden voyage, was the first on the scene after the Shaheed went down. The Shaheed's executive officer, Commander Mohsen Saeed, was in the communications center behind me when desperate radio messages saying the Shaheed was under torpedo attack started to arrive. Just minutes after the Shaheed went off the air,

Commander Saeed boarded the Shaheed's helicopter and flew to the Shaheed's last know position. They sadly reported that no survivors were found among the wreckage. They could not determine from the cursory aerial examination why the Shaheed sank.

"However, based on the radio transmissions from the Shaheed, officers in the communication center behind me believe this disgusting sneak attack was the work of the Imperialist Dogs or their vile Jewish lackeys. Listen with respect, dear viewers, to the tragic last few seconds of radio transmissions from the Shaheed.

A recording of a frantic, shouting voice came out of the TV speakers,

"This is an emergency distress call from IRGC Navy Destroyer Shaheed. Please send help! We are under attack! We have multiple torpedoes inbound and we cannot escape them, we are south of Qe." There was a squeal of static, then the audio clip being played on the TV abruptly terminated.

Jafari clicked off the TV.

He picked up the encrypted cell phone he used to communicate with his cousin and dialed Mohammed's number. It rang and rang. Lieutenant Jafari left a message.

"Mohammed, it is Majid. I am about to head into the command center. The Qods team is doing well: they found Rahimi, and he was already dead by his own hand. They are still looking for the sailor Ziyaii, but are sure, Inshallah, that they will catch him soon. I think you should make the announcement of the investigation immediately. The TV finally aired the news. I need to take control and make sure nobody gets close to the wreck. Also, one important thing I saw on the news: The Shaheed's executive officer, Saeed, was not on board when it sank. He flew out and looked for survivors in a helicopter. We need to talk to him. He *shouldn't* know anything dangerous to us, but with this game, we can take no chances. If he becomes a problem, he can easily be dealt with, but the sooner we control him, the better."

Jafari hung up and started heading out the door.

Everything in Jafari's voicemail message to the General was eminently logical: there was no reason to assume Commander Saeed would be a problem when the IRCG and the Supreme Leader controlled all major pieces on the *shah* board of Iran. Nevertheless, even as he spoke the words, knowledge that Saeed did not go down with the Shaheed caused Jafari to feel a ripple of unease. Saeed's survival was not part of the plan. He also should not have had the opportunity to survey to the wreckage before the news broke and Jafari could clamp down access to the site. Did Saeed know anything dangerous? Had the plan been deviated from in any other unanticipated ways?

The first seed of worry took root in Jafari's dark soul.

The Lieutenant decided tracking Saeed down to "interview" him was his highest priority. The Qods force team could handle finding and disposing of Ziyaii with no help from Lieutenant Jafari. As soon as he took command of the investigation, Jafari's second action would be to immediately dispatch IRGC Navy speedboats to the waters above the wreck of the Shaheed. As lead investigator, it would naturally be Jafari's duty to "preserve evidence, and ensure a solemn peace around the most holy resting place of the martyred Council of Guardians and crew of the Shaheed." The Shaheed "could never be allowed to be contaminated by any snooping *kaffirs*, infidels."

In other words, only those who had been personally chosen by Jafari would be given an opportunity to get anywhere near the Shaheed.

CHAPTER EIGHT-ROCKETS

Joe asked the duty officer in the Ops Center what he knew about the loss of the Shaheed beyond the CNN coverage. Cerrato received the usual response for emerging crises, "Nothing." It was time for Joe to cast out his nets to see what he could catch. Joe headed down to his desk in what was once again called the Iran Task Force, the biggest section in the Near East Division of the Directorate of Operations.

For a while, the Iran Task Force had been the Iran Division, while the Directorate of Operations had been dubbed, "The National Clandestine Service." The Iran Division had been an experiment in the previous decade to try to improve operations against Iran by creating a division focused on that one country. How or why anybody thought efficiency could be improved by a mere cosmetic reorganization was a mystery to Joe…unless the reorganization had included shooting a large percentage of the politicians who insisted the CIA take risks to gather vital intelligence, then punished the CIA on the rare occasions it did so.

Joe had no earthly idea what the National Clandestine Service name change was supposed to have accomplished. To Joe, that name suggested a nationwide group of covert concierges, valets, and dry cleaners, so he had been very pleased when last year it had reverted back to the earlier name, the Directorate of Operations, or DO. Human intelligence *operations* were what the DO really was all about. Why obscure that with bureaucratic bullshit?

Once he reached the cubicle farm of the NE Division he rapidly walked by his co-workers, taking no notice of their cubicle walls, all of which were decorated with some mixture of political cartoons, wanted notices for various terrorist groups, and posters detailing the range and payload of different Iranian missiles. He sat down at his desk, piled high with orange personnel files of

Iranian agents who had once or currently worked as spies, sometimes unwittingly, for the CIA.

As he sat on his lopsided chair, he muttered rhetorically under his breath, "How come CTC has money for the fancy Herman Miller chairs, while I'm stuck with this piece of crap," but then reflexively blocked-out the rickety condition of his chair as he fired up his desktop computer. He typed in his password and the randomly generated code number taken from an electronic token he carried around his neck. Taken together, the password and random code verified Joe's identity to the top secret computer network.

Joe sifted through the incoming cable traffic and NSA signals intelligence reports to see if anything related to the Shaheed had yet appeared, but it was too early for any substantial information. There was some preliminary chatter among political leaders in the Middle East, wondering what had really happened to the Shaheed, but it was apparent that the chatter was simply ping-ponging speculation. Nobody knew enough to draw firm conclusions or react.

The Shaheed had sunk below the waves of the Persian Gulf less than three hours ago. Even if a case officer had caught the initial news flash on CNN and called an emergency meeting with an asset who had insight into the Iranian Revolutionary Guard Corp Navy, that meeting would still be going on, or the case officer would still be writing the information up.

Joe lifted his STU-III encrypted phone and called a contact over at the Office of Naval Intelligence. "Mark, this is Joe. You ready to go secure?"

"Yup. Why don't you push the button."

Joe pushed a button on the phone. This would synchronize the two phones' encryption keys, and allegedly made the conversation secret and secure. After a pause, Joe could hear Mark's voice again. The voice was now tinny, punctuated by random bits of digital static, and accompanied by very annoying signal attenuation. Mark now sounded like he was speaking to Joe from behind a wall. "Joe, you there?"

"Yeah, buddy. Say, Mark, you didn't happen to notice that little thing this morning. With Iran? They seem to have misplaced one of their ships on the bottom of the Persian Gulf. No biggie, but penny for your thoughts?"

Every phone call between Mark and Joe somehow became a contest to see who could pull off the most understated irony. It was childish, but fun.

"Joe, yes, I do believe I heard something about that on CNN. Mighty sloppy of them. I mean, you have to save up a lot of cereal box-tops or green stamps to get a destroyer, no? Children can be so careless with their toys."

"Mark, I don't want to be *indelicate*, but, ahem, you good folks at the US Navy didn't *sink* the Shaheed, did you? And accidentally forget to tell us?"

Mark paused before answering. "Joe, I am shocked, shocked I say, that you would ever consider such a thing."

"Well, you know, Mark, one hates to pry, but I had to ask. And just so we are clear, those huge whiz-bang revamped Ohio class subs that lurk in the Persian Gulf carrying a bunch of SEALs and swimmer delivery vehicles. Those SEALs have a lot of time on their hands. Our friends in the Navy Special Ops community didn't decide to get frolicsome and give the Shaheed a special explosive gift of some sort?"

Dropping out of his "understated irony" voice, Mark replied, "Joe, no BS. It absolutely wasn't us. We are still trying to figure it out. Best guess is the Israelis, but we don't have an iota of evidence to prove that theory, either. Nothing besides a hunch."

Joe responded, "Mark, I'm sure our *beloved* congressional oversight committees will be glad to know that ONI and CIA stand shoulder to shoulder in the solidarity of complete ignorance on this matter. You get anything, you let me know. I'll do the same."

"Right, buddy. Gotta go. I got a meeting, about, drumroll please, you guessed it, the sinking of the Shaheed!"

"If it makes you feel better, I am sure the inventor of the staff meeting, whoever he was, is roasting in the ninth circle of Dante's inferno, Mark. That's the one reserved for traitors."

Mark barked a quick laugh.

"Where do you come up with this stuff, Joe?"

"It's a gift." They hung up.

The whole STU-III setup always reminded Joe of the comically impractical "Cone of Silence" from the spy-spoof TV show "Get Smart." The Cone had been a Rube-Goldberg gadget that made every "classified" conversation a giant leap backwards in effective communications. As miracles of modern spy technology went, the STU-III was almost on par with the "Cone of Silence." Today he had been lucky, but Joe often spent ten minutes trying unsuccessfully to get a STU-III call to "sync-up" before giving up and deciding simply to physically go see the person he had been trying to call.

Joe was the first senior Iran Task Force case officer in the office today. Given Mark's confirmation that the US Navy had nothing to do with the Shaheed, Joe decided to start drafting a tasking "cable" to CIA's "World Wide Stations and Bases" asking for information about the loss of the Shaheed. When Joe had been in the field, he hated reading cables from Headquarters saying "please provide information about this major incident." From the field officer's perspective, messages like that came across as blindingly obvious, redundant, and mildly insulting of the field officers' intelligence.

Obvious though they were, they also provided one necessary thing to the field: official justification to shift case-officer attention and budgetary resources to a new target. Both were always in critically short supply. Every new cable from CIA Hqs demanding information meant something the station had already been working on was probably going to slip through the cracks.

When someone from "hindquarters" later asked the field station, "Hey, what about that *other* problem we asked you about a month ago," the field had the WWSB cable to point to. Having the WWSB on file meant the field could politely tell Hqs to fuck off by responding, "We dropped that other thing, because you told us this new thing in the WWSB was more important. If you want us to go back to doing the old thing, send us a cable asking us to do that."

But of course, it was never that simple. Such a response from a field station, even when fully justified, would simply trigger back-channel sniping in classified, but unofficial, email.

Joe recalled the first time he had received an email like that from a desk officer in CIA Hqs, asking Joe, "Why aren't you doing what we ask you to do? You have to learn how to juggle your cases better."

Joe had hit the roof, particularly as the desk officer who sent the email, Jim Dunston, had never spent a day in the field. Dunston had not even received the basic training course at the Farm that would allow him to find his own ass, *sans* flashlight, operationally speaking. Yet he was trying to give Joe orders, merely because he was behind a desk in Hqs. Joe forwarded the email to his branch chief, who sent it to the Chief of Station. The Chief had told Joe he would handle it. Joe later saw a copy of his Chief's reply to Dunston.

"Dunston, if you want to provide me more case officers, more money, and more authority to act independently, I will be happy to satisfy all the demands for information you make upon my case officers. However, until that day, I have a threadbare operational budget, and I am short staffed. My case officers are overworked as it is. To make matters worse, you personally, and Hqs in general, has a very bad habit of jerking me and my case officers around by changing what you want from this station roughly three times a day, then second-guessing every decision I make."

"If you don't like how this field station or my officers are performing, why don't you get off your fucking fat ass and come show us poor, benighted idiots in the field how *real* case officers do their jobs, since you seem to hold yourself as an authority on the subject. Until that day, kindly butt out and allow us to tend to our knitting.

Hugs and kisses, Chief of Station."

Back channel feuding was a cycle of demand and complaint as old as the spook trade. Fortunately, the old demands and complaints were usually forgotten or ignored with every new crisis.

Given his own distaste for the often imperiously-phrased cables he had received from Hqs when he had been in field stations, Joe went out of the way to make sure anything he sent out from CIA Hqs was straightforward, innocuous, short, and to the point. He had too much bureaucratic drama in his life as it was; he didn't need any more.

SECRET

IMMEDIATE

TO: WWSB
FROM HQS NE/ITF

WNINTEL OPS RYZAT

1. ACTION: TEL AVIV, SEE PARA 3. AMMAN, ABU DHABI, BAGHDAD, BAHRAIN, DOHA, DUBAI, ISTANBUL, KABUL, MANAMA, MUSCAT, TEHRANX, SEE PARA 4. BEIJING, SINAGAPORE, AND TAIPEI SEE PARA 5. MOSCOW, SEE PARA 6.

2. REQUEST ANY AND ALL INFORMATION WITH REGARDS TO SINKING OF THE IRANIAN REVOLUTIONARY GUARD CORP NAVY DESTROYER SHAHEED, SUNK 12 JUNE 2014 NEAR THE STRAIGHTS OF HORMUZ IN THE PERSIAN GULF. IRANIAN CLAIMS TO THE CONTRARY, THE SINKING OF THE SHAHEED WAS NOT/NOT DUE TO US NAVY COMBAT ACTION OF ANY SORT.

3. TEL AVIV, REQUEST YOU IMMEDIATELY CONTACT THE CHIEF OF MOSSAD FOR ANY/ALL INFORMATION ON THE SINKING OF THE SHAHEED, INCLUDING WHETHER ISRAELI ARMED FORCES HAD ANY/ANY INVOLVEMENT OR PRIOR KNOWLEDGE OF THE SINKING.

4. ALL IRAN-REGION STATIONS: IN ADDITION TO ANY INSIGHTS YOU MAY GLEAN FROM IRGC NAVY AND REGULAR IRANIAN NAVY SOURCES ABOUT THE SHAHEED, PLEASE WORK TO CONFIRM WHETHER ALL MEMBER OF THE COUNCIL OF GUARDIANS ACTUALLY WERE ABOARD THE SHAHEED WHEN IT WENT DOWN. WE ARE INTERESTED IN THE POTENTIAL POLITICAL FALLOUT IF THE COUNCIL WAS ABOARD THE SHAHEED

WHEN IT SUNK. REGIME STABILITY IS A MAJOR CONCERN SINCE THE GASOLINE RIOTS LAST FALL IN TEHRAN.

5. BEIJING, SINGAPORE, TAIPEI AND ALL STATIONS WITH ASSETS WITH INSIGHT INTO THE CHINESE PEOPLE LIBERATION'S ARMY NAVY (PLAN): IRGC DESTROYER SHAHEED WAS PURCHASED BY IRAN IN EARLY 2014 FROM THE PLAN. PLEASE QUERY ANY PLAN SOURCES ON POSSIBLE MECHANICAL MALFUNCTIONS THAT COULD LEAD TO CATASTROPHIC LOSS/SINKING, ANY PROBLEMS DURING THE RECENT ACCEPTANCE TRIALS OF THE SHAHEED, AND/OR ANY RECENT MODIFICATIONS TO THE SHAHEED.

6. MOSCOW: REQUEST NAVAL ATTACHE ASK WHAT RUSSIAN COUNTERPARTS HAVE TO SAY ABOUT POSSIBLE DESIGN FLAWS OR OTHER PROBLEMS WITH THE SHAHEED. THE SHAHEED WAS ORIGINALLY BUILT IN RUSSIA. WE CAN'T HELP BUT RECALL WHEN THE RUSSIAN SUBMARINE KURSK WAS LOST IN THE BARENTS SEA IN 2000, IT WAS NOT LONG BEFORE FALSE RUMORS WERE CIRCULATING THAT THE US NAVY HAD TORPEDOED THE KURSK, BECAUSE THE RUSSIANS DIDN'T WANT TO OWN UP. WE WOULD LIKE TO HEAD ANY SIMILAR UNFOUNDED RUMORS ABOUT THE SHAHEED OFF AT THE PASS.

REGARDS.

FILE: BRLAMPSTEAD CLASS: XI HUM 4-82

SECRET

     In the internet age, writing in all caps was considered to be "shouting," but that was the way all CIA cables had always been written. Perhaps that was just a coincidence…although in reading some of the more exquisitely subtle barbs that have passed between CIA Hqs and field stations in official cable traffic, one could make the case that a lot of the official cable traffic between Hqs and the field stations *was* nothing more than two groups shouting past each other. Cables with particularly memorable exchanges of verbal fireworks had come to be called "rockets" and were treasured and tacked to the walls of the cubicles at CIA Hqs.

As a rule, Joe had never suffered fools lightly. When he had been a junior case officer serving abroad, he had written his fair share of rockets, and caused no shortage of trouble for himself thereby. Back then, Joe had a regrettable tendency to "write angry" when replying to obtuse cables from Hqs. After an incident that had his then-Chief of Station yelling at him for twenty minutes because one of Joe's snarky cables had pissed off CIA Hqs all the way up to Deputy Director of Operations, Joe started following a suggestion from Claire. He forced himself to send all his angry cables to a buddy for review. The buddy would thoughtfully drain the venom out of Joe's printed words before sending the cable on its way.

Joe now believed he probably would have been fired or forced to serve five back-to-back tours in Baghdad as punishment if he hadn't adopted this practice long ago. Insults in unofficial emails are one thing, but CIA Hqs does not react well to sarcasm in official cable traffic from the field stations, *particularly* when the sarcasm is merited.

Joe's boss, the NE division Chief of Ops, Fredrick Sandler, arrived and stopped by Joe's desk. "Joe, staff meeting about the Shaheed in 10 minutes."

"Okay, Fred. Got a WWSB about it for your coordination. I'll send it over."

"Right. White House is crapping their pants over this. The sooner we get some info on this, the better."

CHAPTER NINE- *RUBAH'* -THE FOX BEGINS HIS HUNT

The investigation did not start well for Lieutenant Jafari. After the loss of the Shaheed, the communications center at Bandar Abbas was crowded with curious officers. Iranian Navy Admiral Sayyari had ordered most of them out, and told the guards to restrict access to essential personnel which did not include logistics officers such as Jafari. He almost had to bludgeon the guard before gaining access.

Once inside, Admiral Sayyari only allowed Jafari to stay because Jafari promised that a call relevant to the Shaheed would be arriving from his cousin, Major General Jafari. Admiral Sayyari harrumphed at the Lieutenant's claim, before humiliatingly ordering Jafari to stand against the back wall until the call came. Sayyari worked for the rival Iranian Navy, and therefore did not directly command Jafari, but an Admiral could make a lot of trouble, which was something Jafari did not need right now.

The Lieutenant stood against the back wall, quietly seething, until his idiot cousin, the General, finally called and relayed to Sayyari that since the Shaheed was an IRGC ship, the IRGC would be leading the investigation. Furthermore, Sayyari was told, the General's cousin, Lieutenant Jafari, would be in charge of the investigation. This did not sit well with Sayyari, who despised just about everything to do with the IRGC Navy, particularly the corrupt Lieutenant Jafari, but his hands were tied: the Iranian Navy had no jurisdiction over the IRGC Navy.

Lieutenant Jafari immediately ordered that a small IRGC gunboat be posted above the wreck of the Shaheed at all times to keep away the curious and "Any spies of the Great Satan." Jafari then began questioning the duty watch officer, IRGC Navy Lieutenant Junior Grade Assad Mumtaz, about the course of events. "Mumtaz, you were here when the distress messages from the Shaheed came in?

"Yes, sir."

"Had the Shaheed experienced problems of any sort before the messages about being under attack arrived?"

"No sir, everything was functioning normally."

"Who was in the communications center then?"

"Myself, Commander Saeed, a few radio operators, and a few members of the press with their escorts from the Ministry of Islamic Guidance."

"Did Commander Saeed explain why he was not on his ship?

Mumtaz paused before answering slowly. "Sir, the Commander said Captain Akhlagi sent him ashore."

"Mumtaz, why do you hesitate? Do you not understand the importance of this investigation? We must learn why the Shaheed was sunk. Iran has suffered a grave blow."

"Sir, I understand, but Commander Saeed ordered me to discuss this with no one."

"Lieutenant, I am acting now as the direct representative of Major General Mohammed Jafari, *my cousin*, who commands all of the IRGC, including me, you, and Commander Saeed. If I ask a question in the course of this investigation, it is as if Major General Jafari were asking it. I think you would agree that the Major General outranks the Commander?"

"Sir, yes, he does."

"Then kindly answer my questions immediately and with no more nonsense, or I will get my cousin on the phone, and ask him to order you to cooperate directly. Shall I disturb him now? Would you like to come to the attention of the General? Because I promise you, it will not be a pleasant experience for you. Nor a career-enhancing one. Is that clear, Lieutenant *Junior Grade* Mumtaz?"

Subdued, Mumtaz replied, "Yes, sir. Of course sir. I am happy to answer all your questions."

"A wise choice, Mumtaz. Now, did Commander Saeed say anything about why Captain Akhlagi ordered him ashore?"

"Sir, he said Captain Akhlagi ordered them ashore to prove that the Shaheed was so modern and the crew so well trained that the Shaheed could be sailed with a skeleton crew. He also wanted to reward as many of the men as he could. He sent them ashore so they could watch the Iran-Turkey football match."

Jafari was appalled. The "reward" scenario sounded transparently false. Had Akhlagi suspected something? Jafari had to handle this carefully, react very carefully. News that men had survived, when all were thought to lost, would be greeted with joy…unless you were among those who expected all the crew to be dead.

"*Khoda* be praised, Mumtaz, what blessed news! Surely this was the blessed hand of *Imam-e zaman,* the hidden Imam whose coming we await. Many of our brave sailors were saved from a terrible fate! How many were offloaded? Where are these fortunate men? And where is Commander Saeed? Why is he not here? I must speak with him."

"Sir, I regret to say that I do not know. Commander Saeed never told me how many men offloaded, and I have not seen any crewmen from the Shaheed since Commander Saeed left. Except for Lieutenant Khani. Lieutenant Khani from the Shaheed came by fifteen minutes ago, shortly before you arrived, and said that Commander Saeed had taken the Ababeel to Tehran to report to IRGC headquarters. He said the Ababeel would be landing at Mehrabad Airbase."

The seed of worry that Lieutenant Jafari felt at the first news of Saeed's survival was rapidly growing deeper roots. Jafari did not like that Saeed was running loose with a helicopter. He did not like the uncertainty over how many crewman from the Shaheed had survived. Now the fact that the diver, Ziyaii, was still drawing breath began to seem more ominous, as well. He had to take immediate action to master this situation before it spun out of his control.

With a deliberately casual tone of voice, he said "Mumtaz, send a runner over to the IRGC Navy barracks and have him round up as many crewmen from the Shaheed as he can and bring them back here so I can speak with them. Including Lieutenant Khani. Also, radio the Ababeel, and order them to turn back to Bandar

Abbas in the name of Major General Jafari. The investigation is centered here, I need the expertise of Commander Saeed here in Bandar Abbas, not wasted briefing the General Staff or Admiralty in Tehran. Any questions?"

"No sir. I will carry out your orders immediately, sir." As Jafari began to turn away, he saw Lieutenant Mumtaz raise his hand to wave over the duty runner and heard Mumtaz begin relaying the orders to gather crewmembers from the Shaheed.

Jafari needed to find a quiet place to use the encrypted cellphone to call his cousin and pass along the unsettling news about the survival of a large portion of Shaheed's crew. Jafari found a vacant cubicle to use; the walls were thin, but thick enough to muffle the details of his conversation if he spoke quietly. He pulled out his encrypted cell phone and dialed his cousin. The phone only rang briefly, then Mohammed's gruff voice answered.

"Majid, how goes it? What is the latest?"

"Mohammed, all is secure for the moment, but we may have a problem. I need you to send more Qods Force teams here, in case of need. I just learned that Commander Saeed has headed to Tehran on the helicopter from the Shaheed. I ordered the communication center to radio the helicopter, the Ababeel, to return to Bandar Abbas so I can speak with Saeed. Also, something very peculiar, and slightly worrying. It was not only Saeed who was not aboard when the Shaheed sailed. Apparently, Akhlagi only had a skeleton crew aboard when it sailed. Akhlagi ordered most of the crew off! The watch officer here said this was to reward the men for their hard work in preparing for the christening by letting them watch the Iran-Turkey football match ashore. I..."

The General cut Jafari off with a roar. "What? What is the meaning of this? How could you let this happen? You were supposed to manage events down there! What were you doing instead, off visiting your favorite prostitutes? You donkey!"

Lieutenant Jafari interrupted the General's tirade before it could get fully underway, interjecting with a calm tone of voice that was at odds with how he really felt. "General, I did *all* we agreed upon in our planning meetings, including staying away from the Shaheed so I did not appear to be hovering like a vulture!

Thus I did not see the crew disembark. I notice that Ansari's man, Nouri, said nothing of this, the idiot. If you want to blame anyone, blame him. He was set to watch the Shaheed, not I."

The Lieutenant paused to grab a breath, and continued in a mollifying tone of voice, "The key events we planned move apace. The Shaheed is gone. Rahimi is gone. Whatever the reason the crew was put ashore, it is unlikely that Akhlagi explained his orders to the crew. Saeed will soon be back here, where I can question him, and if *your* Qods Force teams are not incompetent, Ziyaii will soon be dead. Every plan has unanticipated developments. We must remain calm and continue to move behind the scenes quickly and quietly. I have someone out rounding-up the disembarked crewmembers so I can talk to them to see if any know *why* they were disembarked. Depending on what I find out, Qods Force Teams may need to take more 'direct action.' The team already down here still has not located Ziyaii, who has his cell phone turned off and cannot be tracked by it. One of the reasons I want more men is so they can flood the area and be sure to catch him. It is critical that Ziyaii be dead soon. How many can you send? When will they be here?"

The General, slightly calmer now, responded smugly, "I do not wear these stars by accident, Majid. I anticipated the unexpected. I have ten Qods Force teams of five men each standing by, all with their own vehicles and communications gear. They can get photographs and descriptions of Ziyaii from the Qods Force team already in place and be combing the streets of Bandar Abbas within 45 minutes."

The Lieutenant replied with an oily sycophancy that was second nature to him, "Wise, Cousin Mohammed, very wise. Truly those stars are justified. I request that you send nine of the teams to coordinate with the one already looking for Ziyaii. The tenth, I ask that you send to report to me. I will keep them nearby to escort Saeed to me when the Ababeel returns to Bandar Abbas."

"Very well, Majid, it shall be as you wish. Keep me informed of what Saeed has to say, as well as the other crewmembers. I will talk to Ansari, and let him know how things stand. And ask him why his man Nouri failed to report how many were crewmembers were offloaded from the Shaheed!"

"Excellent, General. Inshallah, any worries we now have will be laid to rest within a few hours."

General Jafari gave a grunt of acknowledgement to his cousin Majid and hung up.

Lieutenant Majid Jafari would soon recall his soothing reassurances to his cousin the General as the last moment of time when he still truly believed the events they had conspired to set in motion could be managed. Both Jafaris had been riding the tiger. They did not yet understand that both had already fallen off, because they had not yet felt the impact of the ground or the slashing claws of the maddened beast.

CHAPTER 10-ZIYAII

Explosive Ordinance Disposal Technician 2nd Class Javid Ziyaii of the Iranian Navy Destroyer Jamaran stumbled away from the apartment of Captain Rahimi in shock. He moved mechanically, as if he were a marionette guided by an inept puppet-master. Without real thought, his footsteps carried him back in the direction of a bus that went to the naval base at Bandar Abbas.

Although they had both his picture and a detailed description, the Qods Force team headed for Captain Rahimi's apartment raced by Ziyaii as he was boarding the bus without noticing him. The bus obscured Ziyaii, who was on the other side of the street from the rapidly moving Qods Force team. The bus had three stops to make before depositing Ziyaii at the gates of Bandar Abbas. Ziyaii was in a state of such mental numbness that he did not remember Commander Saeed's advice not to return to Bandar Abbas until two stops had already passed.

Ziyaii stumbled off the bus at the last stop before Bandar Abbas Naval Base. The area had many cheap restaurants and some less-than-legal and highly tawdry entertainments favored by sailors and yard workers from Bandar Abbas. Ziyaii turned up a narrow side-street with no sidewalks and crumbling blacktop pavement. The street was graced with a lone, bedraggled tree. After a short two-minute walk, he arrived at one of his favorite restaurants, The Beirut, which served impeccably authentic Lebanese food. The Beirut was about to close for the afternoon rest period when Ziyaii shambled in.

The Beirut's owner was a short, white-haired refugee from the political violence of Beirut's civil war, Melham Hanood. Ziyaii was a regular at Hanood's inexpensive eatery. The décor was faded posters of the Lebanese coastline set above cracked plastic tables, but patrons always forgot about the tacky decor after the first bite. The Beirut had turned Ziyaii into Lebanese food addict; he had eaten there dozens of times in the past two years.

Hanood had become so fond of the good-natured Ziyaii, who had started to bring large crowds of friends every time he stopped in, that he had invited Ziyaii to private family dinners three times in the past two months.

One look at the vacant stare on Ziyaii's face transported Hanood decades in time and thousands of kilometers in space. Hanood had a terrible familiarity with the blank stare of shock common to the faces of people who lost a husband, a son, or a brother to the vicious cycle of car bomb explosions during the Lebanese civil war in the 1980s. Melham had left Beirut in early 1990, hoping never to see that look again, but recognizing it immediately when he did. He knew it had been on his own face after the Christian Marionite militia had blown up a cousin with a car bomb; the bombing was retaliation for a Hezbollah car bomb planted in a Christian neighborhood by his cousin.

The mixture of politics and religion had sickened Hanood ever since.

Melham knew instantly that something was gravely wrong. He parked Ziyaii at a table in the back, shooed out his only other customer, and closed up the restaurant. He dashed into the kitchen to speak to his wife of 36 years. "Maryam, tea, immediately! Javid is here, and he looks sick, as if he had just lost both his parents and grandparents at once. Put some *davaa* in the tea. A healthy amount!"

Alcohol was publicly banned in Iran, but private consumption was as common as sand in the desert. Having grown up in Lebanon where alcohol was routinely consumed by those of all religions and ethnicities, Melham had come to believe the Islamic Republic's rules on alcohol consumption were pointless and hypocritical. In Hanood's mind, alcohol was not an evil scourge to be blamed for bad behavior. As with all other pleasures, it was the lack of self-control in those who overindulged that created problems. Maryam tipped two big slugs of fine Armenian brandy into a large mug of tea drawn from a battered samovar and rushed out to Ziyaii's table with it.

Ziyaii took the cup with a hand that trembled slightly as Melham and Maryam seated themselves opposite from the young sailor.

Maryam urged, "Drink, Javid, drink! It is medicine."

Javid took two big swallows, heedless of the heat of tea, enjoying the burn of the alcohol and the sense of insulation from harsh realities that came with it.

The Hanoods studied Ziyaii closely, waiting a few minutes until the alcohol took effect to before Melham begin gently probing, "Javid, what is it, my young brother? I can see tragedy in your face. Tragedy comes to us all, until we are fortunate enough to leave this life for Paradise. Share your sorrows with us."

With a ghost of his normally exuberant grin and tone of voice, Ziyaii belatedly addressed Maryam with a fond familiarity, "*Naneh Jaan*, dear mother of my heart, thank you for the fine medicine. I think we could power our ship turbines with such tea. Many in Bandar Abbas have great sorrows today, and I more than most. There is much I cannot say, which *must* remain unsaid for your own safety. I can see the news has not spread to you yet, otherwise you would not look puzzled. Do you recall my friend, Izad Vahdat? I brought him here two or three times."

"Yes, Javid, of course. A fine young man. What of him? Has he been hurt?"

"Mr. Hanood, it is not just Vahdat. Vahdat was a sailor on the Destroyer Shaheed. Less than 90 minutes ago, the Shaheed sunk. All aboard are dead, Vahdat included."

Clearly, the news of the Shaheed had not yet reached the Hanoods. Their faces crumpled. Melham interjected, "I am a witness that Allah is merciful and infinite in his wisdom, but how could such a tragedy happen! Was this an accident? What happened? How could such a fate strike so many fine young men?"

"Agha Hanood, there is more…" Ziyaii fell silent. He desperately yearned to unburden himself by telling everything about the sinking of the Shaheed, but knew doing so could only leave the Hanood's in grave danger. Ziyaii started again, "There is more, I…." Ziyaii was struck again by an overwhelming sense of guilt. He could not compound it by involving the Hanoods. "All I can say is, I am an *nafham,* a fool and a buffoon. Vahdat is dead because of me. Directly because of my foolish actions. I must leave soon, and I can never come back."

Melham and Maryam looked at each other, alarmed. Ziyaii's voice spoke of finality, of a permanent parting of ways. Maryam reached over and clasped Ziyaii's hand. Looking him in the eyes, she spoke with a kindly weariness to her voice that marked her as a woman who had known no shortage of regret and pain in life, "Javid, nobody who has drawn breathe upon *Allah's* earth has done so without at sometime hurting those we love. That is the human condition. If you are foolish, it is that you have a good heart, one too trusting to survive easily in a world that is cruel. Inshallah, whatever is wrong, you will someday put it behind you. Sometimes a dark thing is thrust upon you so that you may learn from it, and in doing so, set an example for others."

The Hanoods could see alcohol and emotional fatigue acting upon Ziyaii like a powerful sedative; the most powerful protective mechanism of the mind when confronted by crushing guilt is sometimes to simply deny consciousness. The Hanoods got Ziyaii on his feet and brought him back through the kitchen to a small, screened-in porch off the kitchen. The porch, a part of the Hanood's small house which connected to their restaurant, had low divans and a lazily rotating ceiling fan. This was where the Hanoods took their midday rest between the lunch and dinner crowds. Ziyaii had barely stretched his full length on a couch before a black tide of deep sleep pulled him into its depths.

The Hanoods hurried to the TV in their house. Twenty minutes later, news of the loss of the Shaheed was broadcast. When they heard that the Council of Guardians had been aboard, they were shocked. Melham knew this could ignite a firestorm. He did not understand why Javid was berating himself about the Shaheed, which the news reported as being sunk by torpedoes of the Great Satan. But then again, both Melham and Maryam had lived in Iran long enough to place no faith whatsoever in official news broadcasts.

Melham turned to Maryam, "If Javid is connected to this in any way, or even knows something about it, his life may be hanging by a thread. This is too big. Too important. Whatever has happened is political in some way, that I know! For all his lively spirits and pranks, Javid has never been one to lie, exaggerate, or make something out of nothing. If he says he must leave Iran, we must help him."

*   *   *

When Javid Ziyaii awoke, he could tell it had been dark for at least a few hours. Sitting up slowly and looking through a screen door, it took him a few seconds to realize he was looking into the Hanoods' kitchen. Maryam was stirring a pot of rice, but in an unhurried way. Her slow pace, the dim murmuring of voices and quiet clanks of dishes, and the unusually subdued street sounds filtering into the sleeping porch all combined to create a funereal feel, a mourning air. The silence was penetrating; this area was usually filled at night with the raucous voices of sailors. Clearly, The Beirut, and the whole neighborhood, were almost empty.

Muttering to himself, Ziyaii said, "And why should it not be like a funeral, like a tomb?" Are not many dead this day? And at my hands!" Thinking on Iran's most famous serial killer, Ziyaii mused with black humor, "Would not Ashgar the Murderer look on me with great esteem, awe, and jealousy for my work this day?"

Ziyaii had the disconnected feeling that comes from sleeping for too long at an odd time of day. The sleep had not been especially restorative, but at least it allowed him to put a small amount of emotional distance between this morning's events and now. He knew he had to put his grief aside and move; every moment here with the Hanoods put them in danger. He got to his feet and entered the Beirut's kitchen.

He greeted Mrs. Hanood, "Good evening, *Naneh Jaan*. How are you?"

"I am well. For once I am not pulling my hair out trying to feed an army; tonight is a slow night, very few customers. How are you feeling, Javid?"

"Well enough, *Naneh*, but I must leave. I must leave Iran, tonight. Within the hour, if possible. I have no time to discuss this, and it is safer for you if I do not. "

Melham bustled back into the kitchen with a few dirty plates in his hands. "Javid, you are awake. Good! You had us worried. What shall you do, now? How can we help?"

"You can get me some strong coffee or tea; I must clear my mind and think about what I must do next."

Maryam made Javid a cup of coffee strong enough to be used as paint stripper. He retired to the porch to sit and think, slowly sipping at the bitter brew. It was simple, really. There was only one way out. He was a sailor and a combat diver. He returned to the kitchen.

"Naneh, can you get me some plastic garbage sacks and a length of rope? And a bit of food and water in separate containers? Agha Hanood, I need to get rid of these clothes. Do you have any men's clothes I might use?"

Melham replied, "Javid, this is very simple, we have these things. You can use my son's clothes; he leaves some here for his visits. He is close enough to your size. The food and other things are easy; this is restaurant! Is there nothing else we can do? Do you need money?"

"Agha Hanood, Naneh Maryam, this is truly all I need. Money will not help me now. My course is clear. Worry not. Inshallah, within two days, I will be safe with family, and beyond the reach of harm. But quickly now. The sooner I go, the better for us all."

Melham scurried away to get Javid the clothes. On his way back, Melham stopped at his stash of currency, withdrew five crisp US one hundred dollar bills, and slipped them into the pocket of the jacket he was bringing to Javid along with a hastily scrawled note that said, "Be safe and well, dear Javid." Javid was too proud to ask for money, but Melham knew most problems could be eased with money, and there was no other help he could think of to offer Javid right now.

This was not a traditional leave-taking. There was no time for an evening of tearful goodbyes. No time to prepare or eat the *ash-e posht-e paa,* the special noodle soup eaten at the beginning of journeys to ensure a safe return. Javid changed into the clothes, gave each of the Hanoods a fierce hug. He made a simple declaration.

"I love you as I love my own parents. *Khoda hafiz,* May God Keep you. I must go."

Not trusting their voices not to crack with emotion, the Hanoods stood mute as they watched their young friend stride out the kitchen door, cross the courtyard of their tiny home, and let himself out into the alley behind The Beirut.

The dirt alley was lined with a mixture of structures, judging from padlocked outdoor storage bins, some were small businesses, while others, with plastic toys scattered on the ground, were obviously homes. Most of the buildings backing onto the alley were guarded by man-high, unpainted, rough cinderblock walls. Almost no light filtered into the alley, which was littered with discarded bottles and random bits of construction materials, fragmented wooden boards, damaged concrete blocks, and loose bricks, shattered and obviously unusable anywhere outside of a riot. Moving at a cautious pace, Ziyaii crept south down the alley, ever mindful of the debris that could trip him up.

When he reached the main road closest to the beach, he stayed in the shadows for a few moments, studying, looking for parked cars or police nearby. Seeing none, he casually but quickly jogged across the road. He walked east for a few hundred meters, clinging to the shadows cast by the trees in the sidewalk, then turned south into the long driveway leading to the luxurious beachfront Homa Hotel. He walked like a man with a purpose, as if he was heading to the Homa's beachside coffee shop for an important meeting. When he got to the beach, he continued east along the shoreline. In the shadow of the Homa's pedestrian pier, he stripped down to his underwear, sticking all his belongings into the plastic sacks Maryam had given him. He nested one sack inside the next, tying each one tightly to keep his belongings dry. He tied the sack to his waist with the length of rope. He looked up and down the beach and found it empty of people.

As Ziyaii strode towards the gentle surf of the Persian Gulf, his grief fell away. He was a combat swimmer. He was in his element now. This was what he was trained for. Ziyaii swam out into the Persian Gulf with strong, confident strokes. The mouth of the breakwater to the harbor that was Ziyaii's destination was less than a kilometer a way; a mere warm-up for a man trained to swim five kilometers, carry out a demolition mission, then swim back. Ziyaii fell into an easy rhythm, the exercise delivering a peace from his weighty thoughts that nothing else could.

Maryam Hanood had more insight into Ziyaii's character than she knew. Lieutenant Jafari had specifically suggested to Captain Rahimi that Javid Ziyaii should be used to set the mines. In researching who might be best suited to the task, Lieutenant Jafari had learned that Ziyaii loved to laugh and play practical jokes, and was so trusting that he had repeatedly been taken advantage of by his fellow sailors in games of chance. Ziyaii was open by nature. By Jafari's calculation, this made Ziyaii little better than a naïve fool, but a fool with the diving skills necessary to the plan against the Shaheed.

Javid Ziyaii was a fisherman's son. His father, Rashid, had lost a leg in the war against Saddam and retired to his ancestral fishing village with a small pension. A man with a decent prosthetic leg could still fish, and Rashid did, helping to give his son Javid a boyhood untroubled by politics or the mullahs. Ziyaii spent most of his early years drawing in nets with his father, and learning the tricks of sailing the waters of the Persian Gulf.

Then a recruiter for the Iranian Navy arrived. Like millions of rural young men since the dawn of time, Javid listened to the recruiter, rapt with his tales of promised adventure, camaraderie, the patriotism of defending the blessed *Neza-e Moghaddas,* the Holy Regime. He signed up enthusiastically. Ziyaii's intelligence tests quickly identified him as someone capable of missions requiring a high degree of intelligence and skill; Ziyaii picked demolitions. Javid Ziyaii's demolition instructors subjected him to harsh treatment to simulate combat conditions. Although they never told him so, his instructors had quietly marveled over Ziyaii's attitude. Ziyaii never quit, even in the harshest conditions, and always maintained his cheerful, joking demeanor. Ziyaii had learned explosives, sabotage, escape and evasion, firearms, and small boat handling, and many other things. The sea was in his blood; he took to the diving and demolition training like a duck to water. Ziyaii had never been more proud than when he won his assignment to the Jamaran, the best ship in the Regular Navy.

Lieutenant Jafari had no real conception of what it took to become a skilled EOD technician like Ziyaii. Jafari was a military officer in name only; he had picked logistics as a specialty and worked his connections to get assigned to the shipyards at Bandar Abbas because no other position offered such rich opportunities for graft on military procurement contracts. Jafari had no real military skills, beyond the ability to use naval jargon to simulate competence. Like all narcissists, Jafari assumed others were no more talented or skilled than he was. Jafari's connections to his cousin, the General, had always saved Lieutenant Jafari from the consequences of underestimating others.

Until now.

Once within the protected harbor, it took Ziyaii an hour to identify a suitable craft. The first two pleasure boats were large enough, but did not possess sufficient fuel for Ziyaii's needs. The third craft was a trim 24-foot-long cabin cruiser outfitted as the toy of a rich man. It was perfect. It had outsize fuel tanks that were full and two three-hundred-horsepower motors. Releasing the boat from its anchor and stripping the wires of the ignition to start the motors was child's play to Ziyaii. He had trained for far more difficult missions in far more hostile conditions. Showing no running lights, he slowly motored out of the quiet harbor. When he was four kilometers out to sea, he switched on the boat's running lights and picked up speed. The Persian Gulf was one of the most heavily traveled shipping channels in the world. Traveling with no lights could be extremely dangerous, and could also draw the wrong sort of attention. Nobody but smugglers ran without lights.

Ziyaii headed away from Bandar Abbas to the southeast, instinctively staying far from the wreck of the Shaheed, hugging the southwestern edge of Hormuz Island until he was in open water. Once Ziyaii had traveled 30 kilometers, he shifted his course to due south. By the time the sun was rising, Ziyaii had sighted the tip of the Oman Peninsula. The fuel was holding out well; Javid increased his speed to 12 knots as he hugged the western coast of the Omani peninsula headed southwest.

As the late afternoon sunlight began painting the Persian Gulf with beautiful hues of gold and blue, a tired Javid Ziyaii dialed back the throttles and slowly chugged into the serpentine entrance to Dubai Creek in the United Arab Emirates.

Ziyaii had had plenty of time to think during the voyage. As the hours had passed, a change had occurred and the harsh lesson had been learned. He had cursed himself for a fool, and swore it would never happen again. Forever gone was the boyish openness, which so many of Ziyaii's friends and relatives had admired and enjoyed. He had finally acquired the thin veneer of mistrust common to theocratic Iran. He still loved his family, his country, and his countrymen. He enjoyed his military service, and treasured the skills he had learned. But he knew, now, that he could never serve mullahs that were capable of such massive treachery. Better the mullahs had never been born, than that they lived do such things to their own countrymen. Ziyaii's grief was being shouldered aside by his anger.

This act of betrayal was not something that could be allowed to pass. He had no idea how, yet, but he would have his revenge.

Ziyaii continued up Dubai Creek until he saw a cluster of pleasure boats similar to the borrowed ship he was piloting off his port bow. He carefully eased his boat into a slip at Marina One, then went into the Dubai Creek Marina Clubhouse. He did not bother to go to the Club's office to pay for a slip; it was not his boat, after all. He felt guilty about borrowing it, but knew that once it was reported stolen, the Marina's staff would track down the registered owner and contact him. Ultimately, the owner would be out nothing more than the cost of a ticket to Dubai to pick up the boat, and the cost of a few hundred gallons of marine-grade fuel.

The obsequious Clubhouse concierge ordered Ziyaii a taxi. When the taxi arrived, Ziyaii stepped in, and used his limited Arabic to say "Downtown, please." He pulled out his cellphone and powered it on for the first time in over 24 hours. He pulled up a number from the phonebook and dialed it. "Hello, Salim! It is cousin Javid. I am well, thank you. I, too, look forward to seeing you someday, soon. Ha! In fact, this is your lucky day, cousin. *Khoda* has granted your wish. Guess who has come to Dubai to visit you, Salim!"

CHAPTER 11- *RUBAH'* -THE FOX

Lieutenant Jafari wondered if all investigations were this difficult. The people he wanted to interview had evaporated like morning dew in the desert. The runner had only managed to round up three crew members from the Shaheed, all of whom had been in the process of packing sea-bags to depart the area. The sailors had initially been reluctant to talk to Jafari, but after some browbeating, they had confirmed that they had been ordered off the Shaheed and sent to watch the Iran-Turkey football match on TV.

They had not been given any explanation for why they were offloaded.

None of the sailors knew how many of the crew had come ashore.

They knew nothing of Commander Saeed's actions after the Shaheed went down, besides gossip that was based on the TV news coverage.

During the football match, they had seen news that the Shaheed has sunk. Half an hour later, they had all had been granted emergency leave and ordered to leave the area and not discuss the Shaheed with the press. They claimed they knew nothing more.

Jafari had no reason to disbelieve the sailors, but having them offloaded just before the Shaheed sailed to its doom was simply too big a coincidence to be plausible. Something was wrong; Akhlagi must have suspected an attack of some sort was coming. Jafari had the duty runner going through the barracks with a crew manifest from the Shaheed. At this point, Jafari had no better way of learning who might have offloaded from the Shaheed than having the runner go to each room and check out the gear and clothes lockers of the sailors. Those lockers that were missing uniforms and civilian clothes presumably belonged to those who survived. The lockers that still had a full complement of uniforms and civilian clothes belonged to those who went down on the Shaheed.

While Jafari was narrowing down the list of who remained alive from the Shaheed, he allowed himself a moment of honesty, and admitted that he didn't know what to do with that information. The sailors from the Shaheed were *probably* unimportant, but he could not say that with absolute surety until he talked to all of them. Jafari couldn't think of how to do that. He didn't want to divert any of the Qods Force teams from the search for EOD Tech Ziyaii. Ziyaii's death was absolutely essential, that much Jafari knew. Jafari was getting updates every half-hour from the Qods Force teams, who were slowly driving the streets of Bandar Abbas, looking for anyone that met Ziyaii's description.

Although he didn't realize his error, Jafari was not thinking like a legitimate investigating officer with vast resources to draw on. Because Jafari didn't want any kind of law enforcement involvement that he did not control, he didn't think to ask the local police to send officers to the airport and bus station at Bandar Abbas to round up crewmembers from the Shaheed, many of whom were still waiting to catch a bus or plane out of the area. Jafari had one Qods Force team at the airport and another at the main bus terminal. Both were doing nothing but looking for Ziyaii. Of course, those teams could also have rounded up sailors from the Shaheed, but Jafari ordered them to concentrate solely on searching for Ziyaii. Ziyaii was the immediate priority; everything else was secondary.

*　　　*　　　*

Just as Commander Saeed had ordered, after the Ababeel set down Rescue Diver Erfan and EOD Tech Kazimi had tried to leave Bandar Abbas in the Pride they owned. Unfortunately, the battery had been dead and when they had managed to jump-start the car, it sputtered and died again repeatedly; the sailors suspected there was a problem somewhere in the fuel lines, fuel pump, or injectors. In any case, they had no time to fix it. The only alternative they could afford was a bus.

Rescue Diver Erfan was the only crewmember of the Shaheed, besides Commander Saeed, who knew the Shaheed had been mined. In the Bandar Abbas bus station, a team of hard eyed men holding photos looked hard at Erfan and his companion, EOD tech Kazimi. Both sailors walked by the Qods Force team unmolested and boarded a bus for Shiraz. The Qods Force team took no notice; neither Erfan nor Kazimi matched the description or photo of Ziyaii.

*   *   *

When he was obsessing about Ziyaii, Jafari was able to forget for several minutes at a time that he did not know where Commander Saeed and the Ababeel were. Jafari's orders to return to Bandar Abbas had not been acknowledged by the Ababeel.

When Lieutenant Jafari started screaming at the duty officer at the IRGC communications center about his incompetence, Lieutenant Mumtaz had inquired meekly, "What would you have me do, Lieutenant? Our radios are working. The Ababeel is not answering. That means their radios are broken, they are out of range, they have crashed, have adopted radio silence, or are otherwise unable to respond. None of those things are conditions which I can change from here. We have been radioing the Ababeel every five minutes for the last two hours. Would you like me to call for an airborne search party?"

Jafari managed to reign in his temper. A search party would accomplish nothing beyond raising many awkward questions at an inopportune time. He would have to take Commander Saeed at his word for now, and assume the Ababeel was heading for Mehrabad Air Base in Tehran. "Mumtaz, we will assume for now that the Ababeel is experiencing radio problems. Call the control tower at Mehrabad Airbase and inform them that the Ababeel is probably inbound and may be experiencing radio problems. I will arrange their transportation to IRGC headquarters for debriefing there until I can have Saeed returned here, or I can join them in Tehran."

Jafari was then forced to have a short, ugly conversation with his cousin, the General, informing him the Ababeel had not acknowledged the orders to return to Bandar Abbas, and may have been experiencing radio problems. The General arranged for two IRGC security teams to take Saeed into "protective custody" the second the Ababeel touched down at Mehrabad Air Base. Jafari was not able to report any success on finding Ziyaii. The phone call terminated with the General threatening to have Lieutenant

Jafari's manhood removed with rusty barbed wire if there were any more problems.

There did not appear to be anything more about either Saeed or Ziyaii that Lieutenant Jafari could do at this point. The Qods Force teams would either find Ziyaii, or they would not. The Ababeel would reappear somewhere, and when it did, they would grab Saeed. Jafari did not want to expand the search for Ziyaii beyond the Bandar Abbas area right now. That would require police cooperation and probably lead to questions being asked.

Besides, he had one more important aspect of the plan to initiate.

He summoned in the commander of the IRGC Navy mini-sub Karaj, Lieutenant Commander Behrouz Sadiqi. "Sadiqi, we are ready for you to play your part. Is your boat ready?"

"My boat is ready. As agreed, it will only be myself and my first officer and that disgusting *kaffir* Russian mercenary of yours. I will have to have my boat fumigated, he stinks so badly."

Lieutenant Jafari had a hard time figuring out where the Russian organized crime syndicates stopped, and the Russian government began. His military procurement contacts dealt with both, and both had proved consistently willing to provide to Iran all the weapons, equipment, or skilled personnel Iran desired, as long as the price was right. And they did not just provide Russian equipment: for the right price, they would get weapons and munitions of almost any type. The price for the Russians to obtain two US Mark 48 torpedoes and provide one skilled Russian deep-water demolitions expert, absolutely no questions ever to be asked, had been three million Euros. A pittance to the Supreme Leader.

"Commander Sadiqi, you may not care for the Russian infidel. I don't care for him myself. But his reliability and skill have been guaranteed. Without him, I would be asking *you* to do is his job. Are you a trained deep-sea demolitions diver? Do you want to be handling torpedoes at that depth, in a pressure suit you are not trained for? Do you know how to remotely detonate a torpedo safely? No? Then cease your nattering."

Jafari paused his tirade long enough to drink some tea, then continued, his pique unabated.

"You are being rewarded quite well enough to do what is asked of you and maintain your silence. You get a promotion, a better boat, a large new house to keep my cousin, your wife Elham, happy. Not to mention guaranteed admission for your son to Amir Kabir University. Do your job, then forget today, and live your life. Give my cousin another son to make her happy!"

Lieutenant Jafari considered Sadiqi's complaint ridiculous, all things considered. Sadiqi had to do none of the "heavy lifting." Sadiqi had only to pilot his minisub to the wreck of the Shaheed. He was an underwater taxi for the Russian diver. Once the Russian, Slobodchikov, exited the pressurized diving compartment of the Karaj, it was up to Slobodchikov to accomplish the mission. Sadiqi merely had to wait for Slobodchikov to return.

Jafari continued, "Sadiqi, phone me when you are ready to depart, and the instant you return. After you have completed the mission and Slobodchikov is in the decompression chamber, I want you to personally bring the video footage, wreckage, and photos to me so I can review them. After that, your part is done. Unless the footage is bad and we need to send Slobodchikov down again. Clear?"

Lieutenant Commander Sadiqi disliked taking orders from a mere Lieutenant, let alone one that was an incompetent pervert, and apparently drunk with power to boot. Nevertheless, Lieutenant Jafari was right about one thing: Sadiqi was getting paid more than enough to do the job and keep his mouth shut. Politics weren't his business. And Jafari was family, of a sort. The mini-sub skipper replied, "Yes, *Lieutenant* Jafari. I'll let you know. We will depart shortly, at dusk. Don't forget to notify the patrol boat above the Shaheed that they will hear some blasting tonight. I don't want those fools to panic and start dumping depth charges on my head." Lieutenant Commander Sadiqi turned and left to double check the preparations for this trip.

Lieutenant Jafari dearly hoped that at least this part of the plan went well. If rumors in the IRGC were correct, The General's barbed-wire threat was not a hollow one.

*　　　*　　　*

Even as Jafari and Sadiqi were discussing him, the Russian deep-sea demolitions diver, Vadim Slobodchikov, formerly of Russian Baltic Fleet Naval Spetnaz Unit No. 10617, was in the mini-sub Karaj's small compression/decompression chamber. Slobodchikov had already lashed the Mark 48 torpedoes and his powered dive sled to the Karaj, and then shielded them from view by canvas tarps. He was now loading his diving equipment into the Karaj's compression chamber, and triple checking it.

As soon as the Karaj departed, he would lock himself into the compression chamber and start pre-breathing a normoxic trimix, a precisely calibrated combination of oxygen, helium, and nitrogen. The mixture would help Slobodchikov avoid the deadly condition known as nitrogen narcosis during the dive. At depth, concentrated nitrogen in the blood becomes an intoxicant. In a deep sea environment, where one mistake can mean death, being "drunk" on nitrogen was a life-threatening danger. Breathing the low- nitrogen trimix was crucial to Slobodchikov's ability to successfully complete this dive.

Slobodchikov had arrived in Bandar Abbas from Saint Petersburg two days ago, and had been isolated from outside contact for nearly the entire time. His only human contact had been a welcome from Lieutenant Jafari, and a mission briefing from Commander Sadiqi on what was required: set off two American torpedoes on the hull of a downed ship, and then film the results in a way that pointed the finger at the Great Satan.

After the briefing, Slobodchikov had planned the dive in minute detail. After "locking out" of the compression chamber into the Persian Gulf, he would release the US Mark 48 torpedoes lashed to the hull of the Karaj, and with the aid of buoyancy devices and his powered-diving sled, haul them over to the wreck of the Shaheed. He would place the torpedoes in two of the holes punched by mines in the hull of the Shaheed. Slobodchikov would then retreat to a safe distance and trigger detonation of the torpedoes remotely.

Slobodchikov's would next return to the Shaheed, and set up a small but powerful bank of lights to film and photograph the results. If all went according to plan, instead of distinctive mine-shaped holes, the Shaheed would then have a couple of the much larger, more ragged holes common to torpedoes. Mark 48 torpedoes were very powerful; he knew that the Shaheed might even be blown into three separate pieces by the blasts. Slobodchikov would photograph and film the torpedo holes from the appropriate angles, making sure none of the other mine-holes showed in the camera frame. The last step was to pick up several pieces of torpedo debris, to be displayed later to the world as appropriate "evidence" of the Great Satan's torpedo attack.

Slobodchikov did not know the downed ship was the Shaheed, nor who had been aboard when the Shaheed went down. Even had he known, he would not have particularly cared. He hated Iranians, particularly the Ayatollahs; most of the Russian experts hired by Iran did. That never stopped them from going to Iran to share their expertise. Given the 150,000 Euros he would be earning for his part, Slobodchikov was more than happy to undertake the dive. If he created some trouble for the damned Americans in the bargain, so much the better! Slobodchikov only wished he had a chance to plant mines on a real American or Iranian warship that was actually afloat, not play out some political charade on a sunken wreck with these religion-crazed Persians.

Still, at least they went out of their way to give the Americans fits; Slobodchikov grudgingly admired them for that. He was eager to start the dive.

*   *   *

When he met him, Lieutenant Jafari had surmised that Slobodchikov would not have objected to actually sinking the Shaheed himself, even had he known it involved the murder of The Council of Guardians and hundreds of Iranian sailors. That would have been a tidy solution, if Rahimi and Ziyaii hadn't been needed as potential scapegoats.

Jafari was not afraid that Slobodchikov would have balked at sinking the Shaheed out of ethical considerations. It was just that engaging Slobodchikov to sink the Shaheed might have caused the Russian to leap to the right conclusion: any group of people willing to kill hundreds of their fellow citizens, not to mention a dozen of their own senior leaders, would have no qualms about disposing of a *kaffir*, an infidel, after his usefulness had ended. Jafari had purposely kept Slobodchikov, "in the dark" about the

Shaheed, and Jafari knew that ignorance was not going to be bliss for Slobodchikov. But that was for later.

CHAPTER 12-THE BIRD ALIGHTS

Commander Saeed briefly reflected that there was no such thing as a "good" ride in military helicopter. Helicopters built for the commercial civilian market include the comfort of passengers as a consideration in the design. Military helicopters, particularly those built by Russians, do not. Even on day like today, with clear weather conditions, the Russian-built Ababeel had the ride characteristics of a school bus with no shock absorbers driving over a potholed road, with a few jackhammers strapped to the passengers' seats for good measure. The extended bouts of noise and vibration usually lead to crashing headaches in anyone not acclimatized to helicopters.

Creature comfort being low on his list of priorities at the moment, Commander Saeed was able to largely ignore the noise and vibration of the Ababeel. His hopes were tentatively rising: Saeed's big fear had been that other helicopters or planes would approach the Ababeel and force it to land in a remote area. With no witnesses, who would ever be able to say what had become of those aboard the Ababeel? Now, the Ababeel was only thirty minutes from arrival in Tehran.

Saeed had made good use of his hours aboard the Ababeel. He had his next steps well planned out. On reflection, Saeed cursed himself for not taking the diver Ziyaii's cellphone so he could make a copy of the sound of the mines detonating on the Shaheed. That would have been a solid piece of evidence corroborating the suspicions in Akhlagi's letter. But one could not remember everything in moments of haste and stress. Saeed thought he had done well to react so quickly by getting to the wreck of the Shaheed, then getting to the cursed Rahimi to confirm Akhlagi's suspicions. If fate was kind for just a little longer, Saeed believed he had a good chance of survival. And surely, some good luck was due: what could it be called but massively bad luck, that Akhlagi had thought to have the Shaheed swept for mines, yet had missed the emplacement of mines by less than two hours?

Saeed switched his headset back to channel four so he could talk directly to the pilot without the rest of the crew overhearing. "Saboori, we're half an hour out from Mehrabad Air Base. In fifteen minutes, I want you to switch the radios back on, talk to the control tower, and request clearance to land at the western part of the Air Base. Request an approach that will swing you north of the civilian air terminal at Mehrabad International."

"Aye, Aye, Commander."

"Saboori, are you familiar with the area around Mehrabad? Have you flown in there often?"

"Hundreds of times, Commander, for both helicopter and fixed-wing training courses. Why do you ask?"

"Saboori, we will not be landing at Mehrabad Airbase. Nor will we be landing on the civilian heli-pads at Mehrabad International Airport next door."

The pilot's voice came back over the intercom, sounding confused.

"What? I mean, ahh, excuse me, Commander Saeed, if we are not to land at either Mehrabad Air Base or Mehrabad Airport, where will we be landing?"

"Due north of the civilian terminal at Mehrabad International is a football field and a track. Do you recall that, Saboori?"

"Yes, Commander."

"As we are sweeping north on our approach, I want you to declare an in-flight emergency and make an emergency landing on that football field. You pick the emergency. Just make sure it is something you can convincingly fake: your life, and that of the crew of the Ababeel, may depend upon it. Can you do that?"

Baffled at the request, the pilot replied, "Commander, yes, of course it is *technically* possible, I can always say our oil pressure sensors showed a catastrophic loss of pressure. That sensor is notoriously faulty, and our S.O.P. is to make an emergency landing rather than chance that it is a false reading." Saboori paused. He was not argumentative by nature, yet felt he had to object. "But, Commander Saeed, Sir, such a plan is very dangerous. Landing anywhere that has not been prepared for landing is always dangerous: there could be power wires I do not see until too late, foreign objects could get sucked into my engine intakes, a million things can go wrong. Is this really necessary?"

Saeed wished Saboori would not argue, but he could hardly fault the pilot for doing everything he could to maintain the safety of the Ababeel. "Saboori, I assure you, this is a military necessity. Things will be in great turmoil after the sinking of the Shaheed. Enemies of the people of Iran are everywhere, our only hope of confounding them and reporting the truth about the Shaheed to the proper authorities is to do the unexpected. Follow my orders. The risks we take landing in this manner are justified, I assure you."

Sounding disgruntled, but not ready to openly disobey, Saboori replied, "Aye, aye, sir. May *Khoda* protect and preserve us."

Fifteen minutes later, Saboori relayed back to Saeed that he had contacted the tower at Mehrabad Airbase, which had acknowledged the Ababeel, cleared their approach to the north, and informed Saeed that an escort was waiting to take him to IRGC Headquarters. That bit of news sent a chill through Saeed. Inshallah, if Saeed's plan worked, the men of the security escort would never lay eyes on the Commander.

Saboori came back on the intercom. "We are five minutes out, Commander. Are you sure you want to go through with the emergency landing? And if so, what am I to do with the Ababeel after we set down?"

"Yes, Saboori, we must make the emergency landing. You and your crew stay with the Ababeel and radio for mechanical assistance after you are down. I will be departing as soon as we touch down. Tell the crew chief to be ready to open the hatch for me the second we are down. I imagine it will take an hour or two, sitting on that football field for you to 'confirm' that you had simply had a faulty oil pressure gauge or sensor. After that, you can take off and land over at Mehrabad Airbase. See to the servicing of the Ababeel, then go to the transient officer barracks at Mehrabad and await further orders from IRGC Naval Command."

Saeed hesitated, not wanting to share any more information, but then continued, feeling obligated to protect his subordinate; Saboori was a good officer and an excellent pilot. Reluctantly, Saeed went on, "Saboori, politics are involved here. *Make sure* the copilot and crew chief know that if they do not stick to the story of the in-flight emergency, it might be the last mistake they ever make. When they ask you, 'Where is Commander Saeed,' say I did not explain myself to you, but that you presume I went to IRGC headquarters to report in. Also, for the time being, keep your other passenger, the staff driver from Bandar Abbas, with you."

Saeed withdrew the driver's cell-phone from his pocket and handed it to Saboori over the pilot's shoulder. "Here is the driver's cellphone. You may release him to find his way back to Bandar Abbas and give him back this cell-phone as soon as you get the Ababeel off the football field and finally set it down at Mehrabad. Do you have any questions?"

"No, Commander. I will inform the crew chief and co-pilot about our impending 'oil pressure' crisis. Be ready. When things happen, we will be dropping in very fast."

Saeed's heart started racing. He knew that Lieutenant Commander Saboori was a brave man and his concerns over declaring an in-flight emergency and making an emergency landing on ad-hoc landing field were legitimate. Saeed hated to risk both his men and the Ababeel itself. But he could see no alternative.

Two minutes later, Saeed could see Saboori shouting into the microphone of his headset. Playing his part to the hilt, Saboori then came on the general intercom circuit and said with an excited but controlled tone of voice, "We have lost oil pressure. I have declared an in-flight emergency. We are setting down immediately. All Hands, strap yourself in and brace for impact!"

Saeed thought this was a nice touch. The rest of the crew knew there was no in-flight emergency, but the staff driver from Bandar Abbas, who had a headset on in the rear of the helicopter, did not. This bit of theater would add authenticity to bogus emergency when the staff driver and Saboori were interviewed, and Commander Saeed was sure they would be.

The Ababeel dropped like a stone, and for an instant, Saeed thought it really would crash. At the last second, Saboori went into an emergency power flair maneuver that scrubbed off vertical descent speed, and touched the Ababeel down with a gentle bump. During the second it took for the crew chief to fling open the hatch, Saeed yelled some parting words on the private intercom channel to the pilot, "Saboori, that was brilliant. You are truly a master pilot. May *Khoda* preserve you and the crew of the Ababeel."

Saeed threw off the headphones. In an instant, Saeed was on the grass of the football field and jogging south now. Saeed had forgotten that a tall chain-link fence surrounded this football pitch. Three minutes and another fence later, a winded Commander Saeed was hailing a taxi-cab from the inbound traffic loop for Mehrabad Airport. The Commander did not notice that his fence-climbing adventures had left him with a rip in his uniform pants leg that was trickling blood. A cab screeched as it came to a quick halt. Saeed jumped into the back and said "Laleh Park, Driver, and please be quick."

The cabbie replied, "Of course, Sir! It is my pleasure, Sir."

The cabbie thought the Commander's ripped uniform was a bit bizarre. Even more bizarre was his passenger's unorthodox choice to hail a cab from the inbound traffic loop while dodging traffic. Why not go to the nearby Mehrabad Airport taxi stand? But the driver kept his opinions to himself. It doesn't do to antagonize customers in a job dependant on tips.

Saeed looked more closely around the interior of the cab. This appeared to be an official cab, not one of the thousands of unregulated cabs that plied the streets of Tehran. This cabbie even has a license with a name and photo posted, Reza Hamidi.

Saeed sighed with relief and allowed himself to relax a bit as the cab swept through the traffic loop at Mehrabad Airport, past the taxi stand, and back out onto the streets of Tehran completely unmolested. By avoiding the taxi stand, none of the drivers there, who Saeed guessed probably knew each other, would be able to report seeing a man in an IRGC Navy uniform being picked up by their old comrade Reza.

Twenty minutes later, as they were approaching Laleh Park, Saeed said, "Thank you for stopping to pick me up. I was in a terrible hurry and did not have time to get to the taxi stand. I would like to return the favor. Have you a family, driver?"

"Yes, Sir, a wife and a fine young son."

As in many countries with weak banking systems, credit cards had not caught on widely in Iran. Many Iranians, Commander Saeed included, did not trust Iranian banks. Saeed usually carried significant sums of cash with him against the chance opportunity to purchase bargains. That stash of money now came in handy. Saeed passed over a sheaf of tomans equivalent to a whole night's wages, including good tips, to the driver.

"Driver, we should all take the opportunity to spend the time we can with our precious families. Take this, not as a gift from me, but from the hand of *Khoda*. Do not return to the airport tonight. Instead, go and enjoy your wife and your son. How many such unexpected opportunities does fate send your way?"

The driver actually was unmarried. He had no family to return home to. He did, however, know of a dice game that needed an extra player. Why not enjoy the windfall of a fat tip from this rich fool at the dice game, and see if he could further enhance his luck tonight?

The cabbie replied, "Sir, my deepest thanks! You are most kind. I shall do that very thing, return to my beloved wife and son. *Khoda's* blessings on you and your whole family for your kindness and generosity! I shall tell my wife and son of your kindness."

"Driver, no thanks are necessary. I merely share my good fortune, as Khoda himself has commanded."

Saeed was almost certain the driver was lying about the wife and son. Male children were the pride and joy of Iranian family men, if the driver had really had a son, there would have been at least ten pictures of the son taped to the dashboard and other parts of the cab. There were none.

On more than one occasion, Saeed had heard foreigners complain that Persians speak in a confusing, round-about, elliptical fashion. For those with only a shallow understanding of the Persian language, that may be true. If a listener concentrates only on the *words*, the average conversation in Farsi may appear to be overly flowery and inconclusive. But to anyone who understood the societal and conversational conventions of Iran, the real meaning of the exchange between Commander Saeed and the cabbie would have been crystal clear.

Commander Saeed: "Here is a nice amount of money. Don't go back to the airport tonight. Okay?"

Cabbie: "You got it, pal."

When Saeed got out of the cab at the south west corner of Laleh Park, he set off at a brisk pace down the path heading deeper into the park. An isolated part of his mind was still able to appreciate the beauty of the meticulously maintained trees, lawns, shrubs and fountains that decorated the park; the entire setting had European feel to it, as if Munich's elaborate "English Garden" had been moved whole to Tehran. A brisk twenty minute walk brought the Commander to the upscale Hotel Laleh, located near the north-east corner of the park. He entered the lobby of the hotel and approached a payphone. He dialed a number long committed to memory. Saeed whispered a brief prayer for the phone to be answered quickly.

"Allo?" Masoud Bahktiar said.

"Thank *Khoda*," Saeed said quickly to himself, before continuing loud enough to be heard. "Masoud, it is Mohsen." Saeed had barely said his name before he was bombarded with questions.

"*Khoda* be praised! You have survived! Were you injured? Where are you? What is going on? What happened to the Shaheed? Was it really the Americans?"

Saeed interjected, "Speak slower, my friend, slower! Two things. First, come get me. I am in Tehran, in the lobby of the Hotel Laleh. Second, before you come, call my wife and my brother and make arrangements for them to come to your house as soon as they can. This is an emergency; time is of the essence. The sooner I see Mohammed and my wife, the better."

"But Mohsen, you know the old plan! They are already here!"

Saeed's heart leapt for joy within him. "Truly *Khoda* has been with me this day. That is wonderful news. Why is Mohammed there and not in Qom? Never-mind, never-mind, just come as soon as you can. And turn off your cell-phones before you come."

"Oh, Mohsen! Or should I say, 'My Dear Uncle Napoleon!' Don't worry, Mr. Paranoid! Lily and Mohammed remembered your constant harping. They turned off their phones long before they ever got here. They just showed up on my door, unannounced, bless them! Ha! I am on my way. Inshallah, I will be there in 15 minutes."

Ever since Saeed had learned from a TV program four years ago that people's movements could be tracked through their cellphone, Saeed had been a fanatic on the subject of keeping them turned off when not in use. He knew both the Iranian Ministry of Internal Security, the MOIS, and IRGC Security would be interested in routinely tracking his movements, as well as the movements of his brother, Mohammed. Both Saeed brothers had high security clearances; both did sensitive work for the Iranian government. One never knew what those crazy MOIS and IRGC "Security Bastards" would consider suspicious. Best, then, not to give them any potential ammunition at all! Mohsen Saeed loved his country, but had vowed long ago to make life hard on the security services, whom he considered, with good reason, to be little better than thugs.

Good as his word, sixteen minutes later, Masoud Bahktiar pulled up in a luxurious Peugeot. Commander Saeed could see his brother, Mohammed, and his wife, Lily, side by side in the back seat. He had to fight back tears of joy at seeing his family after this day of tragedy.

Twenty seconds later they were pulling away from the curb, and Commander Saeed was being peppered by questions from his brother, Mohammed. "Mohsen, what happened? Is true? Is the Shaheed sunk? Are all dead? Was the Council of Guardians aboard? Was it the Americans?"

"Mohammed, slow down! We can cover this in detail when we get to Masoud's home. For now, yes, it is true, the Shaheed went down. All who were aboard when she sunk were lost. I myself welcomed aboard the Shaheed all the Ayatollahs from the Council of Guardians this morning. As for how she sunk, let us wait on that a while. I have a question of my own. I know Lily was in Varamin visiting friends, so I am not surprised she made her way to Masoud's, but Mohammed, how is it *you* are here and not in Qom?"

The Commander's brother replied, "Mohsen, I am here for work. I came to Tehran to give the quarterly status briefing on our project to the head of the Atomic Energy Organization of Iran, Gholam Reza Agazadeh. He prefers such briefings to happen in person, so there are no communications about the project that can be intercepted by electronic means."

Relief plain in his voice, Commander Saeed exclaimed, "Mohammed, this is most fortunate; *Khoda* was smiling on the Saeed family this day. When we get to Masoud's, I will explain all. Suffice it to say, when the Shaheed sunk, our life changed. Forever. Now, if you would all be so kind, I would like to rest my eyes a bit until we get to Masoud's."

Commander Saeed had been moving on pure adrenaline since he spotted the Council of Guardians arriving at the side of the Shaheed. It now felt like that was years ago. He felt a strange sense of unreality enfold him as he closed his eyes and marveled with dismay how quickly someone's world could be turned upside down. Commander Saeed was asleep less than a minute later.

CHAPTER 13- MEETINGS

It was not yet nine AM. Joe Cerrato was muttering to himself that this meeting about the Shaheed *should have* taken five minutes because nobody knew anything right now. A time should have been set for an update meeting later in the day, say three or four PM. They needed time to cull incoming signals intelligence and have the photo-recon experts look at satellite imagery of the Shaheed and the area where it sunk. Most importantly, the delay would give the CIA's case officers scattered around the world had a chance to meet with their assets and report what they had heard to Hqs.

The meeting started well; everybody agreed that nobody knew anything right now and should meet later today. For a brief moment, Joe entertained the hope that the meeting could end right there, an outcome which might have allowed the meeting participants *to actually go work on gathering relevant intelligence,* so they could be prepared for the real meeting later.

Instead, the meeting immediately degenerated into an exercise in the oldest bureaucratic sport: CYA. Covering your ass. Joe wanted to shoot himself.

NE Division Chief of Ops, Fredrick Sandler, made the first bureaucratic sally. "Okay people, we know squat. And as far as I can tell, that is not just the CIA, that is the whole 'Intelligence Community.' The White House, Congress, and our *many* admirers in the press are going to want to know *why* we know squat. I haven't heard 'intelligence failure' being bandied about yet on CNN, but I think that's because it's early in the day. After all, it is Thursday morning; almost the weekend. Most Congress-members and intelligence pundits are still sleeping off their hangovers at the residence of their mistress or prostitute of choice."

The joke got Sandler a quick laugh.

Brett Howell, a reports officer from the Counter-Proliferation Division, spoke up. "Fred, I can give you a partial answer on that. In case you don't know, I work on the Iranian Delivery Systems desk. When we learned that the "Shaheed" was going to be sold to the Iranians, we got together with the guys as State and prepared some *demarches* to block an aspect of the sale. Sovremenny destroyers like the Shaheed used "Mosquito" anti-ship cruise missiles. Those things are damned dangerous; they're so fast, some estimates up to Mach three, that they're nearly impossible to shoot down. Navy stuff is not normally my area, but I'll look into anything that is capable of delivering 'Weapons of Mass Destruction,' and the Mosquito is definitely set up to deliver nuclear warheads, as well as conventional stuff."

"Iran has been trying to get hold of more Mosquitoes for years. They already had some direct from the Russians, but we've been trying to hold the line and prevent any new sales; the fewer of those damn things in Iranian hands, the better. Enough of em' could put the US 5th Fleet on the bottom of the Gulf if it comes to a shooting match. Anyway, we helped the State Department's Bureau of Non-Proliferation set up some demarches to China and Russia to make sure they knew we were watching, and reminding them that transfer of Mosquitoes as part of the transfer of the destroyer would be a violation of Category One of the Missile Technology Control Regime which Russian and China *claim* to adhere to it. And sometimes they do… as long as we watch their every move."

"We managed to verify that the Chinese offloaded the Mosquitoes before transferring the Shaheed to Iranian control. That was a good day; the Iranian's were reportedly very pissed off at both the Chinese and us. The Iranians thought they were going to slip that one by us."

"Okay, since then, satellite imagery of the Shaheed showed the Iranians hadn't loaded any replacement for the Mosquitoes aboard yet. We knew today was just a cruise for the Shaheed, that the cruise would be full of dignitaries, and that it almost certainly wouldn't be doing any weapons test-firings or naval maneuvers worth watching. As far as I know, the guys at the Office of Naval Intelligence and the National Geospatial Agency decided it wasn't worth diverting resources just to watch a cream-puff christening ceremony, one that was going to be covered by CNN in any case. So nobody was watching. We may not know jack, but there is a *reason* we don't. Nobody thought there was going to be anything worth seeing."

Those who encountered Brett Howell were blown away by his knowledge of the minutia of Iranian delivery systems. And he didn't just know the *Iranian* stuff inside and out. Once again, he had just proved he had a better than passing knowledge of Russian and Chinese missile systems, too. Brett was like a walking encyclopedia, very handy to have in meetings like this.

Sandler replied, "Thanks, Brett. I'll pass that along to the 7th floor. Maybe by tap-dancing a little and reminding the White House that we blocked the Mosquito sale, we can buy ourselves some breathing room to investigate further. Okay. Item two: why did we *not* know the Council of Guardians would be aboard…"

"Please God, kill me now," muttered Joe to himself as Sandler droned on.

CHAPTER 14-BURN NOTICE

Cynthia Marks knew her next few days were shot straight to hell as soon as she heard that the Shaheed had gone down that morning. For a case officer whose job it was to stop the spread of "Weapons of Mass Destruction," or WMD, Dubai was definitely the place to be. The Pakistani AQ Khan nuclear smuggling network was only one of several WMD smuggling rings that had transferred money and the raw materials to produce nuclear weapons through the United Arab Emirates, or UAE. For a Counter-Proliferation Division case officer like Cynthia, there was no better place to be than Dubai but, naturally, that came with a cost. Dubai's proximity to Iran meant that anytime something involving Iran happened, the US Consulate in Dubai was flooded with people claiming to have the inside scoop, information they would be happy to share, if only the CIA would give them a green-card, a million dollars, and a blonde trophy wife.

In the new millennium, Dubai had joined the ranks of the great historical espionage capitals, grabbing the place of prominence that Berlin had once possessed as a spy capital during the height of the Cold War. As a huge shipping, banking, and media center, untold quantities of money, legal and illegal goods, and secrets flowed through Dubai. The government of the United Arab Emirates devoted far more effort to insuring that Dubai received adequate electricity for their mammoth air conditioning systems than to tracking espionage or illicit commercial activity. Consequently, the two biggest cities in the UAE, Dubai and Abu Dhabi, had become espionage "free fire zones," with intelligence services from all over the world devoting major resources to tracking the flow of information and goods through the United Arab Emirates.

For Cynthia, being stationed in the United Arab Emirates was like being in the Major Leagues in baseball; having to waste a chunk of her valuable time fielding "walk-ins" was the price she willingly paid to play in the big leagues. Thousands of "walk-ins" appeared on the doorstep of the CIA every year. The problem for every case officer in Cynthia's position was figuring out how to weed out the 98 percent of liars from the two percent of walk-ins with information that was *A.* authentic and *B.* actually of interest to the Central Intelligence Agency.

One in 200, maybe one in 500, had genuinely important secrets that they were willing to share with the CIA, if the price was right. Those were the moments that every case officer lived for, but few got to experience. Cynthia had yet to meet a walk-in that was worth the cost of the tea she gave them while she interviewed them.

When the duty officer cell-phone rang, Cynthia was just settling down to dinner. "Cyn, Dave. Sorry to bother you. They're 'playing your song' again. Emergency Services operator just gave me a heads up. Someone who claims to have information about the 'you know what' from this morning. Here's his phone number. I'll send the Marines over to "The Room." He said it was, quote, 'Life or death urgent.' "

Cynthia looked at her rapidly cooling lasagna, sighed, and said, "Yeah, don't they all. Okay, I'm gonna take five minutes to eat dinner, five more to dress, then head on in. Tell the Marine I'll be there in half an hour."

After eating a large portion of lasagna at unlady-like speed, Cynthia made a beeline for her bedroom. There were a dozen exquisitely tailored Dolce and Gabana silk skirts and dresses in her closet, all guaranteed to turn heads at 100 yards. She ignored them. Instead, she pulled out one of three identical navy light-weight wool-silk blend pant suits, accompanied by a simple long-sleeve white blouse of finely woven but plain Egyptian cotton. She tossed both on the bed.

She was so used to donning this particular outfit, what she thought of as her "walk-in uniform," that she no longer bothered to lament to herself how uninspired it was as a fashion choice. While posted in Paris on her previous tour, Cynthia had been on a first name basis with the clerks in the Chanel Boutique at 25 Rue Royal. There, she wouldn't have been caught dead in this outfit; the Chanel girls would never have let her live that down. In Dubai, despite it being one of the most liberal places in the Middle East, Cynthia found it paid to dress in as sober and professional manner as possible. She attracted less unwelcome and outright hostile attention if she dressed like a middle management banker with taste as bland as the pureed peas in baby food. No makeup, no jewelry, no stylish purses: nothing that caught the eye and might cause someone to remember her.

As she shucked out of her threadbare but comfy blue and yellow sweats bearing the logo of her alma-mater, Bryn Mawr, one foot got tangled in the elastic at the left ankle of her sweat pants. She barely avoided falling over while trying to simultaneously step out of the bottoms and pull the sweat top off over her head, a near miss which merited a mumbled, "Sonofabitch, these goddamn things!"

Minor wardrobe malfunction aside, six minutes after walking into her bedroom, she was back on the way out, after quickly drawing her long hair into a severe bun.

Twelve minutes after getting the call, Cynthia yanked shut the door of her apartment behind her and headed for what the CIA's Dubai Base referred to simply as "The Room." Some US Embassies and Consulates have small rooms set aside where discreet interviews between intelligence officers and walk-ins can be held. These rooms are away from the prying eyes of the rest of the embassy staffers. In places with a fair amount of hostile surveillance, like Dubai, the CIA found it wiser to create a "walk-in room" in a place that had no official embassy affiliation, a set-up which further cut down on the number of prying eyes who might identify either the CIA case officers or walk-ins.

"The Room" Cynthia was headed for wasn't really a room; it was an apartment leased to the CIA, through a series of cut-outs, at the Dubai International Hotel Apartments. Frequented by wealthy corporate travelers, the location and clientele provided excellent cover for handling a steady stream of "walk-ins." The hotel owners might have been a bit surprised at a few of the modifications the CIA had made to the apartment, though. The walls and doors of "The Room" had been discretely reinforced with Kevlar blast shields. The CIA's Directorate of Science and Technology folks had also slipped concealed explosive/toxin sniffers into the adjoining apartments, including those above and below "The Room," to prevent a disgruntled walk-in from returning and attempting to take it out by stealth attack. Some of the more prosaic upgrades were a phone that could dial out into the local phone system while blocking traces of its origin and substituting another, an airport-style metal detector built into the frame of the door, and a concealed cubicle with a feed from a closed circuit camera.

The camera system had been installed so a US Marine borrowed from the nearby US Consulate could watch, but not listen to, the interviews conducted in "The Room." If the walk-in made any threatening moves towards Cynthia during the interview, he would quickly discover the Marines that provided security received extensive training in close-quarters combat shooting.

Cynthia hoped that never happened; even a top-notch dry-cleaner probably couldn't get stains from a walk-ins' splattered blood and brain tissue off of her "walk-in uniform."

Cynthia arrived at "The Room," checked that the backup recorder was in working order, and that the fridge had adequate snacks and beverages to sustain a long interview. She sat in the large chair behind the interview desk and pulled out some pens and yellow legal pads from the desk drawer. Ready for action, she called the walk-in's phone number. It took five minutes to give him directions to the lobby of the Dubai International Hotel Apartments and tell him he would be met in the lobby.

Fifteen minutes later, a fat, bespectacled man of indeterminate age with a scraggly salt and pepper beard and beady porcine eyes was escorted into the room by a Marine in plainclothes. The Marine retreated into the cubicle while the fat man wheezed his way across the room.

Cynthia stood and said, "Good evening, my name is Samantha Peters. You can call me Sam."

She leaned forward and extended her hand over the desk in an offer to shake. This was her first test. In the Middle East, strange men and women more often than not did not shake hands in greeting, nor did they exchange first names. That is precisely why Cynthia did it: it was against the local cultural norms. The proffered handshake and first name were the quickest ways for Cynthia to see if a walk-in understood his position, and that position was as a supplicant. The proffered hand said, "You want to talk to me, you will play by *my* rules. I'm an American, and this is how we do things." Naturally, Cynthia took a different, less confrontational approach when dealing with men that she was *pursuing* to recruit as spies. But for walk-ins, it was important to establish up-front who was in change.

The man looked at Cynthia's extended hand with distaste. He crossed his arms in front of him, a common practice in the Muslim world to indicate a preference not to shake someone's hand.

Test one failed. Shit. Cynthia had to suppress a fleeting dislike. She did not want the emotion to color her evaluation. Still, it was not a good sign. In Cynthia's experience, every man in the Middle East who refused to shake her hand, or who shook her hand only with great reluctance, had later become a major pain in the ass for her to deal with. For some men, their cultural prejudices simply made it impossible to treat a woman as an equal, no matter how tough, skilled, or intelligent she might be.

Cynthia gestured to a chair in front of the desk. The fat man sat. Cynthia took a seat, picked up her pen, and said, "You told the Emergency Services operator that your name was Mostafa Moeen, and that you had information on the Shaheed. First off, I need to confirm your identity. Do you have a passport or identity document with a photo?"

Without deigning to speak, the man withdrew a battered Iranian passport from his pocket and, holding it just by the edges to insure their hands did not touch, passed it to Cynthia. She took five minutes to note down the passport number, and flipped through the visa section in the back, writing down on her pad dates and locations of entry and exit in various countries.

The fat man remained silent the entire time, but Cynthia could feel his heavy gaze on her like a clammy blanket. She continued in Farsi, "I have three simple questions for you. How did you get access to the information? What do you want for it? How can we verify the truth of the information?"

Clearly unused to dealing with non-deferential women, and startled at Cynthia's command of his native tongue, he started speaking haltingly. "This information, it is from the cousin of a friend. My friend does not want to meet with Americans; he is afraid for his life if he was seen. His cousin, the man who told him the information, does secret work, very secret, for the government of Iran. I cannot tell you where he works, but it is a branch of the security services. This secret man, he talked to his cousin, my friend, about what the Iranian government knew about the Shaheed. My friend wants ten thousand US dollars for the information. As for how to know it is the truth, my word of honor is the only proof you need!" The last was stated with a tone of voice he probably thought conveyed an air of wounded dignity and reproach, but which sounded more like defensive whining to Cynthia.

Cynthia replied with no hesitation, "Mr. Moeen, this is the way it works: You tell me the information. I will evaluate it and attempt to confirm it. If I can confirm some or all of the details, the US government may consider the information to be unique and important enough to merit a cash payment, the amount to be determined based on the quality of the information. Period."

Bristling with offense at Cynthia's brusque and businesslike tone, the man leaned forward in his chair and retorted with flushing cheeks, "Shameless woman! Do you take me for a fool? Am I to give you my secrets for nothing? With no guarantees? This is very valuable, very important information! Only *I* can tell you this information, nobody else outside the Iranian government knows this!"

Maintaining a calm demeanor in the face of Moeen's contrived anger, Cynthia replied, "Mr. Moeen, there is something you need to understand. We did not come to you, you came to us. You are asking for a lot of money, but you're not offering any way for me to verify your information. You *have* to tell me the information, so I can check it out. Then, and only then, will the subject of money be discussed. There is a colloquial saying in the US that is appropriate for this situation, 'My way, or the highway.' What that means is that if you want to do business with the US government, which I represent, you will do it our way, or you can take your information elsewhere."

Flesh jiggling as he jumped to his feet, gesturing wildly, he retorted with outrage, "This is foolishness; I demand to see a man! I cannot do business with a woman, you are ignorant, you have no idea of how business is conducted, and you do not show proper respect!"

The outburst was abruptly halted when the Marine came out of his cubicle and asked with a razor edge to his voice, "Ms. Peters, is there a problem?"

Startled, Moeen jerked his head around in the direction of the Marine's voice. He quickly apprehended two facts: the first was that this young American man, whoever or whatever he was, looked strong enough to break Moeen in half. The second was that, given the menacing looks he was now shooting Moeen's way, the muscular man would obviously enjoy the breaking. Although he stayed on his feet, Moeen's demeanor deflated like a popped balloon.

Mildly bemused, Cynthia waved the Marine back to his monitoring cubicle and said, "No problem, Tom, nothing I can't handle." With a sterner tone, speaking slowly and directing her comments back to the walk-in, she continued, "Mr. Moeen, you need to sit down and calm yourself. Sit. Down. *Now.*"

Casting fearful glances over his shoulder in the direction of the Marine's cubicle, and muttering something that sounded suspiciously like the Farsi words for "shameless harlot" under his breath, the fat man plopped gracelessly back into the chair with a grunt. He glared across the desk at Cynthia, who returned his gaze with a directness that conveyed clearly that she was neither intimidated nor remotely impressed by the man's theatrics.

With a sour tone, Moeen sighed and said. "As you will. I will tell you some of the information. It is very secret. Excellent information. Very important, *priceless* information, as *Khoda* is my witness. I know who blew up the Shaheed." He leaned forward with a gleam in his eye, his voice dropped to a conspiratorial whisper. "It was the Jews. A cowardly sneak attack from a Zionist submarine. What you do not know was that after the attack, Iranian Navy boats tracked the Zionist submarine and sunk it with torpedoes. The Jews, they do not want to admit one of their submarines has been sunk, particularly by the Holy Regime of Iran. They will never admit it to the world."

"Same shit, different day," Cynthia thought to herself as Moeen's recitation ended. As soon as the theatrics had started,

Cynthia had the usual sinking feeling: that she was dealing with another time-waster. Yet another guy with an overinflated sense of his own cleverness, thinking all Americans were naïve, weak-natured, and gullible, nothing but rich marks to be conned out of cash. Moeen's narrative had just confirmed those suspicions.

Standing up to signal that the interview was over, Cynthia said with a resigned weariness, "Thanks for your time, Mr. Moeen. We won't be doing business. Your 'information' is worthless to the United States. You can go now."

Moeen was back on his feet in an instant, shouting, "I've told you my information and now you try and rob me by saying it is worthless! This is excellent information from a man who knows many of Iran's secrets. You must pay! I am owed! You cannot cheat me!"

Walking slowly around the desk towards the man, Cynthia casually, almost gently, grabbed his left arm near the elbow. Then she pushed at one precise spot. Instantly the man gave out a wail of anguish from the nerve pinch Cynthia was inflicting on him and dropped back into the chair.

Her face now mere inches from Moeen's, looking straight into his eyes, she enunciated very clearly, as if speaking to a slow child. "You are lying to me, Mr. Moeen. Do you know how I know this? Because America has satellites, and as of right now, most of them are trained on the Persian Gulf. If the Israelis had lost a sub, wreckage would have floated to the surface. One cannot hide that from a satellite. Also, we have hydrophones throughout the Persian Gulf. If there had been another explosion, a successful torpedo attack on a submarine, we would have heard it."

"We have heard nothing. We have seen nothing. Therefore, you are trying to sell me lies. I don't need any, thank you very much. It is time for you to leave, and never come back. Not here, or to any other US Embassy or consulate."

Just as casually as before, Cynthia strolled back to her side of the desk, sat down, and continued matter-of-factly, "If you *do* return to a US embassy with more ridiculous lies, I will personally see to it that the story leaks out that you were attempting to sell Iranian state secrets to "The Great Satan." I'll make sure that information finds its way into the hands of the Iranian Ministry of Intelligence and Security office here in Dubai."

Moeen's face paled as the implications of Cynthia's threat sank in. Although many conspiratorial-minded Iranians saw the CIA's hand everywhere, controlling everything, it was rare to find an Iranian who could ever report a first-hand encounter with an actual CIA officer. The CIA was feared in a kind of second-hand, distant way. Like the threat of someday dying from cancer.

The organizations that the average Iranian was *really* worried about in a very immediate and visceral way were homegrown: the MOIS or IRGC Security. Crossing them was a quick way to give your life a Hobbesian flavor: it would become nasty, brutish, and short.

Cynthia pressed an intercom button and said to the Marine, "Tom, can you come in here and escort Mr. Moeen off the premises?"

The Marine returned to interview room and quickly frog-marched the fat man out of the interview room. Cynthia noted with a certain satisfaction that Moeen's visage on the way out was painted with an expression of shocked dismay at the outcome of his first encounter with an American woman, one who clearly and against all previous experience obviously did *not* believe that his maleness entitled him to deference of any sort.

Cynthia sighed and picked up her note pad in preparation for going back to base. The real aggravation to Cynthia was that even though she'd seen through Moeen's tissue of lies in short order, that did not absolve her of the requirement to go back and write up a "burn notice," which would consist of Moeen's name and the travel information gleaned from his passport, the details of his attempted scam, and the statement that Moeen was henceforth to be considered a "known fabricator." The burn notice guaranteed that if he was dumb enough to come back to any US Embassy or Consulate, he would be immediately be shown the door again.

Of course, though Cynthia would and could play hardball when needed, truth be told, she wouldn't really rat Moeen out to the MOIS, even if he came back. Yes, he was a fat, lying, sexist scammer, a toad of a man by anyone's measure…but that didn't mean he deserved to die, which is what would probably happen if the MOIS really believed the man was attempting to peddle Iranian state secrets, instead of rather transparent lies. She'd just said that because many walk-ins have the habit of reappearing at other embassies, trying to peddle the same trash, unless they were discouraged from doing so in the strongest possible terms.

She would admit to nobody the other reason she had made the threat was that she secretly delighted in the opportunity to jerk an asshole like Moeen up short and put the fear of God into him. With that kind of guy, a little fear can go a long way in reforming his character. She thought of it as her good deed for the day.

CHAPTER 15-THE GENERAL

"I want Saeed found! Not next week! Not tomorrow! Tonight! Take the crew of the Ababeel to our special cells in Evin. No need to be gentle about it, either. Call in Jalili to question them, and have Jalili phone me before he begins."

General Jafari slammed down his phone in disgust.

The two IRGC security teams sent to meet the Ababeel at Mehrabad Air Base had just informed the General that the Ababeel had made an emergency landing North of Mehrabad International Airport. After that, according to the security teams, Commander Saeed had vanished as if abducted by the djinn of legend. The security teams frantically searched the area. Saeed hadn't gone into the airport. As far as they could tell, Saeed hadn't gone to the taxi stand at Mehrabad International, either. It was as if Saeed had someone waiting to meet him yet Saeed's cell phone had been off for several hours, and it was practically impossible to make a cell-phone call from a noisy helicopter in any case.

The crew of the Ababeel *claimed* to have no idea where Saeed was. They guessed he was heading to IRGC headquarters. The pilot, Saboori, swore up and down that the all-too-convenient "emergency landing" that allowed Saeed to escape was nothing but a coincidence. The security teams didn't know enough about helicopters to shake Saboori's story, at least not yet.

Jafari's phone rang. He picked up.

"It's me, sir. You wanted to speak to me before I began?"

He recognized the voice of Jalili. The General had first met the now-infamous interrogator more than twenty years ago, in the closing days of the Iran/Iraq war. Jalili had low-ranking Iraqi prisoners staked out on the ground, limbs spread-eagled and tied to an elaborate system of pulleys, all of which were connected via ropes to the back bumper of an Iranian military truck. Then-Col. Jafari had asked Jalili what in the name of *Khoda* he was doing. Jalili had answered in a matter-of-fact tone of voice that he was trying to see if something he read about the medieval torture of pulling someone apart with several teams of horses could be replicated with a system of pullies and a single truck.

There was no intelligence value in the exercise; the prisoners were of low rank and the war was nearly over. Jalili was simply a bored corporal with access to Iraqi prisoners and a particularly inventive psychopathic personality.

Jafari was simultaneously appalled and intrigued; he knew he could find a useful place in his service for a man with absolutely no moral compunctions whatsoever. And so the General eventually had, as his own private interrogator at Evin prison. "Jalili, the four just delivered to you. Start slow, but unless they start talking soon, use any and all necessary means to loosen tongues about the Shaheed and the whereabouts of Mohsen Saeed. Clear?"

Responding with a relish in his voice that was sickening, considering the topic under-discussion was torturing his own countrymen for information, Jalili replied, "Absolutely, General. It shall be exactly as you wish. As soon as I have anything to report, I shall call you immediately."

Not bothering to reply, Jafari hung up the phone.

The General would see how well Saboori's stories held up when Jalili started asking his questions.

Even in a country run by theocratic despotism, respected military officers like Saboori or Saeed were not normally just hauled in for "persuasive" questioning. But this was an emergency. And when the General finally got his hands on Saeed, Saeed would quickly learn just how willing the General was to resort to brutal tactics. Jafari didn't have time for niceties right now, and as the Commanding General of the IRGC, General Jafari was virtually a law unto himself.

Especially now that the Council of Guardians was conveniently gone.

The General remained astonished that the Supreme Leader had approached him for help in eliminating the Council of Guardians. Out of the blue, the querulous old idiot claimed that the Guardians' refusal to disqualify every candidate he wanted off the ballot in the last national elections was evidence the Guardians were plotting against him, instead of a routine difference of opinion. The old man never considered that once the Guardians were dead, he could never remove the General, or even deny General Jafari anything he wanted. By asking the General to eliminate the Council of Guardians, the Supreme Leader had undermined his own power, *and* eliminated one of the few major power centers in Iran outside of the hands of the General.

General Jafari wondered aloud to himself with an audible sneer in his voice, "When 'Our *Dear* Supreme Leader' looks at Iran, what does he see from his isolated palaces? Does he worry about the poverty of the people, does he fight corruption, does he do anything at all which might actually shore up support for the Islamic Revolution? No. He counts on the iron fist of the IRGC to maintain control, and instead obsesses on petty squabbles with the Council of Guardians."

That wonderful inattention had opened the path to power for General Jafari.

Although it had always been powerful, the IRGC had truly begun its ascendancy in 2004, when the rhetoric-spouting buffoon Ahmadi-Nejad had been elected President. The first thing Ahmadi-Nejad did was install IRGC cronies at all levels of the Iranian government. Successive Presidents had found ejecting the IRGC appointees from their entrenched positions nearly impossible. Thanks to Ahmadi-Nejad, General Jafari, as head of the IRGC, now had his fingers in almost every pie in Iran.

*   *   *

Taking a break that evening to escape from a diplomatic reception hosted by the French Embassy in Tehran, the General ducked into a side corridor off the main reception hall to answer a phone call on his encrypted cell from Regular Iranian Navy Admiral Sayyari. Sayyari did not use any of the typical pleasantries, and instead launched right into attack.

"Jafari, it is bad enough that you took the money for the purchase of the Shaheed from my budget. Now your so-called cousin is in charge of the investigation of the Shaheed? This is outrageous." Walking past a mirror with an ornately carved gilt-edged frame, looking to either side to make sure he was alone,

Jafari allowed himself a quick, devilish grin in the mirror, but then responded to Sayyari's assertions with a tone of voice that was sober, attentive, and entirely fabricated on the General's part.

"Admiral, I understand your concerns, but you know as well as I that budgetary allocations are in the hands of the Supreme Leader and the Majlis. I have nothing to do with them. As for the use of my cousin in the Shaheed investigation, well, the investigation is too important not to be headed by someone personally known to me, someone I trust. That is how it must be, too much is at stake. I hope you can understand my action in that regard is entirely motivated by my desire for justice for the Shaheed."

Sayyari just gave a dissatisfied grunt and switched off. Jafari allowed himself a small chuckle at Sayyari's disbelieving response. Sayyari was smart enough to suspect that the maneuvering which placed the Shaheed under the command of the IRGC Navy, while the money to pay for it had come from the operating funds of the Regular Navy, had something to do with General Jafari. In fact, taking the money for the Shaheed from the budget of the Regular Iranian Navy was part of the quid pro quo he insisted to the Leader's aide, Hamid Ansari, for IRGC help in removing the Council of Guardians. But the General had carefully covered his footsteps.

Sayyari may have been right in his assumptions that Jafari was to blame, but Sayyari had no way to prove it, and more importantly, had no idea that Jafari was only getting started in his campaign against the Regular Navy. Soon, Jafari would advocate that Iran build a replacement for the Shaheed, the funds, again, *quite* regrettably, to be drawn from the operating budget of the Regular Iranian Navy. Jafari estimated that as the Regular Navy ships started to sit in dry-dock for lack of funds to operate, and sailor's families started to starve because the Regular Navy had no money to pay their salary, the Regular Navy would eventually acquiesce to being subsumed into the IRGC Navy as an alternative to extinction.

Sayyari's Regular Navy was just one more piece on the Shah-board that was Iran. The Regular Navy posed an inconvenient challenge to Jafari's supremacy, and therefore needed to be either removed or controlled. Jafari has similar schemes underway to subsume the Regular Army into the IRGC. And all was going according to plan.

*   *   *

Sitting in front of the Expediency Council, early the following morning, General Jafari concluded his prepared remarks on the progress of the investigation into the loss of the Shaheed. "I have made the full resources of all branches of the IRGC available to the person heading the investigation in Bandar Abbas. No expense is to be spared in this vital investigation as *Khoda* is my witness. I believe we will soon be able to acquire definitive evidence of the responsible parties and plan our just retribution for this most heinous of crimes."

He closed his remarks with a somber tone, artfully leaving unsaid to the Expediency Council what most of them assumed to be true: that the Great Satan was responsible for the loss of the Shaheed. The members of the Expediency Council gave him polite thanks and asked for frequent updates in the course of the investigation. He nodded to them graciously like the humble, obedient servant he pretended to be, and swept out of the council chambers to return to the motorcade of gray armored Mercedes 500 SUVs which would return him to his office.

As his motorcade shouldered aside lesser mortals on the streets of Tehran with the aid of roaring of sirens from his police escort, it was clear from the solicitous treatment he had just received that the Expediency Council had no idea about the Jafari's plans to consolidate power in Iran. The Expediency Council was one of the few remaining power centers outside of the General's grasp. But they would not remain that way for long. Jafari had no intention actually eliminating it; such a move would be too clumsy and it would tip his hand. The most elegant kind of coup, one that could not be stopped, was one that did not appear to be a coup at all.

No, Jafari would use the death of the Council of Guardians as justification to expand the "praetorian guard" he personally controlled, the Ansar-ol-Mahdi Corps, to give every member of the Expediency Council a security detail from the IRGC to "Protect them from the Great Satan and the Jews." And if the Council of

Guardians was eventually reconstituted, they, too, would have such protection.

Soon all would realize that they were virtual prisoners of their protective security details. Such men were proud; they would insist that the protective security details be withdrawn. Obedient servant that he was, the General would naturally comply.

Of course, when those suddenly left unprotected began to be tragically struck down by "agents of the Jews" after their security details were gone, could the General be held to blame?
No.

He knew who would be first to go: Rafsanjani, Larijani, Habibi, and Mousavi in particular. All senior members of the Expediency Council; all assumed they were untouchable. They, and their colleagues who were left alive, would soon learn otherwise. He already had some of his best sharpshooters practicing attack scenarios with highly accurate and easily obtainable Russian-made Dragunov sniper rifles at an abandoned mine in the sparsely populated desert of Semnan province. General Jafari was sure that after such "tragedies" struck five or ten times, the remaining members of the Expediency Council would resign themselves to the new shape of government in Iran, one in which the General quietly, but very firmly, held the reins of power.

In a year or two, the final consolidation would begin. The General would then move on the Assembly of Experts, the body that elected the Supreme Leader. When they were firmly under his control, the General would have them vote out the doddering fool who was currently Supreme Leader, and have them install a new Supreme Leader, one who owed his allegiance to the General, not vice versa. Then the General's transition to the ultimate power in Iran would be complete.

He had hoped that today would be a day of rejoicing, one where he could celebrate taking a major step towards complete control. Yet these two insects, Ziyaii and Saeed, somehow managed to avoid being found and swatted into oblivion. The General was sure that would soon change. It must. He was fated to control all of Iran; he felt that destiny deep within him.

CHAPTER 16- MY UNCLE NAPOLEON

Mohsen Saeed awoke to a gentle shaking from his friend, Masoud Bahktiar.

"Wake up, Mohsen. We are here. Let us go inside."

Bahktiar's three passengers, Mohsen, Mohammed, and Mohsen's wife, Lily, trailed Bahktiar inside. As always, Mohsen admired the gleaming marble floors and fine Persian rugs in Bahktiar's house. Mohsen had always found the other furnishings a little jarring, though. Bahktiar had lived in Europe for several years, and had developed a penchant for Danish Modern furniture. The simple, clean lines of such furniture seemed to clash with the astoundingly elaborate patterns of the antique rugs in Bahktiar's house. Bahktiar didn't care that Danish Modern had a hard time merging seamlessly with Traditional Persian. He liked both, and ever since he was a boy, he had always had an unusual disregard for how people perceived him, his family name, or his home. Bahktiar was first and foremost himself, and decorating issues aside, that was a very good thing to be.

Bahktiar's steadfast nature was why Commander Saeed's first call after arriving in Tehran had been to Bahktiar. Three decades ago, an incident vividly taught the Saeed brothers about the worth of Masoud Bahktiar as a friend.

The Saeed brothers first encountered Masoud in elementary school in Kerman, Iran, in the fall of 1984. Mohsen was ten years old, and Mohammed was nine. The brothers soon found that their favorite classmate and playmate was the impish ten year old Masoud Bahktiar, son of one of the wealthiest families in Kerman.

By all social conventions, Bahktiar should have spurned the Saeed brothers. Whip-smart though the Saeeds were, they had committed an unforgivable sin in the elevated social circles in which the Bahktiar family traveled: the Saeed boys were the sons of a poor tradesman of no particular family lineage. Time and again, as the boys were growing up together, Masoud's father warned him of the horrible consequences to the Bahktiar family honor of playing with the poor Saeeds. Masoud completely ignored his father's scolding.

The young Bahktiar, well aware that Mohsen and Mohammed Saeed were by far the two brightest students in their school, always retorted,

"Papa, what, are you afraid I might learn something? Inshallah, their intelligence is a disease that I might catch."

Much as the Saeed brothers and Bahktiar had enjoyed playing together after they met, it was the boys' secret reading of the banned novel, "My Uncle Napoleon" that drew them together. They spent hours together reading passages from the book and laughing uncontrollably at the whimsical comedy. Soon the boys were comparing the absurd characters in "Uncle Napoleon" to people they knew, and reveling in glee as they realized the fictional characters were not fictional at all, but true portraits of character types extremely common in Iran.

The boys joked how Bahktiar's grandfather was like the ultra-paranoid, honor-obsessed Uncle Napoleon, and how their teacher, Mr. Shariat, was like the idiotically officious police detective in the book.

The strength of the friendship between the Saeeds and Bahktiar was greatly reinforced on a spring day in 1988. During class, Mohsen leaned over and joked to Masoud with a bit more volume in his voice than was wise, "When are you finally going to San Francisco with sweet little Donya?"

Although "Uncle Napoleon" had long been banned, it was literally impossible to find an Iranian who didn't know that "Going to San Francisco" was a code phrase for "having sex" drawn from "Uncle Napoleon." As soon as the words were out of Mohsen's mouth, the sharp-eared teacher, Mr. Shariat, had whirled around and stalked over to Mohsen, screaming and ranting. Shariat had guessed, correctly, that Mohsen had made the joke.

Mr. Shariat lived to torment Mohsen. Although Mohsen was only fourteen, it was apparent to everyone in the class, including Shariat, that Mohsen was a good deal smarter than his teacher. Shariat strode to the back of the classroom, and started to reach for the branches of a pomegranate tree that he kept soaking in a large vase full of water. Shariat thundered that that the only suitable punishment for making obscene, un-Islamic jokes was *falak*.

Falak was really nothing more than bastinado, a severe beating delivered to the soles of the feet. In Kerman, it was traditional to use pomegranate branches which had been soaked in water. The water made the branches supple, so they would not break while administering the beating.

Interrupting the wild-eyed Shariat in mid-rant, Masoud Bahktiar jumped to his feet. Before the whole class, Masoud swore on the honor of his family that he had made the joke. Shariat's fury at being denied his prey was palpable, but there was nothing the teacher could do; Mr. Shariat could not punish Mohsen Saeed when Masoud Bahktiar insisted on taking the blame.

Mohsen, being poor, could be targeted by the vindictive Shariat with impunity. Masoud Bahktiar, coming from a family of great wealth and prestige, could not. Shariat knew that any attempt to levy an excessive punishment like *falak* on Bahktiar would quickly see Shariat fired.

Later that day, when Mohsen, Mohammed, and Masoud were gathered together, Mohsen told his brother, Mohammed, how Masoud had come to the rescue. Not wanting to be critical of his brother's savior, but having an irrepressible curiosity, Mohammed had inquired timidly,

"But Masoud, how could you swear on your family honor? That was a lie!"

Masoud's earnest reply that day won him the undying respect of Mohsen and Mohammed Saeed. "How much honor would my family *truly* have if I *could have* saved Mohsen from our bullying idiot of a teacher, *but didn't*, just for fear that a little lie might somehow tarnish the "grand" Bahktiar name? We would have *no* honor! Yes, I lied, but I would do it again, a million times over, to deny that dog Shariat his cruel satisfaction. That *is* honorable. What is a family name by comparison? Nothing."

The Saeed brothers knew they had found a friend for life.

Over the years, Mohsen, Masoud, and Mohammed never missed on opportunity to dust off and use jokes from "Uncle Napoleon", which had so drawn the boys together.

*   *   *

Sitting around a battered but highly burnished oak table in Masoud's kitchen with Lily, Mohammed, and Masoud, Mohsen noticed that Masoud had a new picture mounted on the wall, a blow-up of an infamous photo from the demonstrations at Tehran University two years ago. It showed a female student, pain and fear unmistakably etched on her face, sprawled on the ground while being hit in the head and stomach with truncheons. Her "crime" was having the effrontery to appear in public without a headscarf and for demanding the right to dress as she wished. The Regime had tried to suppress the photos of their Basij headbreakers beating down the defenseless women, a futile effort given the reach of the internet. Recognizing Masoud's handwriting, he could just make out the caption his friend had scrawled underneath the photo. "We will not forget what you have done."

Mohsen started to say, "Masoud, having such a photo can get you in trouble," when Mohsen stopped himself, suddenly realizing that the trouble Masoud might encounter for having an illegal photo was as nothing compared to what would happen to the man if IRGC Security discovered Bahktiar had provided refuge to him and Mohammed.

Better to focus on explaining how he came to be sitting in Masoud's kitchen.

As a senior officer, Mohsen had learned a thing or two about teaching. Particularly when dealing with stubborn, intelligent people who are used to relying on their own judgment, trying to force a conclusion on anyone, even if you happen to be correct, often backfires. As his small audience sipped tea and nibbled biscuits, Saeed methodically laid out the events of the past week to Masoud, Mohammed, and Lily. "I flew to the site of the Shaheed, and my diver discovered limpet mine holes, and then I went to Rahimi's apartment, who confirmed the plot, and then I flew here in the Ababeel."

He did not explain why he followed the course he had unless one of the three asked a question. By the end of Mohsen's recitation, his tale had been interrupted by plenty of interjected curses coming from the listeners.

Mohsen then carefully asked one question: "Mohammed, Lily, what shall we do, now?" Mohsen knew there was only one possible answer, but he had had hours to mull things over aboard the Ababeel; Mohammed and Lily were still struggling to absorb the ramifications of the day's events.

Masoud Bahktiar was a highly successful importer, and part of that success was due to his ability to understand the myriad layers of the Iranian government. He knew the palms to grease, those to ignore, and understood how things in the national and international political realm would affect his business.

Masoud replied instantly, "You must leave Iran and not come back. Not for years, if ever."

Trying to create a Socratic dialogue, Mohsen prompted, "And then what, Masoud? Where shall we live? How shall we support ourselves? Put those aside. Mohammed and I were raised very poor, and we are resourceful. We can provide for our families in some fashion."

Bahktiar interrupted, "My dear Mohsen, you, Mohammed, Lily, your children, need never worry for money. I have more than I can spend in my lifetime. I can give you $100,000 dollars to start this very…"

Mohsen softly cut off his friend, Masoud. "There was never any doubt in my mind that you would help us in a moment of financial need, Masoud. But what of the matter of Zahra Rajabi?"

Zahra Rajabi had been a senior leader in an anti-theocratic-regime group called the Iranian National Council of Resistance. Most Iranians, including Mohammed and Mohsen, didn't care for the tactics of the Iranian National Council of Resistance, not least because the group had taken money from the despised Saddam. In fact, the group was almost as widely loathed in Iran as Saddam himself had been. But Rajabi had been the second cousin of a friend of Mohsen's. To Mohsen and Mohammed, Rajabi's death had been a chilling personal reminder of the ongoing willingness of the Ayatollahs to ruthlessly murder any Iranian, anywhere, who dared speak out against them. Throughout the 1980s and 1990s, there had been literally hundreds of attacks against exiled Iranian dissidents living in Europe and elsewhere. Rajabi had been assassinated while living in Turkey.

Mohsen knew the information he was privy to was ten times more damning to the Supreme Leader than that which usually earned the Ayatollahs' wrath, more than damning enough to justify repeated assassination attempts.

In response to Mohsen's question, Masoud and Mohammed exhaled a low groan jointly,

"Ahhhhhh."

Mohsen continued, "You see, Masoud, it is not just a matter of money. There is nowhere I can go that I will not be hunted. Mohammed, being my brother, is guilty by association. They would never take the chance in letting him live. *Be omid e Khoda*, putting my faith in God, there is no reason those hunting me should have any idea I have been here, and as long as that is the case, you will be fine, Masoud. But as far as I can see, there is no safety for any Saeed in Iran. Nor is there safety anywhere else, as long as we are on our own and unprotected."

Mohammed interjected, "What are you saying, Mohsen?"

"Mohammed, if no place is safe when we are on our own, we need powerful protectors, ones beyond even the reach of the Ayatollahs. We need to be able to disappear and not be found, to give our families a chance to live without fear. Please ask yourself, who can do this for us, Mohammed? Who? And what is the coin we have to purchase this new life? Despite the generous offer of dear Masoud, we are not rich, nor will we ever be. He cannot indefinitely support our two families as we live in hiding and dodge assassins for the rest of our lives. Even if he could, without protectors, we would still not be safe."

Mohammed was slowly shaking his head, not in disagreement, but because part of him unconsciously still did not want to acknowledging the truth of Mohsen's words. Mohsen continued softly, "And then, my brother, there is the matter of the Shaheed. More than 150 people died today, not counting the Council of Guardians. They may say the Great Satan did it, but we both know that is not true. But for the wisdom of my friend,

Captain Akhlagi, Lily would be dressed in mourning clothes, and you would be grieving the loss of your elder brother. Those on the Shaheed truly are martyrs, and their blood cries out for vengeance. No matter the robe he wears, or the rank he bears, any man who tries to kill me is my enemy. And any man who would protect the Saeed family and help me fulfill my duty to avenge the blood of the innocents spilled this day is my friend."

"Our government has turned against us. We have no choice but to seek refuge among those who can give it, and pay any price we must to earn it."

There was dead silence in the kitchen. Mohsen could hear the ticking of a clock in the next room. Mohsen saw Mohammed's face silently leaking tears, and he knew what Mohammed was mourning the loss of his country. He was mourning that the Saeeds should have to flee from the land they loved, the culture they treasured. Never again could they attend a family party with all the cousins, never again would they share the camaraderie of co-workers. Mourning that the life of their wives and children would be brutally uprooted, and that all would have to live in *ghorbat,* an alien land. Finally, he was mourning that the government both he and Mohsen had served so loyally would be so ready to sacrifice them in their games of power.

Mohammed was not stupid, nor had he ever been one to sugar-coat the truth. This was one of the reasons why, as an Iranian nuclear physicist, he had succeeded where so many others before him had failed.

Mohammed looked up at Mohsen, and reached over and clasped his brother's hand. With a low voice, he asked, "Tell me, Mohsen, what must we do now?"

As an adult, Mohsen was not normally one to make bawdy jokes, even among close family. But he had always had a gift for lightening the mood when it was darkest. He replied with a small grin, "Well, first, Mohammed, as I haven't seen my dear wife Lily in three weeks, we will be making a trip to San Francisco. After that…"

*　　　*　　　*

Commander Mohsen Saeed considered it the hardest thing he had ever done. Just sixteen hours after escaping from Mehrabad Airport, he was returning to another airport. Saeed felt slightly better that this time; he was going to Imam Khomeini International instead of Mehrabad International, so it felt less like he was returning to the scene of a prison break. Still, despite the preparations for the trip, it was no less than nerve-wracking.

Lily and Mohammed assured him that he looked completely different. And looking in the mirror, he had to admit, there *had* been a remarkable change in his appearance. The strain of his military responsibilities had heavily salted Mohsen's beard and hair with gray; Mohsen had looked several years older than his thirty-nine years. Gone was the beard, now he sported only a mustache. Mohsen had not seen himself without a beard in over a decade, and it completely changed the look of his face. He felt that he had lost 10 years of age, particularly as his hair and mustache, had, with the aid of some hair dye, regained the glossy, coal-black sheen of his youth. His face was further changed with the addition of some stylish titanium-framed tinted glasses. Completing the transformation was a suit borrowed from Masoud, one that cost more than Mohsen made in a year. The disguise was rounded out by an elegant attaché case, and a small wheeled carryon bag. He now looked every inch the successful businessman. Equally as important, he walked like one. Masoud had recommended Saeed practice a more fluid, loose-limbed gait than he was accustomed to using as a military officer.

The assurance that he looked completely different was cold comfort as a taxi pulled into disembarkation area, and he headed slowly but inescapably towards the ticket counters and the security checkpoints.

Mohsen strode through the entrance, past the huge banks of floor-to-ceiling windows that made up the front wall of Imam Khomeini Airport. He casually turned to the right towards the kiosks sheltered under massive rectangular canvas umbrella sun-shades that sold snacks and drinks. He bought a small sack of pistachios to munch; the transaction gave him time to casually survey the terminal without seeming to do so. The light blue, cavernous roof supported by massive white pillars created an open, airy feeling. Mohsen shot a casual glance towards security and passport controll, manned by men in semi-military looking uniforms with mint-green pastel long-sleeved shirts. They looked almost innocuous, like ticket-takers for a movie theater.

Mohsen knew they were anything but innocuous. For all he knew, each passport control officer had a picture of him taped to the inside of his cubicle. He did not see any visible evidence of IRGC security, but he knew that if they were there, they would be lurking out of sight, waiting for a passport control officer to signal a possible match.

Mohsen put the pistachios in the attaché and strode towards the ticket counter. Luckily, the ticket on Emirates Air was issued with no fuss. He mentally composed himself, took a deep breath, and rounded the corner from the ticket counter, moving towards passport control. This would be the ultimate test of the new identity.

Masoud, Mohsen, and Mohammed had put their heads together late last night. Airline travel was obviously the quickest way out of the country, and Dubai was the obvious place for Mohsen to put the first stage of the Saeeds' escape plan into effect. The question was, could Mohsen fly out safely? Mohsen knew the IRGC would be turning over every rock to find him, and the airports, in particular, would be getting a lot of attention.

Once again, Masoud Bahktiar came to Mohsen's rescue.

Masoud's import business was a large, thriving concern. He required that all his top salesman and managers keep their passports in the company safe, along with a change of clothes at the office, to allow quick day trips to regional business hubs like Dubai. Much of the business of the Middle East was conducted in face-to-face meetings. Phone conversations were a supplement, but could never an adequately substitute for a face-to-face meeting; this was an unavoidable custom. At least one of Masoud's sales or managerial staff was traveling at all times.

Masoud had driven into the office and examined the passports in his safe. One of Masoud's top salesmen was fortunately a good likeness for Mohsen, once the razor and hair-dye had worked their magic. Masoud had briefed Mohsen on his new name, background, and job. With every step Mohsen took forward in the passport control line, he repeated to himself internally: "My name is Aziz Bagheri. I am 33 years old. I was born May 22, 1980. I am married to my wife, Nasreen. We grew up in Esfahan. I am flying to Dubai to work on importing equipment for a powdered milk plant for Bahktiar Imports and Engineering. I have worked at Bahktiar for six...."

Mohsen knew he could never remember the infinite number of details of Aziz Bagheri's life if he were seriously put to the question, but he kept telling himself that he had three things going for him. One, Mohsen really did look like his doppelganger, Bagheri. Two, Commander Saeed had studied engineering and chemistry in college; this would allow him to easily mimic the jargon of someone who dealt in industrial food processing equipment if questioned. Three, he had been friends with Masoud so long that he had unconsciously picked up a lot of knowledge about Masoud's business, and could convincingly describe "Bahktiar Imports and Engineering's" product line, staff, offices, etc. For a hastily contrived disguise, it was actually a very good one.

There was one more person between "Aziz" and the passport control officer. Mohsen said a brief prayer under his breath. Suddenly, Mohsen was looking at the passport control officer, answering barked questions, all while the passport officer compared Mohsen's face to the photo on Aziz Bagheri's passport.

"Your reason for travel?"

"Business."

"Length of your trip?"

"Three or four days. Depends on how the meetings go. I am negotiating the import of equipment for a powdered milk plant." Mohsen had to force himself to bite his tongue and go silent. He had been just about to launch into a detailed explanation of the powdered milk plant deal provided by Masoud.

Before coming to the airport, Masoud and Mohammed had pretended to be a passport control officers so Mohsen could practice his answers. He gave silent thanks to *Khoda* they had done so; it saved him now. Masoud traveled extensively on business, and was able to coach Mohsen on the correct attitude to assume and what to say. Masoud explained that business travelers had no desire to waste time speaking with passport control officers, who businessmen generally regarded as low-grade bureaucrats. Businessmen kept their answers short to speed through the lines. They would provide detail on their travel if asked, but *never* volunteered it.

By way of contrast, nervous or guilty people blathered on at length, providing such detail about their "legitimate" travel that passport officers became suspicious. Masoud realized that if he had spoken even two or three more sentences about the powdered milk-plant deal, those extra details might have been enough to make the passport control officer send Mohsen for a secondary interview, one he might have failed.

In preparation for passport control, Lily had had the brilliant idea of smearing Masoud's palms, face, and most particularly his forehead, with an odorless, colorless antiperspirant. She suggested that even if Mohsen's performance were perfect, one thing that might tip off a security officer would be excessive nervous sweat. Mohsen believed he could control other overt signs of nervousness, but was glad Lily had come up with the antiperspirant trick; it gave him an extra bit of confidence that he could pass undetected. Whether the antiperspirant idea truly worked, or it was merely the placebo effect brought on the extra bit of calming confidence, Mohsen's brow remained blessedly dry.

The passport control officer looked at Mohsen for another second, then down at the passport, then flipped to the departures page and applied an exit stamp. He wordlessly handed the passport back to Mohsen, who took it and gave a brief nod of acknowledgement. He did not let relief show on his face as he strode through the terminal towards the men's prayer room. He was not in the mood to pray, but he was very much in the mood to stay out of sight of roving patrols and/or airport surveillance cameras.

On second thought, a *Shokr,* a prayer of thanks for *Khoda's* mercy and guidance in transiting passport control, would not be amiss.

Ninety minutes later, as the Emirates Air jet climbed out of the heavily polluted air of Tehran, Saeed felt tension drain away. There were many more steps to bringing his family to a new homeland, but he had just taken the first, and one of the most dangerous.

CHAPTER 17-THE MIRACLE OF MODERN COMMUNICATIONS

Given the time difference between Dubai and Washington, he was surprised to see Honey-Bunny logged on to the Agency's instant messaging, or IM, system.

Christ almighty, Joe thought, it had to be midnight or later there, what was Cyn doing in the office in Dubai?

In the privacy of his own head, Joe referred to Cynthia Marks as "Honey-Bunny." He had not dubbed Cynthia that as a term of disparagement; more in admiration, really. Pulp Fiction was one of Joe's favorite movies, one in which Amanda Plummer had played a female sociopath called Honey-Bunny with a scary intensity. When Cynthia was pushed, she could get a crazed gleam in her eye that suggested a willingness to commit bodily harm far more effectively than the shouted threats of Plummer's nut-job character.

Although Joe hated IM with an unholy passion, he considered it a time-waster that interrupted his train of thought and let lazy people ask him questions to which the already knew the answers, he made a rare exception to his vehemently anti-IM policy and logged on to see what was making Cynthia burn the midnight oil.

"Ahoy, Cyn, how's my favorite squid? What the hell are you doing in the office at this hour?"

Joe, a former Army man, always made a point of teasing Cynthia about her naval background.

She zinged him back with the traditional insult for Army soldiers, "Hiya, dogface. I'm writing up the latest burn notice on my second fucking LLPOF piece-of-shit walk-in of the night." LLPOF was an acronym Cynthia had coined for walk-ins that were fabricators. It was short for "Liar, Liar, Pants On Fire."

Joe laughed aloud when he read Cyn's answer: he had noticed at the Farm that angelic-looking Cynthia had a propensity for swearing like a drunken sailor when she was tired or frustrated. Of course, given Honey-Bunny's stint in naval intelligence, once upon a time, she had been a sailor; that's probably where she picked up the habit.

"Cyn, I already saw your cable on the Moeen character, are you saying you had to field another one after that?"

"That's affirmative, Joe. Just after I finished the cable on that sleaze Moeen, I got another call, had to go back to 'The Room,' only to be graced with the presence of yet another lying bastard. Now I'm writing up *that* meeting. I swear to God, what would be wrong simply shooting these LLPOFs, then dumping their bodies in Dubai Creek? Pretty soon, word would get around and the fabricators would dry up!"

Joe knew one of Cynthia's biggest challenges as a case officer was that she was cute as a button, and many men, particularly in the Middle East, equated cuteness with being weak, soft, or stupid, which was definitely not the case with Honey-Bunny. While she was no martial arts expert, Cynthia had obsessively studied pressure points and nerve pinches and used that knowledge to great effect when necessary.

Joe grinned to himself. He knew Cynthia was just blowing off steam and would never actually shoot someone, except in self-defense. He had been in her position often enough to know exactly the frustration she was feeling with the process of winnowing through the BS that almost every walk-in tried to peddle. He would lay odds that one of her recent walk-ins might have been ejected from "The Room" by Cyn with a bit more "assistance" than was strictly necessary.

He typed back, "Your master plan to rid the world of intel fabricators is intriguing, my dear swabbie, but have you thought that it might also cause the few legitimate walk-ins to dry up?"

She immediately came back with, "It's two AM and I still have a half-hour of work left to do, typing up the latest meeting notes from talking to the another jerkoff. Just like Moeen, this guy was trying to peddle a variation of 'A supersecret Zionist submarine sank the Shaheed' story. I have to be back at work at seven AM!! Right now, I'd be willing to take the risk of scaring off the tiny number of potentially legit walk-ins. In fact, I'm shooting the next one that even looks at me sideways! Has the number of Iranian walk-ins trying to con us out of a buck shot through the roof since the gas riots last year or what?"

Joe felt sympathy for Honey-Bunny, but knew that long hours were par for the course if you were a field officer for the CIA; at least, if you were a *decent* field officer, and Cynthia was one of the best.

Sick as Cyn was of walk-ins at the moment, Joe knew that despite her rhetorical threats, she'd handle the ones who came in tomorrow, next week, or next month, with the same professionalism she always displayed. Because that's what he would do. Even when she was pissed off, like now, she wouldn't allow that anger to interfere with her work.

Joe typed, "Cyn, Walk-in numbers for Iranians have been climbing across the region since riots after the 'Holy Regime' cut the gasoline subsidy in half last year. If it makes you feel any better, the case officers in Beirut Station and Baghdad are reporting the exact same thing: a flood of Iranians trying to sell anything and everything since last November's gas riots. Nothing for it but for you to 'muddle on through,' as the Brits say."

Being a big believer in "soldiering on in the face of adversity," Joe's last line of text held a note of encouragement. "Hey, Cyn, the odds aren't great, but *somebody* has to win the walk-in lottery. Maybe soon, it'll be you. TTYL."

And to Cynthia's everlasting surprise, the next very day, it was.

CHAPTER 18-MEETINGS PART TWO

Joe had finally managed to get a few hours of work done before being dragged back to the NE division conference room for the three PM. meeting on the Shaheed. The conference room had a long, highly polished wooden table; the walls were lined with stylized logos of various US intelligence agencies and counterterrorism units. Pricey Herman Miller Aeron chairs surrounded the table; 9/11 had seen the CIA's funding increase vastly. Joe knew from personal experience that didn't mean that field personnel got all the money they needed to run operations. Instead it meant that big wigs in headquarters got $500+ ergonomically correct chairs.

Field officers overseas still got what they usually got: the shaft.

All the main players from the morning meeting were there, as were hordes of newcomers that served no apparent purpose, as far as Joe could tell. There was a species of CIA headquarters dweller that deluded themselves into thinking that attending a meeting was actually doing work, and furthermore believed if they attended a meeting on a breaking crisis, they were helping solve that crisis, even if they had contributed nothing but carbon dioxide and methane to the meeting.

Yes, if questioned, they would all have a legitimate *sounding* reason to attending the meeting, and thus could not be summarily ejected, but in reality, they did nothing.

When Joe had a choice, he scheduled important meetings at four or five PM. This weeded out those more concerned with getting out of the CIA Hqs parking lot before it gridlocked in the evening rush than with national security.

Once again, Fredrick Sandler, Near East Division Chief of Ops, opened the proceedings.

"Okay, people, what do we have? Joe, you first?"

Joe quickly launched into his summary, briefly referring to printed emails and cables as he went along. "Still don't have much. I expect that will change overnight as folks have a chance to meet with their assets. I think most people here have already seen the email from Chief-of-Station Tel Aviv that made the rounds this morning. For those of you that missed it, COS said the Head of Mossad is swearing up and down that Israel had nothing to do with the sinking of the Shaheed, not that it hadn't crossed their mind. COS said the Israeli General Staff had already talked about taking out the Shaheed, and decided not to do it. Their reasoning went like this: taking out the Shaheed might provoke a confrontation between Iran and the US Navy's 5th Fleet, stationed in the Persian Gulf. The Israeli admirals know the Fifth Fleet's dirty little secret: since the IRGC Navy has so many small speedboats crewed by "martyr" trained crews, the 5th Fleet could never knock them all out during a swarming attack, which is the IRGC Navy's favorite tactic."

"Hundreds of speedboats packed with explosives and kamikaze crews would decimate the Fifth Fleet, even the Fifth Fleet's own war games showed that."

"No matter how many boats the Iranians lost during a confrontation, any confrontation that caused *us* to lose an aircraft carrier or other capital ship would make us *very* pissed. A confrontation which started as a result of Israeli action might make us so pissed off that we would cut our military aid to Israel. So the Israeli admirals decided the Shaheed was a threat they could live with. After all, the Shaheed was based in the Persian Gulf, not the Mediterranean. The Israelis' view was that the Shaheed was really the Fifth Fleet's problem, not Israel's."

"Tel Aviv Station is still preparing a formal response cable. They're waiting for an official written assurance from the Chief of Mossad that Israel had nothing to do with it. In the meantime, COS Tel Aviv says that he is confident that the Israelis are telling the truth."

Joe riffled his papers and picked his next item.

"Okay, next, one of Singapore's assets sent in something via COVCOM about the Shaheed. The Iranians paid a computer geek from the Chinese People's Liberation Army Navy to help write a software update for the Shaheed six weeks ago. The source said it had something to do with training simulations. I asked Singapore to write back to the asset for more details on software, which I am sure they were already doing in any case. Next, Hizboll…"

Sandler cut into Joe's recitation, "Joe, what do we know about the Chinese source?"

"Fred, I'll be happy to give you details later. The Singapore case is Restricted Handling, and I know at least half a dozen people in this room right now are not cleared for that RH compartment." This statement was as close to a stab at the several do-nothing meeting-crashers as Joe would allow himself. Fred Sandler took the hint about "Need to Know" and let the question about the Chinese source drop.

"Okay, Joe, proceed."

"The Counter Terrorism Center forwarded me a Restricted cable from Beirut Station. Station there has a source with Hezbollah contacts. The source says orders for retaliatory attacks against Israel or the US have not come down yet. He didn't know if that was because none will be ordered, or whether the Ayatollahs will want major retaliatory strikes, which require some planning and can't be done on the spur of the moment. Despite lack of orders from Iran, the local Hezbollah leaders decided the sinking of the Shaheed was a good excuse for an anti-Israel riot in southern Lebanon, so look for that tomorrow. Just in case, our embassy in Beirut is evacuating all non-essential personnel to Italy until things settle down."

"Next, my buddy Mark at the Office of Naval Intelligence called just before the meeting and said that ONI's seismic and sonar registers picked up some underwater blasts just two hours ago. ONI can't be precise, but the triangulation puts the blasts within a coupla' miles of the Shaheed. What caused them, ONI doesn't know. Maybe the Iranians are blasting as part of salvage operations for the Shaheed. Mark did say ONI is still working to pick apart the original acoustic blast signature from the blast when the Shaheed sunk, but they don't have anything on that yet. Acoustics can be pretty tricky under water, I guess."

"Finally, and I can't claim to have seen every single message, but so far, I haven't seen any signals intelligence from Iranian leadership or military comms that show a major retaliatory strike is being planned. People are still absorbing the reactions."

"Here is my read of the whole deal so far: if you turn on CNN, you can see the mullahs are beating the old 'Great Satan' drum again. Reportedly a million demonstrators are flooding the streets of Tehran to protest the sinking of the Shaheed. If the sinking has any internal political effect so far, it is that regime hardliners will benefit from the 'rally round the flag' effect. If they want to launch a wave of retaliatory attacks, as of right now, the Iranian populace will support it."

"We have to wait and see if that support drops away when the populace learns we didn't do it, and neither did Israel. If the average 'Ali' on the streets there remembers that their economy, which was *already* dysfunctional before the gas riots last year, is even worse now, and that the blame lies in the Ayatollahs' mismanagement of Iran's oil reserves, things will cool down in a few weeks. The average guy there has more immediate concerns than the 'Great Satan.'… Namely, his own economic survival."

"Of course, making up conspiracy theories is the national sport of Iran. Even if the Supreme Leader went on TV and swore on a stack of Korans that the USA didn't do it, at least a quarter of Iran would still be convinced we had. Unfounded rumors are easier to start than stop over there. Hard to tell how this will play out."

"That's it for me. Oh, wait. One more thing. So far, we have had five 'walk-ins,' two in Dubai, one in Beirut, and two in Baghdad. All five were information peddlers claiming to have information on the Shaheed. All five said it was 'The Zionists.' Cynthia Marks, for one, is fit to be tied and swears she's gonna shoot the next fabricator that darkens her door."

This earned Joe a laugh from those who knew her reputation.

"All five were given the 'Don't call us, we'll call you speech' and if I know Cynthia, the two she met were probably booted in the ass on the way out the door, too." Another laugh. "Okay, that's it for me."

Fred Sandler said, "Thanks, Joe, nice summary," then turned to a frumpy forty five year old woman whose impossibly bright red hair could only have come from a bottle.

"Maggie, what have you got?" Maggie worked National Geospatial Agency, which analyzed the satellite imagery from the US's satellite "eyes in the sky."

"What I have is bubkis. We didn't have any eyes on the Shaheed when it went down. We managed to get one pass from one of our electro-optical birds before we lost daylight. We saw a debris field with oil and fuel slicks, bobbing pieces of wreckage, and that's about it. The IRGC has a few of their little speedboats circling the area where the Shaheed went down. What they are doing, we have no idea. They were all in motion when we saw them, so they did not appear to be dropping off divers to go down to the Shaheed. We guess they are probably there to keep away the curious."

Fred turned to look at Mark Barnes, an up-and-coming analyst in the Directorate of Intelligence's Near East and South Asia group.

"Mark, any surprise in what you just heard? You guys whipping something up for the big boys?"

Mark replied, "Yeah, we'll be burning the midnight oil on a sitrep and ad-hoc estimate on the implications of the loss of the Shaheed for tomorrow's President's Daily Brief. It will say pretty much the same thing Joe just said. Will you Directorate of Operations guys have anyone minding to store to send us relevant Restricted Handling stuff that may come in before 10 pm tonight?" Access to RH cases, which often produced the best and most sensitive reporting, was so tightly controlled that only people specifically "read-in" on the "compartment" would even know the compartment existed, let alone what information was *in* the compartment.

Joe would normally be stuck with such a task, but in this case, he had a way around it. Joe spoke up quickly, so Fred didn't order Joe to stay, "I'll take care of that, Mark."

Fred Sandler looked at Joe with mild surprise on his face. Fred knew Joe had happily worked crazy hours when operating overseas to collect intelligence himself, but never took kindly to headquarters bureaucratic drudgery like waiting to see if other case officers 'in the field' were going to send in something of interest. Still, Fred was not one to look a gift horse in the mouth. Fred could see some of the useless chair-warmers who had attended were just about to start asking questions. Like Joe, Fred knew better than to let that get started.

"Thanks, Maggie, Joe, Mark. Okay everybody, that's it. Unless anybody here knows who sunk the Shaheed, but has neglected to mention it, we are done here for right now."

"It is calm-before-the-storm time, people. Be back in this room tomorrow at nine AM for an update. Things will start happening tonight as reaction sets in around the world. This Shaheed thing isn't going away; it will probably just start getting hotter for the next couple of weeks at least. Warn your wives and husbands that they won't be seeing much of you in the immediate future."

Joe wasted no time getting to his feet and out of the conference room; he knew if he got buttonholed by any one of the ten superfluous chair-warmers who had sat in on the meeting, he would be forced to have a twenty minute conversation on the implications of the sinking of the Shaheed, a conversation that would teach him nothing he did not already know.

Unfortunately, you can't dodge your boss when he knows where your desk is. Fred Sandler ambled up to Joe's desk five minutes later and said, "Joe, let's go to my office. Background on the Chinese source."

There weren't many perks available for those below Division Chief in the Directorate of Operations, having an office with a door that could actually close out the distractions and bustle of the NE Division cubicle farm was one of them. Joe followed Fred to his tiny office, which didn't seem too much larger than a box of animal crackers. As with most offices in NE Division, the walls of Fred's small office were covered with leadership diagrams of various Middle Eastern government organizations and/or terrorists groups. Of course, in Iran's case, it was sometimes hard to tell the difference between the two.

Joe spent the next ten minutes filling Fred in on the Chinese source, an accountant in the People's Liberation Army Navy who helped funnel the graft money from the PLAN's many illegal enterprises into the pockets of various senior officers of the PLAN. Since some of the illegal enterprises involved trading with Iran, Joe had been "read-in" on the RH case by China Ops. Decent Chinese sources were rarer then gold. Consequently, the boys in China Ops jealously guarded all information on their sources.

Joe modestly accepted Fred's thanks for volunteering to monitor the Restricted Handling channels for information about the Shaheed. Joe knew Fred *assumed* that meant Joe would be sitting in the office until 10 or 11 pm tonight waiting to see if any interesting RH cable traffic came in.

Joe had no intention of sitting in the office tonight. Joe neglected to remind Fred about Steve Billings. Steve was one of the Iran Task Force's case officers, and Steve had all the relevant access to Restricted Handling cases. Steve was currently filling in for a buddy on the 4pm-midnight shift at the Ops Center watch office. Since Steve was going to be in the building anyway, Joe had already asked Steve come down a couple of times during his shift to see if anything good had arrived in RH channels. Steve agreed to do that.

Joe figured it probably violated some obscure regulation to have Steve working in both the Watch Office and in the Iran Task Force at the same time. Just about everything at the CIA that made sense or actually worked violated a regulation of some sort. So Joe had fallen back on the old adage, "Better to ask for forgiveness than permission." If Fred found out, it would be after the fact, too late to stop it.

Instead of staying in the office, Joe was going home at a reasonable hour tonight. He was going to watch some TV, have some nice "goodbye sex" with Claire, and pack his bags for a trip. Like Fred, Joe had a feeling "The Shaheed" was going to require a lot of late nights for everyone involved. Unlike Fred, who enjoyed serving at CIA Hqs, Joe hoped and prayed those late nights would include travel overseas to meet with sources. In Joe's estimation, Human intelligence, or "Humint," was not collected by sitting behind a desk in CIA Hqs, but by CIA case officers "in the field" meeting with human sources. When the first real lead on the Shaheed came in, Joe planned to be on a plane within hours to pounce on it. That's why he had to get his bags packed.

CHAPTER 19-EVIN

Despite the Iranian government's repeated efforts to portray Evin Prison as a humane facility, nobody was fooled. Evin was shrouded with an aura of mystery, brutality, and dread. Saboori couldn't help but think back to the incident with the Canadian photojournalist. Photography was prohibited in the area around Evin. Ten year ago, a female Canadian photojournalist had been arrested for taking photographs in front of Evin, an imprisonment which led to her beating and death in Iranian custody. Doctors examining her body found evidence of rape and torture. They also found her skull fractured. Forensic evidence to the contrary, the Iranian government claimed she died from a stroke.

Evin's reputation had not notably improved in the intervening decade.

Saboori felt a deep stab of fear as he realized the IRGC security team was not taking him and the others from the Ababeel to IRGC Headquarters, but rather to Evin Prison. He knew enough about interrogations to know that his only chance was to cling to the emergency landing story as Commander Saeed had told it. While the emergency landing of the Ababeel *was* faked, emergency landings provoked by false readings in the temperamental helicopter avionics occurred regularly; nobody could gainsay him on that point as long as the co-pilot and crew chief had the wit to stick to the same story.

And it *was* true that he had no idea where Commander Saeed was, if they asked.

Saboori hoped his co-pilot, Lieutenant Firouz Shafaq, and his crew chief, Petty Officer Maani Tolui, understood the change in the situation going to Evin implied. Saboori had figured they would have an administrative debrief at IRGC Hqs, not a trip to Evin. Unfortunately, the crew of the Ababeel was being transported to Evin in separate vehicles. Separate transport was itself a very bad sign; it meant the IRGC Security was already thinking of them as criminals who needed to be isolated so they could not "get their stories straight."

So focused was Saboori on the crew of the Ababeel, he had already forgotten about the other passenger on the Ababeel, the Iranian navy staff driver, Seaman 2nd Class Abdul Khatami.

*   *   *

IRGC interrogator Ebrahim Jalili was disappointed. He had been given four men to interrogate. He had looked forward to days of playing one off the other, slowly destroying their will to resist by extending hope of freedom or surcease from pain, only to withdraw those hopes. Perverse though it was, Jalili's knowledge of human psychology, or at least the darker arts of human psychology, was unrivaled in Iran. In Jalili's view, there were only two categories of inmates at Evin: those who were guilty of crimes against the Iranian state and would admit to those crimes, and those who were guilty but would not admit to their crimes. Jalili usually took great joy turning the latter into the former. His position as the IRGC's chief interrogator insured a steady supply of material upon which he could practice his "art," which is the way he thought of his job.

The moment of most exquisite pleasure for Jalili was that instant when the person he was interrogating finally realized, and they all eventually did, that it didn't matter what they told Jalili. The very fact of being sent to Evin meant you were defacto guilty of crimes against the Holy Regime. Some prisoners he killed. Some sat for years, uncharged with any crime. A few he released. The fate of prisoners was more closely tied to whether Jalili had an alcohol or amphetamine hangover than any notion of actual guilt or innocence.

Jalili was therefore very disappointed when he was told to release his four newest prisoners in the morning. He had only spoken to the Navy Staff Driver, Khatami, and Khatami had been pathetically cooperative from the very beginning. Jalili hadn't even had a chance to be "persuasive." Khatami had obviously not held back a single detail.

Jalili had really only said one thing to Khatami, "Tell me everything about today. What you did. Where you went. Who you saw. Where you saw them. Who you spoke to. Everything you heard them say."

The details had come spilling out, with Jalili only stepping in occasionally for clarification. He had reported the information to the General, who had only seemed interested in two particular details. The General asked Jalili to confirm that Khatami had seen a diver board the Ababeel before it flew off to the wreck of the Shaheed, and that the diver's gear had been dripping water when the Ababeel returned. The second detail that Jalili confirmed was that Commander Saeed had visited Captain Rahimi before taking off aboard the Ababeel for Tehran. Khatami had freely confirmed both, with no coercion needed.

The General had ordered the prisoners to be put in the nicer cells, those showcased to the international media. They were to be treated well, and given decent food and a chance to take a shower. Jalili was ordered to tell them that they would be released in the morning to return the Ababeel to Bandar Abbas. The General had even forbidden Jalili from questioning the Ababeel's crew. Jalili felt cheated, but knew he could not go against the General's wishes on this matter.

After all, the General had always provided well for Jalili. He was sure the General would soon see fit to provide replacements for the four from the Ababeel.

CHAPTER 20-JACKPOT

To his chagrin, Commander Saeed stood in front of the locked door to the US Consulate in Dubai at the enormous Dubai World Trade Center. It was Friday, and the Consulate was closed. Saeed had been so overwhelmed with relief at his easy passage through Iranian and then Emirati passport control that he had temporarily forgotten that US Consulates around the world don't follow the US standard work week of Monday-Friday, but follow local schedules. In Dubai, the work-week is Sunday-Thursday, and the US Consulate follows suit.

Mohsen cursed under his breath and studied the notices and forms posted on a bulletin board near the Consulate, which had instructions on how to apply for various kinds of US visas, wait times for visa interview appointments, documentation requirements for visas, etc. In one corner of the board was a small notice: "If you are a US Citizen and are experiencing an Emergency, you may call the American Citizen Services unit at 971 2 414 2550."

"Khoda bozorg ast, God is great," he thought in relief!

Of course, Saeed was *not* a US citizen, but he was hopeful that if he could only talk to a live person, instead of a maddening automated answering service or computer, he might be able to make contact with the right person.

Mohsen scribbled down the number and went in search of a pay-phone, then remembered that Masoud had told him that all employees of Bahktiar Importing and Engineering had access to the ultra-plush World Trade Club Dubai, which was also part of the Dubai World Trade Center complex and not far from the US Consulate. Mohsen fished the out the card Masoud had given him, which identified Mohsen as an employee of Bahktiar Importing.

Mohsen was chagrined for the second time in less than an hour as he discovered the World Trade Club Dubai was *also* closed on Fridays.

Mohsen found his way to the nearby Fairmont Hotel and found a private phone booth off the lobby. Withdrawing a Bahktiar Importing credit card given to him by Masoud, he inserted the card and dialed the number. He had to endure the typical five minutes of recorded explanations that the Consulate was closed, that this was not the correct line to call for visa information, and admonitions not to call this number unless the caller was a US Citizen experiencing an emergency before getting forwarded to the US Consulate duty operator. Finally, a voice came on the line.

"Emergency Citizen Services, how may I be of assistance?"

Mohsen took a deep breath before responding. If he started down this road, there would be no turning back. Just making this call was enough to earn him a death sentence. But then again, what choice did he have? Luckily, Mohsen's English, while rusty, was still serviceable. He had been brushing up lately, as senior bridge crew often had to exchange navigation information with the crews of various ships in the Persian Gulf, exchanges that were often conducted in English.

"Hello. Please listen very carefully. I am not a US Citizen, but this is an emergency. I am a Naval Officer in the Pasdaran Navy." Damnation! As soon as he said it, he remembered the Pasdaran was the *Iranian* term for the IRGC, not the phrase the US used. He started again.

"Excuse me. I am an officer in the *Iranian Revolutionary Guard Corps* Navy. I would like to speak directly to a representative of the Central Intelligence Agency. I have information about the sinking of the IRGC Navy Destroyer Shaheed yesterday."

He expected to spend the next twenty minutes wheedling his way to the next level of contact; all bureaucracies existed to create such impediments, did they not? Commander Saeed was therefore surprised when the operator replied, "Very well sir. Can you provide me your name and a contact phone number?"

Mohsen read off the phone number of booth he was sitting in, then said with urgency in his voice, "My life is in danger from the government of Iran. I do not feel safe giving you my name over the phone. I can say I am a senior officer and I will be happy to meet any place and follow any security measures you require, including a full search and x-ray of myself and my belongings. I will provide all required information in person. I ask only that someone contact me as soon as possible. This is a matter of the utmost urgency, and time is of the essence."

An hour later, long after Mohsen had started to wonder how long he could occupy the private phone booth before being ejected by the Fairmont's staff, the phone began to ring. Although he had been anxiously awaiting that ring, he was startled when it finally happened. Swallowing deeply again, he picked up the phone. "Hello? Yes, I work for the government of Iran. I have information about the Shaheed."

*　　　*　　　*

Mohsen Saeed glanced around the lobby of the Dubai International Hotel Apartments with an unease he hoped he concealed. He was the only man waiting in the lobby, tucked away from the flow of foot traffic in one of the comfortable chairs in the waiting area. He surreptitiously eyed the desk clerk behind the circular wraparound check-in counter, the two porters near the front entrance, and all guests passing through. After only a few minutes wait, a muscular Caucasian man with short hair, dressed in a tan polo shirt and khaki pants, appeared from the direction of the elevators. He strode directly towards Mohsen. The man halted a few paces away and waved Mohsen forward with a slow beckoning gesture while saying in English with a placid demeanor "This way, please, sir."

Mohsen clambered to his feet and followed the burly man to a bank of elevators, where they stepped into a vacant elevator car. Once inside the elevator, the man pantomimed, "Arms up." Mohsen complied with the directive, and the larger man quickly and dispassionately patted Mohsen down. After arriving at the sixth floor, Mohsen followed the man to the fourth door on the right. The muscular man unlocked the door, gestured Mohsen inside, closed the door to the hallway behind them both, gestured towards the desk and chairs directly in front of Mohsen, and then disappeared behind a narrow cubby built onto the wall of the apartment.

Mohsen looked in the direction of the desk and was surprised to see that behind it was seated a beautiful woman with blond hair and a flawless porcelain complexion that said she was of northern European stock and that, like many in Dubai, she avoided exposure to the blistering heat and light of Dubai's summer as much as humanly possible.

Mohsen strode towards the desk. The woman got to her feet, and he noted that although she wore a presentable navy business outfit, it was rather loose fitting and not tailored to her figure at all, which surprised him. She was American, was she not? Why dress in such a way?

Because of the Ayatollahs' harsh dress codes, Persian women of the urban educated classes dress somberly in chadors in public, much against their natural inclination. In the privacy of their own homes, particularly during private parties among a close circle of friends, the opposite trend prevails: fashionable Iranian women wear chic and sometimes even daringly revealing clothes, not to mention meticulously applied makeup. When his own wife, Lily, was dressed for a celebration at home amongst friends, away from the prying eyes of the Hizzbolla'hi, the religious fanatics, she was as polished and perfumed as any Persian princess of antiquity.

By way of contrast, he noticed that the woman before him not only wore a rather plain outfit, she lacked eye-shadow, lip-stick, nail polish, and jewelry of any sort. Mohsen knew his wife well enough to know that were she in a country that allowed women freedom to dress as they would, as in Dubai, Lily would never dress as plainly as the woman before him.

He was far from qualified to discuss the intricacies of modern women's fashion, but his instinctive comparison to Lily's dress habits brought him a flash of insight: the woman before him had the freedom and the money to dress however she wished. She was unmistakably attractive and feminine, and could easily have dressed to accentuate that, but did the opposite. Her plain manner of dress was a mark of discretion, a way to hide in plain sight and avoid attention. They had not yet exchanged a word, yet he found himself strangely reassured.

She spoke a greeting, leaned forward over the desk, and extended her hand.

*   *   *

The walk-in glanced at her hand for the merest fraction of a second and then shook it firmly. Test one passed. He spoke to Cynthia, "Thank you for agreeing to see me, Ms. Peters. I mean Ms. Sam. I have information that I believe will be of great value to the US."

Cynthia replied, "Well, that remains to be seen. Let's begin at the beginning. Please, relax and have a seat. Can you tell me your name and what brought you here? Also, can you show me some form of identification, a passport, a driver's license?"

The man said, "My name is Commander Mohsen Saeed of the Iranian Revolutionary Guard Corps Navy. Until yesterday, when it sank, I was the executive officer of the IRGC Navy Destroyer Shaheed. I know what sank the Shaheed, and it was not US torpedoes, as the Iranian news had been suggesting. Nor was it the Zionists, as many are saying. I am sorry, but I do not have my real passport right now; I left it in Iran with a friend. I fled from Iran after changing my appearance to fit a borrowed passport. However, I will be happy to answer any questions necessary to establish my identity to your satisfaction."

Cynthia had thought there was something familiar about his voice when she first heard it on the telephone. A thrill of electricity shot through her when the man identified himself as an IRGC Navy officer. Long before joining the CIA, Cynthia Marks had been a Farsi linguist for the Office of Naval Intelligence. She had spent four very boring years in Bahrain listening to Iranian Navy and IRGC Navy radio chatter. She could identify three quarters of the current senior Iranian Navy and IRGC Navy officers by voice alone after thousands of hours spent listening to Iranian Navy communications intercepts.

Never in her wildest dreams had she expected to meet one of the men she had been once eavesdropped on, but his voice was undeniably familiar.

Careful to keep her demeanor calm and her voice non-committal, she said, "Commander Saeed, without identity documents, I hope you understand I am going to have to go to some length to verify that you are who you say you are." She handed him a yellow legal pad and a pen, and continued, "Please fill out for me every position you have held in the Iranian military. Start with your first service, describe all the training you have ever had, the name of every unit you served in, along with your commanding officer at the time. Either English or Farsi is fine, I read both. Please omit nothing. I realize this may take a while. While you are working on that, can I offer you something to drink, coffee, tea, water?"

This was Cynthia's second test, and the biggie. A real IRGC Navy officer would easily be able to answer these questions. A phony would be tripped up in about 10 seconds. After hearing Cynthia, the man nodded as if to acknowledge the reasonableness of her request, leaned forward and took the pad from her, and propped it on his knee. His eyes took on the faraway look of someone searching their memory, and he absently replied as he started to write,

"Yes, of course. Thank you for the offer, Ms. Sam, I would welcome some tea."

Cynthia spent ten minutes heating water and steeping the tea. She watched him out of the corner of her eye, noting that he continued writing at a furious pace. She set down a tea service with two cups on the edge of her desk. The man paused his writing to look up. He smiled with pleasure to see that the tea service included large rough chunks of crystallized sugar. This lady obviously knew how Iranians took their tea.

Instead of putting sugar into their tea, Iranians will often dip a lump of crystallized sugar into tea so it absorbs a small amount, and then place the lump of sugar in their mouth as they sip their tea from the cup.

The sugar trick, of course, was only one of many Cynthia knew to increase a walk-in's faith in her. When speaking to Iranians, for example, she would make sure to use the phrase *Inshallah,* or God willing, which both Arabs and Iranians use, but also knew to use the Persian for God, *Khoda*, the majority of time. If the walk-in had been a Russian, instead of Iranian, she would have put out a bowl of fruit preservers instead of crystallized sugar; Russian drank their tea while holding a spoonful of fruit preserves in their mouth. It was all part of winning a stranger's trust by demonstrating you knew something about their culture, which was Cynthia's job, even though she was far from sure *she* could trust *him*.

Cynthia poured him a cup, then said, "That will be enough detail for right now, Commander. Please let me see what you have written so far."

As Cynthia started to read over what he had written, she had to hide her growing excitement. Training at Bandar Abbas, check. Service on the missile boat Paykar, check. Service on the Destroyer Jamaran, check. Transfer to IRGC Navy six months ago, which included a promotion to full Commander and assignment as executive officer of the Shaheed. Every detail fit. She recognized the names of ships he had served on, and the Commanders he had served under. Of course, she would have to do a lot of digging to verify what he said, but this guy sure seemed to be who he claimed he was.

Cynthia said, "Excellent, Commander, that will be enough on your background for now, although we will revisit it later. Let's get down to business. Please tell me what brought you here today. What is the nature of the information you have? You mentioned that you know what happened to the Shaheed. Please elaborate." Cynthia picked up her pen, and prepared to begin taking notes.

"Miss Sam, as to what I want, that is simple. Relocation in the West for myself, my wife, my brother, and my brother's wife and child. As to why I am seeking this, that, too, is simple. I know the US did not sink the Shaheed, because I know who did. The Shaheed was sunk by fifty limpet mines attached to the hull yesterday just before dawn. They were put there by order of the Supreme Leader. Because I discovered this information, my life, and the lives of my family, are now at risk."

Commander Saeed noticed that the woman "Sam" raised her eyebrows in surprise when he said the Supreme Leader was responsible for the sinking of the Shaheed, but she did not stop her furious note-taking as he continued to relate the history of the last 48 hours of his life. She didn't stop until he got to the topic of his brother, Mohammed, and Mohammed's job.

"Miss Sam, as I said, since I am in danger, my whole family is in danger as well. My brother Mohammed also works for the Iranian Government. He is a nuclear physicist. Are you aware that a uranium enrichment facility was built underneath the mountains near Qom late last decade?"

Cynthia nodded warily and replied, "Yes Commander. The centrifuge cascade at Fordow has been inspected and monitored by teams from the International Atomic Energy Agency, the IAEA. Does your brother work there?"

"Not exactly, Miss Sam. He works nearby. The facility you know of is a cover for the facility where my brother works. In exchange for relocation for his wife and child, my brother Mohammed will share information about this second nuclear facility. This facility is, we believe, unknown to the IAEA and the United States. Certainly, my brother and others have exercised great ingenuity to make sure it remains undiscovered. The second facility is much larger than the one monitored by the IAEA. It contains four cascades, each composed of 2,500 IR-2 centrifuges. Mohammed has informed me that it has been in full operation since early 2011."

"Over the last three years, these centrifuges have enriched enough uranium for six low yield nuclear weapons."

Cynthia could not hide her shock. Unwillingly, she interjected, "What? What are you telling me? Say that again!" She could hardly believe her ears. As early as 2008, the IAEA had assessed that Iran had enough low enriched uranium that, were it to be sufficiently enriched, a single atomic bomb could be produced. But that uranium was under IAEA seal, and nowhere near pure enough to be "bomb grade."

Where did the extra uranium come from?

Even more important, how the hell did the Iranians enrich it to weapons grade without the US finding out?

Every intelligence estimate going back a decade had concluded that Iran continued to have problems getting their older uranium enrichment centrifuge cascades to operate reliably, and getting enough parts to build newer cascades without either the US, UK, Israeli, or German intelligence catching on. Centrifuge cascades were some of the most complex and delicate networked systems in the world, which made tracking parts purchased for centrifuge programs much easier for the CIA than it would have been if parts for them were readily available COTS (commercially-available-off-the-shelf). Even the slightest imperfection in the materials or assembly could cause them to fail, often in a way that spewed around the toxic uranium hexafluoride gas they were trying to enrich. They were a technical nightmare.

Even though the cascades Iran had built using carbon fiber centrifuges worked, they were unreliable, and US and other international sanctions had put a stranglehold on the high strength carbon fiber and filament winding tools necessary to build the newer centrifuge rotors. Failures of the old generation of centrifuges (with more than a little help in their failure from CIA sabotage) and lack of parts for the new one were the reason why the 2010 National Intelligence Estimate, or NIE, on Iran's nuclear program had stated that while Iran would have a fair pile of uranium enriched to 19.75% by 2013, that level of enrichment was less than one fourth the level needed to make a nuclear weapon. Outside of a few alarmists and the hawks who believed there was no foreign policy problem that couldn't be solved with 2,000 lb JDAM bombs, the general consensus in the intelligence community had been until Iran managed to secretly get both enough parts *and* uranium feedstock for the new models, Iranian progress towards the bomb, while not halted, had slowed to a glacial pace.

If that had changed, if Iran had secretly obtained both centrifuge parts and enough raw yellowcake uranium to start a parallel and covert program under the cover of the one monitored by the IAEA, that information would create shockwaves around the world. First off, it meant there were major gaps in the sanctions on Iran and US efforts to monitor them, and also meant the NIE was way, way off, another huge embarrassment for the US intelligence community. That alone would cause heads to roll back in Virginia...

When Cynthia stopped taking notes two hours later, her arms ached at the fierceness with which she had been gripping her pen and pad. She had taken eight pages of single spaced notes. She realized she had either just netted the best walk-in of the decade, or one of the worst, most cunning double agents the CIA had ever seen. Joe had warned Cynthia over and over at the Farm:

NEVER promise a walk-in anything, until his information has been verified, and the higher-ups in the CIA have signed off on a deal. She knew that, had always followed that advice to the letter. Still, she could not help herself, "Commander, *IF* what you have told me in the last few hours can be verified, the US government may indeed agree to some sort of arrangement which could *potentially* involve resettlement. It will take several hours for me to report the details of this meeting, and certainly at least a day or two for my Headquarters to respond. Where can I reach you?"

"Miss Sam, I will be staying at the Fairmont Hotel. I will check in under the name I have traveled under, Aziz Bagheri." Commander Mohsen Saeed paused for a moment. For the last two hours, he had been businesslike, unemotional, objective in his recitation of facts. He came across very much like a military officer giving a detailed briefing, which, of course, he was. For the first time, no matter how hard he tried, he could not keep the desperation from his voice.

"Miss Sam, I will be there day and night until I hear from you. You must realize, I am a hunted man, and soon my wife and my brother will become hunted, too. If you cannot help us, I very much believe that I and all my family will soon be dead. Even worse, those who destroyed the Shaheed will get away with their crime. That cannot be allowed to happen. My life and the lives of those I hold most dear are in your hands. Please help me."

Cynthia would say one thing: if he was faking desperation, he was the best damn actor she had ever seen, on or off the silver screen.

Once again, she extended her hand for him to shake. As he stood to do so, she said, "Commander, I do not control the CIA, but I promise you *I* will do everything in my power to make sure your information gets to the right ears." Switching to Farsi, she continued, "Inshallah, we will do what we can to make your family safe."

As Commander Mohsen Saeed got to his feet, he felt slightly ashamed to have been so emotional with a stranger. Yet he knew he had to do everything he could to impress upon this American that he and his entire family were on a knife-edge of peril, balanced over an abyss of death. He nodded in response to the American's statement, shook her hand, and retreated to the door.

*   *   *

Although the meeting with Commander Saeed had just ended, Cynthia's evening had just begun. She left "The Room," and did an elaborate series of maneuvers designed to identify any surveillance that might have been following her. Finally, she arrived back at CIA's Dubai Base, hidden behind the façade of a European shipping company. She knew it would take at least three hours to type up the meeting; she would be typing well past midnight. Before she started drafting the formal cables that would report every detail of her meeting with Commander Saeed, she took the time to draft a quick email to her oldest friend at the CIA, Joe Cerrato. "Ahoy, Cap'n Ahab. Thar she blows, the White Whale. Ishmael. P.S. Get your ass on a plane here. Yesterday."

CHAPTER 21- THE GENERAL, PART II

General Jafari was seriously considering the pros and cons of shooting his cousin. Ideally, it would be most enjoyable if the General invited Majid for a cruise on the Gulf, shot Majid in the stomach, strapped him to a flotation device, then threw him into the Gulf and watched while the sharks ate him. But the General was not sure he could fit that into his schedule right now. With a sigh, he realized that he was stuck with the bungling Majid for another few weeks until the "investigation" of the loss of the Shaheed was over. The General chided himself for not thinking ahead of time to have a replacement for Majid ready in case the lieutenant proved unable to manage his responsibilities in this plan which was definitely proving to be the case.

True, Majid had brought off the actual sinking of the Shaheed, and the part of the plan involving the Russian diver, Slobodchikov, had gone quite well. Yet that was not enough. Like many senior military officers, the General considered good follow-through and the ability to make decisions under pressure key qualities in a subordinate, and it was apparent that Majid had neither. Majid had let the diver Ziyaii escape. Then he let the other diver, Erfan, escape. Then he let Commander Saeed escape. Instead of having *no* divers with incriminating knowledge, the General now had two running around on the loose, plus Commander Saeed. Majid had no idea where this Erfan might be, and none of Majid's bumbling suggestions had helped locate him.

If Majid had thought to simply divert a few of the Qods Force teams to round up every sailor from the Shaheed as soon as he learned that some had survived, the General suspected that either Erfan, or somebody who had a good idea where Erfan might go to hide, would have been netted as well. But that opportunity had been missed. Now Erfan's picture was being quietly circulated by the IRGC to local law enforcement, but Erfan had not turned up.

This was really turning into an exquisite mess. The General would be feeling depressed if he hadn't received a couple of pieces of good news about the Russian diver, Slobodchikov.

The General had viewed the underwater video of the Shaheed that Slobodchikov had shot. He had also seen the torpedo fragments Slobodchikov recovered, one of which clearly said "Mark 48". Both were perfect for the General's needs. While the US had sold the Mark 48 torpedo to several allies, nobody would believe the Dutch or the Australians fired a torpedo at the Shaheed. The General quite looked forward to the feigned outrage he would display tomorrow during the press conference at which he would announce the "preliminary" findings: that the Great Satan was responsible for the attack on the Shaheed.

And as for the Russian, Slobodchikov, whose diving skill had provided the damning false evidence? He received what he deserved. As soon as Majid had verified that the torpedo fragments and underwater video satisfied the General's requirements, Majid had cracked open the pressure chamber where Slobodchikov was decompressing. Had the General cared about such things, he probably would have considered it a testament to the Russian's superb physical condition that Slobodchikov had managed to live for ten minutes after the lethally abrupt pressure change. Of course, given the unbelievable amount of pain involved in dying from decompression embolisms, the Russian himself undoubtedly wished he had died immediately.

The General thought Slobodchikov's end rather fitting: he knew most of the technical experts Iran hired from Russia hated Iran and Iranians. The foolish Russians nevertheless prostituted their skills out to the Iranian government which, if ever given the chance, would be glad to see Russia wiped off the map. While the General was more immediately focused on "The Great Satan," like many Iranians, he had neither forgiven nor forgotten Russia's humiliating colonial meddling in Iran in the early 20th century. Even the Great Satan had not physically invaded Iran and stolen pieces of Iranian territory; Russia had. Paying the greedy Russians back, even in a small way, by killing Slobodchikov, brought a feeling of warmth to the General's heart.

Still, aside from Majid's reasonably competent handling of the Slobodchikov issue, it seemed like the General was the one fixing all the unanticipated problems with the plan, and that was not satisfactory. After all, it was not Majid, but the General's interrogator, Jalili, who had discovered that Saeed had dangerous knowledge about the Shaheed.

It was from talking to the staff driver, Khatami, that Jalili had *also* discovered that the crew of the Ababeel was probably complicit in helping Saeed evade capture. If the pilot, Saboori, had reported on the radio that the diver Erfan had examined the wreck of the Shaheed, a Qods Force team would have taken both Saeed and the crew of the Ababeel into custody before the Ababeel departed for Tehran. Saboori had not, and that made him complicit.

Now the General had to personally fix the problem of the crew of the Ababeel. He called one of the many specialists in the IRGC who reported directly to him and who had no other duties beyond the occasional special missions he assigned them. This cadre was greatly rewarded for their competence, loyalty, and above all, silence. He left a bare-boned message in a voice mail box located on an encrypted server. The Qods Force operative who checked that box three times a day was expert with explosives, and had access to documents and false, but authentic-looking, credentials that would let him move through virtually any controlled zone in Iran. The message Jafari left was short. "Helicopter Ababeel. Hanger Omega, Mehrebad Airbase. Some time before 0800 hours tomorrow morning."

Upon release from Evin, Saboori would be given orders to fly back to Bandar Abbas and put himself and the Ababeel at the disposal of the investigation into the loss of the Shaheed. He would not arrive.

Jafari did not need to describe to the Qods Force specialist what he wanted done to the Ababeel. The General had used the same Qods force expert to attach explosives to an Anatov airplane that had crashed in 2007, killing 33 members of the IRGC, including two rivals of the General. It had also worked perfectly on the Falcon jet that had crashed in 2006, conveniently removing another rival, the then-commander of the IRGC ground forces,

General Ahmad Kazemi. He had no doubt it would work again on the Ababeel. The Qods force operator would send a text to the General's encrypted cell when the explosive charges were in place, which would probably be before midnight tonight.

Luckily, the diver Ziyaii's cell phone had popped back up on the grid in Dubai, but it was another mess that should not have happened, which the General would take immediate steps to fix. After his secretary confirmed that his next appointment awaited him in his private conference room, he stood up from his large dark-stained mission-oak desk, an antique with solid lines and smooth beveled edges imported from America over a century ago, and headed towards an unobtrusive door set in the side wall of his office.

The room he entered was Spartan in its appointments. The dingy white-painted walls were unadorned by art of any kind. In the center of a room was a cheap pressboard table covered with plastic laminate that tried unsuccessfully to suggest the table was made of real wood. Sturdy but cheap green plastic chairs lined the table. This was not a room for receiving important visitors or high-ranking meetings. This was the room where he gave his subordinates orders too sensitive to be given over the phone.

Seated around the table, drinking tepid tea in a desultory way, was a group of six men in their late twenties. All were tall and lean, with dark eyes and black hair. There was a shared lupine quality to their countenances, as if they were wolves used to chase down their prey in a pack together. Once again, the General kept it short; this team had worked directly for him before, and knew he had no time or taste for unnecessary chatter. He could see they had all been given a copy of Javid Ziyaii's service record, including a recent photo.

"Men, the traitor Ziyaii is in league with enemies of the Islamic Republic. He must meet lethal retribution for his crimes, quickly and quietly. His cell-phone has surfaced in Dubai; a truck is at the loading dock in the rear waiting for you, it will take you to a plane at Mehrabad. Less than three hours from now, you will be landing in Dubai. My representative in our consulate in Dubai will provide you weapons, money, a vehicle, and the appropriate cell phone tracking equipment. Find the traitor. Send him home to the fires of Shaitan. Report to me when you are finished. Questions?"

They had none. They had carried out similar missions, in environments far more challenging than Dubai, which was, after all, just a short hop across the Gulf, practically a suburb of Tehran to most Iranian elites. They kept the photos of Ziyaii, shredded their copies of Ziyaii's service jacket, and filed out, headed towards the loading docks at the rear of IRGC Headquarters.

The General shook his head in disgust after the meeting ended. It was not that the General objected to such measures, it was that if Majid had handled things competently, they would not have been necessary. Cousin or no, such sloppiness could simply not be allowed to continue.

CHAPTER 22-THE WHITE WHALE

When Joe checked his email at noon, he was surprised to see a message from Honey-Bunny.

Joe immediately understood Cynthia's email reference to the "White Whale." They had had several long conversations when Cynthia had been a trainee about some of the CIA's legendary walk-ins of the past, like Soviet electronics engineer Adolf Tolkachev, who had provided the CIA an incalculable wealth of information about Soviet jet fighters.

The many problems with distinguishing legitimate walk-ins from the legions of amateur fabricators were compounded by the fact that almost every major hostile intelligence service in the world deliberately sent very convincing *fake* walk-ins to the CIA. These fakes had legitimate credentials, and often even provided the CIA information that was true, at least in the beginning. After being accepted as legitimate, these double-agents would then start to feed the CIA carefully crafted lies.

The point of the elaborate charade was to get the CIA to swallow disinformation. Even more important, the hostile intelligence services hoped that when the deception was finally discovered, it would make CIA officers so wary of future walk-ins that they would reject legitimate walk-ins when they came along. Sadly, the tactic worked pretty well, as history had demonstrated.

In 1992, Vasili Mitrokhin, a KGB archivist, had walked-in to the US Embassy in Tallinn, Estonia. As Mitrokhin had appeared disheveled, slightly dotty, and had no actual documents, simply heaps of handwritten notes, the CIA case officer in Tallinn had concluded he was "fabricator" whose notes were amateurish forgeries. Ten years ago, Joe had a chance to talk to the case officer who turned away Mitrokhin in Estonia. After that chat, Joe privately admitted to himself that in the same situation, he probably would have turned away Mitrokhin, too. It was a depressing conclusion.

After the CIA turned him down, Mitrokhin then approached the British Secret Intelligence Service, who correctly evaluated Mitrokhin as eccentric, but genuine. Mitrokhin subsequently provided the British SIS the single greatest haul of information about the foreign and domestic activities of the Soviet KGB that any defector had ever provided.

As Cynthia's training officer at the farm, Joe had likened the effort to spot a legit walk-in to Captain Ahab's ultimately futile quest for the White Whale in Moby Dick: one could spend a whole career waiting to find a real walk-in with truly great information, only to come up short, or have your career destroyed for buying into a clever fake. Cynthia's White Whale reference could only mean one thing: she *thought* she had the real deal.

Joe responded to Cynthia's email with a simple: "What's up, Cyn? You got something going on?"

Cynthia replied with a cryptically, "Watch the incoming RH queue. Things should start popping into it about four p.m. your time. In the meantime, you might want to call Central Travel and book a ticket for Dubai. I guarantee that you will want to be here as soon as you read the intel reports I am writing right now." Central Travel was the CIA's in-house travel service, one that could make reservations while dealing with the intricacies of booking travel for CIA case officers, who use a variety of false and true identities.

Even though Joe was a senior case officer with a lot of latitude, and he could ask Central Travel to make a reservation for him, he couldn't get a ticket unless he had a legitimate operational reason; an excited email from Cynthia wouldn't cut it. Joe's hands were tied until Cynthia sent the intelligence reports in through official channels. He had to be able to justify his travel to the ever-present bean-counters. He called Central Travel and requested an evening flight to Dubai. With the reservation made, the ticket could be issued in moments if Joe came up with a real reason to get on the plane.

A few hours later, when Joe saw Cynthia's first two reports appear in the Restricted Handling compartment dealing with Iran's leadership and nuclear program, Joe was almost frantic in his efforts to get hold of Central Travel and get them to issue the ticket immediately.

Cynthia's hot-potatoes had just provided more than enough justification to criss-cross the globe a dozen times over.

Intelligence reports from walk-ins are generally treated as, well, crap. In fact, Joe had loudly proclaimed to colleagues on more than one occasion, usually after he had a couple of beers in him, that wiping your ass with reporting from walk-ins would allow the reporting to serve a far more useful function than it normally did. Problem was, after 9/11, the CIA had implemented a regulation that required that all "terrorist-threat" information from walk-ins be reported, no matter how ridiculous, implausible, or outright loony it was. This blatantly butt-covering approach to terrorist threat reporting had done nothing to improve the CIA's intelligence on terrorism, and had instead insured that a huge quantity of false reports would make its way into the CIA's channels.

Joe had seen first-hand that once those reports were in the pipeline, they clogged it up and generally diverted attention from real information about terrorist threats. The false reports were also used by various politicos to justify just about any national security policy the politicians wanted to pursue.

Because the initial reporting from walk-ins was so poorly regarded, it was not usually very restricted, and almost anybody in the intelligence community, even those with a lowly secret clearance, could see it. By sending reporting from a walk-in via the super-secret RH channel, Cynthia was telegraphing to Joe that she thought the information was either so groundbreaking, or sensitive, or both, that it merited very narrow distribution until its authenticity could be verified. Looking at the titles of the intelligence reports that Cynthia was sending in, Joe immediately understood why Cynthia was sending it via RH channels.

Joe was so flabbergasted when he read them that he never realized that he said,

"Jesus *Cheee*rist on a popsicle stick," loudly enough to be heard six cubicles away.

SUBJECT: IRANIAN POSSESSION OF SUFFICIENT ENRICHED URANIUM FOR SIX NUCLEAR WEAPONS.

SOURCE: A WALK-IN

AS OF JUNE 2014, A WALK-IN WITH INDIRECT ACCCESS TO THE INFORMATION STATED THAT A COVERT IRANIAN URANIUM ENRICHMENT FACILITY HAD PRODUCED ENOUGH ENRICHED URANIUM FOR SIX/SIX LOW YIELD NUCLEAR WEAPONS. THE URANIUM HAD ALREADY BEEN REPROCESSED FROM HIGHLY ENRICHED URANIUM HEXAFLOURIDE AND CAST IN A MAGNESIUM OXIDE AND GRAPHITE CRUCIBLE. SIX BOMB PITS HAVE BEEN PRODUCED AND MACHINED; THE PITS INCLUDE DEPLETED URANIUM TAMPERS. THEY ARE READY FOR INSERTION INTO THE "PHYSICS PACKAGE" OF IMPLOSION DEVICE ONCE MANUFACTURE OF THE ACCOMPNAYING NEUTRON INITIATORS IS COMPLETE....

*   *   *

SUBJECT: LOCATION OF A COVERT URANIUM ENRICHMENT FACILITY IN IRAN

SOURCE: A WALK IN

A WALK-IN WITH INDIRECT ACCESS TO THE INFORMATION STATED THAT AS OF EARLY 2011, IRAN HAS BEEN OPERATING A COVERTLY-CONSTRUCTED

URANIUM ENRICHMENT FACILITY IN THE MOUNTAINS NEAR QOM CONSISTING OF 10,000 HIGH SPEED IR-2 CENTRIFUGES. THIS FACILITY HAD BEEN CONCEALED BY BURYING ITS EMISSION SIGNATURES WITHIN THOSE OF THE FORDOW FACITILITY THAT IS ALREADY BEING MONITORED BY THE IAEA. ALTHOUGH THE OPERATING PROBLEMS THAT HAD PLAUGUED EARLIER P-1 CASCADES HAD BEEN RESOLVED WITH THE IR-2 CENTRIFUGE DESIGN, DUE TO PROBLEMS OBTAINING THE NECESSARY CARBON FIBER AND REPLACEMENT PARTS FOR CNC FILAMENT WINDING MACHINES, MANUFACTURE OF 8,500 OF THE CENTRIFUGES ROTORS IN THIS COVERT FACILITY WAS SECRETLY

SUBCONTRACTED TO NORTH KOREAN AND CHINESE SOURCES...

*   *   *

SUBJECT: SINKING OF THE IRGC NAVY DESTROYER SHAHEED

SOURCE: A WALK IN

AS OF JUNE 13 2014, A WALK-IN WITH DIRECT ACCESS TO THE INFORMATION STATED THE IRANIAN REVOLUTIONARY GUARD CORP DESTROYER SHAHEED HAD NOT BEEN SUNK BY ENEMY ATTACK, BUT RATHER AT THE BEHEST OF THE IRANIAN SUPREME LEADER. SOURCE WAS UNSURE OF THE MOTIVATION BEHIND THE ATTACK BUT SURMISED THAT GIVEN THE PRESENCE OF COUNCIL OF GUARDIANS; THE LIKELY MOTIVE WAS ASSASSINATION OF THE COUNCIL. THE LOSS OF THE SHAHEED WAS CAUSED BY THE DETONATION OF FIFTY LIMPET MINES EMPLACED BY IRANIAN NAVY EXPLOSIVE ORDINANCE DISPOSAL DIVER JAVID ZIYAII AT THE BEHEST OF IRANIAN NAVY CAPTAIN ALI RAHIMI, COMMANDER OF THE IRANIAN NAVY DESTROYER JAMARAN.

*   *   *

SUBJECT: OPIUM USE OF THE IRANIAN SUPREME LEADER

SOURCE: DOCUMENTARY, FROM A WALK-IN

AS OF EARLY JUNE 2014, BASED ON DOCUMENTARY EVIDENCE OBTAINED FROM A WALK-IN WITH INDIRECT ACCESS, THE SUPREME LEADER OF IRAN WAS USING OPIUM. DURING AN EARLY JUNE 2014 MEETING AT THE SUPREME LEADER'S RESIDENCE, THE LEADER HAD AN OPIUM PIPE AT HIS SIDE, AND SOURCE STATED THE SMELL OF VAPORIZED OPIUM IN THE ROOM ALMOST CERTAINLY MEANT THE SUPREME LEADER HAD BEEN USING THE PIPE TO SMOKE OPIUM. IT WAS UNCLEAR HOW OFTEN..."

The little corner of his mind where Joe's vanity resided was tickled when he saw that, as usual, Cynthia's reports were nice and short, each two pages or less in length. When he had been her instructor at the Farm, Joe had repeatedly drilled Cynthia to keep her reports as short and easily digestible as possible. From his own time as a junior case officer in the foreign field, Joe had come to realize that nobody in Washington DC would read something longer than five pages, no matter how important it was. If the phrase "Russia will be launching a sneak nuclear attack next week" were ever buried back on the ninth page of an intelligence report, Joe was virtually certain that the nation would be radioactive embers long before anyone got around to reading the warning.

Joe shook his head as he started to grasp the magnitude of the information. Cynthia had sent in a total of eight reports, each more sensational than the last. Assuming the nuclear information had even a grain of truth, this could not help but become a huge political football. The foaming-at-the-mouth neo-cons would say the reporting proved that Iranian nuclear facilities should have been pounded into rubble years ago, and that immediate attacks were now called for. The rabid liberal pantywaists would say the reporting was complete bullshit, another effort by the CIA to drag the United States into a costly and unnecessary war that would damage US credibility and prestige even more badly than the Iraq fiasco had. Being caught square in the middle of the debate, the CIA would be alternately praised and reviled by those on all sides, depending on how well each new report Cynthia sent in justified the policy each side wanted to follow.

Nobody would actually allow information this sensational to be evaluated *on its merits*; that had stopped being possible long ago in Washington DC. Joe realized that more than anything, Cynthia would now need someone to watch her back and help her guide this case where it needed to go. If the walk-in was real, Joe needed to help deflect the efforts of the political animals who would try to suppress information they didn't want to hear. Just as tough would be the struggle to reign in those who wanted to exaggerate the information and use it as a bludgeon to force the US to bomb Iran.

If the walk-in turned out to be a fake, Cynthia needed to "kick him to the curb" quickly, and without getting splashed by any of the muck that comes from having reported information that seemed extraordinary, but turned out to be false. Joe composed a quick email to Cynthia,

"Cyn, on my way, leaving eight PM tonight, will arrive around seven PM local tomorrow. Keep your head down until I arrive. We will set up a meeting at the Novotel as soon as I get in. Joe.

Joe considered it a stroke of luck that his boss Fred Sandler was down on "The Hill" briefing Congress. It meant Fred would not be back into the office today, and thus he could not tell Joe not to go to Dubai. Not that Sandler necessarily would have forbidden Joe to go, but why take the risk? Joe figured it was better to present Sandler with a fait accompli. By the time Sandler got into work tomorrow and read the email from Joe that he was headed to Dubai to back up Cynthia, Joe would already be half-way there.

Joe reserved such cavalier tricks for his boss; his wife Claire would have strangled him in his sleep if he left the country without telling her. The last thing Joe did before leaving the office was call Claire and let her know that he was heading over to the region where that "boat thingee" had happened, but that he would be back in a few days.

CHAPTER 23—ZIYAII'S REVENGE

Ziyaii's cousin, Salim Ghiassi, was the big success story of his extended family. Against great odds, Ghiassi had amassed quite a respectable fortune. These days, Salim styled himself a "major commodities exporter," but as he always delivered that phrase with self-deprecating mockery, nobody, least of all Ghiassi himself, took that claim seriously. Calling Salim an exporter was like calling a bank robber a cash-removal technician. Salim was, quite simply, a smuggler. He was successful enough now that he no longer needed to personally engage in smuggling activity, but he commanded a fleet of ten fast "cigarette boats" that smuggled Polish vodka and single malt Scotch into Iran.

Both Salim and Javid had enjoyed relatively idyllic childhoods as the sons of fishermen in one of the traditional fishing villages near Jask, Iran. That happy time had become a distant memory for Salim by the time he had reached fifteen years of age. As so many disasters do, the problem started with the spite of a petty, mean-spirited man. When Salim was 13 years old, a jealous neighbor reported Salim's father, Kazem Ghiassi, to the *Hizzbolla'hi*, the religious fanatics. The charge was drinking alcohol and "other un-Islamic practices," namely, refusing to force his wife to strictly adhere to the *hejab,* the strict dress codes for women, which Kazem considered ridiculous.

Kazem was sentenced to a public flogging of 10 lashes and fined as much as he normally earned in a month of fishing. Kazem knew precisely who had informed on him, as soon as he had sufficiently recovered from the lashes, Kazem administered a beating to the neighbor-turned-informant that left the man with a broken arm and a dislocated shoulder. That beating, while more than justified, earned Kazem a sentence of three years in prison for assault.

While there, Kazem caught tuberculosis. Given the poor diet and medical treatment in prison, the three-year sentence turned into a death sentence.

As a teenager, Salim had realized his prospects in Iran as the child of a dead "criminal" were not good. He hungered for money, respect, and most of all, to pay back the perverse and hypocritical legal system that had killed his father. By the age of sixteen he was a mate on one of the coastal smugglers that plied the Persian Gulf. By the age of nineteen, he was running his own ship. Now aged 26, Salim owned ten ships and was planning to purchase two more, as soon as he could find reliable crews to man them.

Salim specialized in smuggling alcohol into Iran, not only because it was very lucrative, but because he considered it a fitting way to help subvert the system that had killed his father. Salim commonly referred to the Ayatollahs as "turban-wearing cockroaches than needed to be stepped on." He considered every shipload of alcohol he sent into Iran an act of patriotic defiance against the mullahs he felt had ruined his family, his childhood, and his country.

When his favorite cousin, Javid, unexpectedly appeared in Dubai, Salim had no trouble believing the Supreme Leader was capable of such a monstrosity as sinking the Shaheed. Any doubts Salim might have entertained were removed after Javid played him the voice mail from Izad Vahdat, which included the sound of detonating limpet mines.

Salim's only reaction had been to say, "Ahh, Javid, you should have taken the boat I offered you two years ago! I am sure your friend on the Shaheed would still be dead; after all, the crazy mullahs can always find someone to do their dirty work, witting or unwittingly. But if you had been working for me, you would not have learned the lesson not to trust those cockroaches in such a painful way. But don't worry, Cousin! Today is a new day, *Khoda bozor eh*, God has been merciful! He has given you an opportunity to help revenge yourself upon the mullahs who have perverted Islam; such an opportunity is not to be wasted!"

Ziyaii inquired, "Salim, what do you mean? What opportunity?"

Salim, as a successful smuggler, was skilled in all the techniques of evading the watchful eye of the Iranian government. As soon as he heard the Izad Vahdat's chilling last words, Salim realized that the Iranian government would be sending someone to eliminate his cousin. Salim also realized the most likely way of tracking Ziyaii down would be through his cell phone.

"Cousin, the opportunity is simple. We know they will be sending a team of assassins for you; there is simply no chance those murderous cockroaches can let you live, knowing what you know. As soon as you turned your cell phone on, Emirates Telecommunications knew you were here. That information will be shared with Irancell as part of reciprocal billing information exchange that enables Iranian travelers use their phones here. But here is the catch: This is Dubai, not Iran. The IRGC does not *control* the cell-phone system here. Unless the IRGC or the MOIS has someone on the inside at Etisalat, they won't be able to triangulate your location like they can in Iran. Unless they send a team here with specialized tracking equipment, which is what they will probably do. So, turn your phone off. When we *want* them to find you, we will turn it back on. Then we can hunt the hunters!"

Ziyaii asked, baffled, "Salim, how do you know such things?"

With a proud smile, Salim responded, "It is my business to know such things. I am a smuggler, cousin! I have to know all the tricks that police use. Not one of my ships has ever been caught, for the simple reason that I turn the tricks of law enforcement against them. Knowing how cell-phones can be used to track someone is the simplest of those tricks. If I did not understand that, the mullahs would have caught me and executed me long ago."

Javid replied with sincere admiration, "Most impressive, Salim! Truly, I think *Khoda* has guided me to you. And how shall we, 'hunt the hunters,' as you say?

"Ahh, there, Javid, you will have to guide us. I am not a military man. My skills are skills of stealth and evasion. I was not trained in how to kill my enemies, as you were; I have merely learned how to avoid them. Surely there is something you learned in all your training with bombs and other things that may be of use?"

Javid pondered his options before responding. He did not have access to guns or military explosives; he would therefore have to improvise. Luckily, he had been trained to do just that. The hazy outlines of a plan began to form in his head.

"Tell me, Cousin Salim. Do you have a warehouse that I might use? One that may suffer extensive damage, if all goes well?"

"Cousin Javid, if I can help squash some cockroaches, I would personally burn down every warehouse I own, with a smile on my face!"

Getting into the spirit of the planning, Ziyaii replied with a sly grin, "That will not be necessary, cousin Salim. But speaking of cockroaches, we will need some bug-killing supplies."

*   *   *

The six-man Qods Force team assigned to hunt down Ziyaii arrived in Dubai on June 14th. A quick trip to the Iranian consulate equipped them with guns and cell-phone tracking gear that had been shipped over from Tehran in the diplomatic pouch, which was not technically a "pouch" at all, but actually a very large crate with Iranian diplomatic seals on it. The team sat idle for almost four days, enduring daily calls from General Jafari. The General asked, in tones whose stridency increased every day, why Ziyaii was not dead yet. When they tried tracking down the number Ziyaii had called in Dubai, they found the phone had been bought with false documents and was registered to a non-existent address.

When Ziyaii's cell phone finally went active on June 18th, the team breathed a sigh of relief. The Qods Force team leader called the General to inform him they would soon have their prey. In his arrogance, the team leader had forgotten that the person they were hunting was not the kind of timid target he was used to killing: exiled journalists or political leaders. They were now hunting someone who was quite as well trained in the art of killing as they were.

They might have launched themselves on their hunt with considerably less zeal had they understood that EOD Tech Ziyaii, for all his native affability, was at the peak of his lethal profession, knew they were coming, and was very, very angry.

CHAPTER 24-SABOORI'S FLIGHT

When he had been at university, Commander Saboori had taken more than one course on religion. He had no intention of training to become a mullah or Ayatollah, but had always been fascinated by various belief systems. This was a rather unexpected hobby to those familiar with his gruff, taciturn demeanor, but Saboori was far from the only man to show one face to his military colleagues, and have another in his own private life.

It was because of his studies that Saboori was familiar with many sections of the Old Testament, particularly the Psalms. Islam considers many parts of the Jewish Torah and Christian Old Testament to be valid prophecy; and Persians tend toward a deep appreciation of poetry. It was perhaps natural that Saboori was most drawn to the beauty of the Psalms, which were, after all, lyric poetry as well as solemn prayer.

When he had arrived at Evin prison the day before, Saboori had struggled to remain outwardly calm. Inwardly, he was reciting one of the most famous Psalms, one well used by soldiers and sailors for many centuries, "Yea, though I walk through the valley of the shadow of Death, I will fear no evil. For thou art with me; thy rod and thy staff, they comfort me. Thou preparest a table before me in the presence of mine enemies. Thou anointest my head with oil; my cup runneth over. Surely goodness and mercy shall follow me all the days of my life, and I will dwell in the house of the Lord forever."

To anyone familiar with the horrors perpetrated in Evin prison, the phrase "Valley of the Shadow of Death" seemed as apt a phrase to describe it as any. Saboori know that *Khoda* would not reject a legitimate prayer simply because it was one also used by Christians and Jews. The pilot had never heard of anyone being brought to Evin prison and then being released, seemingly without prejudice, the following day.

Saboori greeted his return to Mehrabad Airbase and the Ababeel with wary astonishment. As soon as he returned to the Ababeel, Saboori talked to his co-pilot, Lieutenant Shafaq, and his crew chief, Petty Officer Tolui, about the strange experience. Both seemed as baffled by the arrest and release as he was. Only after a few minutes did it occur to Saboori to ask the Iranian navy staff driver, Seaman 2nd class Abdul Khatami, who had been ordered to return to Bandar Abbas on the Ababeel, if he had been questioned at Evin.

Khatami, who was thinking he had been dragged into something ugly when Commander Saeed ordered him to accompany the Ababeel to Tehran, answered reluctantly. When Saboori finally thought to ask if there were any questions whose answers the interrogators had seemed particularly interested in, Khatami admitted that the man who questioned him had asked him three different times to confirm that there had been a diver aboard the Ababeel when it flew to the site of the Shaheed's wreck, a diver who had returned carrying equipment that was dripping water. Khatami also related how interested the interrogator had been in Commander Saeed's trip to visit Captain Rahimi before the Ababeel had departed for Tehran.

As he had been flying, and then in custody, Commander Saeed had no way of knowing that Captain Rahimi was dead. Not having any idea that the Diver Erfan saw limpet mine holes, not torpedo holes, Saboori also had no idea of the real significance of the questions Khatami had been asked. But given the extraordinary events of the last 36 hours, Commander Saboori felt spooked: his ship and many of his shipmates were gone, Commander Saeed had disappeared, Saboori and his crew had been arrested with no explanation, and released the same way. Unhappy as Saboori was, there was nothing he could do to change his state of ignorance until he returned to Bandar Abbas and started asking his friends in the Iranian and IRGC Navy questions what was really going on.

What he *could* do was do an extra thorough pre-flight, as that ritual had always been effective in calming his nerves.

*   *   *

It was in the "cleavage" that Saboori found them: two small metal objects that resembled small upside-down bowls. The sheet metal that formed the engine cowlings of the Ababeel dipped down a bit between the two circular air intakes for the Isotov turboshaft engines; more than one Kamov pilot over the years had jokingly compared that dip between the two rounded engine intakes to the cleavage of a woman. Saboori would never have spotted the additions to the Ababeel without doing a particularly thorough pre-flight: the "bowls" were not large, and they were painted precisely the same battleship grey as the Ababeel. Some tugging proved that, whatever they were, they could not easily be removed; they seemed welded in place.

Saboori was a pilot, not an explosives expert, but one could not spend more than twenty years in the military without picking up bits of information about many different things, particularly when one ferried about EOD divers, who often toted various kinds of demolition charges. To Saboori's eye, the "bowls" looked very much like small shaped charges, which is precisely what they were.

The discovery caused feelings of panic and nausea to well up in Saboori. In the last ten years, there had been several Iranian military aircraft crashes that had killed a variety of high ranking Iranian military personnel. Iran did not have a reputation for high aircraft maintenance standards, but even so, the crashes had caused persistent rumors of sabotage within the small circles of Iranian military aviation. Here, then, was proof-positive that they were more than rumors.

He looked around casually and he could not spot any watchers. The Ababeel was parked in a hanger. There did not appear to be anyone else in the hangar besides his own crew and Seaman Khatami.

After pre-flight, the normal procedure would have been to have the Ababeel towed out into the open air, where it would start its engines and taxi under its own power to a strip of runway, then lift off, headed for Bandar Abbas. Saboori realized with dread that even if his hunch was right, and these *were* explosives, he was still going to have to take off with them aboard. If someone had affixed explosives, they would be looking to see if he took off as normal. He assumed that whoever set these explosives wanted to detonate them at a time and place where the destruction of the

Ababeel would be absolutely assured, and in an area outside of Tehran, to avoid gawkers who might examine the wreckage. Refusing to take off would simply result in re-arrest.

If Saboori's assumptions were true, the explosives would be set to detonate once the Ababeel was in the vast open stretches of desert between Tehran and Bandar Abbas. Saboori's only way out was to take off as normal, then do precisely what Commander Saeed had done--set the Ababeel down unexpectedly and get away.

Twenty minutes later, the Ababeel was airborne, heading southwest. At first, the Ababeel's luck held. Lieutenant Commander Saboori was correct in his assumptions: the mysterious "bowls" he had found were small linear shaped charges. The explosives were concealed under the small bowl which helped direct the blast like an explosive lens. The charges had been placed where they could send two knives of superheated plasma into the compression blades of the turbine engines, and then continue on thorough into the pilot's compartment. There the plasma jets' temperature and pressure would have instantly killed the whole crew. The detonators had a barometric trigger and a timer; the explosives would detonate 15 minutes after the Ababeel went more than 400 meters "above ground level." Assuming a normal cruising speed of 200 knots, this meant the charges would have triggered over sparsely populated farmland 50 kilometers to the south east of Tehran.

Instead, three minutes after flying over Highways 6 and 7, which ran south-west out of Tehran, Saboori had flipped off the Ababeel's transponder and made his second emergency landing in 24 hours. To anyone tracking the Ababeel via its transponder, the Ababeel would have seemed to have vanished.

Excellent though Saboori was as a pilot, his virtues as a critical thinker were limited. After thinking the matter through on the way to Tehran, Commander Saeed had ordered the Ababeel to make an emergency landing in an area near Mehrabad Airport, which Saeed knew would give him virtually instant access to taxis. By way of contrast, Saboori set down in a farm field just south of Tehran, a place with no ready access to taxis to aid in escape. Saboori compounded his error by moving several hundred meters away and then waiting to see if what he suspected were explosive charges actually *were* explosive charges. Ten minutes later, Saboori and his crew were rewarded with grim conformation as they saw twin darts of flame lash through the engine cowlings and into the crew compartment. The fire quickly ignited the Ababeel's fuel and the helicopter began to burn fiercely.

By the time Saboori and his crew had jogged two kilometers north to the freeway that forms the southern boundary of western Tehran, a pillar of smoke had already risen several hundred meters in the air. Fire and rescue crews were dispatched to the scene of the downed helicopter, and soon determined that there had been no crew aboard when it burned.

Saboori and the other men had no trouble flagging down one of the thousands of unlicensed cabs in Tehran and leaving the area, but in the end, that didn't really matter. True, General Jafari had made the flawed assumption that his aircraft sabotage would be as effective against Saboori and the Ababeel as it had against his previous targets, forgetting that his previous targets had been caught unawares, whereas Saboori had just lost many shipmates and had the unexpected terror of a trip to Evin prison to elevate his paranoia to record levels.

The General's false assumption was, if anything, only a minor delay in his plan to rid himself of the Ababeel's crew.

When Saboori, his crew, and Seaman Khatami had been in Evin prison the night before, their cell-phone numbers had been logged by IRGC Security as a matter of course. Not realizing how easily they could be tracked by their cell phones, all four men had left them on, and been re-arrested within three hours of the Ababeel's second emergency landing.

When he was driven back though the gates of Evin Prison a second time, Saboori assumed that this time, he would not leave alive. The cruel smile upon the face of IRGC interrogator Ebrahim Jalili when Saboori next saw him confirmed that Saboori's anguished assumption was correct. Ironically, the crew of the Ababeel would probably have been better off if Saboori had never spotted the shaped charges. There are worse things in the world than a sudden, fiery death; many of them happen at Evin.

CHAPTER 25-FACE TO FACE

Joe blessed the policy that let him book a business-class seat for long flights *if* he had to work immediately upon arrival. He had no idea how people managed to sleep in coach seats, but it was a knack he had never acquired. After the Emirates Air cabin crew served a fairly respectable dinner, a couple of stiff drinks helped Joe enter the Land of Nod. When he awoke the following day, the cabin crew was serving lunch. The electronic in-flight map showed they were smack over central Europe, still several hours from Dubai. Even in business class, the flight's fourteen hour duration was grueling. Joe was thankful that Emirates Air had been allowed to add some direct Washington DC-Dubai runs last year; the flight was long enough as it was without having to change planes in New York, London, or Paris.

Two hours later, fed and caffeinated to within an inch of his life, Joe was standing in the open space near the galley and doing deep knee bends to restore his circulation and jump-start his mental process. He reviewed in his mind everything Cynthia had written in her intelligence reports and operational or "ops" cables, which described all the aspects of the meeting which could not be released to the wider intelligence community. The intelligence community saw the intelligence reports, but, with some exceptions, only people in the CIA's Directorate of Operations got to read the ops cables that gave all the nitty-gritty details describing how a particular piece of intelligence came to be in the CIA's possession.

He knew something had been nagging him about Cynthia's ops cables, and the knee bends helped jar it loose. This Commander Saeed guy was on the run, and he and his nuclear physicist brother Mohammed both wanted to defect because what Commander Saeed knew endangered both brothers. So how was the brother, who allegedly had been seconded from the Atomic Energy Organization of Iran to a nuclear weapons program run by the Iranian Revolutionary Guards, still walking around drawing breath? Wouldn't IRGC Security have picked up Mohammed Saeed the instant they realized he was the brother of Commander Mohsen Saeed? And if they did grab him, what did Mohsen have to sell? Only hearsay about the Iranian nuclear program.

If Mohsen Saeed was legit, he could provide a lot of valuable insight into Iranian Navy and IRGC Navy operations, but those had regional significance only. Commander Saeed came in proclaiming access to both IRGC Navy information in his own right, and nuclear weapons info through his brother. If his brother was unable to support the story because he had been arrested, then Mohsen would have inadvertently cast doubt on everything he had said, and people in CIA Hqs would be inclined to doubt *both* the IRGC Navy information and the nuclear information, which was going to a political hot-potato in any case.

Joe pulled out pen and paper and made a couple of cryptic notes to himself; things for follow-up when he met Commander Saeed.

Joe flipped out the small TV stowed in the arm of his seat. BBC News was carrying a feed from Al-Jazeera. The immaculately coiffed BBC anchor announced at the top of the hour with a melodramatic flourish,

"Once again, General Mohammed Jafari, Commander of the Iranian Revolutionary Guard Corps has just released "preliminary results" from the Iranian government's investigation in the sinking of the Shaheed."

A translation of General Jafari's words flowed across the bottom of the screen.

"There can be little doubt that the Great Satan was responsible for this abomination. To the audio tape of the attack that has already been widely aired, I now add videotape footage of the wreck taken yesterday."

The screen cut to murky underwater footage. Despite the low-light conditions underwater, a jagged hole that was clearly at least five meters wide was shown near the huge props of a submerged ship. Next, the camera zoomed in on the Farsi text for "Shaheed" spelled out on the bow of the sunken ship. After the footage had aired, General Jafari continued, "And lest there be any doubts, these torpedo fragments were recovered from the area of the wreck." The General gestured to a table, on which metal fragments had been carefully spread and tagged like pieces of evidence in a criminal trial. The Al-Jazeera cameraman zoomed in on one of the fragments, which clearly said "Mark 48".

"The whole world knows the Mark 48 is one of the devilish torpedoes used by the Navy of the Great Satan."

Joe felt a sinking sensation in his gut. He knew this coverage was going to give his buddy Mark, ONI, the US Navy, and pretty much the whole US foreign policy machine fits. We know we didn't blow up the Shaheed, but how do we prove a negative? Particularly if the opposition was willing to fabricate evidence to support the lies? This could get ugly, real fast.

Indeed, as if Joe's thoughts were words of prophecy, the BBC feed cut to shots of hate-filled demonstrations that were dangerously close to riots being held outside the US Embassies in Beirut, Damascus, Cairo, Riyadh, and Islamabad. The BBC broadcaster continued, "The US Department of State has sharply denied these accusations, which their spokesman characterized as completely unfounded. The US Navy has even gone so far as to offer the services of one of their salvage ships, the USS Grapple, to investigate and help salvage the Shaheed. The US Navy has offered to invite sailors and clerics aboard from Muslim countries to see that the recovery operation is carried out with due sensitivity to Islamic practices. Iranian General Jafari outright rejected such an offer."

The screen shifted back to the press conference with General Jafari, "Do these infidel American dogs, having murdered so many holy men and fine patriots, think we would be so foolish as to give them a chance to defile the final resting place of so many heroic martyrs? We spit on this offer."

The broadcaster continued, "In other news, oil prices topped $135/barrel in trading on the Hang...."

Joe clicked off the TV. Reading between the lines of Cynthia's intelligence reports and the news, a big jump in Iranian-American tensions, not to mention oil prices, could only benefit the hardliners in Iran. One school of thought in the US "intelligence community" said that the Iranian hardliners might want to go right up to the edge of war with the US, simply to shore up their power base among the Iranian populace, most of whom had come to despise the mullahs with an exquisite passion.

When the unsustainable gasoline subsidy system in Iran finally collapsed for lack of funds last year, despite record oil prices, that simmering tension had approached open rebellion. The gasoline riots near the Majlis, the Iranian parliament, had been suppressed with ruthless brutality, but need for such tactics to keep a lid on virulent anti-government anger demonstrated, even more than the 2009 post-election riots, that public opinion in Iran was shifting inexorably away from the mullahs. Defense Intelligence Agency analysts speculated in the last year's National Intelligence Estimate that the Iranian hardliners might seek to provoke a conventional war to benefit from the "rally round the flag" effect. And why not, the DIA's logic went, as long as the hardliner's had adequate leadership protection facilities for themselves? A callous attitude, but then again, Ayatollah Khomeini had certainly proved willing to sacrifice countless young Iranian men in ill-advised mass suicide charges during the war against Saddam in the 1980s. What was a few hundred more?

Still, Joe was skeptical of the DIA analysis. The mullahs had sponsored plenty of terrorist and subversive acts outside Iran, but they had always shied away from direct armed conflict with the "Great Satan." For all that Americans had been calling the hard-line mullahs "crazy religious fanatics" for years, there had always been a method to their madness, at least once you understood their thought processes and points of reference, which were vastly different from those of an average American. Had something changed, he wondered?

Despite her use of RH channels, news of Cynthia's reports, if not the reports themselves, would have started to spread through the intelligence community rumor mill. Joe wondered how the reports were playing back home. He hoped that they could keep a lid on this for at least a week. If not, any possible operation involving exfiltrating the Saeeds from Iran would probably be blown before it started.

*　　　*　　　*

Joe breezed through Emirates Customs, as he usually did. He was traveling under one of his favorite aliases, Irish national Sean Brennan. Three months spent as an exchange student in County Sligo, Ireland had given Joe enough exposure to fake an Irish lilt to his voice that would pass muster everywhere outside of Ireland and the UK.

Joe loved traveling on his Irish passport. Given Ireland's neutrality and the explosion of the Irish economy in the previous decade (before the collapse of Irish banking), the Irish were one of the few groups of English speakers who still received a warm welcome just about everywhere. How different from being a US passport holder. Overt Anti-Americanism had receded since the widely unpopular Bush Administration had left office six years before, but the legacy lingered. In half the countries he traveled to, when Joe handed over a blue US passport, the passport control officer still looked at him as if he had handed him a steaming turd. Such pervasive hostility formed a kind of collective psychic pressure which had gradually caused many US citizens simply to stop traveling abroad altogether.

Joe had picked up a rental car, run a brief surveillance detection route, and pulled into the Novotel. He noticed along the way that Dubai's skyline was no longer dotted with the incredibly profusion of high-rise cranes which had fed the construction boom of the last decade. The Emirati passion for using seeming unlimited resources to make their dreams a reality, like an outdoor *refrigerated* beach in a place where summer temperatures reached 120 degrees, or an indoor ski slope, had finally run aground on the rocky shoals of economic reality.

The Novotel was nice, although there were plenty of even fancier hotels in Dubai. Joe preferred the Novotel because he had always been able to get a room without a reservation by slipping the desk staff a $50 bill, even during convention season.

On the way inside, Joe noticed another sign of Dubai's burst economic bubble. Young men, obviously of southeast Asian origin, probably Pakistanis or Bangladeshis, were lurking under the shade of the Novotel's awning for a few minutes, at least until Novotel's security noticed them and shooed them away with angry gestures and raised voices. Joe figured the poor bastards had only been seeking some respite from the brutal heat. They were probably from the ranks of the thousands of young men stranded in the Emirates when the construction jobs that lured to Dubai suddenly went away.

On one level, Joe truly pitied them. On another, they were his worst nightmare: economic hardship could make young men with time on their hands easy pickings for the fundamentalist mullahs who proclaimed that wherever economic prosperity slipped away, it did so through deliberate action of the West, particularly the US, to keep the Muslim world poor and needy. That was patently bullshit…but in a world where Jim Jones talked a couple hundred people into drinking poisoned Kool-Aid, it was hard to put limits on human credulity. If you told people what they wanted to hear, and gave them a cause to fight for or against, more often than not, they'd believe whatever BS you told them.

When he got to the front desk, Joe pulled out a wad of cash to pay for the room upfront. He preferred to leave as few electronic footprints when traveling as possible. If he was not in the reservation computer, and he paid for the room and room charges in traveler's checks or cash, it would make anyone tracking the movement of his Brennan alias have to work just that much harder to figure out what Brennan was doing in Dubai. There was no such thing as being invisible in the age of computers, but every shred of information you were able to keep out of international commercial and government databases made his backtrail harder to follow.

Joe showered, put on a fresh shirt and underwear, and called up Cynthia on one of her disposable cell-phones. "Cyn, it's your old pal. I'm in Suite 1212. Do you have time to collect your new friend and drop by?"

Joe thought he could hear the barest hint of relief in her voice as she answered, "Ahh, glad you made it alright. I think we can be there in an hour or so. Does that work for you?"

"Fine, Cyn, fine. Ciao."

She had the constitution of a stainless steel Energizer Bunny. If she was relieved Joe was here, that must mean she was feeling some heat from DC about the reports she had submitted. He had arrived just in time to give Cyn some back-up by providing the professional gravitas of a senior case officer. Joe and Cynthia had always worked together very well, partly because Joe remembered that while he was the senior officer, loyalty was a two way street. It was Cynthia's job to run the case, but it was Joe's job, a harder and less satisfying task in truth, to make sure she had the freedom to do so without getting bogged down in office politics and other similar bullshit. Joe took off his suit jacket, loosened his tie, set his alarm clock to wake him in forty five minutes, and lay back on his bed to run through his head everything he wanted to cover in this meeting. For both Cynthia and Joe, this meeting could be one of the most important of their professional lives.

*   *   *

When Joe heard a knock on his door, he went and checked the peephole. Sure enough, it was Cynthia accompanied by an unfamiliar man. Joe opened his door and greeted them both.

"Welcome, welcome. Please come in. Samantha, it is good to see you; it has been awhile." Both Joe and Cynthia knew each other's favorite "throwaway alias," which was a false name with no documentation to back it up. Cynthia's was Samantha Peters, Joe's was Hank Statler. Joe had taught Cynthia to always use throwaway aliases with a walk-in until they had proven themselves; too much effort went into the creation of a documented false identity to casually risk it on a walk-in.

After the door was firmly closed, Cynthia responded, "Nice to see you as well, Hank. Commander, may I present my friend and a case officer of vast experience, Hank Statler. Hank, I have the honor of presenting to you IRGC Navy Commander Mohsen Saeed, late of the destroyer Shaheed." In most any situation, it was a chancy thing to bring up a major personal loss, but Joe knew why Cynthia had done it. First, she wanted Joe to have a chance to see how Saeed reacted when she mentioned the Shaheed. Second, she wanted to give Joe an opening to make a good first impression by offering his sympathies, which he promptly did. Joe extended his hand to shake and said, "Commander, I am honored to meet you, although I wish the circumstances were happier. To have suffered such a loss, both a ship and many fine men…that is a tragedy.

That it happened the way it happened is nothing less than an outrage."

Joe noted that the Commander attempted to keep a rigid control of his emotions, but he could not entirely suppress an expression of pain at the mention of the Shaheed, and an expression of anger when Joe referred to how it was sunk. Case officers set great store by such impressions, and Joe's gut told him that whatever else this Saeed guy might be, he probably *had* served on the Shaheed.

Joe continued, "Commander, if you could take a seat in the conference area here, Sam and I are going into the room to catch up for just a minute, then we will be right back and get things started."

Joe and Cynthia retreated into the bedroom and closed the door. Joe asked, "Any reaction from Hqs to what you sent in yet?"

Cynthia replied, "Just the standard 'we need more information' response. The problem at this stage is that the Commander's brother Mohammed is the guy with the nuclear information. Mohammed only filled Mohsen in on the bare bones details about the program two days ago, when they decided that defecting was their only chance. Before then, they hadn't talked much about it, because it was so highly classified. Two positive things did come in, though: name traces on the Commander did come back with a Commander Mohsen Saeed as the exec on the Shaheed. Name traces on Mohammed Saeed show someone with that name taking a Bachelor's Degree in high energy physics from Shaheed Behesti University about 15 years back, then no further information. That is exactly the profile of guys who are recruited into "black" WMD programs. They drop off the radar screen, sometimes they are even sent out of Iran to finish their studies under another name so we can't track 'em and recruit them while they are abroad.

"Also, a buddy from ONI pulled up something nice. I digitized a snippet of the interview I had with the Commander, then emailed it to a friend at ONI who has access to the archives of radio chatter between Iranian naval officers. I didn't tell him who it was from, just asked him to find a match. He came back a few hours ago and said it was 90 percent probable match for

Commander Mohsen Saeed. So, I think we can agree Commander Saeed probably is who he says he is. Now we only have to figure out if he was sent to sell us a bill of goods."

Joe quipped, "Hell, Sam, finding that out is the fun part! Let's get back in there."

One could never be too careful in Joe's line of work. Any phone could be turned into an "infinity mike" with the right expertise in phone switches, and any conversation in a hotel room could be eavesdropped on by bouncing a specialized laser off a window, a laser which could read the vibrations of the window pane and translate those vibrations into sound. As a precaution against such tricks, Joe flipped on the TV to a low level to make sure that any recording devices would be baffled by having to separate the voices of Joe, Cynthia, and the Commander out of the background noise provided by the TV, a virtually impossible task. Joe then ordered some snacks from room service, after which he unplugged the phone to render it safely inert.

Soon they got down to business. Joe spent an hour taking the Commander over his story step-by-step. Having multiple interviews that cover the same ground is an old cop trick that spooks like to use as well. When people are creating elaborate lies, they often mix up details when asked to repeat the story. When they are telling the truth, the story stays the same in all the major details. Of course, there are ways around this. The really good "fake" walk-ins sent by hostile intelligence services will spend days or weeks in practice debriefings making sure they had their story straight. In a lot of cases, they were even trained to pass polygraphs with "No Deception Indicated" scores.

Mohsen's story did not change, although new details emerged as Joe went over the same ground. That was a good sign, but not conclusive. Joe decided it was time to start throwing out the questions he had thought up on the plane.

"Mohsen, one thing is confusing to me. If you are here, and Mohammed is home, won't he be arrested as soon as someone figures out you have disappeared and he is your brother?"

Commander Saeed responded, "Ahh, a shrewd question. The answer is, yes, he will be arrested, but he should have at least a few more days of freedom. You see, the fact that Mohammed works in a covert nuclear program is highly secret. None of my work colleagues know it. A couple of years back, I bribed an acquaintance in Iranian Naval Security for a look at my classified personnel and security files. Under siblings, it only says "Contact IRGC Security for this information." Even an IRGC security officer conducting an investigation on me will have to call the particular office that holds the highly sensitive personnel records. That office is then required to personally obtain permission, in writing, from the Commanding General of the IRGC, even if the person requesting the information is doing so on behalf of the Commanding General. So, from the moment they decide to start tracking me down by digging into my personnel file, it should take at least a week, if not longer, to unearth Mohammed's name and his connection to me. They *will* get the information, but it will take a while, no matter how much pressure is applied from above. Their own security rules will work against them."

Joe chuckled inwardly at Saeed's description; it never hurt to remember that your adversaries have to struggle with bureaucracy, too. But there was one more issue he had to bring up. There would be no need to dig into his personnel file if they could simply dig into his cell phone billing records and track down Mohammed through that.

"Commander, I am glad to hear your brother has some breathing space but there is another issue that puts your brother and your family at risk. Cell phones. You and your brother can be..."

Commander Saeed held up a hand and cut Joe off. Joe was interested to note that the Commander actually had a small grin on his face.

"Ha! Mr. Hank, I laugh with some irony at your concern on cell-phones. Because my brother and I both have high security clearances, we became aware long ago that our own security services would always be trying to keep an eye on us. Mohammed works on nuclear weapons, so they watch him even more closely than they watch me. They read his email, tap his phone, put bugs in his house, they do everything they can to watch him to make sure he is not giving away their precious nuclear secrets.

Do you know, Mr. Hank, a man can love his country and want to serve it, yet still *hate* many parts of the government? My brother and I, we have long despised the thugs who are in the Iranian security services. The MOIS. IRGC Security. Qods Force assassination teams. It is a great sadness to us that these groups spy on and intimidate their fellow Iranians. Truly, they are a greater enemy of the Iranian people than America could ever be. There may be elections, but Iran can never be a real democracy while these groups exist.

Mohammed and I decided long ago to make life hard for the bastards, excuse me for the language Miss Sam, but that is what Mohammed and I call them: the Bastards in Security! We both have cellphones for work, but that is all we ever use them for, work. No personal calls. We keep them switched off, otherwise. We do have personal cell-phones, but we cannot be tracked through them, because nobody knows Mohammed and I have them. My friend, Masoud Bahktiar, the same man who loaned me the passport of one of his salesmen, bought these personal phones for us long ago through his company. They are registered to his company, and our names are not associated with them. Whenever I need to talk to my brother, Mohammed, or my wife, Lily, we use the phones we got from Masoud.

The irony is that we only went to all the trouble to get cell-phones from Masoud simply to stick a thumb in the eye of the Security bastards. We just wanted to be able to talk like a normal family and not worry about being overheard. But you know, perhaps it is the guiding hand of *Khoda*, or perhaps it is a sad side effect of growing up in a country that forces everyone to become paranoid for their own protection. I think the fact that Mohammed and I have unregistered cellphones may have saved our lives."

Joe shook his head in admiration and replied. "Commander, it is more than luck, I think. We have a saying in English, 'Fortune favors the prepared.' The most amazing part of what you have told me is simply that instead of falling to pieces after losing your ship, you managed to conduct a quick investigation, fly to Tehran, disappear, assume a new identity, and come here. I know trained intelligence officers who would have great trouble pulling off such a feat."

Commander Saeed dipped his head in acknowledgement of the compliment.

Joe continued, "Amazing as that all is, you are not out of the woods yet. I have to tell you honestly, we find your information very interesting, but what you have told us is not enough. Mohammed's information about the nuclear program is sure to send shockwaves throughout the US government. We will need proof, concrete proof, that what he says is real. As you know, the CIA has been burned before by people peddling information about Weapons of Mass Destruction programs that did not exist. There is going to be extreme skepticism over anything Mohammed says. What kind of documents or evidence can you produce to back up your story? Keep in mind, I would like to help you, but you are asking for a lot from the US government: you want a new life for your whole family and protection from your enemies. You and Mohammed are going to have to give a lot in return."

Amazingly, Joe noticed that Commander Saeed was grinning again. "Ahh, Mr. Hank, my brother Mohammed is a *very* smart man! The night I flew into Tehran on the Ababeel, the helicopter from the Shaheed, Mohammed and I were up late into the night. He asked me the question, 'What do you think the Americans will want from us?' So we sat for a while. We imagined we worked for the CIA, and some crazy man we never met came to tell us some fairy tale about nuclear bombs. And we decided that you would want just one thing from us: proof. So this is how Mohammed decided to get it. You will appreciate this, Mr. Hank, because he got the idea from your President Reagan."

*   *   *

They had sent Commander Saeed back to his hotel in a cab. Joe and Cynthia were using her car, a purposely nondescript dark-brown Nissan Altima, to do a "surveillance detection route" back to Dubai Base to write up the meeting. Although a good surveillance detection route required much more intense concentration than normal driving, Cynthia was adept enough at them by now that she was able to spare enough attention to ask Joe a one word question. "Well?"

Joe pondered a minute before responding. "Why don't you break it down for me, Cyn? What are the possibilities?"

Cynthia responded quickly; it was obvious she had already given the matter some thought, said, "Joe, I see five possibilities. First is that he is genuine. That is what my gut tells me. Second is that he is not genuine, but wants to lure the CIA into swallowing a nice chunk of disinformation. Third is that he is not genuine, and was simply sent to "burn" one or more case officers to cripple our operations in Dubai. Fourth is that he was not sent by a hostile service, but is lying to us just to get his family relocated because, for whatever reason, they decided they don't want to live in Iran. Fifth is the "X" possibility, the possibility we can't see, 'cause we don't know all the facts. I consider possibilities two and three remote. I have no problem believing the Supreme Leader wouldn't hesitate to kill masses of Iranian sailors if it served his purposes, but I have a real hard time believing a serving naval officer could be so cavalier and uncaring as to participate in a ruse that would involve the loss of his own ship.

"After talking to him and getting the voice print analysis confirmation, my gut says there is an eighty percent likelihood he is genuine. Also, the guys who are 'dangles' sent by hostile intelligence services, those guys are loners, singletons. They don't want to bring their families out. Doesn't mean he is telling the truth, but the fact that he wants to bring his family is strongly suggestive to me that he isn't a dangle. If he isn't a dangle, the risk for us is much less. So?" Cynthia asked, with a question-mark in her voice.

Joe, who was gazing out the windows at the spectacularly lit facades the countless luxury hotels in downtown Dubai, replied slowly, feeling his way through his own reasoning as he spoke it, "Cyn, I think he is the real deal. I'm glad I came here 'cause seeing is believing. I don't really buy the idea that Saeed would voluntarily take part in any plot that involved the loss of his own ship and a big chunk of his crew just so he could sell us a bill of goods on the Iranian nuclear program. He would have to be a psycho to do that. I just don't get that from him. He is not psycho, just pissed off at his government, and can you blame him?"

They pulled into a subterranean parking garage beneath a large, non-descript office building that housed, unbeknownst to the building's owners, CIA's Dubai Base. Looking around the deserted parking garage to make sure they were alone, they headed for the bank of elevators and continued the conversation in low voices.

"Having met him in person, it'll be easier for me to take up the fight back in Headquarters to make sure this case doesn't get shit-canned, which is a major possibility. I think that even though the stuff about the Shaheed is big on the news right now and there are riots and demonstrations going on, even if there are some small terrorist attacks, the Shaheed thing will ultimately blow over, in a week or a month. It is important, but the loss of a single ship is not *strategic*. That makes it less controversial."

Joe paused while the elevator doors opened until he was sure it was empty, then continued.

"The nuclear angle is whole different kettle of fish, on the other hand. You know as well as I do that the administration that just got voted into office 18 months ago won on domestic issues. Their campaign made it pretty clear that the US would not be an international buttinski. So the very last thing they'll wanna hear is information that revives the drama over Iran's nukes, which might force a military response. Mohammed Saeed, assuming he is real and can get the goods, will blow the isolationists out of the water. Which means a lot of the politicians and political appointees in Washington are going to want to squash this case."

Cynthia asked, "So, if the politicos want to squash this, who is going to do it, and how?"

Joe thought some more before answering, "Cyn, hard to say. They could come at it in any of a dozen ways. I will say the story of how he got out of Iran is friggin' amazing. I definitely think the guy is smart enough to pull it off, but that may be the first thing people attack. They will say it is too implausible, ignoring the fact that most of the really good walk-ins had interesting tales to tell on what it took for them to contact the Agency. Sure as God made little green apples, some of the fuckers back there are going to say the Shaheed was sunk just to get us to swallow lies about the Iran's nuke program, and that if we take the bait, it will be an even bigger fiasco than the Iraq WMD.

"Long story short, we need to get our hands on Brother Mohammed, and he needs to bring some good evidence with him. But for now, we just worry about the next step. I can write up this meeting, and I will give a detailed "case officer assessment" in my cable that reinforces yours and says I think Saeed is probably genuine, that the clock is ticking, and that we need to move fast to get the Saeed brothers out of Iran. I want to meet with him one more time before I fly back to DC."

CHAPTER 26-MAKING MOVIES

Mohammed Saeed sat waiting for two days in a hotel in Tehran. Every minute since his brother Mohsen had boarded the airplane for Dubai, Mohammed had feared "the knock on the door." He knew that sooner or later it would be coming, the only question was when. It did nothing to help his anxiety level that he was staying in the Hotel Paradise in Tehran, which was constructed for the use of police and security officials, and for those, like Mohammed, with ultra-high security clearances, who the Islamic Regime wanted to keep an eye on. How better to do that than by sequestering him in a hotel full of policeman? The security requirements of his job mandated that he stay at the Hotel Paradise whenever he visited Tehran for work.

Mohammed desperately wanted to take action, to set the wheels in motion that would get his family out of Iran. But he couldn't, not yet. He had arrived in Tehran on the 13th, the same day the Shaheed sank. After news of the Shaheed spread, most of the Iranian government had shut down; Mohammed's planned meeting with Gholam Reza Aghazadeh, head of the Atomic Energy Organization of Iran, had been cancelled and postponed until June 16th. After meeting with Mohsen at Masoud Bahktiar's home later that day, Mohsen had checked into the Hotel Paradise under his own name on the morning of the 14th and had begun climbing the walls with anxiety.

Mohammed ended up going for a long walk so he could use one of Masoud's cell-phones to call his wife, Fatameh, and tell her to leave Qom, come to the Hotel Paradise, and bring their daughter, Marjan. They arrived the next day. As they always did, the sight of his beloved wife and daughter distracted him from his cares and worries. They also reminded him of the necessity for carrying through on Mohsen's plan. Frightening as Mohsen's proposed course of action was for both the Saeed brothers, Mohammed knew that unless they could bring it off, Fatameh would be a widow, and Marjan be an orphan. If they survived at all.

*   *   *

On the morning of 16 June, Mohammed fought to keep his expression businesslike as he entered the Atomic Energy Organization of Iran's Headquarters in the Amir Abad district of Tehran. Mohammed's destination was the private office of AEOI President Reza Aghazadeh who had headed the Atomic Energy Organization of Iran for over thirteen years. Mohammed was there to deliver the quarterly briefing on the status of the secret project he headed in the mountains 30 kilometers from Qom.

Mohammed Saeed and Reza Aghazadeh were two of the three participants, the other being the Deputy Head of the AEOI, whose name was, coincidentally, Mohammed *Saeedi*. Mohammed Saeed had grown so used to having a name that was almost identical to the deputy head of the AEOI that he no longer even noticed it. In Iran, such name overlaps were commonplace, and no wonder: if one counted all male children named either Mohammed or Ali in Iran, the numbers would top thirty percent. While Saeed was not quite as common a surname in Iran as, say, Smith or Johnson was in America, variations on the surname Saeed were common enough that Iranians did not assume two men named Saeed were related. Mohammed Saeed thanked *Khoda* for that. If he and his brother Mohsen had shared a more distinctive last name, it might actually have occurred to the senior AEOI officials to ask Mohammed if he was any relation to the Shaheed's missing executive officer. That was not a question Mohammed wanted anyone asking right now.

As usual, both AEOI Chief Aghazadeh, and his Deputy, Saeedi, were glowering at Mohammed Saeed when he arrived. Saeed was in many ways a personal affront to both AEOI officials. Aghazadeh had attempted to guide Iran through a covert nuclear weapon development program, with notably mixed results. Not only did security lapses mean that Iran was repeatedly caught by the US and IAEA undertaking highly suspicious nuclear activities, Aghazadeh had proven himself unable to reign in the corruption in the bomb program, and equally unable to tame the massive egos of the bomb physicists and convince them to work in a cooperative manner with one another.

When control of the bomb development program had been stripped from the AEOI and given to the IRGC, Aghazadeh had hoped in the worst way that progress would remain as glacial under IRGC administration as it had under AEOI control. It hadn't, and Mohammed Saeed was one of the main reasons it had not. Saeed had resolved several outstanding technical hurdles in the centrifuge program. Just as important, he had also proved adept at soothing egos and imbuing the scientists who built and manned the covert nuclear facilities under the mountains of Qom with a spirit of cooperation rarely seen in Iranian academic and technical circles.

Therefore, Mohammed Saeed's quarterly report to the Chief and Deputy Chief of the AEOI on the status of the nuclear weapons program was a trial for all men involved. Mohammed Saeed did not want to be there, and neither AEOI official was happy to see him. He was about to greet the AEOI officials and launch into his speech when Aghazadeh brusquely raised his hand and cut off Saeed.

"A moment, Saeed. The usual oral report will not do this time. I just got a call from the Supreme Leader's chief aide, Mr. Ansari. He said the Supreme Leader is agitated, and wanted a detailed briefing on the security and progress of the program. This includes bringing in each section chief at Qom, as well as head of IRGC Security detail in Qom. The Leader is afraid that the Americans will try to deflect blame for sinking the Shaheed by renewing their accusations that we have a bomb program. He wants to make sure we leave them no opening to do so. How long will it take for you to get the various section heads up here for a briefing?"

Mohammed Saeed could hardly believe his luck. Instead of coaxing the meeting around to where he needed it to be, he could present the idea he and Mohsen had conceived two days ago as a logical alternative to what Aghazadeh had just suggested. Mohammed Saeed paused a minute to feign giving Aghazadeh's question serious consideration. As Aghazadeh also held the title Iranian Vice President for Atomic Energy, and Saeed knew

Aghazadeh preferred that title, he answered, "Mr. Vice President, I think it will take a week or more. The main problem, as I am sure you know, is the delicacy of each of the centrifuge enrichment cascades. They are very large, very sensitive closed loops of machinery. We cannot simply flip them on and off with the flick of a switch. If we want to bring up several of the men who run those cascades to brief the Supreme Leader, we will have to shut the cascades down for safety reasons. That shut down will take several days. And, after the scientists return to the facility, it may take as long as three weeks for the cascades to be restarted, to reach system equilibrium, and be able to resume enrichment activity. Still, if that is what the Supreme Leader wants, we will carry out his wishes."

As Mohammed had hoped, both Aghazadeh's and his deputy's glowers had intensified at the mention of as much as a month down-time on the cascade operation. Clearly, both had forgotten the difficulties involved in powering down and powering up something as complex as four cascades of 2,500 precisely balanced centrifuges. Mohammed continued, "Sirs, I can see from your faces that you are not happy with the idea of taking so long to get a report for the Supreme Leader, nor with shutting down the cascades for so long. May I presume to offer an alternative?"

Aghazadeh and Saeedi both considered Mohammed Saeed too clever by half, and their faces adopted a wary look as Aghazadeh barked out a gruff,

"Proceed, Saeed, what is this idea?"

Mohammed replied, "Mr. Vice President, I remember watching a documentary some years back about the early days of the glorious Revolution. As you recall, Ronald Reagan was the leader of the Great Satan at the time, and the documentary talked about Reagan at some length. It explained that instead of giving him detailed briefings, Reagan's staff had learned to prepare short films on different topics. Reagan used to be in the American cinema when he was young, and he seemed to grasp complex material more easily when it was presented as a short film. I think that idea has merit in this situation."

"I propose we contact Ali Hosseini, head of IRGC Security at our facility near Qom. He can set up a video camera, and get a one minute status summary from each section head of our facility. Then Mr. Hosseini can show a brief example of each of the deception measures we are employing to maintain secrecy around the project, and how we are diverting attention from our covert facility by focusing international attention on the nearby Fordow facility instead. This film should take no more than a few hours to prepare. I am sure Hosseini could do this tomorrow, and he could personally hand-carry the film to us here by the 17th. If you can get me an appointment with the Supreme Leader on the afternoon of 17th, I can play this brief status update video for him and then answer any questions he might have. This way, we will not have to shut down the cascade, disrupt operations, or delay getting the Supreme Leader his information. Would this be an acceptable alternative?"

Mohammed noticed Aghazadeh and his deputy shooting glances at each other. He knew that it galled them to accept any suggestion from him. Fortunately, Mohammed also knew that both men considered the Supreme Leader a very unpleasant old man, one who grew progressively more unpleasant when his whims were not instantly satisfied. Until now, the routine had been that Saeed briefed the two senior AEOI officials, and they, in turn, briefed the Supreme Leader.

Even before hearing of the Supreme Leader's request for a detailed status briefing, Mohammed had been planning to propose this video idea, and had been counting on the AEOI officials' well-known dislike for briefing the Supreme Leader to sell it. The fact that this video would also turn out to be the fastest way to get the Supreme Leader the information he had requested was simply icing on the cake.

Neither Aghazadeh nor Saeedi could see a palatable alternative to Saeed's plan. Instead of answering, Aghazadeh picked up the phone on his desk and dialed a number. Aghazadeh said, "Mr. Ansari? Aghazadeh here." He proceeded to outline the plan for a video briefing, pointing out the disruption that shutting down the cascades could cause, then asked, "Would this video briefing meet the Supreme Leader's needs? It would? Very good. One of the chief scientists, Mohammed Saeed, is sitting in my office right now. I will send him over to the Leader's office on the afternoon on the 17th. He will wait there until the head of Security from Qom hand-delivers the video-tape to him there. As soon as Saeed receives it, you can get him in to brief the Supreme Leader. Saeed can answer any questions the Leader may have that the video does not cover. Very well. *Khoda* be with you. "

Aghazadeh turned to face Mohammed Saeed again. "Mr. Saeed, I am sure you heard that. The Supreme Leader's office has agreed to the video briefing. Be at the Leader's Central Tehran compound at noon on the 17th and be prepared to wait as long as it takes until the video-tape shows up and the Supreme Leader can fit you in. You could be waiting several hours. You may use my phone to call Mr. Hosseini in Security at Natanz to tell him what we need. He can refer to Mr. Ansari if he feels he needs the Leader's authorization to make such a tape."

Mohammed Saeed made the call to Natanz over Aghazadeh's secure phone. Hosseini took the instructions in stride. Technically, as Head of IRGC Security at the underground facility buried in the mountains near Qom, Ali Hosseini should have checked with General Jafari before videotaping Iran's most sensitive nuclear secrets for a briefing. But as the video-tape was to be hand-delivered by Hosseini to Mohammed Saeed at the Supreme Leader's residence, Hosseini assumed the project had all the authorization it needed.

After Mohammed Saeed had replaced the telephone receiver in its cradle on Aghazadeh's vast desk, Mohammed looked at the head of the AEOI with upraised eyebrows as if to say, "Are you satisfied?"

Aghazadeh replied to the non-verbal question with a gruff,

"Very well, Saeed. We are done here. Report back to me after you have briefed the Supreme Leader. You may go."

Mohammed gave a simple nod of acknowledgement, stood, and strode out of Aghazadeh's office. His first thought as he wiped his brow and found it dry was, "Bless dear Sister Lily and her antiperspirant trick!"

CHAPTER 27-WHICH WAY THE WIND BLOWS

Joe shook his head in disgust, and then quickly hid his expression. He hated reading this kind of crap from CIA Hqs, but he had to keep his spirits up so that Cynthia would do the same. If he started acting like the Saeed case was a lost cause, she would too, and the case would self-implode.

For anyone unfamiliar with the bureaucratese that made its way into CIA cables, the cable Joe just got from Hqs would seem like a cautious, measured response. Joe's experience told him, however, that the real message of the cable was not in what it said, but in what it *didn't* say.

.....FIND THE INFORMATION PROVIDED BY MOHSEN SAEED ABOUT THE SHAHEED AND THE IRANIAN NUCLEAR PROGRAM TO BE POTENTIALLY INTERESTING. HOWEVER, EVER MINDFUL OF THE POSSIBLITY OF A WALK-IN UNDER CONTROL OF A HOSTILE INTELLIGENCE SERVICE, WE WOULD LIKE TO PROCEED SLOWLY AND COMPLETELY VERIFY SAEED'S BONA FIDES BEFORE DICSUSSING POSSIBLE EXFILTRATION.......

Joe had seen it many times over the years. Where there should have been a response full of passionate zeal, he instead received something chill as a high plains winter wind. CIA Hqs would rarely come right out and say, "Drop this case, we don't have the inclination to support it," because such a bald statement could be battled by logic and facts. Instead, the baffled case officer in the field who had proposed an operation that Hqs didn't want to authorize would simply get a tepid response.

When he had been a junior case officer receiving such cables, Joe had wondered if everyone in CIA Hqs was a moron, had wondered if they *did not grasp* the concept that many operations had a very narrow window of opportunity, which, if missed, never came again. With experience, Joe had come to realize that while Hqs did not lack for morons, in fact, the vast majority of people in CIA Hqs really did "get it." When they sent a tepid response cable, they *were* responding to the proposed operation. The case officer in the field just had to be good at reading between the lines to understand what the response really meant.

In this case, the message was: we don't want to hear what Mohammed Saeed may tell us about the Iranian nuclear program.

Joe knew that was the real message, because if CIA Hqs had really been interested in reaping a potential intelligence harvest, while still maintaining a healthy skepticism of the Saeeds, the cable would have said something else entirely. It would have said, "We need to get the Saeeds and debrief them in a third country. If, and only if, their information thoroughly checks out, we will then agree to resettle them. If they turn out to be fabricators, we'll just give them the boot." That approach would have embraced the opportunity the Saeed brothers represented, while still treating their information with deliberate caution.

Joe had warned repeatedly in the assessment cable that he had sent in from Dubai Base twelve hours ago that if the CIA wanted to cash-in on the intelligence bonanza that Mohammed Saeed potentially represented, they had only one chance to do so. Joe had stated that they had to start planning the exfiltration of the Saeeds from Iran immediately. If they weren't out of Iran in less than a week, chances were they would be dead or in Evin Prison.

Therefore, the cable from Hqs saying, "We are going to take our time evaluating the Saeeds" really meant, "We are pointedly ignoring the fact that this case has a literal 'deadline' until the opportunity to grab the Saeeds is lost. We will then shake our head and say 'tisk tisk' and pretend we did not deliberately shoot this operation in the foot."

Joe knew someone in Hqs was trying to kill the Saeed case; that didn't surprise him. What was not clear was who was doing it and why they were trying to kill it. Joe would have to fly back to Hqs to find out. But before flying back, he and Cyn had to have one more meeting with Mohsen Saeed. Joe was damned if he was going to let this case founder because some Hqs jackass, or group of Hqs jackasses, cared more about politics than performing the original mission of the CIA: collecting secret information on strategic issues.

Joe turned to Cynthia and said, "Okay, we got some crappy news here. Let's go grab the car and go stretch our legs. Let's go to Burjaman mall. I should pick up some trinkets for Claire in any case."

After a 15 minute ride in the withering heat of Dubai in June, the pair arrived at Burjaman mall, a massive-multi-level structure topped by a glass roof that terminated in a slender metal and glass arches running the length of the structure. As they strode past a trendy boutique, Cynthia suggested the stylish red and gold Hermes scarf in the window. Joe, not needing to break his stride or even turn his head to look at the scarf, noted that he could take Claire out for three nice dinners for the cost of a Hermes scarf. He stopped at a food stand and bought a large sack of Iranian pistachios for Claire instead. Not knowing the alternative might have been a gorgeous Hermes scarf, he figured she'd probably be happy with the pistachios, as she had an addiction to them.

Cynthia bought them both lemonades, and they stationed themselves side by side at a railing on the upper level, looking down at the shoppers on the lower two levels, which ran the spectrum from wealthy, western shoppers to fashionable Muslim women who looked western in every regard but for the addition of a head-scarf all the way to women clad in all-enveloping black burqas. The Middle East in microcosm. Having no further excuse to avoid discussing the implications of the cable from Hqs, Joe dove right in. "Cyn, don't let it get you down. I'll get back to Headquarters and get this turned around. In the meantime, we need to have one last meeting with the Commander to plan things out. One way or another, we are getting the Saeed family out of Iran. But Cyn, there is something you *really* need to think about first; you have a decision you have to make."

Joe tried to project an earnest intensity so Cyn would comprehend that he was dead serious. "If we plan to get the Saeeds out, and that *is* what I intend to do, we may be doing so without official support, if Headquarters doesn't change its mind. That means if the Saeeds turn out to be 'dangles' who were sent with disinformation, both our careers will be over. We could even be prosecuted for running an unauthorized operation."

As Joe continued, he could hear in his own voice that he was fed up with and sick of the often dysfunctional intelligence bureaucracy they worked for.

"Cyn, this is a 'risk all to win all' proposition. You probably shouldn't have to risk your career just to do the job you were hired to do, but sometimes, that's the way it is. This is one of those times. You need to think very, very carefully about whether you want to jump on board here. There is no shame in deciding this risk is not for you; that's probably the smart thing to do, in fact. If you go down in flames on this, you won't have the chance to 'live to fight another day,' and you'll be sacrificing everything else you might achieve during your career. If you decide you don't want to roll the dice on the Saeeds, then we need to go meet with Commander Saeed, thank him for his time, wish him good luck, and send him packing."

Cynthia didn't answer Joe directly. Some part of her knew that he was deliberately giving her a chance to "chicken out," although he would never call it that, and that he would not reproach her in any way if she did so…but also know that he would be deeply disappointed in her. Things would never be the same between them again. She maintained a gaze off into the middle distance, as if contemplating a vision that only she could see. After a minute, she said,

"Joe, did I ever tell you who my favorite President was?"

Joe replied,

"No, Cyn, I don't think you did. Who was he?"

"Teddy Roosevelt. There was something he said once, I read it when I was in high school. I liked it so much I read it over and over until I had it memorized word for word. Teddy said, 'The credit belongs to the man who is actually in the arena, whose face is marred by dust and sweat and blood, who strives valiantly, who errs and comes up short again and again, because there is no effort without error or shortcoming. But who knows the great enthusiasms, the great devotions, who spends himself for a worthy cause; who at best, knows in the end, the triumph of high achievement, and who, at worst, if he fails, *at least he fails while daring greatly*, so that his place shall never be with those cold and timid souls who knew neither victory nor defeat.'"

From time to time, Joe became so discouraged with the bureaucracy at CIA Hqs, he started asking himself what the hell was he doing there. With his experience, he knew he could be making twice the money with half the stress as a security consultant in private industry. Cynthia's response reminded him why he stayed. It was not that he forgot the CIA's many faults, it was just that she reminded him that many of the case officers he worked with were the smartest, most dedicated, most outstanding people it had ever been his privilege to know.

He was so proud of Honey-Bunny's answer he was fit to bust, but like a lot of men, he didn't know how to express his respect or affection to a female colleague in a direct way. So instead, he just joked, "Jeez, Cyn, you make me feel a little shallow that my favorite historical figure is Ben Franklin, and that's mainly just because he was a babe-magnet."

Cynthia couldn't stifle a bark of laughter at Joe's response. She said, "Joe, did I ever tell you that you were a jerk?"

He responded, "No, but don't worry, sweetheart. My wife Claire does if for you all the time. Okay, Cyn, here's what we need to do…"

*   *   *

"Right about there should be best" Mohsen Saeed said, pointing to a spot on the satellite image. Joe, Cynthia, and Mohsen were in Mohsen's hotel room, crowded behind Cynthia's laptop, which was open to Google Earth.

The utility of Google Earth was very much a mixed blessing, in Joe's view. The CIA had missed three terrorist attacks in 2013. One of the planners of the attacks was later captured in a raid on a terrorist training camp in Afghanistan. He said he often no longer bothered to send a reconnaissance team to "case" a target in preparation for a terrorist attack. He just used Google Earth to case the targets instead. Since many attacks were foiled because the terrorist were caught while casing the targets, less direct casing meant Google Earth was making it even harder for the CIA and law enforcement agencies to get the bad guys.

Mohsen had pointed to a dock about three miles northwest of the city center of Qeshm, Iran. The dock in question had a large L-shaped breakwater. Joe began to gently object, "But Commander, this is less than ten miles from the wreck of the Shaheed, not to mention less than twenty miles from the main naval base at Bandar Abbas. Don't you think this area will be a little…ahem, hot? In terms of patrol activity? We know the IRGC has patrol boats directly above the wreck of the Shaheed; I've seen them on satellite imagery myself."

Mohsen Saeed chuckled in response. "Mr. Hank, I can understand your hesitation. But I am proposing this area precisely because I know it, and patrols in it, so well. Qeshm Island is many things. It is a popular tourist destination; the water there is a beautiful shade of light blue, and there are many historical monuments there, including forts from when the Portuguese held the island centuries ago. It is also one of Iran's "Free Trade Zones" meaning customs controls are much more lax. Most importantly for our needs, it is a center for smuggling imported goods into mainland Iran. The Iranian government looks the other way, because all the palms have been greased."

"The Bonyad Mostazafan makes a great deal of money from these smuggling activities. The Bonyad pays to make sure that dock I pointed to never receives any kind of official attention. The Bonyad doesn't care who uses it, as long as Iranian customs stays away from it."

"As for the patrol boats you mentioned, the wreck of the Shaheed is ten miles away from this dock, off the other side of Qeshm Island, the south side. Those patrol boats will never come near this dock, I promise you. Nor will any other official Iranian boats. The sinking of the Shaheed may have changed some things in Iran, but not the corruption."

The scales fell from Joe's eyes at the mention of the Bonyad Mostazafan. That title loosely translated as "Foundation for the Oppressed," which was a laughable description to those who know what the Bonyad really did. The Bonyad was a huge, shadowy commercial organization. It *claimed* to be an Iranian charitable foundation, and did do some charity work, but the CIA had repeatedly found the Bonyad tangled up in procuring parts for Iran's nuclear program, and countless other shady deals. The Bonyad Mostazafan was also tax exempt, and got a million special breaks, because the Supreme Leader got a huge chunk of the profits. The Bonyad was a great example of the kind of corruption that had caused more and more average Iranians to loathe "The Ayatollahs." Joe thought an exfiltration plan which made use of the corruption of the Bonyad Mostazafan was a delicious irony.

He responded, "Mohsen, I like it. In fact, I love it! You have style, Commander."

The planning meeting went extraordinarily well. Commander Saeed had explained in detail why he felt Qeshm would be the easiest way to get his and Mohammed's family out of Iran. Joe and Cynthia found his logic impeccable. Joe had planned several exfiltrations over the years and it was a joy to plan one where the person you were exfiltrating was a cool-headed, clear thinking military professional who knew all the ins and outs of the area where the exfiltration was being conducted. It didn't eliminate risk, but it greatly mitigated it, and that was what successful intelligence operations were all about.

Joe and Cynthia carefully avoided mentioning to the Commander that CIA Hqs had not bought into an exfiltration plan. They had decided they were going to get the Saeeds out of Iran, come hell or high water. If that meant they had to show up with inflatable boat from Wal-Mart and paddle the Saeeds off of Qeshm, they would. Joe figured they could worry about the debriefing and the politics of Mohammed's nuclear information once the Saeeds were out.

Luckily, the dock Commander Saeed had indicated would easily be able to handle the kind of smuggling ship that Joe and Cynthia planned to use to get the Saeeds out, so messing with rubber boats would not be necessary. That would make the exfiltration both safer and faster, and make it far less likely that the Saeed family would inadvertently take a dunking in the Persian Gulf. Rubber boat exfiltrations can be tricky when some of the passengers have never gotten into or out of a rubber boat before. Joe and Cynthia went over the exfiltration plan with the

Commander many times. Commander Saeed impressed them with his recall and attention to detail. Joe felt the growing hope they might actually pull this balls-to-the wall "exfil" scheme off.

After their previous meeting with the Commander, Joe and Cynthia had come to the conclusion that Mohsen Saeed was a real defector. In setting up an exfiltration operation, they were betting their lives on that judgment. Heading unarmed into Iranian waters on a smuggling boat was one of the riskiest things Joe had ever planned. He knew if he and Cynthia were caught, there would be no "prisoner exchange." Joe would probably be tortured to death. Cynthia might meet the same fate; except that her torture would also involve being repeatedly raped by the thugs in Iran's security or intelligence services.

Both case officers had strong incentive to make sure their planning missed nothing.

Finally, after four grueling hours, every detail of the plan had been checked and rechecked. Cynthia gave Mohsen a stack of cash for expenses and a "clean" cell-phone so he could signal Joe and Cynthia once Mohsen, Mohammed, and their families had arrived in Qeshm.

Joe climbed creakily to his feet, as Commander Saeed and Cynthia followed. "Commander, I look forward to seeing you in a few days and meeting your family. If you can get your family to Qeshm, I promise Samantha and I will do everything in our power to get you out of Iran. If you can't get there, I'm sorry; there is nothing we can do for you. Though few in Iran would believe it, the CIA doesn't have agents everywhere, and we aren't 10 feet tall. Our capabilities are very limited. But if you *can* get to Qeshm, Sam and I will come for you. That much I can promise." Joe broke into Farsi, *"Khoda posht va panaah baashad*, God is behind you and your family. Go with God, my friend."

The Commander shook Joe's hand with vigor, and then pulled both him and Cynthia in for a hug. He said, "Mr. Hank, Ms. Sam, when I came to you in need, you helped. I know of no better definition of 'friend' than that."

They left the Commander's hotel room in the Fairmont without looking back.

It was two a.m. when Cynthia, Joe, and Commander Saeed finally parted. Joe had a flight to catch. Cynthia had a smuggling boat to find and hire. And the Commander had a plane to catch back into Iran, where thousands of men were quietly searching for any trace of him.

CHAPTER 28-BELLY OF THE BEAST

The years of Commander Mohsen Saeed's early life were beset by deprivation and adversity. He had met no shortage of petty tyrants who tormented him for their own amusement. As a young boy, the Commander witnessed first-hand how his father, a man both bright and talented, had been relegated to the role of common tradesman. Every attempt by his father to elevate his family's financial or social standing had been quashed by status-conscious "social superiors," people who believed success was a zero sum game, and that if the *lowly* Saeeds advanced, their own glory would not be quite as bright. After seeing such a fate befall his beloved father, Mohsen had to struggle not to become a fearful boy, not to believe that the natural order of the world was set against him.

Mohsen and Mohammed Saeed had both climbed out of that dangerous mental trap, mainly due to natural talent, but also with the benefit of gentle nudges and aid from Masoud Bahktiar. Masoud had helped open doors for the Saeed brothers that otherwise would have remained closed, no matter how brightly the stars of their intellect and ambition had shone.

Boarding the plane to Tehran, Mohsen Saeed felt like he had returned to that earlier era in his life where fear and hopelessness had been constant companions. Seemingly in an instant, everything he had achieved, from obtaining a university education to climbing the ranks of the Iranian military, had been stripped from him. The self-appointed rulers of his country were no longer just trying to hold him down, now they would be trying to kill him and his family. Fear gripped him. He desperately did not want to go back to Iran.

In Dubai, under a false name, he was safe. At least for the time being, he was beyond the reach of the Ayatollahs. If he returned to Iran, he would be back on the territory they ruled. He had racked his brain to think of a way that he could stay in Dubai and bring his family over directly, but could think of none. It was lucky enough that Masoud Bahktiar had one passport that Mohsen could borrow to flee to Dubai, but there was no chance that Masoud would have had enough passports of suitable age and gender to outfit Mohsen and Mohammed's families.

Mohsen, a professional military officer, felt shame at his own fear as he was purchasing his return ticket. But he was determined not to let that fear rule him. He could not leave Mohammed to find his own way to the pick-up point in Qeshm, burdened with both wives and Mohammed's daughter. Commander Saeed knew Qeshm and the surrounding areas; Mohammed didn't.

Also, Mohsen did not want to risk conveying the escape plans to Mohammed via phone or email.

All reasons that meant he *had* to go back into Iran.

He felt some comfort when he thought of the two Americans. He liked the two, he truly did; both had seemed professional, which he had expected. What he had not expected was the compassion for his family's plight, and their impressive knowledge of Iran. To trust two people you had only just met with the lives of your family was a tremendous risk, but one he now felt better about after having met Mr. Hank and Ms Sam. They were going to risk their lives to help him escape because it was their job to do so. Black as the CIA's reputation was in Iran, Saeed could not help but admire that courage.

Mohsen took a deep breath as he settled into the seat of his Tehran-bound flight. Though a short flight in terms of mere duration, his ceaseless anxiety about making his way back through Iranian passport control seemed to be a mental torture designed in the very depths of hell.

*　　　*　　　*

Back in the international arrivals terminal at Imam Khomeini airport, Mohsen had resumed the internal litany that had gotten him through passport control on the way out of Iran. To bolster his flagging courage and maintain the proper calm, bored demeanor, he kept mentally reminding himself that he looked completely different now than he used to, and that furthermore, any security net spread to catch him would be focusing on outbound flights, not on inbound returns.

After all, who among the "Security Bastards" would anticipate that, having successfully escaped Iran, the Commander would voluntarily return. He hardly believed he was doing it himself.

Just before coming into view of the customs officers, he reminded himself to relax and move with the more fluid, loose-limbed gait of a civilian. Mohsen was proud that his hand did not tremble when he passed over the Bagheri passport, nor did he flinch when the passport officer examined the Bagheri passport and closely compared it to Mohsen's face. When the passport control officer slammed the mechanical entry stamp onto the borrowed passport with a clatter, so tautly were the Commander's nerves drawn that he almost leaped out of his skin at the sound.

Saeed had hoped his anxiety would fade once he had the passport back in his hand, but with every step he took beyond the passport control booth, he kept on expecting squads of airport police or IRGC Security to swarm out of hiding places and arrest him. He felt like he had a bull's-eye painted on his back. When he finally passed through the Airport doors into the summer heat of Tehran and entered a taxi without incident, he slowly felt the iron bands of fear encircling his heart begin to dissolve.

Mohsen changed cabs at three locations to avoid drawing any kind of straight line between the airport and Masoud Bahktiar's house before finally hailing a cab to take him to Masoud's. Masoud and Lily had awaited Mohsen's return anxiously, not having heard from him for four long days.

There were tears of relief in Lily's eyes went she opened Masoud's front door.

*　　　*　　　*

It was 5:43 PM on the17th of June when the text message arrived on the cell phone Mohammed had received from Masoud. Mohammed breathed a sigh of relief when he realized that the text message originated from Mohsen.

"I'm back. Things went well. Azadi Tower, under the arch, eight PM."

Built in 1971 to commemorate the 2,500th anniversary of the Persian Empire, the Azadi Tower was one of Iran's biggest tourist attractions. The Tower, which has a huge arch at the heart of it, looked like a combination of France's Arc' de Triumph and a gargantuan battlement from a medieval castle, yet a battlement designed as only a modernist architect could envision it. Since the Azadi Tower swarmed with both tourists and Tehran natives, it was as inconspicuous a place to meet as could be found. When Mohammed spied a grinning Mohsen under the looming arch of the Tower two hours later, he realized he had been mentally "holding his breath" awaiting Mohsen's return. Mohammed felt himself relax a little.

Mohsen and Mohammed quickly caught each other up. Mohsen described his meeting with "Mr. Hank and Ms. Sam," and explained the bare outlines of the plan to leave Iran by boat from Qeshm. Mohammed explained that if all went well, they would soon have the iron-clad proof they needed for the Americans. He recounted with no small glee to Mohsen how the Supreme Leader's last minute request for a detailed briefing had actually given weight to his video briefing suggestion.

Mohammed then sheepish admitted to Mohsen that despite the confidence he had expressed in the notion when he and Mohsen had planned it just days earlier, Mohammed had not been at all sure of his ability to sell AEOI President Aghazadeh on the video-tape briefing idea.

"You see, brother, Aghazadeh doesn't like me. He resents my success in administering the nuclear program, where he often struggled. He often blocks my initiatives out of spite. Luckily, the video tape notion gets him out of briefing the Supreme Leader, a task he hates." Mohammed paused to grin broadly at Mohsen, "He will come to regret that laziness! I admit that I relish this last chance to be a pain in Aghazadeh 's backside. He may have senior rank, but the man is a complete donkey. He is nothing but a politician, and not a particularly bright one: he understands neither nuclear physics nor nuclear physicists. Do you know, he didn't even write his own dissertation? It was a sham, written by someone else. If we can manage to vanish from right under Aghazadeh 's nose, with crucial proof he helped us obtain, he will be doubly humiliated, which is no less than he deserves!"

Mohsen and Mohammed spent another twenty minutes planning. Mohsen and his wife Lily were going to leave tonight, heading towards Bandar Abbas overland. Mohsen would travel on the Aziz Bagheri passport in one of Masoud's Mercedes; the police were less likely to trouble a wealthy man than a poor one. Once he reached Bandar Abbas and caught a *lenj*, a launch, to Qeshm Island, he would rent a large suite at the Qeshm International.

Mohsen explained, "Every time we have stayed in Qeshm in the past, we stayed in the Sara Hotel or the Nasim Hotel. They are cheap. But I am pretending to be a rich businessman, and I want to stay in a big hotel where I am not known. The Qeshm International makes sense. *Beh omid-e Khoda,* if, God willing, you get to Qeshm and cannot find us at the International, try the Diplomat Hotel instead. But we will go there only *if* there is some problem checking into the International." With a bit of black humor, Mohsen continued, "Personally, I won't feel the weight of the fear off my shoulders until we are all in Dubai, but I am sure Lily will enjoy the luxury of the International!"

Mohammed quipped back, "I am sure Lily will like that if you get there in one piece. I think, my brother that your wife has always dreamed of being a race car driver! You will split the long driving shifts with her, yes? I don't think she has ever gotten a chance to drive a car as fast as Masoud's Mercedes! Have a care!"

Mohsen chuckled and admitted ruefully, "Point well taken, brother. Much as I love her, Lily can be impulsive, not to mention a demon behind the wheel. It would be just like her to wait for me to fall asleep in the passenger seat, and then see if she can really get the car up to two hundred kilometers per hour!"

Mohsen paused, and then continued in a more serious tone. "Mohammed, I know what you face tomorrow is difficult. It was a fearful trial for me as well, passing through customs on the way in and out. Now more than ever, our fate rests in the hands of *Khoda*. I cannot believe he would let us get so far, only to rob us of hope now. This is beyond our mere survival. We have a holy mission: to make sure the world knows the truth of the Shaheed, and that a leader who would do such a thing should not be trusted with your weapons of great power, yes? I know you can do it, brother. Just stay calm, stick to the plan, and all will be well."

Time was up. Then knew they must part; each had their own tasks to perform.

The Saeed brothers embraced, both unashamed to have tears in their eyes. Both knew the odds were formidable, and that if the police discovered Mohsen's true identity and whereabouts, he was dead. Mohammed was at equal risk when the "Security Bastards" finally realized that Mohammed was Mohsen's brother. The fact that they might never see each other again remained unspoken. Mohsen turned away without looking back. Mohammed returned to the Hotel Paradise to await the following day.

*   *   *

Three hours later, as Mohsen Saeed blasted down Highway Nine towards Qom with Lily behind the wheel, Mohsen shook his head in despair at his fiercely grinning wife. He said, "In the name of the Prophet, woman, slow down!"

Lily pouted and brought the racing Mercedes back down to within five kilometers of the speed limit. Mohsen shook his head in exasperated affection. "Please, my dear wife, keep it there!"

CHAPTER 29- BEHIND EVERY GOOD MAN

Claire Cerrato shook her head with a sensation of mingled relief and vexation. On the one hand, she was glad to have received the Skype voicemail from Joe. For all his faults, he was diligent about letting her know where he was going and when he would be back so she wouldn't worry overmuch while he was out doing whatever it was that spies do.

The voicemail said he was on his way home. It also said, "Honey-Bunny and I have discovered what we think is a gold mine. The idiots, both Honey-Bunny's and mine, think it is crap. Time for 'Showdown at High Noon.'"

Claire sighed again when thinking about the message. She stopped chopping the garlic for her homemade marinara sauce and headed towards the home office she shared with Joe to start looking for her Rolodex. This was going to take some fixing.

She knew she shouldn't be surprised by the message, it was classic Joe. Anyone who didn't agree with him was an idiot, and the way to deal with idiots was to confront them head on. Claire loved her husband deeply, and respected the incisive intelligence, dedication, and creativity he brought to his job. Those same qualities, though, sometimes made Joe a maddening man to be around, whether you were a colleague or his wife. He deeply believed in the CIA's mission. His unspoken attitude towards colleagues was, "If you aren't as smart as me, as dedicated as me, as experienced as me, or as willing to take risks as I am to accomplish the mission, you get the hell out of my way."

Joe reserved his compassion and understanding for the "assets" he met in the field; winning over potential spies was the core of being a good case officer. However, unless they were a close friend or a junior case officer still learning the ropes, the understanding Joe showed his "assets" had never extended to his

CIA colleagues. He expected them to always be on their "A Game."

Because Joe was a risk-taker by nature, he didn't understand that not everyone could be like him all the time, not everyone could do what he did. The reason he got along so well with Cynthia was that she was just like her mentor, Joe: tough, smart, and determined to make operations succeed. To Joe, any CIA officer who was not willing to push themselves to the limit to get the mission accomplished was merely an obstacle. One to be avoided, if possible, but driven over, if necessary.

Claire had never been certain if Joe's outlook derived from a certain inherent hard-headedness, or whether it was a product of his education. Joe had earned his master's in political science from Carnegie Mellon. Claire felt her own degrees from Virginia Tech in history and sociology had given her a more balanced and realistic view of what humans and human institutions were capable of. Even while she had studied and admired the achievements of the great men and women of history, Claire had understood that they suffered from the same flaws of pride, ambition, pettiness, weakness, etc, as any common man. All were, on some level, quite ordinary. Even the "great" had spouses and children, concern for which sometimes made them timid and fearful when they should have been bold and decisive. Those weaknesses were simply human nature, something to be accepted and worked around.

Claire had tried to talk Joe around to her viewpoint on several occasions, to get him to start cutting his colleagues some slack. The conversations usually went something like, "Don't you realize that humans are imperfect and flaws are part of their humanity?" To which Joe would reply, "These weaknesses you talk about, ego, pettiness, greed, laziness, to name just a few. Are these things that someone can change for the better?" "Yes," she'd reply. "Then, given the fact that they can change into a better person, and choose not to, why should I not hold the people demonstrating those flaws responsible for the consequences of their actions or inactions?"

And that was that. No budging him on the topic.

After a few such conversations, coming at it from a variety of perspectives, she had eventually concluded that, at least on the subject of allowing for flaws in himself or his CIA colleagues, there was not a lot of give in the man. He expected the people he worked with to get the job done, with "No bullshit excuses" accepted.

Claire remembered a few years back when Joe had come home complaining that an extremely important operation, a once-in-a-lifetime opportunity to bug the Chinese embassy in Rome, had been cancelled because it happened to be September, the last month of the fiscal year at CIA. There was no money left in the CIAs budget for new ops until Congress passed a new budget resolution in October. Claire inquired what Joe had expected the senior case officer who cancelled the operation to do. After all, there was simply no money available.

Joe had replied, "Running the operation, planting the bug, collecting the "take," getting out the intelligence from it to the people who needed to know, that was my job. It carried a risk, but that's part of the job, and I was ready to do it. My boss' job was shaking loose money to fund the operation. We have no money, ergo, he ain't doing his job."

And of course, Claire knew this was not just idle chatter on Joe's part. If Joe had been in the position where he was the "money man," he would have found the money. By hook or by crook, by means fair or foul. Claire had no trouble imagining Joe assembling a coterie of his admirers and saying, "Okay people. We need to fly to Vienna to rob a bank."

Admirer number-one would ask, "Uhh, Joe, why are we robbing a bank in Vienna?"

And Joe would respond," Because banks are where the money is, people! We need money to fund a very important operation, and it would be against US law to rob a US bank, so we need to go someplace where we aren't bound by US law. And as to why Vienna, that's simple: The Viennese piss me off." Which they did. Joe hated the Viennese, for some reason he had never explained. On more than one occasion, when on they were on vacation in Vienna a year ago, she had caught him staring at branches of the bank Credit Anstalt with a predatory look on his face. When she had asked him what he was up to, his response was nothing but a grin, and the jaunty reply, "Nothing, my dear. Just thinking about some rainy-day contingencies for work."

She knew him well enough to know exactly what he meant by that.

At Agency cocktail parties, after a few of Joe's colleagues were "in their cups," some of them had sidled up to Claire and given her vague but eye-popping accounts of a couple of the operations Joe had pulled off, including one that had helped put an end to the Peruvian terrorist organization known as The Shining Path. Agency officers weren't supposed to share details of their operations with their wives, but from a few snippets Joe had let drop over the years, augmented by similar cocktail-party whisperings, she knew of at least three operations where he had obtained information that saved dozens of lives. He would do a lot more than rob a bank if that's what it took, particularly when American lives were at risk.

Claire was an Agency brat herself; her father had been a case officer. She accepted that Joe had a very important job, one that he was very good at. She also accepted that, good as Joe was at the "field" part of the job, his refusal to cut his colleagues any slack and "play well with others" hurt his career and his effectiveness.

A few years back, while stationed in Jakarta, Indonesia, during Joe's three-millionth rant about the stupidity and incompetence in CIA Hqs, as Joe was driving them home from a diplomatic reception, Claire had a "eureka" moment about Joe and his job at the CIA. What she figured out that day had everything to do with why she was hunting through her Rolodex looking for the number to Joe's boss' wife. And there it was. Denise Sandler's number, a good place to start.

She picked up the phone and started punching in the digits on the keypad. Neighbors thought they used that phone for its "retro" look. In fact, Joe insisted they keep around the ancient phone, with its faded yellow plastic housing and long-curly cord connecting the handset to the body of the phone, simply because cordless phones were too easy for eavesdroppers to intercept.

"Denise? Hi, it's Claire. I need a favor, sweetie. Yeah, it's about Joe. Can you call Fred at the office and…?"

CHAPTER 30-HIGH NOON

Although the entire fourteen hour flight back to Washington DC happened in daylight, Joe had no trouble getting several hours sleep. He had been up straight through the night after meeting with Commander Saeed. He managed to stay awake long enough to eat the breakfast the cabin crew served him, then he reclined his chair, broke out the sleeping mask from the little bag of goodies that Emirates Air provided to business class passengers, and took a sleeping pill to ensure that he would get some solid sleep even if they hit turbulence, thunderstorms, or hurricanes.

When Joe boarded the plane in Dubai, it had been 6 a.m. When he awoke, his watch told him that he had slept seven hours, but from the sun's position in the sky, it was only mid-morning. The in-flight electronic flight map showed that he was over the Atlantic Ocean. Although Joe was not a nervous flyer, and had crossed various oceans dozens if not hundreds of times during his career, he could admit to himself he always found the notion of being in a plane above many thousands of miles of empty ocean a bit unsettling.

Joe usually dealt with that unease by firmly focusing on other things. It was impossible for Joe to focus on the one thing that was consuming his thoughts. Until he knew who was bringing pressure to bear, he had no way of figuring out how to circumvent it. But, with a little luck, he soon would know. Before leaving Dubai base, he had sent an email to his boss Fred requesting a late-afternoon meeting which would include only Fred, Joe, and Norman Bates, the Chief of Ops for the Counter-Proliferation Division, or CPD.

Joe had always found the usefulness of any meeting was in inverse proportion to the number of participants and the amount of time it took. Short meetings with just a few people got things done. Anything else degenerated into a sort of bureaucratic purgatory.

Although Joe had slept for several hours, he felt himself flagging as he pulled back into the CIA's Hqs North Lot. As Starbucks had managed to penetrate even this sanctum of the nation's secrets, he stopped at the Starbucks in the CIA's cafeteria and got a *large* coffee from the local branch.

He liked their coffee, but refused to use that confusing "grande, venti" bullshit when ordering. Small, medium, and large were perfectly adequate words to describe a cup of coffee in an English-speaking country. Anything else was yuppie pretention.

As Joe gingerly sipped the scalding brew on his way to Fred Sandler's office, he mused on the ubiquity of Starbucks and figured if the CIA had only managed to get Starbucks to believe that Osama Bin Laden was a potential franchise owner, the behemoth of corporate coffee would have had that bastard tracked down in about a week instead of the nearly 10 years it had taken the Agency. And two weeks after Starbucks had found him, the guy probably would have been brainwashed and learning the Arabic phrase for "Should I leave room for cream?"

Joe was pleased to see that Norman Bates from CPD was already in Fred's tiny office when he arrived. Norman's predictable sensitivity to "Psycho" jokes aside, Joe considered Bates a fairly decent case officer. He had attained his lofty position of Chief of Ops, a title usually shortened to "COPs" when spoken, by recruiting several valuable penetrations of WMD networks. Joe knew that not all of Bates predecessors had had such a distinguished operational pedigree: at least one former CPD COPS had been given the position after a major screw-up as Chief of Station in Croatia which had led to the exposure of several assets. That previous COPs had been living proof that, sometimes, if a screw-up is bad enough, and the person who screwed up is really plugged-in to the 'Old Boy Network,' a major mistake could be a big career move.

Like a lot of bureaucracies, the CIA sometimes found it easier to transfer a screw-up and promote him; it was the easiest way to pretend the screw-up never happened.

Not being one to waste time, Joe launched right in as soon as he had taken a seat. "Fred, thanks for setting this up, Norman, thanks for coming. I know you both read the stuff Cynthia sent in, and my assessment backing her up. I am sure you both noticed that there is a ticking clock here. If we don't get the Saeeds out in a few days, we will have lost our shot. I also noticed the time factor was completely ignored in the reply cable you sent out to Dubai. So, what gives? I think he's real, Cynthia thinks he's real, we got a voice print match that confirms his identity, and we got a friggin' Iranian destroyer on the bottom of the Gulf that we know we didn't sink, and which provides Saeed a pretty compelling reason to defect. So why didn't your cable say 'let's get 'em, debrief 'em, and see if their story holds up?'

Fred Sandler answered briefly, "Seventh Floor." Sandler was referring to the seventh floor of the CIA's Old Headquarters Building, the floor that held the office of the Director of Central Intelligence and the office of the DDO, the Deputy Director of Operations.

Joe replied, "Okay, Seventh Floor. But I'm sure the DDO didn't wake up yesterday and say 'Today is a good day to piss all over a promising case just for fun.' So where is the heat *really* coming from?"

This time, Bates replied, "Pants Boy."

"Oh Shit!" Joe cried, "I might have friggin' known!"

"Pants Boy" was the widely used derisive nickname for Charlton Baker. In late 2000, several CIA CSTs, Clandestine Service Trainees, had been carousing in a bar when Baker, who was in the CST program, had decided that dropping his pants would be an appropriate way to impress the female CSTs. The ladies were less than impressed; Baker had been summarily ejected from CIA employ for sexual harassment.

Baker had nevertheless managed to weasel his way up in the "Intelligence Community" by going to work as a staffer for HPSCI, the House Permanent Select Committee on Intelligence, pronounced "Hip-See" by insiders. By virtue of his near-completion of the CST program, Baker had billed himself as an expert on human intelligence, despite never having recruited a single asset or run a single operation.

With the change of administrations, Baker's decade-plus of relentless self-promotion and pandering to any politician that would have him had earned Baker a position as Assistant Deputy Director for National Intelligence in the new administration. Now, when the White House or the one of the Congressional oversight committees wanted to pressure the Directorate of Operations into doing something, or not doing something, Baker did their dirty work by passing along unattributable messages, leaving no official traces.

The unstated iron fist in the velvet glove was always that if the DO ignored the messages from Baker, they might find their budget cut to the bone the following year.

The very thought of Pants Boy made Joe want to puke.

He responded, "Fuck Pants Boy. They can't punish us if we pull off a major intel coup. I'm telling you guys that Saeed is probably the real deal, and we have to find out if he is. We need to get him and his brother out, and then we can stuff the fucking nuclear intelligence down Pants Boy's throat and hope the sonofabitch chokes to death on it. I volunteer for that mission."

Fred and Norman both barked out a laugh at Joe's comment. They enjoyed Joe's acerbic wit, when they weren't on the receiving end of it.

Joe continued, "Seriously, Fred, Norm, we can't let this one get away. It is a fucking crime against humanity and a complete abrogation of our mission if we don't pursue this."

Fred sighed. This was going to be yet another in the series of "bureaucratic facts of life" chats that he had with Joe. Smart as he was, experienced as he was, Joe couldn't get it though his head that telling the White House or Hip-See or the Senate Select Committee for Intelligence to go fuck themselves could seriously damage the Agency.

Fred began in what he hoped was a soothing tone of voice, "Joe, I agree with you. Norman agrees with you. But the Director of Central Intelligence, who, as you may recall, serves at the pleasure of the President, does *not* agree with you. He said we needed to nip the Saeed case in the bud, because 'Renewed tensions in the International Community over Iran's Nuclear Program might destabilize several important diplomatic initiatives.'"

As Joe was about to open his mouth, Fred raised his hand to cut Joe off and continued,

"I know, Joe. I know. Its bullshit. There are no 'diplomatic initiatives.' This administration doesn't trust the CIA, so they don't want to have anything to do with information that might provoke an international confrontation right now. Long story short, the Seventh Floor said, 'Delay, delay, delay, and when that stops working, send out a cable saying we don't have the budget for it.' My hands are tied, Joe."

Joe knew if he had been a cartoon character, steam would be shooting out of ears at this moment. He spoke hotly, "How can you sit there and tell me we are fucking knuckling-under and not doing our job? Every time we cave to political pressure, it makes it that much more likely that someone else is going to pressure us to knuckle under. This is complete bullshit. We need to fucking report 'Pants Boy' to the FBI for trying to subvert national security, not roll over like well-trained dogs every time he fucking visits the Seventh Floor."

The normally unflappable Bates replied to Joe's tirade with a little anger of his own.

"Joe, you need to get it through your head: that is not going to happen. The Director has decided not to fight for this. Like it or not, the Director gives us the orders, and he ordered us to delay. I don't know about Fred, but I decided a long time ago that no case was worth getting fired, losing my pension, and not being able to send my kids to college. That is the real fucking world. We admire your dedication to mission, Joe. But why don't you get off your high horse? Didn't you notice that the cable we sent out *didn't* say terminate all contact with the Saeeds? And it could have. Baker didn't want anything in the official records to be so obvious, so he said just delay the case. That means that *officially* speaking, the case is still alive: there's your opportunity. If you're so fired up, so willing to 'risk careers' for it, go ahead and do so."

Bates paused to calm down, and then continued.

"Right now, Mohammed Saeed is some guy none of us has ever met, you included. To Pants Boy, that means he doesn't exist, and that he and his bosses can afford to ignore him, no matter what he may know about Iranian nuclear weapons. He's just an inconvenient abstraction. But guess what, Joe? If the Saeeds show up somewhere in the West, with some solid evidence, Pants Boy won't be able to sit on that. And then we can back the case to the hilt."

Joe answered warily, "So are you telling me I can run this op, just keep it out of official channels? What the fuck?"

Bates shook his head in frustration and replied, "I'm not telling you anything of the sort, Joe. I'm telling you there is an open door. You can go through it, or not. If you get to the other side, and find something worth bringing back, Fred and I will go to bat for you to make sure the case isn't quashed, even though we were *ordered* to subtly quash it. Be fucking thankful that we are doing that much. You want to get them out, get them out!"

Bates tone abruptly shifted from frustrated to deadly serious.

"Before I finish, let me remind you of something, Joe. I know you're friends with Cynthia Marks. Before you consider getting her involved in anything, think about the fact that if something goes wrong, her career is over. She's one of my best case officers. She could go far if she keeps her nose clean. If this goes bad, she'll be looking for work, and a lawyer, come this time next month. So will you. And if the political pressure over a 'flap' gets bad enough, so will Fred and I."

The mention of Cynthia drained off Joe's ire. He worried whether keeping her involved was the right thing to do. But she was a big girl, big enough to make up her own mind. Joe replied, "I wouldn't worry about Cynthia. She has more balls than three quarters of the case officers in this place. She knows how to make a difficult decision and stick with it." Joe carefully omitted mentioning that Cynthia was already hip-deep in working on the exfiltration, which Joe knew couldn't be pulled off without her.

Joe continued, "Okay, I'm 'walking through the door.' Where do I get the money? This kind of operation can't be run with the measly few thousand bucks I have in my revolving-fund account."

This time, Fred answered, "As Norman said, Joe, an open door is all we have for you, and be thankful for that. I can't give you money I don't have, and the Seventh Floor already called down to the budget section of both NE Division and CPD and specifically ordered the bean counters not to release any money for this case. If you want to do this, you are going to have to figure out how to do it on your own."

Joe replied, "Come on, dammit, what about the covert action money? You know damn well we have twenty million dollars sitting in an account for any activity that 'destabilizes the theocratic government of Iran.' You don't think Commander Saeed's news that the Supreme Leader ordered the Shaheed sunk will help destabilize the Ayatollahs?"

Fred Sandler replied with a resigned tone, "Joe, you know that money is fucking 'fenced' by Congress. We are specifically prohibited from using it for the collection of intelligence. We can only use it for cross-border paramilitary ops to destabilize Iran, and there is nothing about the Saeeds that can remotely be passed off as covert action: it is a straight defector case. The bean-counters and 'HipSee' watch 'fenced' money even more closely than my discretionary funds. You're dreaming if you think I can get that 'fenced' money to you without being caught."

Joe sighed, shook his head, and climbed wearily to his feet. He reflected that the grandstanding Congress put so many fucking strings on the "fenced" money it gave the CIA that the money was often practically useless. It would sit there, unspent, while real operations died for lack of money because real operations were risky and unpopular. It was a sad fucking day when the best his bosses could do for him was offer him almost no support, no money, and the chance for he and Cynthia to ignominiously end their careers.

But it was about what he had expected.

Joe said, "I want a week's personal leave. Norman, Cynthia told me she wants a week of leave, too. Can you manage that?"

Norman's phlegmatic demeanor had returned. "Joe, that much I can do."

"Joe," Fred said a question mark in his voice.

Joe, who had been facing away from Fred as he pulled open the office door to leave, turned to face Sandler again. "Yeah, Fred?"

"You should thank your lucky stars you married Claire, Joe. Without her, that 'door' we've been talking about? It would be closed."

*   *   *

Joe was baffled by Bates remark all the way home. But he figured he would have a chance to discuss it with Claire in a few minutes. It was bound to be a touchy discussion. Joe wasn't sure how happy Claire would be to hear the phrases "Home Equity Line of Credit" and "exfiltration operation" in the same sentence. But the conversation had to happen; he didn't have time to fly to Vienna right now.

*   *   *

During Claire's "Eureka" moment years before in Jakarta, Claire realized that she had a major part to play in keeping Joe's career on track. It is normal for CIA case officers to rotate back to CIA Hqs to serve one or two tours at Hqs as they ascend the career latter. But Joe had avoided spending time at Hqs at all costs; he cursed "Headquarters dwellers" as "bureaucratic, risk-averse assholes." In that "eureka" flash of enlightenment, Claire suddenly understood, even though Joe did not, that the upshot of his refusal to spend any time in Hqs was that Joe did not have a social network at CIA Hqs to protect him and help keep his operations on track when they started to meet bureaucratic resistance. Having studied sociology, Claire understood the real value of social networks. As a career case officer, which is a "lone wolf" profession, Joe didn't.

People turned against Joe, not because he was wrong, which he rarely was, but because he was so *damned* aggravating.

In her own way, Claire was patriotic, and not in the shallow, flag-waving, "America, love it or leave it" way. She knew her husband served his country with a skill and dedication few could ever hope to equal. She also knew if she didn't do something, Joe would probably either get fired, or quit the Agency in frustration, if his operations kept getting arbitrarily rejected.

Two years ago, when it came time to pick Joe's next duty assignment, Claire had put her foot down and insisted it was time to return to the US. She insisted that it was of vital importance for their daughter, Emily, to have a chance to go to high school in the US and have some stability in her life. Emily, Claire insisted, had to be given a chance to build a consistent set of friends.

This was all a huge lie on Claire's part.

Although Claire though that though it *was* hard on Emily to have to make new friends every time they moved, the chance to live all over the world and get exposed to a variety of cultures was a great opportunity, one which more than made up for the stresses of moving. Claire had grown up that way herself, and considered her childhood and adolescence to have been filled with learning and adventure.

Claire turned a deaf ear to Joe's arguments. He had countered that living in the US was far more expensive than living abroad, that traffic in the greater DC area was a nightmare, that daily commutes of an hour or more were the norm, and that Emily would be exposed to the vapid emptiness of American pop culture. That emptiness was something Joe and Claire had worked hard to shield Emily from while living abroad.

Claire heard Joe's arguments and inwardly cringed, silently agreeing with every word he said. Just the thought of exposing their sweet Emily to the hormonal pawing of American teenage boys made her mildly nauseous.

Nevertheless, Claire dismissed all Joe's arguments and pulled out the relationship equivalent of the H-Bomb.

She said, simply, "Joe, if you love me, if you love Emily, we have to move back to the US for a while. It is only fair to her. Sometimes your career has to come second."

Naturally, Joe fumed and ranted, but ultimately, he gave in. He could not deny Emily this, not after she and Claire had both been such good sports about their nomadic lifestyle.

After Joe and Claire had moved back to northern Virginia so Joe could work at CIA Hqs, Claire had made a point of bending over backwards to help other people who worked at Hqs in the Directorate of Operations. Claire helped case officers, their wives, and their families, in any way they needed. And she never judged them. Clair helped patch-up marriages rocked by infidelity or substance abuse...like the marriage of Norman Bates, "COPs" of CPD. She helped people cope with teenage daughters who unexpectedly got pregnant. She got people going through bitter divorces into therapy, and had served as an emergency babysitter on many occasions.

If you worked in the Directorate of Operations, or DO, long enough, you develop a "hall file." A "hall file" was quite simply the consensus opinion of the CIA Hqs rumor mill on your reputation as a case officer or a person. Joe's hall file was that he was smart, experienced, had pulled off a lot of great ops, and was a legendary pain in the ass. After a few years in the Hqs area, Claire now had a hall file, too. The DO tribe at Hqs had came to know that if you had personal problems, Claire Cerrato would help, and she wouldn't blab about your woes to other people when she did it.

Of course, as the wife of one case officer, and the daughter of another, Claire knew their tricks. She knew that a lot of people spied for the CIA simply because the case officer who had recruited the spy helped that spy in their time of need. A good case officer was almost like a social worker, a combination of a counselor, banker, boss, and friend. Your case officer could get you to see a doctor when you lived in a place where there *were* no doctors. Your case officer would get you money to send your kids to college. Your case officer would talk you through your messy divorce.

Claire had decided she needed to "case-officer the case officers." Some might have considered that cynical, but Claire didn't. After all, it wasn't that Claire wasn't happy to help; she was. It wasn't that she didn't genuinely like and care for the DO families she helped; she did. It was just that she cared for her husband even more, knew the work he did was important, and knew she had a part to play in saving him from himself and helping to make sure he could do his job. Joe wasn't the kind of guy who thought to build a social network, so Claire had to. Like a much kinder and more attractive version of "The Godfather," Claire worked to get as many people indebted to her as possible. Unbeknownst to Joe, Claire cashed in those debts on Joe's behalf as needed.

Like today.

After getting Joe's voicemail, Claire had picked up her phone and started dialing. Joe's immediate boss was Fred Sandler. His wife, Denise Sandler, had been in a car wreck nine months ago and had seriously injured her right leg. Claire had driven Denise Sandler to physical therapy for two months, and provided a shoulder for Denise to cry on when she was frustrated at the physical agony that was part and parcel of the recovery process. Fred Sandler had told Claire if there was anything he could ever do for Claire, to let him know. The next call had gone to Cynthia's boss, Norman Bates, whose lovely wife, Sharon, had been talked out of divorcing him and taking the cheating son-of-a-bitch to the cleaners by none other than Claire, a fact that Norman well knew.

Although Joe and Cynthia would never know it, the reason they now had, "an open door to walk through" on Saeed case had little to do with the merits of the case itself, or anything to do with Joe and Cynthia's powers of persuasion. No, it was far more closely tied to the two phone calls that Claire had placed yesterday afternoon.

CHAPTER 31-CHARM SCHOOL

The last thing Joe said to Cynthia before they parted at the Fairmont Hotel was, "Go to Waterston. He'll be the fastest way to get the boat. Tell him I sent you, and that I'm cashing in my marker with him from the Herat thing; he'll know what I mean. And he'll be less suspicious if you invoke my name: he knows I've been a 'troubleshooter' for fast-breaking operations before. But don't forget about the SIS's 'Charm School' course, even for a second! He'll bend over backwards to be accommodating, until the second he thinks the interests of 'His Majesty's Government' and the British Secret Intelligence Service diverge from ours. Make sure you don't give Waterston any information to make him think trying to grab primacy would be a good idea."

This was Cynthia's third field tour, but the first one in which she had been "declared to British Liaison," meaning that Henry Waterston, the Head (or H) of the local British Secret Intelligence Service office, the SIS, knew who she was. Being "declared" came with pros and cons. On the one hand, your level of risk was inherently higher when another intelligence service knew your true identity as a CIA case officer, and the SIS had had no shortage of highly damaging moles planted by the KGB over the years. On the other hand, being "declared to liaison" also meant that you could participate in joint operations with the other intelligence service, which sometimes offered great opportunities.

A year and a half ago, when Joe had learned Cynthia was going to be declared to the SIS on her tour in Dubai, he asked her to stop by his desk in Hqs so he could "bring her up to speed" on Henry Waterston,"H" Dubai.

Joe began, "Waterston is a decent guy, smart, accomplished, has a good record. But you have to remember, all the crap you hear about a 'special relationship' between the US and the UK, and between the CIA and the SIS is just that: crap. Or maybe it is better to say it is both true, and not true. Ya gotta hand it to the Brits, they saw the writing on the wall before World War II; they knew the "Empire" was in decline, and that the best way to catch a new wave and maintain most of their power and prestige was to buddy-up to the US. Broadly speaking, we cooperate a lot, and we both get a fair amount out of it, although the SIS and Brits consistently get more out of the bargain."

"If we both throw most of the intelligence we collect into a common pot, but the CIA has collected a lot more, because we're much bigger, who is getting the better end of the deal? Not us. The 'special relationship' propaganda continues mostly because it is in the Brits' best interest."

"Now that you're gonna be declared to the SIS, you're gonna see first-hand that things aren't always so collegial with our jolly British allies. On a lot of issues, nuclear weapons being just one of them, there are only a few really juicy potential assets out there. Every time both we and the Brits have managed to make contact with the same potential asset, they have tried to 'declare primacy' in the case and grab it away from the CIA control, even if we made contact first, and even if our case officer is in better position to recruit the guy. The only people worse than the Brits about trying to snatch away 'primacy' are The Mossad. The Brits, at least, are polite about it."

"One thing to remember about Waterston or any Brit in the SIS is that you can't be lulled into a false sense of security by their chumminess and seeming willingness to help. They will play the 'historic ties' card, the 'we Anglo-Saxons have to stick together against the WOG hordes' card, and pour as much beer and/or scotch down your throat as they can, to try to turn you into a 'drinking buddy,' if you get my drift. But it's all bullshit, all an act." At this point in the monologue, Joe had paused, leaned forward, and tapped Cynthia on the knee a couple times with his index finger, as if to say, "Pay special attention to what comes next."

Joe continued, "With any liaison service, but particularly the SIS, the thing to remember is, *it's all an act. They are not your buddy*, they are there to leverage you to get information from the CIA on the cheap, *information other CIA officers and assets have fought and bled for*. The SIS has elevated this to an art form.

They actually give their case officers classes in how to appear charming and friendly to their CIA counterparts, so they can wring every last drop out of the relationship. You need to keep that front and center in your mind, and watch every word that comes out of your mouth when meeting with any liaison service. End of sermon."

Cynthia was glad for the warning. When Cynthia had ended up meeting Henry Waterston nine months ago at a "liaison" meeting in the US Embassy in Abu Dhabi, she was immediately struck by his charm and convivial good nature. Joe's warning had allowed Cynthia not to fall under his spell, but to project a pleasant yet professionally detached demeanor that kept the senior SIS officer at arm's length.

After her meeting with Commander Saeed and Joe, Cynthia allowed herself five hours of sleep, and then forced herself to get out of bed and call Waterston. When she requested a meeting, he was, of course, pleased to oblige. They met at a restaurant near the meticulously manicured Mamzar Park north of Dubai proper. On her way inside, she was surprised to see people out strolling in the great half-circle amphitheater in the park. To her, air conditioning was the only thing that made life in Dubai endurable, the notion of a stroll in the mid-day sun was horrific. She reveled in the cool whirring up of the restaurant's air conditioning, the white linen table cloth, and the muted clink of metal utensils on fine china. There aren't too many perks in the espionage business, one of the Cynthia enjoyed was the chance to have business lunches at pretty decent restaurants.

Waterston, already seated at a prime table, grinned a two-hundred-watt smile, as if Cynthia were his oldest and dearest friend and said, "Cynthia, really brilliant to see you! I'm so glad you called. To what do I owe this honor? And how's dear-old Chester?"

Chester Green was Chief of Base Dubai, Cynthia's direct superior. It was standard protocol that meetings between liaison partners took place between people of equal rank. In this case, that meant the Chester Green was normally the person who met with Waterston, not Cynthia. Not that Waterston would stand on protocol; quite the contrary. Waterston saw any deviation from

SOP as a potential opportunity to be exploited, and was fishing to understand why Cynthia had taken the unusual step of contacting him directly. Cynthia, adopting a cordial but direct tone, said, "Henry, Chester's fine. This isn't about him. Joe Cerrato sent me. We need your help on a fast-breaking case. Joe said you have good contacts in smuggler circles and can get a boat faster than we can. Time is of the essence."

Waterston replied, "Of course, Cynthia, of course. Anything for old Joe, the man's absolutely *aces* in my book! Happy to help. What's this all about, then? I'll need a little information to help you plan your little adventure, won't I?"

Cynthia had given a good deal of thought how to play this: how much to reveal, how much to hold back, and what concessions to be ready to give. "Henry, we've had a walk-in. Seems genuine. We've had a voice print match that identifies him as an officer who has served aboard the Shaheed."

Henry's eyebrows shot up with interest. He said with enthusiasm, "That's fantastic! Brilliant. What a bit of luck."

Cynthia replied, dryly, "Yes, we're very excited. It may be a good opportunity for us to find out what happened with the Shaheed, and get a wealth of 'Order of Battle' information about the Iranian Navy and the IRGC Navy."

Cynthia made no mention of Mohammed Saeed or any nuclear weapons information.

She continued, "What we need from you, Henry, is simple. We need to get our walk-in and his family out. We need a smuggler with concealed compartments big enough to hold seven people and convincing enough to pass inspection if stopped at sea. The seven will be Joe and I, our walk-in, and four members of his family. We need to pick them up from a dock near Qeshm city. Because our walk-in was a serving officer, he knows the patrol schedule and which dock to use, one that doesn't receive any official customs attention because the right palms have been greased by the Bonyad Mostazafan. The exfiltration has been planned; we just need a ship capable of pulling it off. We need to be ready to go within thirty-six hours from now. Can you manage that?"

Waterston, the machinery in his head plainly turning, managed to keep an air of amused collegiality on his face as he pondered how to turn this request to his advantage. In this case, the answer seemed fairly straightforward. "I know just the chap, Cyn, bit of a rough customer, most smugglers are, but an honest one, in that once bought, he stays bought, at least for the duration of the voyage for which you have paid him. That's about all you can expect from his lot, I'm afraid. Still, he's earned a nice bit of change from his work for us over the years, so he's likely not going to tattle. More importantly, if I may say, he has nerves of steel."

"I've been on his boat. To the naked eye, it's a pig of a dhow, really. Ancient looking. But it has a few tricks. A few years back, we had to move some people around. This Captain, name of Shirazi, like the wine, you see? He was willing to undertake the charter if the price was right. Problem was, his dhow was of standard design, and the compartments couldn't really hide anything from a determined search. We flew out some shipwrights and carpenters, and they put in false decks in each compartment. They're a bit snug, but you can fit a total of twelve people, if they're well acquainted. It's down in the bilges, which are a bit evil-smelling, I'm afraid, but given my druthers, I'd ruther have a bit of a stink and still be drawing breath, yes?" Waterston chuckled with good humor.

Cynthia purred her reply, "Well, that's so nice to hear. I knew we could count on our old friends," then she shut-up, waiting. She knew Henry had just thrown out some tasty bait, and wanted to set the hook. He was in a strong position. Still, it was best to wait for his opening bid, and then react; she had a few trump cards up her sleeve. She knew he had to bring it up and he did.

"Anytime, Cynthia, anytime. We're in this together, you know. Of course, the 'home office' expects me to 'turn a profit', metaphorically speaking, on such transactions, even with dear friends. Can you tell me, then, what's our cut of the loot? We'd love to put this chap up for a few months, debrief him directly, eh?"

Cynthia smiled a winsome smile she had been saving for this moment. "Well, what's in it for you, Henry, is that you finally get to pay your old comrade Joe back for Herat. He didn't tell me what it was about, but said he knew you'd be eager to repay him for that. As for access to this IRGC Naval officer, Mohsen is his name, by the way, our debriefing teams will be happy to take all your written questions and present them to him. We'll provide you all his answers. When we're done with his initial debrief, and we've had a chance to get him settled in, we'll ask if he would mind meeting directly with some of your officers. If he says yes, we'll be more than happy to facilitate access."

Cynthia had been watching carefully when she used the word "Herat," which was a city in northwestern Afghanistan where she knew Joe had spent some time. Apparently, Waterston had, too, and whatever had gone on there to leave Henry in Joe's debt was still a sensitive subject with Waterston. Cynthia had noticed a look of alarm in Waterston's eyes at the mention of Heart. Cynthia felt a glee that she did not allow to spread to her face; she had finally managed to puncture Waterston's air of effortless bonhomie.

Waterston replied with a weak grin, "Herat, eh? Our dear friend Joe has the memory of an elephant, apparently! And here I thought that little unpleasantness was behind me." With a resigned air, Waterston continued, "Ahh, well, water under the bridge. We all must pay the piper, Cynthia."

Honestly, Cynthia didn't know why they had to play these little games; it's not as if the SIS wouldn't get to eventually see 90 percent or more of whatever information the CIA collected. But some people where only happy unless they felt they had driven a hard bargain. Cynthia could tell that whatever it was Joe had done for Henry in Herat, it was enough to make Waterston back off and conclude his negotiations with Cynthia with a lot less wrangling than might otherwise have been the case.

Nodding to himself, Waterston continued, "Well, then, I suppose a man pays his debts, and Joe had presented a legitimate one for collection. If you can come up with the money for my smuggler Captain, and he doesn't work cheap, *and* you promise my lads a crack at your Mohsen down the road, I think we're in business. I'll ring up Captain Shirazi directly and get the ball rolling."

Cynthia, knowing when to be gracious, replied, "Henry, I'm so pleased. Joe said you were absolutely a man of integrity, and I can see his faith was justified. I promise you that we'll get a fair haul from this Mohsen and your Royal Navy folks will be quite impressed. I spent four years in the Office of Naval Intelligence and I can spot a real naval officer when I see one. There's just one other small matter to discuss."

Henry, with an air of good humored mockery, said, "My dear young lady, you've already picked my pockets nearly clean! Surely you'll leave me a few pence for bus fare!"

Cynthia replied with a genuine grin, even leaning forward to pat Waterston's hand with sympathy, "There, there, Henry, this won't cost you a thing! A few scraps of paper, is all, I promise!"

CHAPTER 32-*RUBAH'* THE FOX IS LOST

Lieutenant Jafari was very afraid. Four days had already passed since the Shaheed had sunk, and still he hadn't located Commander Saeed, or the Rescue Diver, Erfan. Jafari also knew that the wrath of his cousin was growing daily because the Qods Force team the General had dispatched to Dubai had not yet managed to locate Ziyaii. Now Jafari was faced with a dilemma that he had no idea how to solve.

The General had specifically said, "Majid, when I hear from you next, it would be wise to have good news to report about your progress in finding Erfan or Commander Saeed." Lieutenant Jafari knew the General did not make such statements idly.

Unfortunately, Erfan had seemingly vanished. He hadn't gone to visit family, and so many sailors came through Bandar Abbas that none of the commercial airline pilots or bus drivers that staffed the transportation services into the area could recall seeing Erfan.

Lieutenant Jafari was down to one remaining lead to investigate, and he had no idea if that would produce results. In Commander Saeed's personnel file, under 'siblings' was written, "Contact IRGC Security, Personnel File Division, regarding file *87734 Fajr.*" Jafari was hoping that Commander Saeed was hiding with this "mystery sibling," and if the Lieutenant could find out where Commander Saeed's brother or sister was, the General would be able to send a Qods Force team. When Jafari had called the Personnel File Division two days ago, an IRGC Ground Forces Major had answered. When Jafari explained that he was the investigating the loss of the Shaheed, and that he was cousin to IRGC Commander Jafari, he had expected the man to deliver instant cooperation. He certainly did *not* expect the response he received. The man had refused to identify himself by name to Jafari, stating only his rank!

Then, he said, "Lieutenant Jafari, I do not care if you are the reincarnation of Morteza Ali, bless his name. There is only one way that people get names from this particular personnel office. You fill out the form I send you, explaining why you have 'need to know.' I look over the set of guidelines, very *narrow* guidelines, for people with legitimate 'need to know.' If you fall within the guidelines, you get the information."

"Two days after I came to this position, I was visited by your cousin, the Commanding General. I will tell you now what he told me on that day. 'Major, you have been promoted to this position because you are a man who follows orders blindly, and has absolutely no imagination. That is precisely what I want in this position. I want a man who will *follow the rules* about restricting access to these *very* sensitive personnel files.' Your cousin, the General, then presented me with a copy of the regulations in a glass picture frame, as if it were a photo of my family. He placed the frame on my desk, and told me, 'Major, these regulations are your new family. If you don't follow them, *Ghassam mikhoram,* I swear to it! Your real family will suffer! Of course, that might not matter to you, because I will personally shoot you if there is a breach of security. If you release a name outside of the regulations I have set for you, better for you if you had died at birth.' "

Afraid to call the General, Lieutenant Jafari had meekly submitted the form the Major had emailed him. Since only Lieutenant Jafari, the General, and a few others knew the reality behind the sinking of the Shaheed, Lieutenant Jafari could not explain to the Major the real reason he desperately needed to locate Commander Saeed, or why he *knew* the General would authorize an exception to the rules, no matter how restricted the particular personnel files were.

In an unprecedented display of speed for Iranian bureaucracy, Lieutenant Jafari had received the answer in just two days. The form came back with, "Request denied," stamped on it in bright red ink.

Lieutenant Jafari did not know what to do. He needed to make progress in the Saeed investigation, but to do that, he needed his cousin, the General, to order the release of the information on the identity and location of Commander Saeed's sibling.

How to do this without speaking to the General, who would not have forgotten his order that Lieutenant Jafari should only call him if he had good news to report?

Lieutenant Jafari sat in his office pondering the matter for several hours, and could see no solution that would not make matters worse. Finally, at 11:30 p.m., it occurred to the Lieutenant that at this time of night, the General probably had his encrypted cell phone switched off.

With no little amount of trepidation, Lieutenant Jafari dialed the General's phone. The Lieutenant breathed a sigh of relief when it rang directly through to the voicemail. He left a message with an abject apology for disturbing the General, and explained his predicament in locating Commander Saeed without being able to know if Saeed was staying with his 'mystery sibling.' The Lieutenant left the file number of the restricted file twice, to be sure that the General did not mishear, and then switched off.

He prayed that the General was feeling merciful and simply ordered the Major at the Personnel File Office to release the information to Lieutenant Jafari with no further fuss.

After leaving the voicemail, the Lieutenant returned home and lay in bed next to his wife. His mind could not stop churning through the possibilities of what might happen should he fail to find Commander Saeed. No matter how he tried to calm himself and think of something else, he could not attain the sleep he so dearly wanted. Finally, but only with the aid of a very strong sleeping pill and a large tumbler of Johnny Walker Blue, the Lieutenant retreated into slumber.

CHAPTER 33-DUBAI, TAKE TWO

As Joe settled into his seat for his return flight to Dubai, he shook his head in wonder at his wife, Claire. Joe didn't know a married couple alive that hadn't fought at one time or another over money. Certainly, he and Claire had had their share of disagreements on the topic. Claire, having been a CIA brat, had grown up overseas in diplomatic circles. Joe felt that tended to give Claire a rather skewed perspective on money.

When Claire had been ten, she lived in a beautiful house in Egypt, paid for by the CIA. It was not that the CIA *wanted* to house their employees and their families so well, but in a lot of third world countries, there was no "middle class," so there were only two kinds of houses available to lease: dirt-floored shack or a luxurious home in a fenced compound. Given low costs in the third world, such a luxury home cost the CIA about the same to lease as a three bedroom ranch-style house would have in a big US city.

Claire's father had not earned a big salary, but since one could get a maid, a cook, a butler, a gardener, and a nanny for $300/month in Egypt, the money went much further abroad than it would have in the US. Trailing her father from assignment to assignment, Claire had lived in a series of houses that, had they been in the US, would have been classified as mansions. She had had servants for most of her life. Joe felt Claire had led a rather pampered life, with the upshot being that Claire was sometimes ready to spend Joe's salary before he earned it.

They had fought last year when it came time to replace their old car. Joe had pushed for a sensible Camry, Claire wanted to get a new BMW 335i using money from their home equity line of credit, and she had given Joe the silent treatment for two days when he had balked.

Given their past battles over money, Joe had expected Claire to kick up a fuss when he discussed the admittedly outlandish scheme of drawing on their home equity line of credit to fund an exfiltration operation, especially when all he would tell her about it was that it was very important, Cynthia was involved, and at least two men and possibly their wives would die if he couldn't pull it off.

Joe had been amazed when Claire had sat silently for a few minutes after he had made the proposal, thinking things over, before answering, "Well, then, we better get to the bank early tomorrow, you have a flight to catch."

Joe had been so astonished and happy that he clean forgot to ask why the COPs of CPD, Norman Bates, would suggest that he was only willing to go to bat for him because of Claire.

Even if Joe *had* remembered, Claire would have made some vague reference to payback for all the babysitting she had done for Norman and Sharon Bates. And, there would have been *some* truth in that answer, although it probably would have been closer to "the whole truth" to say that Claire had recently called Norman and reminded him that she had talked Sharon out taking their kids and leaving him after Sharon had caught Norm cheating on her.

Claire was privately amused that Joe was so bad at reading her, but not surprised. Claire remembered reading that psychologists are experts at judging other people, but as a group, they aren't noticeably more successful their own personal lives than anyone else. She knew that Joe was just as expert in making judgments as a case officer in the field as the cleverest psychologist was in diagnosing and treating mental distress in his patients. She also knew that Joe's keen abilities didn't extend to understanding his wife, but Claire didn't mind. She preferred to remain mysterious.

The real reason Claire had been a pushover is that when it came to his job, to being a case officer in the field, she trusted her husband's judgment implicitly. If he said a couple of people would die if he didn't get the money, he wasn't kidding. Much as Claire had wanted a BMW, and much as she quietly admitted to herself that she was a bit of a spendthrift, she would never seriously put her desire for a car with heated leather seats and a Blaupunkt stereo in the same class as saving the life of two people who were depending on Joe.

CHAPTER 34-THE FIERY FURNACE

Like the Ababeel's ill-fated pilot, Commander Saboori, Mohammed Saeed had always been fascinated by religion. For Mohammed, the hobby of learning about various religions was not so much a matter of belief as it was an interesting lens through which to examine the sweep of history, which was one of Mohammed's passions. Mohammed marveled to think that tales of Zeus and other gods from Greek mythology had not always been treated as fairy tales, but in their own day been accepted by the Greeks as surely as Mohammed himself believed in *Khoda*.

As he had passed through the security checks at the Supreme Leader's main compound in Central Tehran, Mohammed felt his faith in the justice of *Khoda* was the only things keeping him on his feet. His tumultuous thoughts hit for some reason on the Old Testament tale from the Book of Prophet Daniel, perhaps because Daniel had been buried in ancient Persia: the tale of Shadrach, Meshach, and Abednego. The three men had refused to worship a false idol, and held fast to their faith in *Khoda*. For this effrontery, King Nebuchadnezzar punished them by having the three men thrown into "a fiery furnace," yet so great was the faith of the three that they were not even singed by the flames. Mohammed did *not* compare himself to any biblical figures. He only hoped that his faith would sustain him for the next few hours, and that he would not melt under the weight of his own fear and anxiety.

Sitting in the anteroom of the Supreme Leader, he found it hard to keep his imagination in check. The room was lavishly decorated, but it had no fripperies such as books or magazines to occupy the mind of those waiting to meet the Supreme Leader. Presumably those who waited in this room were intended to reflect on about the honor of meeting the Leader, and thus had no need to distract themselves from the tedium of the wait. Mohammed would have given a great deal to have even a gossip magazine to read as a distraction.

Mohammed had been working on the Fajr Project, as General Jafari had designated the nuclear weapons program, for four years. It had been a time of great struggle for Mohammed, but he and his team of scientists and technicians finally managed to attain a goal that had eluded Iran in previous decades. They had created a real uranium enrichment capability under conditions of blackout secrecy.

Every second spent waiting in this room caused Mohammed to wonder if Ali Hosseini had at the last minute balked at the idea of videotaping the secrets of Fajr without first checking with General Jafari for permission. Mohammed tried to comfort himself with the knowledge that Hosseini was one of the *Hizzbolla'hi, the* religious fanatics. Hosseini was proud of his *unthinking* obedience to the Supreme Leader. Mohammed only hoped that fervor meant Hosseini would fulfill any order he perceived as having come from the Supreme Leader without question.

When Hosseini was finally escorted into the waiting room gripping a small package, Mohammed Saeed breathed an internal sigh of relief. As the guards who had escorted Hosseini in were leaving, Mohammed approached Hosseini and said, "Ahh, Mr. Hosseini, *khateh nabashid,* I hope you are not tired? So good to see you. Were there any problems with the tape? Is it ready for the Supreme Leader to view?"

Hosseini looked awed to be standing in the Supreme Leader's residence, just a room away from the Leader himself. He replied with a sober tone, "Mr. Saeed, there were no problems. The tape is very crude, of course, we did not have time to edit it, but there were no problems. Each department head gave a quick status summary of his operations, and I filmed examples of the concealment measures we have been employing. As you instructed, I kept it short, the entire length is less than ten minutes."

Hosseini adopted an abashed expression totally out of character for one whose fervent religious zeal normally gave him an iron certainty about all his actions. He gestured for Saeed to step closer and whispered, "Mr. Saeed, do you think there is a chance? Would it be improper? Might I stay with you and meet the Supreme Leader when you deliver the briefing? Gazing upon the Leader with my own eyes is an honor I have hoped for since I was in the Basij."

Mohammed was an observant Shia Muslim, but he despised the fanatics like Hosseini, who Mohammed believed were so rigid and intolerant in their beliefs that they perverted the true message of Islam. When Mohammed spoke with his brother Mohsen about "The Bastards in Security," Ali Hosseini was always the illustrative example Mohammed used. As Mohammed was one of the chief scientists of Fajr project, Hosseini spent an extraordinary amount of effort trying to pry into every detail of Mohammed's personal life, including regularly harassing Mohammed's wife and daughter with intrusive questions. The fact that Hosseini had not been more successful in learning Mohammed's secrets proved to Mohammed that not only was Hosseini a bastard, he was a stupid bastard.

As Mohammed had learned from Mohsen just how much "The Leader" himself had already perverted Islam in justifying the mass slaughter of sailors and the Council of Guardians, it sickened Mohammed to hear Hosseini speak with such reverence about "The Leader." Instead of expressing these thoughts, which surely would have been a death sentence, Mohammed feigned an air of sympathy.

With obvious regret in his voice, he said, "My Dear Mr. Hosseini, I am sorry to say that the Supreme Leader's aide, Mr. Ansari, told me the Leader is feeling 'under the weather' today. He specifically requested that the briefing be as quick and uncomplicated as possible. I think bringing an extra person into the briefing might make our Revered Leader uncomfortable."

The hope in Hosseini's eyes died, and then returned. Mohammed could see Hosseini was about to press his case with more fervor.

Mohammed quickly cut him off by saying, "I would prefer to give the briefing as planned, Mr. Hosseini, but I promise you this. At the end, I will emphasize how important the security measures have been to the success of the program, and I will suggest to the Leader and his aide that you be summoned to deliver a more detailed briefing on every aspect of security for the Fajr Project when the Leader is feeling better. That way, instead of merely standing quietly besides me today, you will be able to meet with the Leader on your own and give him examples of how the hard work of Security has enabled the success of the project."

Mohammed could see the gleam in Hosseini's eyes grow brighter. Hosseini had merely hoped for a chance to *see* the Supreme Leader in person, now Mr. Saeed was telling him he might have a personal meeting with the Leader. Hosseini took both of Saeed's hands within his own and shook them vigorously, saying, "Bless you for your kindness, Mr. Saeed! *Khoda dar akherat beh shoma ajr bedeh* May God give you your just rewards! Thank you! It would be the greatest honor of my life!"

Disentangling himself from a near-embrace with the enthusiastic Hosseini, Mohammed responded, "Think nothing of it. Your virtuous hard work on Fajr should be rewarded! It is my greatest pleasure to see that you receive what you deserve. After the briefing, I will return to the Paradise Hotel. Would you like to meet me there for breakfast tomorrow morning, then I will tell you how the briefing went and we can return to Qom together?"

Hosseini looked excited at the prospect and replied, "Yes, Mr. Saeed, that sounds wonderful! I look forward to hearing how the Leader reacts to our project. I am sure he will be pleased with our rate of production."

Mohammed, knowing he had temporarily drawn the poison from this serpent, pressed his advantage and suggested with a smile, "Mr. Hosseini, if you will be so kind, I would like to compose myself for a few minutes in peace and review the high points of the Fajr Project in my head before letting Mr. Ansari know that I am ready to brief the Leader. Might I ask you to depart now, that I could have these few moments alone to better prepare myself? I promise, when the time comes for your meeting with The Leader, you will feel a similar need to compose your thoughts."

Blinded again with the shining promise of a personal meeting with the Leader, Hosseini could only nod his wordless gratitude. Mohammed heard him withdraw into the next room where the guards awaited and say to them, proudly, "You may escort me back out, now, but keep my security pass in your files. I think I will be back, soon!"

Mohammed breathed another inward sigh of relief, and then sat back down. The pause was not "To compose his thoughts," but simply to give Hosseini time to get clear of the Leader's residence. Mohammed did not want to bump into Hosseini on the way out. It took an iron discipline to wait, when all he wanted to do was flee.

After an eternity of ten minutes, Mohammed finally started to undo the double-wrapped envelope Hosseini had left with him. Mohammed had experienced a moment of real alarm when Hosseini had grabbed his hand to shake it. He feared what he had been hiding up his sleeve would come tumbling out into Hosseini's hands. As Mohammed reached into the envelope, he palmed the small digital videotape that had been inside the envelope. At the same time, he allowed a near twin of the tape to slide out of his sleeve and into the envelope. He then moved the tape that had originally been in the envelope into his sleeve. He had practiced the movement dozens of times while standing in the bathroom at the Hotel Paradise with the water running and the lights off, on the off chance that there were concealed cameras or microphones in the Paradise.

In outward appearance, the compact digital video tape Mohammed slipped from his sleeve into the envelope was *almost* twin to the one Hosseini had brought, which he had just concealed in his sleeve. The only difference was that tape Mohammed had brought with him in his sleeve had been thoroughly abused, and clearly was in unplayable condition. As the slight-of-hand switch had taken only a second, and had actually been shielded by the envelope itself, Mohammed was virtually certain that the move could not have been detected, even if a guard was monitoring the room via concealed closed-circuit cameras.

Mohammed made a show of withdrawing the damaged tape from the envelope slowly, and then made an expression of anger and disgust in case the room contained microphones. He pressed the button in the wall that Mr. Ansari had said to press when he was ready to brief the Supreme Leader. Mohammed carefully composed his face with what he hoped was a convincing display of embarrassment.

Two minutes later, Mr. Ansari reappeared and fired off a single word, "Ready?"

Mohammed prayed he could pull off this last scene in the drama he and Mohsen had planned. He spoke, refusing to meet Ansari's eye at first, holding out the damaged tape in one hand for Ansari's examination, "Mr. Ansari, as you can see, I have the tape, but it appears to have been damaged in transit. I don't know what is wrong, but it looks as if it may have been run over by an automobile!" Mohammed looked up briefly to gauge Ansari's reaction; he could see a flush of anger start to spread into the man's cheeks.

Mohammed shot Ansari a beseeching look and interjected, "Wait, Wait, Mr. Ansari, this is my responsibility, I think I can make this right! The plastic casing of the tape is damaged, but the magnetic tape itself is probably in good enough shape to play. If you allow me to leave this tape with you here, for obvious security reasons, I will go to an electronics shop at Mirdamad and get a similar tape and a screwdriver. I will come back, take this tape apart, and spool the magnetic tape into an undamaged case. Then I can test it to see if it is playable, and if it is, we can still have the briefing in a few hours. If not, we can have Mr. Hosseini reshoot the tape."

Ansari was not happy about delaying the briefing, but his time spent getting his MBA in America had caused him to appreciate men who not only recognized problems, something Iranians had no problem doing, but also took personal responsibility for the problem and for fixing it, something Iranians did not do nearly as well. To admit a mistake was to lose face, and many Iranians were unwilling to do that. Americans, Ansari acknowledged to himself, tried to find solutions. They did not accept problems as unchangeable realities inflicted by the hands of fate or *Khoda*. He appreciated Saeed for taking responsibility and having a solution, so he replied without rancor over the delay, "Very well, Mr. Saeed, you may leave the damaged tape with me. I will notify Security that you will be returning later today. When you return, we will see if this tape can be salvaged. Please make haste. The Leader has a full day, and would like to get this briefing finished."

With a tone of contrition, Mohammed replied, "Thank you for your understanding, Mr. Ansari. I will do my best to return quickly.

*   *   *

Mohammed had worked on Iran's nuclear weapons program for the same reasons most scientists work on such programs: they present intriguing intellectual challenges. Mohammed also felt that a country with a history as ancient and proud as Persia needed such weapons, so as not to be at a disadvantage on the world stage. When upstarts like the *Pakistanis* had them, could Iran stand aside like a man with no pride and not rectify that imbalance?

Like a man who has conquered a great mountain, Mohammed was proud of all the hurdles he had overcome in the Fajr Project. The fact that he had changed his mind about the worthiness of "The Ayatollahs" to control the fruits of his labor did not mean he was not proud of his achievement. He still thought Iran had a right to the weapons, but after the loss of the Shaheed, Mohammed now knew that he could only put such might into the hands of a government that was free and open, not one ruled by the *shayyads* in robes and turbans.

As he strolled away from the Supreme Leader's residence, bearing in his sleeve video-taped evidence of Iran's covert nuclear weapons program, he savored the irony and enjoyed the fact that soon, as soon as Mohammed Saeed's deception was discovered, Mr. Hosseini and many of the "Bastards in Security" would *indeed* "get what they deserved." That justice was, perhaps, the crowning achievement of his involvement in the Fajr Project.

CHAPTER 35- THE GENERAL, PART III

Leading a vast organization like the IRGC was a burden even on someone with great organizational gifts. Almost every minute of every hour of General Jafari's day was normally occupied with meetings, briefings, phone calls, and decision making. It was not too surprising, then, that a full 18 hours had elapsed from the time Lieutenant Jafari left his message for the General to the time the General remembered he had not checked the messages on the encrypted cell phone he used for sensitive calls. At 5:30 p.m., the workday was already done for most. As the General dialed into his voicemail box, he reflected that power was a mistress that made great demands; rare was the day he left work before 8 p.m.

The General's philosophical musings on the nature of power were interrupted with a shock when he heard Majid's message. That donkey, Majid, had no way of knowing, but the Fajr Project was Iran's covert nuclear weapons program. When the General heard Majid repeat the file number and Fajr code name twice, he knew there was no mistake: the elusive Commander Saeed obviously had a relative somewhere in the highly secretive nuclear program. The General cursed and called the Restricted Personnel File Division, trying to get hold of Major Ashrafi, the man he had personally selected for the post.

Naturally, Ashrafi had already closed the office for the day, and the General did not have Ashrafi's home phone number on file, personnel file matters were not usually emergencies. The General then had to call the headquarters duty officer of the IRGC ground forces battalion which administratively "owned" the Restricted Personnel File office. From that officer he obtained Major Ashrafi's home number. The Major sounded put-out to be receiving a phone call at the dinner hour, until he recognized the General's voice. He meekly obeyed Jafari's orders to go into his office and await the arrival of the General.

*   *   *

When General Jafari arrived at the Restricted Personnel File Office, his mood did not improve when Major Ashrafi brought the General the file he had requested, and Jafari saw that File 87734 Fajr was the file for Mohammed Saeed, who the General knew to be one of the most senior scientists on the Fajr project, and probably the most effective one. Jafari knew he had to track Mohammed Saeed down, and do so immediately.

While the General had not thought to keep Major Ashrafi's number on file, he did have the number of Ali Hosseini, Chief of Security for the Fajr Project, on speed dial on his encrypted cell phone, yet Hosseini did not answer the phone. The General fumed and vowed that Hosseini would pay for that lapse later, when the General had the time to devise a suitable punishment. The General had ordered Hosseini to *always* be available to take the General's calls. Jafari left Hosseini a message.

When Hosseini called back two hours later, babbling some excuse about how his cell phone battery had died, he had forgotten his charger, and he had just returned from buying a new battery and charger at Mirdamad, the General was in no mood to be forgiving.

He cracked out, "Mirdamad, Hosseini, where are you? Are you in Tehran? Why? Why are you not at Qom at Fajr Hqs? And where is Mohammed Saeed?"

All visions of a soon-to-come glorious meeting with the Supreme Leader suddenly gone, Hosseini answered warily, "Sir, General, yes, I am in Tehran, I was planning to head back to Qom tomorrow, with Mohammed Saeed. General, the Supreme Leader requested a status briefing on Fajr. Mohammed Saeed was to deliver that briefing earlier today. The last time I saw him, several hours ago, Mr. Saeed was outside the Supreme Leader's office, preparing for the briefing."

The General replied, "I understand why Saeed is here for the briefing, it is time for the quarterly report. But why are *you* in town? Did you take part in this briefing?"

The possibility that he had made a grave error in preparing a videotape of the Fajr Project without first consulting General

Jafari was finally beginning to dawn on Hosseini. With obvious reluctance, he answered, "General, the Supreme Leader's office requested that a video-tape on the status of Fajr be prepared as a visual aid for briefing the Supreme Leader. Obviously, with something so sensitive, I wanted to hand-carry that video tape myself to insure that it did not fall into the wrong hands."

In a voice devoid of emotion, which was somehow more chilling than the General's frequent outbursts of temper, the General replied, "Obviously, Hosseini, *your* hands *were* the wrong hands. How you could presume to prepare such a tape without checking with me first? I am nearly speechless with your stupidity. But we will deal with that at another time. Where is Mohammed Saeed now, and where is that tape?"

Mustering courage to answer, Hosseini said, "General, Saeed said he was staying at the Hotel Paradise, which is normal procedure. I was headed there myself when I got your message. We had planned to meet for breakfast tomorrow, than drive back to Qom together. The Supreme Leader's office was planning to keep the tape."

General Jafari replied, "When you get to the Paradise, find Mohammed Saeed immediately. Find out where that tape is. Most importantly, do not, under any circumstances, let him leave or talk to anybody. There are some very important questions that I must ask him. Call me the second you find him."

The General switched off the phone. He was tempted to reach into his desk and take one of the Valiums he had in there to calm himself. He knew he was so angry right now that he might order his Qods Force teams to take overly aggressive action somewhere, just to feel like he was accomplishing something.

Instead of taking the pill, he ordered a cup of tea, took several deep breaths, and thought of how much he would savor gaining absolute control of Iran in a year or two when his efforts to consolidate his power were complete. General Jafari had managed to largely calm himself until his encrypted cell-phone rang. It was not, as he expected, Hosseini from the Fajr project. Instead, it was Hamid Ansari, the senior aide to the Supreme Leader.

The General answered gruffly, "Ansari, what do you want?"

The hauteur in Ansari's reply matched the General's. "What I want, General, is for your people to live up to their commitments. Mohammed Saeed of Fajr was supposed to deliver a briefing to the Leader on Fajr. Six hours ago, he said the video tape that Hosseini in Fajr Security dropped off was damaged. He asked for permission to leave the tape with me, to go get parts to fix the damaged tape. He said he would be back soon, but that was over six hours ago. Are your precious Fajr physicists so unreliable that they don't feel it necessary to keep their commitments to the Supreme Leader?"

The General had been intending to call Ansari soon in any case. Jafari thought he might as well use this opportunity to inform Ansari of the shape of things to come; the General had long been looking forward to deflating the windbag, Ansari.

With relish, he said, "Ansari, allow me explain some things to you. When 'The Leader' asked me to help him eliminate the Council of Guardians, *he gave away his power.* If he tries to remove me, or even gainsay me, I will now admit with tearful regret before the country that as a faithful servant of the Supreme Leader, I carried out his plan against the Guardians and the Shaheed, as ordered, but have since come to believe that the Supreme Leader was misguided in his plan and no longer follows the divine wisdom of *Khoda.*"

"Soon, the Expediency Councils will be under my control, as will the Assembly of Experts. "

"You exist now *on my sufferance* alone. Accommodate yourself to this new reality, or you will find out for yourself just how uncomfortable a visit to my special wing at Evin can be."

The more General Jafari spoke, the more he allowed a goading smugness to permeate his words. "I *used* to think you were intelligent, Ansari. But first you went along with the Leader's foolish plan for the Shaheed; did you not see that would undercut the Leader's power base, while enhancing mine? And now you have taken complete leave of your senses, and requested a video be made that holds all the secrets of Fajr, just to make life easier for that old doddering fool!"

Here Ansari broke in, although his voice did not contain the same degree of surety he usually displayed, "General, the idea was not ours, but rather came from Aghazadeh at the AEOI. We wanted the Fajr scientists to come here for a personal briefing. Aghazadeh phoned two days ago, said that would hurt Fajr operations too much, and offered the video-tape as an alternative."

The General resumed as if Ansari had not spoken, or what he had said was not worth noting. "The Leader no longer deserves his position, if he ever did. I am going to send a Security squad and a courier over right now to pick up that damaged tape. You, Ansari, you are going to stop your ceaseless whining, if you and your precious 'Leader' know what is good for you."

The General had a savage grin on his face as terminated the phone call with a stab to the disconnect button.

The brief buoying effect of the call from Ansari was dashed by the call he received from Hosseini twenty minutes later. Clearly afraid now, Hosseini stammered as soon as the General was on the line, "General Jafari, Sir, Saeed is gone! The front desk at the Paradise said he was gone, that he and his wife and daughter had checked out earlier today. I did not even know his wife and child were in Tehran! I asked to see his room, and the manager let me in. It was empty. I searched every square inch, and all that I found was the cellphone that the Fajr Project issued to him, sitting on top of a wardrobe, towards the back, where a maid probably would not find it. Sir, Saeed is gone, and I have no way of knowing where he is or how to get hold of him."

The General knew at that moment that Hosseini would need to be replaced as head of Security at Fajr. What remained to be seen was whether the man had earned an extended stay in the tender care of IRGC Interrogator Jalili before that happened. Hosseini's fate now depended on whether Mohammed Saeed, his brother Mohsen, and this mysterious video tape could be recovered before they caused the General further headaches.

"Hosseini, report to my office immediately. A courier is picking up the tape from the Supreme Leader's office right now. We will view this tape together. Then you can explain, in detail, why you though it unnecessary to discuss making such a tape with me. That is all."

*   *   *

Two hours later, Ali Hosseini was standing in General Jafari's office, swearing that the badly damaged tape the IRGC courier retrieved from Ansari at the Supreme Leader's office was not the mini-DV tape Hosseini had dropped off, and pleading that Hosseini had only been following the Supreme Leader's order. The General ordered one of his aides that was clever with technical things, Lieutenant Rafiqdoost, to take the mangled tape and attempt to repair it. A quarter of an hour later, the Lieutenant reported that he had been able to transfer the intact film spools from the damaged mini-DV tape case into a similar tape casing he had found; the efficient Lieutenant had even brought a Chinese knock-off of a Sony Handycam to play the tape. When the tape started and static filled the screen, he had but one question for Rafiqdoost, "Rafiqdoost, does the static mean the video tape was damaged?"

Rafiqdoost replied with a subdued tone, "No, General. There was nothing wrong with the spools of tape, once I transferred them into a casing that was not broken. The tape spools were not damaged at all. This is simply a blank tape. One that was damaged, or even demagnetized, would not show such perfectly regular static."

The General had heard enough. He pressed a button to summon the ever-present Security squad that waited in a room adjacent to the General's office. As soon as the squad leader entered, room the General pointed at Ali Hosseini and said to the squad leader, "Take him to Jalili at Evin." Jafari considered the whimpering and wailing with which Hosseini greeted this announcement to be most unsuitable for the *former* Chief of the Security at the Fajr Project.

The General ordered Rafiqdoost from the room and indulged himself in a sixty second tirade at the incompetence of Hosseini, his cousin Majid, the Qods Force team in Dubai, and for good measure, Hamid Ansari.

A few minutes later, feeling wrung out, but with his emotional tides but finally calmed, the General knew what he must do. He found it ironic that instead of using Mohammed Saeed to find his brother, Commander Mohsen Saeed, he would now be forced to do the reverse, and use Commander Saeed to track down

Mohammed Saeed and the missing tape. He could not allow Mohammed Saeed's name, or the Fajr Project, to be discussed even as a faint rumor.

Whatever Mohsen Saeed knew or thought he knew about the sinking of the Shaheed, the General was confident he could suppress that knowledge, or at least lay the blame on the dead Rahimi. What he could *not* afford was for word of the Fajr Project to leak out before it had produced enough enriched uranium for at least twenty "pits", or bomb cores, and before the pits had been weaponized and loaded onto extended range Shahab 4 missiles, which could target both Tel Aviv and Moscow with equal ease.

He cursed the necessity that made him pick up a phone and call the officer that handled the IRGC's contact with the media and the Ministry of Islamic Guidance. The General began, "We need to locate Commander Mohsen Saeed."

CHAPTER 36-ARRIVAL

Mohammed flagged a cab five minutes after leaving the Supreme Leader's compound. Despite his fears, he got to Mehrabad International Airport and rendezvoused with Fatameh and Marjan with no problems. The two hour flight passed quickly, and rarely had Mohammed been as happy as when the three deplaned at Kerman, where Mohammed had grown up. Mohammed knew that IRGC Security would eventually be able to track his movements to Kerman, as he, Fatameh, and Marjan had all had to use their real identity documents to get the tickets.

Still, Mohammed hoped that in Kerman, his trail would go cold. As he had grown up in this city, he hoped IRGC Security would assume he had "gone to ground" with friends or relatives. In fact, using some of the money Mr. Hank had given to Mohsen, Mohammed was able to arrange the loan of a car with no traces left behind. Shortly after arriving in Kerman, he and his family were headed south out of town. The 450 kilometer journey down Highways 10/A79 and 11/A79 to Bandar Abbas was blessedly tedious and incident-free. Mohammed held his breathe as they passed the highway patrol station in Baghain, but there were no roadblocks out. Despite a desire bordering on compulsion to drive straight through to Bandar Abbas, he stopped in Sirjaan to visit a teahouse for snacks and to make sure he had enough fuel. And even on the run, the father in him couldn't ignore the need for little Marjan to take a bathroom break.

Although they did not arrive in Bandar Abbas until midnight, long after the *lenj* to Qeshm had shut down, Mohammed had no intention of checking into a hotel. That would have required the display of an identity document, which eventually would have told IRGC Security that he was not in Kerman.

Nor did he want to drive around aimlessly until the regular ferry service to Qeshm resumed at 5:30 a.m.

In planning for this moment, Mohsen's familiarity with the area once again came to the rescue. He had given Mohammed the name and address of a man with a boat who would take passengers from Bandar Abbas to Qeshm at any time, day or night, for the price of $150, US dollars still being highly prized over the unstable Iranian toman. Mohsen explained that since goods were usually smuggled from Qeshm to Bandar Abbas, and not vice-versa, unofficial water taxis going from Bandar Abbas to Qeshm did not receive any official scrutiny.

In fact, Mohsen could have sent Mohammed to a man who would have taken them all to Qeshm for less than half as much, but Mohsen believed the absolute discretion of the man who charged the higher price more than justified the extra cost.

During the ninety minute sea passage, Mohammed savored the salt smell and the rhythmic feel of the Gulf. Unfortunately, little Marjan, never having been in a small boat, only huddled into her mother's arms, terrified at the vast expanse of black Gulf water.

Once in Qeshm, Mohammed's fatigue, not to mention Fatameh's and Marjan's, finally began to show. Marjan started crying the temperamental tears of childish exhaustion and refused to be comforted. She could not understand why they had to wait quietly in a park until after dawn to go to the hotel, nor could Mohammed explain that he did not want to raise the interest of the staff at the Qeshm International Hotel by showing up with his wife and child in the middle of the night, when there were no regular flights or ferries arriving.

Mohammed took comfort in the fact that June nights on the Persian Gulf were not cold enough to require shelter from the elements.

When Mohammed, Fatameh, and Marjan finally made it to the hotel, and up to the suite of "Mr. Aziz Bagheri," Mohammed was too tired to be happy when Mohsen opened the door and ushered them all in. Mohammed allowed Lily to sweep up Fatameh and Marjan and get them settled, while Mohsen pulled Mohammed by the elbow to one of the suite's three TVs, and turned it on via remote control. A photograph of a bearded

Mohsen in an IRGC Navy uniform was being displayed on the Irinn TV newscast.

The announcer was saying, "Dear Viewers, please help us locate Commander Mohsen Saeed. He disappeared somewhere in Tehran after the loss of his ship, the Shaheed. Though a brave man, and a great patriot, we fear the trauma of losing his beloved ship and shipmates may have unhinged his reason. He may be wandering confused and alone, or may have been injured and admitted to a hospital under another name. If you see a man meeting this description, please report him to the local police. Helping Commander Saeed is our duty to the Revolution"

Not surprisingly, Mohammed noted that Mohsen's eyes were shadowed with worry.

He asked Mohsen, "Have you signaled your Mr. Hank with the phone they gave you?"

"I wanted to wait until you and Fatameh arrived."

Mohammed responded, troubled, "You had better do so now and inform him if they cannot get us out soon, it will be too late for all of us."

CHAPTER 37-THE HUNTERS HUNTED

Despite his habit of referring to everyone associated with the theocratic regime in Iran as cockroaches, Salim was surprised to learn that Javid's plan for dealing with the team of men sent to kill him really did involve little more than some supplies commonly used by insect exterminators.

The real problem had been getting the fumigation tent. While there are plenty of insects in the deserts of the United Arab Emirates, fumigation tents were more commonly used in temperate environments, which Dubai in the summer most certainly was not. Still, almost anything can be had in Dubai for a price. Within three days of ordering it, a fumigation tent big enough to cover a small home had arrived.

Javid's stubborn refusal to tell Salim how all this equipment would be employed nearly drove Ghiassi insane with unsatisfied curiosity for the first two days. When Javid had all the necessary gear assembled and finally let Salim in on the details of the plan so that they might practice it, Salim's already high regard for his cousin Javid went up. Salim doubted that he could have come up with a plan so simple, so elegant, and so beautifully lethal as Javid's, yet he also had a few doubts about whether Javid could pull it off.

Nevertheless, as Salim had no better alternative, he was eager to help Javid set the plan in motion. All the players rehearsed Javid's plan, including three of Salim's smuggler captains that he trusted implicitly, because they, too, hated the Ayatollahs with a passion that could not be feigned. When Salim asked one of the Captains, Shahriari, if he minded the fact that they were trying to kill a group of men who were probably either from the IRGC's elite Qods Force, or from the Iranian Ministry of Intelligence and Security, the man only laughed and asked Salim how much Salim was going to charge him for the chance to take part in Javid's plan.

Javid explained to Salim that the key element in planning any sort of military operation was "Simplicity, Cousin Salim, *simplicity*. The simpler something is to execute, the less likely it will go wrong. We really only need to do two things here: draw them into a trap, and then spring it. We want to do those two things with as few steps as possible, and we want the trap to spring closed with the reliability of gravity."

Salim was about to see, first hand, whether Javid was as clever as he thought he was.

The sun had just gone down, and Salim was sitting in a car unobtrusively parked in the lot of the Althayafah Hotel in Dubai. One of his smuggler captains was checked into a room overlooking the parking lot and hotel entrance. Ziyaii was sitting in a chair in the lobby when he switched his cell phone back on for the first time several days. Now they had only to wait for hunters who would be tracking that phone to arrive.

Ziyaii had assured the nervous Salim that there was no chance of Salim failing to spot either an MOIS or Qods Force assassination team.

Javid explained, "They travel in a pack, and subtlety is not their strong point. Going against solo targets, they rely on speed, numbers, and firepower, not stealth."

When a Range Rover with dark tinted windows wheeled into the parking lot twenty minutes later and disgorged several heavily-built men with odd bulges under their clothing, Salim concluded that Ziyaii had been right. Subtlety was not their strong point.

Javid and Salim had purchased several cheap, reliable Motorola "Talk-About" radios, which had an eight kilometer range, far more than would be needed. Now all five players on Javid's team were in touch. Only yesterday had they finally accepted Javid's lessons in radio discipline and learned not to clutter up the airwaves with chatter when they had nothing of importance to say. Both Salim and the captain watching the parking lot crackled out warnings to Javid within two seconds of the men exiting their Range Rover.

As soon as the warning was out of Salim's mouth, the voice of Captain Shahriari squawked out of the hand radio, "Salim, I am starting the all the sprayers now, as planned."

As the team started moving towards the entrance of the hotel, Javid casually strolled out, forty meters from the group of men, one of whom was carrying a bulky piece of electronic equipment, probably the cell-phone tracker. Salim knew this was the moment of truth, when Ziyaii *had* to be convincing. Salim had worried over this part, but Javid had demurred, and insisted this part would be easy,

"These are predators, Salim. Hunters of men. What do predators do when their prey flees? Chase it! It is an automatic reflex, one that does not depend on my acting skills. And the more panic I show as I flee, the more inclined they will be to follow. Once their adrenaline is flowing with the chase, they will *only* worry about catching me, not where I am going!"

Salim watched as Ziyaii gave an alarmed start as he suddenly appeared to notice the group of men, and then quickly ran to another Range Rover, which Salim had paid extra to get parked as close to the entrance of the hotel as possible. Ziyaii managed to get in the Range Rover and screech off in a cloud of tire smoke as the closest of the men ran to within 15 meters of Ziyaii and started to claw under his jacket for something.

Salim thought the very fact that the men were wearing loose jackets in a place where the summertime heat is literally scalding screamed that they were armed; who wears more clothes than absolutely necessary in such weather? Only men with something to hide under their jackets. They ran back to their own Range Rover at top speed to give chase.

Salim heard Ziyaii's excited commentary over the radio he was carrying, "Ha, they follow, Cousin, exactly as planned! Let us see how they enjoy this!" Salim knew the plan was for Ziyaii to get on the nearby freeway northbound, and then cut across the grassy median to head southbound. Ziyaii's plan was to "Show a reckless desire to escape which any man might, if he were running for his life and being chased by a band of armed killers."

Salim planned to follow in a more law-abiding and sedate pace; he had no other part to play now, he only wanted to be close enough to see the grand finale when it happened.

Ziyaii reported he had cut across the median and was speeding south on the freeway and approaching the Al Garhoud Bridge over Dubai Creek with the men in the Range Rover in close pursuit.

One of Salim's captains, who had been following the byplay and was posted on Al Garhoud Bridge as a watcher, cut in excitedly, "I see you Javid. And yes, the team following you is alone, there is no other vehicle following, *Khoda* be praised!"

A short while later, Ziyaii shouted out that he had made the final major turn, a highly illegal left turn that took him across the median again and then across three lanes of oncoming traffic to enter a road opposite the Dubai Grand Hyatt. Javid raced southeast down the road as fast as he could without losing control. After a kilometer, he approached a dockyard and complex of warehouses situated on the northwestern Bank of Dubai Creek, across from Festival City. The warehouse area was quiet; activity wouldn't pick-up until close to midnight, when the baking heat of the day subsided. Javid made sure to slow just enough that the pursuing gang of men could see which turns he took. Javid screeched to a halt in front of one of Salim's warehouses, one whose main loading door had been left open just wide enough to admit a man. Javid fled through the gap inside the warehouse.

A few seconds later, the voice of Captain Shahriari, who was watching the front of the warehouse Javid had entered from the roof of a neighboring warehouse, yelled excitedly "Javid, they are running in behind you, just as planned!"

Salim had been torn about which role to play himself. On the one hand, he deeply wanted to see the trap sprung first hand. On the other hand, he wanted to be present at the hotel to make sure Javid got the initial warning he needed when seconds counted most. Putting Javid's safety ahead of his own pleasure, Salim yielded the more exciting role to Captain Shahriari.

Shahriari had started the insecticide sprayers as soon as Javid had begun to flee, and then moved out of Salim's warehouse to a perch on the opposite warehouse overlooking it.

Just as they had practiced, as soon as the pursuing men entered Salim's warehouse in pursuit of Javid, Shahriari triggered a remote control that Javid had rigged. The simple control activated the electric motor which rolled the warehouse door closed. The walls and doors of the warehouse, made of thin metal as they were, would not hold heavily armed men inside for long. But then, they didn't have to last long, only for twenty seconds or so.

As soon as the warehouse door was closed, Captain Shahriari followed Javid's advice. He dropped both the radio and the remote control and ran away as fast as he could.

Because he was running, Captain Shahriari did not see Javid come flying out of a side door of the warehouse he had just entered, pausing only to slide shut the external deadbolt that would prevent the pursuing men from following him out this exit. Javid, cellphone in hand, ran as fast as he could for about ten seconds. Then he dove inside a little shelter he had constructed of wood and sandbags behind a neighboring warehouse, hit the number "one" on his phone, and then the speed dial button. At the last second, he remembered to open his mouth, and cover his ears with his hand. He didn't want the pressure wave from the explosion to shatter his eardrums.

Salim was still a kilometer away when Javid's trap closed. Salim's fears that he would "miss the action" proved misguided. He noted with astonishment that the roof of his warehouse seemed to levitate into the sky on a pillar of fire. Even here, the shock-wave rocked Salim's car.

Two days ago, Ziyaii had explained it all quite clearly, but Salim had still had his doubts. He now felt a little foolish that he had questioned what Ziyaii might accomplish with a mere forty liters of gasoline, even though Ziyaii had patiently tried to battle Salim's skepticism.

"Yes, yes, it is true, Salim, as you said: Cars leaking gasoline do not really blow up, as in the American movies! They just burn. That is because *liquid* gasoline is not really explosive. What is quite explosive, however, is gasoline *vapor*. It just takes a few liters of vaporized gasoline, after all, to move a vehicle weighing over a ton 100 kilometers in distance, while travelling at 120 kilometers an hour, playing the radio, and running the air conditioning! That should tell you just how much chemical energy is in vaporized gasoline!"

"Do not be thrown off by the small amount of gasoline! I am actually using far more explosive than you think; you just can't see part of it. Most explosives have a fuel and an oxidizer. Gasoline is *just* the fuel, but we need no oxidizer, we can use the oxygen in the air, *if* the gasoline is vaporized to the correct degree, and *if* the air is saturated with enough vapor. That is why we set up the fumigation tent inside your warehouse: by filling the pressurized sprayers with gasoline, then turning them on to spew vapor into the enclosed space of the fumigation tent, we will quickly reach the vapor saturation point. The tent will keep the vaporized gasoline from dispersing, and also keep the smell of gasoline from leaking out of the warehouse and alerting the pursuers. At that point, the air inside the tent will really be a giant fuel-air bomb merely awaiting a detonating spark! Which I will deliver with a signal from my cellphone."

Javid had prattled on and on about how fuel-air explosives were "the poor man's nuclear weapon." He boasted they were used by the Americans to steal the air from the lungs of Taliban soldiers hiding in near-impregnable tunnels in Afghanistan, and by Russians to flatten the entire village of any Chechen grandmother that looked cross-eyed at a Russian soldier.

Salim had remained skeptical.

He should not have. Pulling up to the smoldering wreckage of his warehouse, which had clearly been shattered by an explosive pressure wave, Salim Ghiassi admitted that seeing was believing. He chuckled to himself that he was glad he had bought the warehouse through a series of cut-out corporations. He suspected the Emirati authorities would be looking for the owner.

Salim, Javid, and Captain Shahriari had to wait a few minutes for the heat to subside before pulling out their video cameras.

CHAPTER 38-OPTIONS

As he put down the phone receiver after talking to General Jafari, Ansari cursed himself. He, of all people, should have realized that even if the Supreme Leader's plan to assassinate the Guardians were completely successful, the Leader had undermined his *own* power over General Jafari by co-opting Jafari to help plan and execute the assassination. The General had been acting the part of loyal subordinate for so long that he had fooled not only the Supreme Leader, but Ansari as well.

The General was plainly still trying to make the initial plan work, but Ansari had the feeling that things were slowly falling to pieces, that they were moving beyond the General's control. Ansari believed their inability to locate Commander Saeed or the diver Ziyaii meant a disastrous leak would occur sooner or later.

Ansari knew it would negate the General's advantage if the General was forced to shift to their back-up story and blame the loss of the Shaheed on Captain Rahimi as "an agent of the Zionists." Yet Ansari saw little chance that would happen, not until it was too late for all of them. Since the Shaheed had been sunk, the Supreme Leader had been crowing in public and private about the demonstrations in the streets against the Great Satan, the greatest in decades. Given that apparent resurgence of popular support, the Leader would want to cling to the initial story, particularly as the Leader still foolishly believed General Jafari was a loyal subordinate.

It was time to make exit plans. Ansari could no longer work for an inept Leader or let himself become General Jafari's pawn. And there was no need to. He knew the General might hunt him if he fled, but also considered that with enough wealth at his command, he could foil any assassination squads the General might send. What did Ansari care if he had to spend five million dollars a year on the finest personal security? Given the amount of money he had siphoned from official Iranian coffers, Ansari could spend twice that and never run out, as long as that money was safely out of Iran when he needed it. Time for some phone calls to Bank Sepah and Bank Saderat. Ansari's already sizeable bank accounts in Lichtenstein were about to receive a major infusion of cash, money Ansari had quietly embezzled from the Leader's Bonyad Mostazafan profits.

CHAPTER 39-INBOUND

When he arrived back in Dubai, Joe found a text message from Mohsen waiting. Joe, Cynthia, and Henry Waterston held a hurried conference in Joe's room at the Novotel. Joe was ecstatic that Henry had come through with a boat. Joe had prayed that Henry would know a suitable smuggler, and thankfully, he had.

Henry said, "Bonus points for daring, both of you, but have you seen the latest from Irinn TV? They're looking for this Mohsen of yours high and low. Are you sure it's worth the risk?"

By way of reply, Joe asked, "Does this Captain Shirazi know who we're going to pick up?"

Henry grinned, "Good God, Joe, do you take me for an idiot! Of course not. He knows you're going to pick up several people. Who they are, he doesn't care. As long as you have his fee, that is: $30,000."

Joe grimaced at the figure and said, "Yes, it's worth the risk. And yes, I have the money."

Henry laughed and quipped, "Cheer up, man! It's not as if it's *your* money, is it?"

*　　　*　　　*

Joe and Cynthia boarded Captain Shirazi's decrepit-looking dhow at two in the afternoon. Both were dressed in "skulking clothes": dark athletic shoes, dark blue jeans, and long-sleeve navy blue shirts. Joe had a black knit cap in one pocket and a small tin of waterproof camouflage face paint in the other. He did not dwell on the fact that if push came to shove, if he and Cyn had to flee on foot or go into the water to hide from pursing Iranian forces, it was likely already too late. He had prepared for contingencies as best as he could; best not to over-think things at this point, which would only create needless anxiety.

The ship's crew did not, at first glance, inspire particular confidence. The Captain's rank was evident only from a battered Captain's cap, the rest of his "uniform" consisted of a grimy green T-shirt bearing the words, "Kiss me, I'm Irish," jean shorts, and sandals. In some ways, that was sensible dress for the oppressive heat of the Gulf, but it was not exactly an outfit designed to convey professionalism. Joe guessed the T-shirt was likely one of the millions of surplus T-shirts shipped to various third world nations by American aid agencies and sold for the equivalent of pennies in the local bazaar; he doubted that Captain Shirazi knew what the T-shirt actually said.

To Cynthia, the man looked distinctly unkissable.

The two other crewmembers visible, young Iranian men in their 20s standing fore and aft, were similarly grimy and ragged around the edges. The one at the bow was in a blazing Hawaiian shirt and shorts, the one near the stern lines was also wearing shorts, but he had on a stained powder-blue T shirt with an arrow on front pointing down towards the belly and the words "Baby on Board," above the arrow.

Cynthia had to stifle a major laugh attack at the sight.

The long, narrow wooden boat was coated with an ancient rime of sea-salt near the waterline. Further up the hull, lengthwise cracks in the timber were visible in the dark, tar-stained wood. Set far forward on the hull was a mast about twenty feet high, it had various lines and pulleys coming off it, but sported no sail; no surprise, as this particular trip could not possibly be completed in the allotted time under sail power. The bridge at the stern of the ship was on a platform elevated slightly above the deck of the ship. The bridge consisted of a small freestanding wooden shack, the walls of which were ringed by a series of small windows set at what would approximately be eye-level for a standing man. The platform holding the bridge was entirely enclosed by a waist-high white wooden railing.

Most field operations involving boats used small boats with hulls of sleek fiberglass or resilient reinforced inflated rubber; Cynthia and Joe's doubts about the sea-worthiness of the old dhow must have been evident in the quiet looks they shot each other after stepping on board. As they moved towards the bridge, Captain

Shirazi was observant enough to note the glances and indignantly assured Joe that the boat was much faster and more seaworthy than it looked. Shirazi boasted that with the oversize engines he had retrofitted, the dhow could drop its sails and cruise at 20 knots. Cynthia, with her naval experience, was even more skeptical than Joe. She knew 20 knots was not particularly fast for a modern ship, but dhows weren't built for speed. Cruising at 20 knots was practically flying for a dhow.

Visibility out the bridge's port holes was good, but would have been better if the windows had been cleaned within the last six months. The ship's instruments were rudimentary, consisting of a large metal ship's wheel to turn the rudder, a compass, a radio, and chrome-stemmed throttle controls with red plastic knobs for the boat's engine. Behind the Captain's chair was a small table with a lip running around the edge of it, presumably to keep objects from sliding off the table in heavy seas. The table was piled with partially-furled navigation and tidal charts, held in place with an incongruous matched pair of "I Love Chicago" snow-globes used as paperweights. Joe was constantly amazed when traveling abroad at just how much refuse from America's consumer culture washed up onto foreign shores, the "Kiss Me" and "Baby" T-shirts and snow-globes being three prime examples.

After looking over the bridge in a desultory way, Joe requested that Captain Shirazi show him and Cynthia the smuggling compartments. Both Cynthia and Joe felt better when they saw their cunning design. All the hinges for hidden compartments were mounted on the inside of the hatch and could not be seen by someone outside. The hatches to the concealed compartments swung open smoothly. Joe was impressed that each hatch cover was buttressed by multiple supports. The whole compartment, and particularly the hatch cover, was also thickly padded with sound absorbing material. Joe swung the hatch to the compartment closed and jumped up and down on it. The buttressing supports made the hatch cover as immobile as a stone floor; the hatch seemed as solid as the real hull. The acoustic padding of the compartment deadened any hollow reverberation which could have given the compartments away. When standing inside the compartment, it was clear to Joe that the dhow had a deeper draft than was apparent from casual external inspection; an illusion that would further help confound anyone searching for smuggled goods or people.

Joe dearly hoped that Shirazi was telling the truth about the speed of his dhow, the *Mowj,* or Wave. Just before boarding the Mowj, Joe had sent the Commander a simple text reply. "Arriving the 21st at 3 a.m." Just in case anyone intercepted the texts and became curious, Joe, Cynthia, and the Commander had agreed on a simple code during their planning meeting. Whatever time and date Joe texted, Commander Saeed actually needed to arrive the day before, and three hours before the listed time. This had momentarily confused Saeed, but Joe had simplified it by explaining to the Commander, "Mohsen, whatever the date and time of the meet is, subtract 27 hours and show up then."

Mohsen had obviously been monitoring the phone Joe had given him very closely. Joe had to wait less than five minutes before the text reply came back: "Affirmative, Mr. Rocco, see you soon." "Mr. Rocco" was the agreed-upon code phrase Saeed had included to indicate he was not under hostile control. If the phrase had been missing, Joe would have known that "the bad guys" had Mohsen and that they were laying a trap for Joe and Cynthia. Shortly after receiving Mohsen's reply, the ragged crew of the Mowj cast off its mooring lines, the boat slowly motored down Dubai Creek towards the Persian Gulf.

*   *   *

When they puttered out of Dubai, Cynthia had been eager and excited to get going. She and Joe had passed the first several hours by swapping war stories and practicing getting into the smuggling compartments at a moment's notice; they needed to be able to demonstrate this drill to the Saeeds in case they were boarded by an Iranian patrol on the return leg of the journey. They agreed that Cynthia would take charge of instructing the women and little girl they would be picking up. Being exfiltrated by the CIA in the dead of night was likely to have the Saeed ladies jumpy as it was, but for them to interact directly with Joe, a foreign man they had never met, might make them panic at a time when seconds could count.

When night had fallen and Shirazi announced they were approaching waters patrolled by the Iranian and IRGC Navy,

Cynthia felt a vast mass of tension in her belly. Joe, looking at Cynthia, merely remarked, "Cynthia, if you weren't scared now, you'd be a frigging nutcase. Don't worry about it. We have a good plan, and a decent ship. Plus, if worse comes to worse, Henry slipped me these."

Joe held up a small tin, like one for breath mints. He gingerly pried open the lid to show several capsule shaped objects, which looked to be made of porcelain.

Curious, she asked, "What are they?"

Joe replied briefly, "L pills. We don't issue them anymore, but for situations like this, the Brits like to keep them handy, and I agree."

Cynthia's eyes widened with surprise at the words, "L Pills." The "L" stood for lethal. With a few extremely rare exceptions, the CIA had stopped issuing cyanide capsules to either their staff officers or their "assets" decades ago.

She asked, "No shit?"

Joe nodded, and then explained, "Henry said the casing is made out of non-reactive porcelain. You have to bite down hard to rupture it, but the pill will kill you quick if you do. Here's the trick, though, if you just swallow the pill, it will pass all the way through your GI tract intact. You can, ahhh, 'recover' it later and use it then, if you decide your situation is hopeless. It's completely inert while passing through you, unless you are beaten hard enough to rupture it, that is. Clever, really."

Joe could think of several cases, such as a few years of torture in Evin prison, in which death was a far preferable alternative to continued life. There were persistent rumors in the halls of CIA Hqs that William Buckley, a case officer who had been kidnapped by Hezbollah in Lebanon, had been taken to Evin prison. As Buckley's remains were found in a plastic sack by the side of the road near Beirut airport years after Buckley had died, nobody could really tell what had happened. In any case, Joe was reasonable certain that if he or Cynthia fell into the hands of any Iranian security service, they would both be *screwed*.

Despite the obvious good reasons for issuing L pills to people heading into the dangerous situations, the practice had been abandoned by the CIA long ago, which is why Joe had to borrow some from Henry. Joe remembered from his own training on surviving interrogation that you had to keep some part of your mind free. Knowing you had the ability to kill yourself if it ever got too bad meant your captors never controlled you 100%. Knowing *that* could ironically buoy your hopes and keep you from falling into despair.

During a barbecue some years back, out of curiosity Joe had asked a buddy in the CIA's Directorate of Science and Technology why the DS&T no longer issued L pills. Joe's techie buddy, George, had just laughed and said that CIA lawyers had become convinced that one day a CIA case officer or asset would use an "L pill" as a murder weapon and the CIA would get the blame. Since CIA lawyers stayed safe at home and though the idea of being captured and tortured was farfetched, their bureaucratic ass-covering had removed the ultimate comfort of an L pills from the CIA's arsenal, even though one had never been misused.

Cynthia took one from Joe, wrapped in several layers of Kleenex tissue, and put it in the pocket of her jeans. It made her feel better to know it was there.

Joe said, "Hey, you were in the Navy. How many SEALS do you think have the guts to hop on a boat piloted by a foreign guy they never met before, to head into hostile waters where being captured might mean very bad things? All while being unarmed, and having no hope of "back-up" or rescue if things go wrong? And to do it, no less, based on their judgment of a guy they had spent maybe a grand total of twelve hours with! You have more guts than any ten HQ desk weenies, Cyn; be proud of that."

At Joe's words, Cynthia felt a warm glow, and responded, "Fuckin' A. You're right, Joe, we rock," which she followed with an incongruous giggle.

CHAPTER 40-TIES THAT BIND

Tired as Mohammed was when he, Fatameh, and Marjan finally made it to Mohsen's suite at the Qeshm International, the sight of Mohsen's picture on the TV screen shocked Mohammed back to full wakefulness better than any amount of coffee could have done. After settling Marjan in one of the suite's bedrooms, Mohammed, Marjan, Mohsen, and Lily met for a 'Council of War."

Mohammed went first, asking, "Why do they say you may be lost or confused?"

Mohsen replied, "I think they want everyone looking for me, but cannot explain the real reason. Also, the phrase about 'unhinged reason' may be meant to undermine anything I say about why the Shaheed sank. Of course, this could mean that the searchers have finally realized that I am your brother and that they decided it is the lesser evil to circulate my name to track *you* down."

Lily said, "My husband, *why* they did it is not as important as what effect it may have upon our plans to escape. Is not this 'Mr. Hank' on the way? Do we not then only need to continue to hide for several more hours, which was already our plan?"

Mohammed, tired as he was, immediately saw a problem. "Mohsen, how were we to get to the dock where Mr. Hank is to meet us?"

Mohsen looked startled, "I was going to rent a car with the Bagheri passport. I planned to drive us there near pickup time, and leave it near the site. When we got to Dubai, I had planned to DHL the passport and both sets of car keys to Masoud, the set for his Mercedes which we left in Bandar Abbas, and the set for the car here. He would send someone he trusts to return the vehicles."

Mohammed asked, gently, "And how comfortable do you feel going to rent a car now that your picture has been circulating on TV for the last 12 hours?"

An appalled silence settled over the room. All immediately knew it was too risky to hope that the "Aziz Bagheri" identity would hold up, when almost every person in Iran was on the lookout for Mohsen. Mohsen only hoped none of the front-desk staff remarked upon the resemblance between the missing Mohsen Saeed and hotel guest Aziz Bagheri. Mohsen believed that as his appearance had changed enough to get through Iranian passport control, he was *probably* safe, but he had stayed in the hotel room since his photo appeared on TV to cut down any chances that the hotel staff might make the connection.

As there was a better-than-even chance that Mohammed's trickery with the tape had been discovered and that a covert search was underway for him as well, Mohammed could hardly rent a vehicle in his own name. Logically, neither Lily nor Fatameh could take that risk, either.

For the family to take a taxi in the middle of the night to a remote industrial area, where the dock was located, was to risk having a cab driver report suspicious behavior, particularly if Mohsen was recognized.

Any late-night caravan of two men, two women, and a child trudging the several kilometers on foot to a remote area might draw the attention of any police officer who happened to pass by.

It seemed they were within a few kilometers of the place they needed to be, and had several hours to get there, yet practically speaking, it was as distant as the moon. All options for getting there seemed fraught with unacceptable levels of risk.

Mohsen had always sought Lily's counsel on major decisions. In Iran, women's rights remained far behind men's, but even under the Ayatollahs, Persian women enjoyed far higher status than women did in fundamentalist Sunni countries like Saudi Arabia or Afghanistan. In Iran, women could drive. They were also doctors, lawyers, engineers, journalists, and members of the Majlis, the parliament. Mohsen had met Lily in university, where she had been studying psychology, and Mohsen never had cause to doubt the sharpness of her wits.

Pensively, Lily said, "We know where we need to go, the problem is getting there undetected. I do not see any way around it. We need help from someone we can trust to get to the dock.

Mohammed and Fatameh remained silent. They had nothing to add; they did not dispute Lily's assertion, but neither had any familiarity with either Bandar Abbas or Qeshm. After a minute of silence, Lily produced a name. "Sima. Sima and Asadollah Bushehri. Asadollah swore to me on his soul when little Kiyan was born two years ago that he would do anything to repay me. Mohsen, do you remember Asadollah?"

He remembered Bushehri, of course; they had served together as lieutenants on the missile boat Paykar. Asadollah had been a pleasant enough fellow and Mohsen knew he was a good officer, but their paths had not crossed much since serving together on the Paykar. He knew that Lily and Sima Bushehri, Asadollah's wife, had been very close a few years back and still regularly socialized, but knew of no reason why either Sima or Asadollah would consider themselves in such debt to Lily.

He answered, "Yes, my dear, but why would he make such a promise? And why are you confident he would honor it now?"

Lily had agreed to respect a confidence, and she disliked going back on that, but Fatameh, Mohsen, and Mohammed had to understand why the Bushehris could be counted on. In Iran, matters of birthing were considered to be mysteries that were the province only of women or trained medical professionals. Men did not meddle in such affairs, and women were often tight-lipped about them.

Lily began, "Mohammed, Fatameh, you do not know the Bushehris. I became close to Sima when Mohsen and Asadollah were serving together many years ago. Did you know, Mohsen, that Sima had a second trimester miscarriage when you and Asadollah were serving on the Paykar?"

Mohsen shook his head no in surprise.

Lily continued, "I thought word might have reached you. If you did not hear of that, then you also probably do not know that it was her third miscarriage. Sima fell into a deep depression after she lost that poor baby. Asadollah called me a few weeks later in tears. He knew I was Sima's friend, and did not know how to help her. He said Sima was listless, would not get out of bed, and was crying all the time. He begged me to come over. I agreed, but I could not see her that day. I saw her the next. She was not at all as Asadollah had described her. She was calm, peaceful, she embraced me, and told me how much she loved me. Then she tried to give me something I knew she held very dear, a silk peshmina from her grandmother. That is when I knew..." Lily trailed off, reluctant to go on.

Mental illness was a taboo subject to many in Iran, as it was often considered a mark of shame, not a medical condition to be treated.

Mohsen prompted, "Please continue, Lily, we need to know."

"Sima had made up her mind to kill herself. She fit the profile exactly."

Fatameh gasped, Mohsen and Mohammed exchanged grave looks. The cult of the suicide bomber has obscured the fact that suicide is considered one of the gravest sins of Islam. To those untutored in the complexities of mental illness, even contemplating suicide is a sin. Lily, of course, had a different understanding of it from her psychology training.

"I warned Asadollah what the problem was, that he could not leave her side. He was shocked, he thought her calmness meant she had started to come to terms with the last miscarriage and had started to move on. I contacted some friends who had completed their psychiatric training. We got Sima started on anti-depressants and talk therapy. Within four weeks, the crisis was past. Three years later, she successfully carried Kiyan to term. She has been well ever since. On the day Kiyan was born, Asadollah promised me, if I ever needed anything in his power to give, he would give it."

The room remained silent, until Mohsen said, "Ahh, my dear wife, I always knew I was a fortunate man, truly blessed by *Khoda*, to have married you. Never, until this day, did I understand the depth of that fortune. The great poet Hafiz himself could not express the words in my heart. "

Given the centrality of family life to Iran, nobody had any question that Lily was right. Mohsen, Mohammed, and Fatameh contemplated the magnitude of the service Lily had done, how she had not only averted a great shame and loss for Asadollah, but made possible a recovery that led to the birth of his son. Asadollah's gratitude would outweigh any tenuous loyalty to the *Neza-e Moghaddas,* the Islamic Republic. Fatameh said, with no hesitation in her voice,

"Lily, you should call Asadollah now."

*　　*　　*

A further fifteen minutes of discussion led to the decision that Lily should make the call from a payphone at a different hotel. Mohsen was determined to do anything to avoid creating links between the name Aziz Bagheri and his own, not least because the innocent and uninvolved Bagheri had no idea Commander Saeed was using his passport. Mohsen only hoped that Asadollah's ship was in port and that his duty schedule allowed him to leave Bandar Abbas and come to Qeshm. The four adults pooled their coins to give Lily enough change for repeated calls and she slipped out of the suite with a determined look on her face.

*　　*　　*

Ninety minutes later, as many shops were starting to shut down for the mid-day rest period, Lily returned, with a triumphant look on her face.

She explained, "His ship is in port. He was scheduled to be the watch officer tonight, but was able to switch shifts. I did not explain why I needed him, just that I needed him to help Mohsen."

Lily stopped and chuckled a bit, "He asked if it had anything to do with what they are saying about you on TV, Husband. I think he was trying to find out if you have gone mad, as the news suggests. I told him it was not that, but that it *was* a matter of life or death, and that he had to get out to Qeshm immediately and tell nobody he was coming to see us. I asked him to bring his suitcases. He said he will be on the 3:30 pm *lenj* to

Qeshm. I will meet him at Zeytoon restaurant in Zeytoon Park at 6 p.m. and tell him what we need."

Mohammed, never having traveled to one of the Iran's Free Trade Zones, asked "Suitcases, why should he bring suitcases, Lily?"

Mohsen laughed and explained for her, "Lily was thinking ahead! This is a duty free area. People travel from the mainland to fill their suitcases with cheap goods, which they can take back and sell. If Asadollah has suitcases, he will be only one of dozens on the *lenj* to carry them. He will fit right in. It is the perfect excuse for a short trip to Qeshm."

Mohsen leaned over and kissed her on the lips, and said, "Clever, clever, dear wife."

*   *   *

Four hours later, Lily was off to meet Asadollah. An hour later, she phoned the suite from a payphone near Zeytoon Park. The ringing of the phone made Mohsen jump, Mohammed and Fatameh, who were dozing on the suite's divan, also were jarred awake.

She said, "He's here. He's puzzled about what we want, but he has agreed to do it. I gave him the last of Mr. Hank's money; he said 700 dollars should be more than enough. He knows to come to the side entrance at 11p.m."

Lily returned to the suite an hour later. She was greeted with applause from Mohsen, Mohammed, and Fatameh. Lily laughed and swept into a bow like an actor receiving an encore.

Mohsen asked, "Did Asadollah get the vehicle? How? Where is he?" One of the consequences of low credit card usage in Iran is that it can be difficult to get a vehicle on short notice. At this hour, most rental car locations would be closed.

Lily answered with pride, "He got one of the taxi drivers from the central square to loan a van. Asadollah is eating a late dinner now. He wanted to know what was going on, but I told him you would explain further when he came to get us, Mohsen. Of course, the taxi driver *was* suspicious. He wanted to know why was Asadollah willing to pay 600 dollars for personal use of the van when it could be chartered all day, driver included, for a less than 100 dollars."

Lily stopped, grinning.

Mohammed was force to asked, "And what happened, how did Asadollah convince the taxi man?"

Lily continued, "I suggested to Asadollah that he show the taxi man his Navy ID, tell the man that he was escorting some Saudi Naval officers and their wives on sightseeing tour as a professional courtesy, and that it was a "pardeh" matter."

No further explanation was needed. Saudis rigidly follow the tradition of "purdah", or "pardeh" as Iranians call it. Pardeh segregates the two sexes, and in particular shields women from contact with strange men. Many in Iran followed "pardeh" to a lesser extent, but most Iranians consider Saudis, who often declare no stranger should *ever* see a Saudi woman, even one fully covered in a burkah, to be fanatics on the issue.

While Saudis are far from beloved by Iranians, few Iranian hesitate to take advantage of the rigidity of Saudi beliefs on "purdah", or any other matter, if accommodating the whims of a Saudi meant a fat profit. Clearly, the taxi driver had no problem making such an accommodation, once Asadollah provided a plausible reason why he needed to borrow the van itself, and could not simply hire the van and driver as a unit. Saudis would not want a strange taxi driver to see their wives, and Saudis were known for throwing their money around. It was the perfect excuse.

Now they had only to wait.

*   *   *

Mohsen was glad the van had tinted windows. The tinted windows made it unlikely that any passing pedestrian or motorist would recognize Mohsen's face as they drove by, no matter how broadly his picture had been circulated.

Asadollah had a bemused look on his face as the Saeeds ghosted out the side entrance of the International and clambered into the waiting van. Mohsen rode on the bench seat directly behind Asadollah, who was behind the wheel.

Bushehri glanced over his shoulder and said, "Mohsen, I am sorry for your loss. The Shaheed was a fine ship; Akhlagi was a fine Captain. I am glad you survived, but tell me, my friend, what am I doing here? Why is your photograph on the TV? You do not look as if you have 'lost your reason.' What is going on? Why are they searching for you?"

Mohsen had known Bushehri was going to ask these questions, how could he not, when he was dragged away from his home with a mysterious phone call to play taxi for a man who the whole country was looking for? Best to avoid giving answers, even if it involved some hints that could be construed as rude.

He answered, "Asadollah, thank you for helping us in our time of need. Lily told me why she was so certain you would help. Like Sima's situation years ago, sometimes things are best left unsaid. In fact, Lily said we could count on you, because she knew you could be trusted to keep your silence, as she can."

Mohsen knew Asadollah would not want Sima's depression to be a topic of discussion, he hoped Bushehri took the hint that prying into Mohsen's current situation was equally unwelcome.

Commander Saeed continued, "In a week or two, all will be clear to you. In the meantime, I advise you to tell *absolutely nobody* that you saw us here, not even Sima. I tell you this for your own safety. There is no reason anyone should connect my name to yours, and that is best for you, believe me. You need only drive us where we must go, and tell none you have done so. If you can do that, you will have more than repaid Lily's long-ago kindness."

Asadollah Bushehri digested that for a moment as the van puttered in the direction of the coastal highway. On the one hand, Asadollah reasoned to himself, Mohsen is obviously not "unhinged." He *is* probably in some sort of trouble, trouble which I do not want to be involved in. On the other hand, in some ways I owe my little Kiyan's very existence to Lily. To repay that debt, I would do much more than drive some friends where they need to go and be quiet about it.

Bushehri answered, "As you like, Mohsen. Unsatisfied curiosity is a small enough price to pay, all things considered. Where shall I take you, my friend?"

Mohsen gave Bushehri directions to the Bonyad Mostazafan's dock.

They arrived near the Bonyad's dock twenty minutes later. By Mohammed's watch, they still had nearly forty minutes before "Mr. Hank and Ms. Sam" were scheduled to arrive. Mohsen directed Asadollah to park the van, lights off, behind a factory across from the entrance road which lead to the dock. Lily occupied Asadollah with small talk about Sima and Kiyan.

At ten minutes to midnight, Mohsen asked Asadollah to head towards the dock, keeping the van's lights off. The Bonyad's dock was so large that it was paved along its entire length, and even had a circular vehicle turn-around point near the end. It was five minutes slow drive before they arrived at the turnaround point. The Saeeds disembarked. Lily reached up and kissed Asadollah on the cheek in thanks.

Mohsen shook Bushehri's hand and said, "Asadollah, obviously, we are making a journey. I cannot tell you where we are going, nor why, but, as I said, I believe you will soon understand I had good reasons for acting as I have, and for asking you to remain silent. May *Khoda* watch over Sima and Kiyan, may he bless you for the help you have give us this night."

Mohsen took both Asadollah's hands in his and clasped them in a firm handshake. Asadollah started to reenter the van when Mohsen said, "Asadollah, I have a question about IRGC patrols for tonight. Also, you should know one more thing. It's about who owns this dock. "

CHAPTER 41-FROM PHARAOH'S BONDAGE

As they approached Iran's territorial waters, Joe and Cynthia donned Gen V night vision goggles, another loan from 'Good ol'Henry,' and scanned the horizon for patrol boats. Joe could clearly see a haze of light pollution from Qeshm City off to the south-east. When they were about 500 meters from the GPS waypoint that marked the dock where Mohsen had said he would be waiting, Captain Shirazi chopped his throttles back to a jogging pace. Joe checked his watch and saw that it was three minutes after midnight. He had to hand it to Shirazi; smuggler or not, the Captain knew his business and delivered them on time.

At two hundred meters out, Joe pointed towards the shore and whispered "There, Cyn, switch your goggs to infrared."

Cynthia switched over, and could see immediately what Joe was talking about. Set against the cooler background, Cynthia could just make out the shapes of five heat-radiating figures standing on a dock. There were two larger adults, two smaller adults, and a fifth that was much smaller.

Trying to keep her voice nonchalant, she said, "Unless IRGC Security has started hiring midgets, that's a kid. We found our lost lambs, I think." Joe loaned his goggles to Captain Shirazi, so he could make towards the group which was still invisible to the naked eye.

Five minutes later, after Shirazi had jockeyed his boat up to the dock, and held it in place with deft engine work, Joe jumped onto the dock, and reflected in a flash that despite a career spent working against theocratic Iran, this was the first time he had ever set foot on Iranian territory. On the one hand, he felt an incredible professional satisfaction. Most CIA officers never set foot in "hard target countries." But Joe had many Iranian friends, and he regretted that sneaking in like this was the only way he would be able to visit Iran until the current regime was gone.

When he saw they were all looking at him expectantly, he realized with a moment of embarrassment that he needed to stop daydreaming and get moving. These people were understandably worried and wanted to get the hell out! With a sweeping gesture, he pointed towards the Mowj, and said to a relieved-looking Commander Mohsen Saeed in Farsi, "Commander, Mohammed, Ladies, and my dear girl, your taxi awaits."

*   *   *

Nearly a kilometer away, Asadollah Bushehri was approaching the exit from the paved road that led to the dock. He turned left onto the coastal highway, and quickly realized he had forgotten to turn the van's headlights back on. At the same instant he flipped on the headlights, he saw a car rounding the bend several hundred meters ahead, coming up the coastal highway from the direction of Qeshm. As the car flash passed him, Bushiri saw that it was a police car. The police car immediately began a U-turn. Five seconds later, it was coming up behind Bushehri, lights flashing.

Asadollah honked his horn twice, and then pulled over.

*   *   *

Sound carries clearly for long distances over the water. The two distinct honks of a car horn were easy to hear.

Joe was surprised to see Mohsen suddenly look worried again and say, "Mr. Hank, we *must* go immediately."

It was faster to board first, and explain later, so they did. Within ten seconds, Captain Shirazi was pulling away from the dock.

Joe asked urgently, "Commander, what is it? Did those honks mean something?"

Mohsen replied intensely, "Mr. Hank, a friend dropped us off. I asked him to drive near the entrance to the dock, which is a kilometer away, and wait for ten minutes. This area is normally very quiet. He was to give two honks if anyone approached."

Joe asked, "Are you telling me the police are coming, or people from the Bonyad?"

Mohsen replied, "Mr. Hank, I don't know who it is, or why he honked. Simply that someone is near."

Joe said, "Stay right here. I don't want Captain Shirazi to see your face, at least not yet."

Two minutes later, Mohsen could feel the dhow start to move at a rate of speed that, considering the wooden-hulled ship looked like it might simply *dissolve* from age, was quite remarkable.

*   *   *

Qeshm Constable 3rd Grade Parviz Anvari was reveling in the freedom. His first night alone! Tonight, there would be no patronizing attitude from his trainer, Sergeant Izadi. Trainee Constable Anvari felt proud that the shift commander, Detective Musavi, had trusted Anvari to patrol Qeshm by himself while Sergeant Izadi was home sick.

In reality, Detective Musavi had no confidence *whatsoever* in Anvari's skills as a police officer. But Musavi had no intention of babysitting the annoying, inexperienced and naïve Anvari all night. That was Izadi's job. Since Izadi was home sick, Musavi needed a task to occupy Anvari. Otherwise, Anvari would spend the whole shift peppering the veteran detective with pointless questions, like a three year old always asking, "But Papa why, why, why?"

Detective Musavi reasoned that as there was minimal crime in the area, Anvari could hardly get into trouble if he were out driving around. Sending the neophyte Constable out to "look for crime" would keep Anvari out of Musavi's hair. Maybe Anvari could issue some parking citations.

The intrepid Constable Anvari had quickly become disappointed at the lack of activity in Qeshm. Not only was there no crime to stop, he hardly saw a soul at all. Which is why he found himself cruising up the coast road toward the industrial area that was likely to be, if anything, even less active than downtown Qeshm at this time of night?

When he saw a pair of headlights suddenly pop on, Anvari thought, "Ahh…this fellow was driving with his lights off! At this time of night? In this area? I must see what he is about!"

*   *   *

When the police radio crackled to life in the police substation that served the northern part of Qeshm City, Detective Musavi mused philosophically that it had probably been too much to hope for, that Anvari would keep himself out of trouble for the whole shift.

The excited youngster said, "Detective Musavi, I have made a traffic stop! The man was on the coast road. I think he was up to something suspicious. He won't tell me what he was doing here."

Detective Musavi unconsciously grimaced, then picked up the microphone of his radio, looked at a map, and asked, "Where are you, *exactly*? And what did this man do that was suspicious?"

Musavi listed to Anvari's excited response, looking at a map. He knew exactly where Anvari was. He turned to Constable 1st Grade Rabani, the only other officer on duty. He pointed to the area on the map, and said, "Rabani, Anvari's right here. Go find our young idiot and see what is going on. If this is what I think it is, I don't want it broadcast on the radio."

Musavi got back on the radio, and said, "Anvari, stay where you are. Return to your vehicle. Do nothing. I'm sending Rabani out there."

*   *   *

Sending Rabani as backup! They must think something suspicious was going on, too!

Ten minutes later, Rabani arrived and questioned Anvari about the "suspicious activity" of the car he pulled over. Rabani then gave Anvari a look of astonishment.

He said to Anvari, "Wait here," and then approached the van pulled over at the side of the road.

*   *   *

Asadollah Bushehri's nervousness grew when he saw a second police car arrive. When he saw the scowling visage of the newly arrived constable approaching in the side mirror, he swallowed and hoped Mohsen's information was correct.

Suddenly, the police officer was at the driver's side window. Asadollah noted with some relief that the Constable was no longer scowling, in fact, he looked rather contrite. Bushehri rolled down the window.

Without preamble, the Constable pointed back towards the dock that Bushehri had just left and asked,

"Sir, you just came from that dock over there, did you?"

Bushehri blinked nervously, hoped what Mohsen had told him right before they parted was true, and said, "Yes, Constable, that is correct."

Bushehri saw a sheepish grin steal over the constables face as he said, "Very well, sir. Sorry for any inconvenience. We have a trainee constable on the loose; he does not know the procedures. I'll see that it doesn't happen again, Sir."

Anvari was surprised to see the vehicle he had detained pulling away, and see the scowling Rabani approach his car, yank open the door, and get in.

Rabani cocked a fist, drew back, and hit Anvari in the arm as hard as he could.

"Ahhk!" yelped the surprised Anvari. "Why did you hit me?"

Rabani only shook his head in disgust, "You idiot, that is the Bonyad Mostazafan's dock! Has Sergeant Izadi told you *nothing*? We don't interfere with that dock! For all practical purposes, it doesn't exist. *If* it is on fire, you can call the fire department, but otherwise, it does not exist, nor do *you* interfere with anyone entering or exiting it. If you delay one of the Bonyad's shipments, the *least* that will happen is that they will take the cost of the delay out of your pay. Do that again, and the Chief Constable will see to it that you clean the station toilets for the rest of your life."

Anvari was deeply offended. Yes, he was a trainee, but he should not have been struck! Did Rabani not know who he was, or more importantly, who Anvari's *uncle* was? As soon as they returned to the police substation, he would call his uncle, Iranian Navy Admiral Sayyari, and report the whole affair.

*   *   *

Joe started to calm down a bit when he returned to Mohsen. The Commander looked calmer, and admitted, "Mr. Hank, I'm sorry. I overreacted a bit. It was just to hear the horn right as you arrived startled me. As I said, the honks just meant someone was coming or was nearby. If it was someone from the Bonyad, the worst that might have happened was that they would have asked us for some money for using the dock, but they would not care otherwise. And the police, well, they know better. It is the Bonyad's dock, that's why I chose it. It's untouchable by the police."

Joe could hardly blame the man for a few jitters.

He laughed and said, "No harm done. Let's go below, there's something we need to show you.

*   *   *

Constable Anvari's call to his uncle, Admiral Sayyari, had been brief. Anvari had gotten no further than saying he intercepted a man coming off the Bonyad Mostazafan's dock near Qeshm when the Admiral exploded,

"*Khoda* give me patience! Nephew, why do you persist in being an imbecile! Is it not enough that I got you the position as a constable, despite your failing police training on three separate occasions! There are some things even an Admiral cannot do lightly, and interfering with the Bonyad is one of those things! And it is one in the morning! Do not call me again unless it is an *emergency*. If you were to spontaneously catch fire, *that* would be an emergency. On second thought, if you catch fire, don't call me then, either."

Click.

The Admiral rolled over and attempted to go back to sleep. He could not. Anvari was undoubtedly a fool, a *nafham*, but he did report something out of the ordinary. As far as the Admiral knew, there was no activity scheduled for the Bonyad's dock on Qeshm that evening. Word of the Bonyad's smuggling operations informally filtered-up the Navy and IRGC Navy grapevine to prevent any interference with Bonyad activities. The Admiral would normally not care what was going on at the Bonyad's dock, but that fool Lieutenant Jafari had been trumpeting throughout the command center with ever increasing stridency, that anything, anything whatsoever, that was unusual in and around Bandar Abbas, and in the general neighborhood of the sinking of the Shaheed, i.e. Qeshm Island, should be reported immediately as part of the investigation of the Shaheed. Little as Admiral Sayyari cared for Jafari, a snake masquerading as an IRGC Lieutenant, he did not want any failure to report something unusual to place the Iranian Navy in an even worse position than it already was in vis-a-vis their rivalry with the IRGC Navy. Sayyari was sure it was nothing; Anvari was an over-eager idiot, after all. But, Sayyari reasoned, Why not tell Jafari and let him chase after shadows to his heart's content? Then none could say the Regular Navy had not cooperated with the IRGC Navy's investigation.

He picked up the phone and dialed the Iranian Navy command center at Bandar Abbas, where Jafari has set up the task force for his so-called "investigation."

*   *   *

Lieutenant Jafari, who just a few days ago had been so smug with his own cleverness and sense of inevitable victory, was now a haunted wreck. He had not yet managed to locate the targets he had initially sought, the divers Ziyaii and Erfan, and even more importantly, Mohsen and Mohammed Saeed. Hindsight conclusively demonstrated, from the damage the elusive Ziyaii had wreaked on the Qods force team sent to kill him, that Jafari had underestimated the young EOD diver, a mistake which let Ziyaii slip away to Dubai and set a lethal ambush for his pursuers. A second Qods force team sent to Dubai found no trace of the diver, only the still-smoldering wreckage at a warehouse leased through untraceable cutouts.

Knowing the temperament of his cousin, the Lieutenant suspected he had less than 48 hours left to live, unless he could report substantial progress in tracking down the targets and plugging the leaks on the Shaheed affair.

He had no solid leads, and no prospects. Fate, extraordinarily generous until recently, had suddenly turned against him.

When Admiral Sayyari called and said a local police officer had noticed someone coming off the Bonyad's docks and reported it to the Navy, the call found Jafari sitting behind a desk in the small private office he had commandeered for the investigation. In front of him was a battered tea-cup with the Iranian Navy logo on it, half full of an amber liquid. The bottle of whiskey hidden in the desk drawer, which Jafari had cracked the seal on three hours ago, was now half-empty.

Jafari grasped at Sayyari's information like a life-line thrown to a drowning man, which, metaphorically speaking, is exactly what Jafari was. He pressed Sayyari for details. Sayyari responded brusquely, his loathing for Jafari clear in his reply, "Lieutenant, the only information I have is that someone came off the Bonyad's dock. We do not know who he was, or what he was doing there. Per standard procedure, as he was coming off the Bonyad's dock, he was not questioned about his business on the dock. He headed in the direction of Qeshm City about an hour ago. I have no further details for you."

Sayyari carefully avoided mentioning that the police constable in question was his own foolish nephew, or that he could probably get more details of the man's appearance and vehicle from that nephew, if he so chose. If Jafari had been someone he respected, he would have done what he could to help him. Since Sayyari would rather see Jafari fail, hopefully in a way that made the Lieutenants spectacular incompetence manifest for all to see, the Admiral simply hung up.

Nobody knew the schedule of the smuggling activities of the Bonyad Mostazafan better than Lieutenant Jafari. He often used the Bonyad to procure sensitive items and weapons in support of Iranian "black ops," not to mention liquor, electronics, proscribed fashions, black market satellite dishes; the list was practically endless. As a logistics officer at Iran's biggest naval base, Jafari got a cut of most of the action. He knew beyond a shadow of doubt there was no Bonyad activity scheduled for the dock that night. Which meant some sort of unauthorized smuggling was going on.

He had no way of knowing how, if at all, the unscheduled activity related to the Shaheed or the missing Saeed brothers, but intuition, or perhaps sublimated terror, told him it did. Suddenly he was gripped with nauseating certainty that struck like a bolt of lightning. Ziyaii was a sailor. Commander Saeed was a sailor. Of course the water would be their chosen method to flee the country; it was what they knew best! And practically speaking, he had no other leads to chase. In the absence of any real progress in finding his targets, the *appearance* of frenetic activity, the simulation of progress, might buy him a reprieve from the looming wrath of the General.

The Lieutenant's judgment had been poor, at best, throughout the course of the so-called "investigation" into the loss of the Shaheed, but even a broken clock is right twice a day. Perhaps alcohol-fueled desperation drove him to the intuitive leap, nevertheless, for the first time in days, Jafari guessed correctly. The activity at the Bonyad dock had everything to do with the Shaheed and the Saeed brothers. Fate had granted him one last chance to save himself, if he had the wit to take advantage of it.

By virtue of the extensive authority delegated to him by the General to find the Saeed brothers and the two missing divers at any cost, Jafari was in the curious position of having considerable naval might at his beck and call, while having precisely zero experience in commanding such a deployment. Thirty seconds after getting call from Sayyari, Jafari was in the commo room of the command center, giving orders that he wanted every vessel in the Persian Gulf that appeared outbound from Iranian shores to be boarded and searched from stem to stern by IRGC Navy fastboats. Having exercised his temporary authority, he retreated to his precious teacup in the little office in the command center, feeling better than he had in days to be taking *some* kind of action. He gulped down the rest of the whiskey in the cup, and then returned to the command center commo room to listen to reports of the IRGC boat crews.

Jafari, being a naval officer in name only, had only the haziest notion of naval strategy; he had never received any kind of tactical training in ship-handling, weapons systems performance, or other skills crucial to a real fighting sailor. He rarely went out on ships that were under weigh; his substantive conversations with real sailors were limited to talking to ships' supply officers to figure out how to pad their requisitions and line his own pockets.

Perhaps more important than his lack of command experience was the Lieutenant's lack of imagination. It never occurred to him that coming on the heels of the loss of the Shaheed, and given wild rumors of Iranian retaliation, a sudden and unannounced deployment of IRGC Naval fastboats under cover of darkness might appear very provocative to the USS Abraham Lincoln Carrier Strike Group, currently approaching the Straits of Hormuz in the Persian Gulf.

CHAPTER 42-ARGUS IS WATCHING

Aviation Systems Warfare Operator Sondra Begley's jaw momentarily dropped as she looked with astonishment at her screen. Quickly recovering her composure, she took the standard corrective action for a malfunctioning piece of equipment: she slammed her fist against the side of her radar console, which was currently tracking surface ship contacts in the Persian Gulf.

The PA-8 Boeing aircraft in which Begley flew, commissioned into naval service a few months earlier, was the replacement for the Navy's venerable P-3 Orion fleet, although many P-3s remained in service. The new radar-bird in which Begley rode had bells and whistles which made P-3 crews turn green with envy. Riding in a P-8A felt like riding in a comfy passenger jet. Riding in a P-3 was like was like riding in the slow, noisy, bumpy, prop-driven commuter aircraft of the kind that typically fed small cities like Idaho Falls, Idaho. In fact, the comfy blue captain's chair in which Begley sat would be greedily coveted by most commercial airline passengers…until they noticed the five-point restraining harness which served in place of a simple lap belt. The serious restraint made one instinctively aware that this aircraft that would fly in even the worst weather and might be called upon to take violent evasive maneuvers if shooting started. Begley was so used to the harness she no longer noticed it; she still reveled in the fact that the interior was quiet enough that she could talk to the crew member sitting next to her like a normal person, without screaming, and without the bulky headset and mike rig necessary on the P-3.

Although the Navy designated their new radar bird "The Poseidon," the aircraft commander of this particular swept-wing 737, Lieutenant Commander George "Loopy" Thomas, had decided he preferred the imagery of the name Argus, the hundred-eyed monster of Greek mythology, a demigod known as "All-Seeing." After all, Thomas reasoned, did not his plane give near god-like omniscience of what was going on in the battle space? Couldn't the AN/APY 10 radar at which Begley sat track an astounding 256 surface contacts at once, just to give one example of its prowess? After Thomas explained his theory about how the designation Argus was a much more fitting nom-de-guerre for the P-8A, the CAG, or Commander, Air Group, Captain George "X-Ray" Gregory, bowed to Thomas' seemingly inexorable logic and directed all P-8As attached to the USS Abraham Lincoln Carrier Strike Group, currently the core of the US Fifth Fleet, to use the Argus call sign. Thomas' bird, since he came up with the idea, earned the call-sign "Argus-One."

Commander Thomas was infamous in the naval aviation community for his quirks; the call-sign "Loopy" had been hung on him by colleagues in his first squadron. But whatever his personal oddities, the general consensus of people who served with "Loopy" Thomas was that he was one determined son of a bitch. He was hardly the kind to stop with a mere *redesignation* of his aircraft; he was just warming up.

Most combat aircraft are painted with dull, radar-absorbent paint to minimize chances of radar detection, including the P-8A. Maybe for fighters and other creatures of stealth, that made sense, but not for the P-8A, in Thomas' view. The Lieutenant Commander had a keen appreciation for the fact that whenever the P-8A went into active mode, i.e. during a combat engagement, the AN/APY 10 radar put out so much electromagnetic energy that it looked like a supernova on the screen of any hostile radar screen, and there was no way a little radar-absorbent paint was going to change that. So after getting Captain Gregory to agree to the new designation, Thomas pressed his advantage and further argued to the Abe Lincoln's CAG that any modification to the paint scheme would have exactly zero impact on Argus-One's combat survivability, which depended on the Argus' electronic countermeasures, their onboard missiles, and luck. Thomas won permission from Gregory to revive the proud tradition of WW II bombers, when air-crews personalized their aircraft with a name, a motto, and a picture. Out of his own pocket, Thomas paid one of the more artistically talented master machinist's mates from the Lincoln to paint an eight foot high full-color image of a ghastly, hundred-eyed monster with horrific fangs onto each side of Argus-

One's cockpit, a picture underlined with the motto "Argus is Watching."

"Loopy" Thomas would probably have been disappointed to learn that Captain Gregory's decision to allow a non-regulation modification had little to do with the persuasiveness of Loopy's arguments. Like Thomas, "X-Ray" Gregory had always loved the logos on the old bombers, and when he had been a fighter pilot herding his own "Super-Hornet" through the sky, he always wished he could have personalized his own fighter the same way. Now that he was in a position as CAG to bend the rules; he did. Yes, not using the radar-absorbent paint marginally increased the risk to Argus One, but a wise commander knows that the little things, like a picture and a motto, have intangible but real effects on the esprit-de-corps that is that heart of any effective military unit. So he allowed Thomas his hundred-eyed monster.

Tonight, both Thomas and Gregory would get to see first-hand whether the moniker "All-Seeing Argus" was an idle conceit.

When Begley's time-tested cure for faulty radar consoles, namely, whanging the hell out of the console until it unglitched, failed to change the information it was conveying, she started to get excited. Clumps of little dots told her that at least 50 small surface craft were suddenly sortieing from various IRGC naval bases. At least two thirds of the new contacts were heading in the general direction of the patrolling Lincoln Strike Group, whose first ships were just starting to transit from the Gulf of Oman to the Persian Gulf by threading their way through the pincer point of the Straits of Hormuz, one of the narrowest points of the Persian Gulf, and the place where the Strike Group would be most vulnerable to missile or ship attack from Iran.

Begley's training immediately kicked in and she followed protocol by notifying Chief Petty Officer Daniels, in charge of aircraft communications, of what her screen was telling her. Daniels radio console came to life as he verified that Argus One's radar feed was being piped down in an encrypted stream to all the Combat Information Center, or CIC, of every ship in the Abe Lincoln Strike Group.

While Daniels was verifying that all the CICs were getting clear signals and could see what Argus-One was seeing, Begley's dismay was mounting as she kept her eyes glued to the console before her. She whispered, "Fuckity, fuck, fuck," under her breath, an exclamation none of her crewmates could hear above the muted purr of the 737's two jet engines. She momentarily reflected that her mother would reprove her for such language. On the other hand, her mother had never seen what might be the opening phases of the biggest ship-to-ship naval battle since the legendary Leyte Gulf in WWII, a bloody affair that had driven the final coffin nail into the ambitions of the Imperial Japanese Navy.

Until transitioning to the P-8A a month ago, Begley had served on a P-3. Unlike the P-3, P-8As operate fairly independently, as they don't fly off carriers, but the 5th Fleet was a special case. The high-threat environment in the Persian Gulf meant that Argus-One had to operate in much closer proximity to the Carrier Strike Group it was protecting than P-8As normally would, which fostered a close sense of connection to the ships Argus-One was watching over. Any possible threat against the ships of the Abe Lincoln CSG felt to Begley, on a visceral level, like an existential threat to her own home and family.

She flipped the intercom switch to "Loopy" Thomas at the stick of Argus-One and said, "Skipper, Begley. Be advised that I'm tracking fifty, that is five-zero, surface contacts leaving Al Farsiyah, Sirri, Abu Musa, and Larak IRGC naval bases and fanning out through the Persian Gulf. Their high rate of speed suggests they are "Boghammer" speedboats. At least 30 of the surface contacts appear to be moving in the general direction of the Lincoln CSG's projected path through the Straits. Iranian shore-base radar installations are also lighting up like Charismas trees. No evidence of hostile aircraft or missile activity, but the radars *are* active, again, the radars are active. As of right now, none are in fire-control mode. "

When in fire control mode, a precursor to missile launch, radars admitted an energy pulse that was stronger, faster, and narrower than normal, making them readily distinguishable from normal scanning. But since the transition time from "scanning" to "fire control mode" and finally "launch" could be well under a minute, the fact that the radars weren't in fire control mode only meant that shooting was probably unlikely in the next 20 seconds, not that it wasn't coming.

Still, those seconds could be the difference between life and death; Missile Technology Control Regime agreements to the contrary, Russia had long ago supplied Iran with both "Yahkonts" and "Sunburn" cruise missiles, both of which boasted a speed of Mach 2.5, stealth technology, and final-phase evasive maneuver capability, not to mention the ability to carry a nuclear warhead. In other words, these particular "vampires," as cruise missiles were often called informally, were ship-killers extraordinaire. In fact, so tricky were the Russian-built vampires that it was anyone's guess as to whether the "SEA-RAM" Missile system, which had replaced the Phalanx 20 MM Gatling gun as the US Navy's primary defense against cruise missiles, would actually work against the Russian ship-killers.

"SEA-RAM" never been tested in combat action actions either the Yahkonts or Sunburn.

Loopy inquired on the intercom, "Begley, any movement of Iranian Regular Navy forces?"

"Negative, Skipper. Not at this time. The ship signatures and locations I'm tracking are all consistent with the smaller IRGC craft. No capital ships."

"Keep me posted if anything changes, Begley."

"Aye, aye, sir."

*   *   *

At first, it had been literally smooth sailing. Cynthia had made a game of practicing scrambling into the smuggling compartments and nobody had balked at the practice; the little girl had even loosened up enough to giggle and enjoy herself. Soon, the whole group was adept at diving into the smelly compartments in less than ten seconds and pulling the hatches closed behind them.

Sailor to the core, Mohsen remarked in passing that it took shipwrights of extraordinary skill to fit smuggling compartments into an old ship and have the new wood appear to have the same rough texture, age, and deep brown color as the rest of the bulkheads of the old dhow. Joe had not considered that before, but once pointed out, he instantly agreed that the Brits must have imported some master shipwrights, possibly even some talented movie set-design people, to fit the smuggling compartments into the Mowj so seamlessly.

Not only had the practice gone well, it also seemed they had dodged an unanticipated bullet. Mohsen had advised them that his friend Bushehri said that a new IRGC patrol boat was going to be deployed between Larak Island and Hormuz Island tonight at "Two Bells in the Middle Watch," which Cynthia had to translate for Joe as "1 a.m. in Navyspeak." That meant an IRGC patrol boat would now be patrolling the area they had passed through on the way to pick up the Saeeds. They would need to take a different route out of the area.

Joe had asked, "Does Bushehri know why the IRGC Navy expanded the patrol? They didn't have a boat patrolling this stretch yesterday. I checked before coming."

The Commander responded with disgust, "Lieutenant Jafari's orders. He is running 'The Shaheed investigation.' The extra patrol is to keep any of the ships from the "Great Satan's Navy" from sneaking up on the resting place of the Shaheed from the east and 'defiling the wreck.' Jafari just wants to keep people from seeing the limpet mine holes. It is overkill; there were already two IRGC patrol boats stationed directly above the wreck, as you know."

Bushehri, of course, had no idea that his encounter with the hapless Constable Anvari would lead Jafari to trigger an all out "blitz" to stop and search every boat the IRGC crews could get their hands on.

Joe and Cynthia borrowed one of Captain Shirazi's navigation charts, and Mohsen pointed to the remaining path left open to them. Instead of dashing quickly east, then south towards Dubai, they would now have to loop around to the northeast and pass between Hormuz Island and mainland Iran, then several miles further east to be safe, and then south. On the map, the passage between Hormuz and the mainland looked narrow, but Mohsen assured Joe it was almost 10 kilometers wide and was rarely, if ever, patrolled. Joe knew the extra distance would add at least 90 minutes to their travel time in waters patrolled by Iran, but figured it was safer than heading through an area they *knew* was patrolled while hoping the IRGC boat did not stumble across them.

CHAPTER 43-THE BRINK

Clad in the comfortably loose "undress" khaki uniform of the US Navy, Admiral Stewart stood in front of the Digital Dead Reckoning Tracer, an electronic plotting device in the heart of the USS Abe Lincoln's Combat Direction Center. The Tracer showed the Lincoln's own position, that of all friendly ships, as well as any other surface contacts nearby. Stewart's watchful eyes were riveted to the blips that indicated inbound Iranian vessels.

A trim man in his late 40s with thinning brown hair and icy pale gray eyes approached with a purposeful stride. "Admiral, I suggest we launch the two ready birds to clear the "cats," then get all our Growlers in the air and orbiting those shore batteries at 'standoff' distance. If any of those search radars go to attack mode, I want them fried the second it happens." The advice from Captain "X-Ray" Gregory, to Rear Admiral Ian Stewart, was no surprise. Every Fifth Fleet tactician, including Gregory, who controlled the Lincoln's considerable air assets, had nightmares about the threat from the Russian-built "vampires" in the Iranian shore batteries. Once launched, they had independent radar-homing capabilities which made them doubly hard to stop.

So the real trick was to stop them from ever being launched.

That's where the Lincoln's squadron of F/A 18 Growler electronic warfare aircraft came in. The planes' jamming pods could direct enough brute force electromagnetic energy at a cruise missile battery that its radars would became hopelessly jammed and useless for the duration of the Growler's electronic attack. "Frying" an installation in this manner was option one; it was annoying and possibly damaging to the battery's radar equipment, and definitely not a friendly act, but ultimately temporary and not lethal. On the other hand, because such jamming was often the precursor to an attack, it was not something to be undertaken lightly. If a more permanent solution to the threat from the cruise missile batteries were desired, the Growlers' AGM-88D HARM missiles, each carrying over 12,000 tungsten fragments capable of turning any radar emitter into a Swiss-cheese of smoking wreckage, would do the trick nicely.

For right now, the Lincoln CSG's current ROE, or Rules of Engagement, said the HARMs could only do their dirty work if ships of the Strike Group were fired upon first. "Frying" a cruise missile installation to prevent it from effectively engaging was thus the Lincoln's only option right now.

Admiral Stewart's reply was instinctual. "Do it. And make sure the Growler boys are getting constant updates from Argus-One. This thing could go sideways in the space of five seconds and if it drops in the pot, I want those "Sunburn" batteries to be a distant memory. And, X-ray, vector the Hawk over. I want eyes on a couple of these boats to see if we can figure out what these sonsabitches are up to."

"Aye, aye, Sir. Global Hawk is on the way. Should have "eyes on" the closest speedboats in five minutes."

*   *   *

"Lincoln, this is Argus-One. Be advised that several of the speedboats have approached other surface contacts and appear to have rendezvoused with them. We cannot tell for what reason. Those that have rendezvoused are currently dead in the water. But at least 20 are still outbound in the general direction of the Lincoln CSG."

"Roger that, Argus-One." After a brief pause, the headphones of CPO Daniels crackled back to life with the voice of the CAG, "X-Ray" Gregory. "Argus-One, I'm diverting the Global Hawk from the closest inbounds over to the closest pair of contacts that are dead in the water. We want to know why they are stopped and what they are up to."

"Copy that, sir." Daniels looked over the array of luminous computer screens which cast an eerie, unhealthy looking bluish pale glow onto Daniels' already pallid skin, and continued, "My systems show our feed to your CDC is still nominal, as is the feed to the two Growlers outbound towards the IRGC Bases at Al

Farsiyah and Abu Musa. They should be orbiting at stand-off distance in five mikes."

"Argus-One, expect two more Growler's outbound our 'pos' in three 'mikes.' Let me know if you have any problems with the feed to them."

"Aye-Aye, sir. Argus-One out.

*   *   *

As always, the Combat Direction Center aboard the USS Abe Lincoln hummed with a quiet efficiency. Only someone intimately familiar with the functioning of a CDC would be able to notice the indefinable air of tension that now emanated from the CDC staff.

"Admiral, Global Hawk is tracking one pair of stopped contacts with its Synthetic Aperture Radar. The electro-optical feed will be up in five seconds. Standby...Live feed. Confirm one IRGC Boghammer speedboat, alongside what appears to be a small commercial vessel, a costal trader." There was a pause, and then the chief bosun's mate relaying the Global Hawk's data to the Admiral on the ship's J-phone said, puzzlement clear in his voice, "Sir, The IRGC sailors...appear to be conducting search operations?"

Admiral Stewart was just as puzzled as the rest of the CDC staff. IRGC boats had never sallied en-masse in the middle of the night to conduct search and seizure operations. He needed confirmation of what was going on. Was this part of a deception tactic to position IRGC fastboats into close proximity to the Lincoln CSG, in preparation for a swarming attack? Too soon to know. He turned back to the CAG. "'X-ray,' get the Hawk moved over to the next closest pair of contacts that are stopped. If they *are* conducting some sort of emergency search and seizure program, I want to know about it."

"Aye-aye, Sir. I'll get it shifted. Hawk should have 'eyes-on' the next pair of contacts in five mikes."

*   *   *

"Admiral, Hawk is coming up on the second pair contacts. Same as before, one IRGC Boghammer fastboat, crew engaged in what appears to be a thorough search of a small trading vessel." Admiral Stewart digested information while Gregory worked to get the latest aircraft updates by consulting a crewman manning the air-traffic control radar console. That particular console emitted a bright jack-o-lantern orange glow which, when reflected onto the skin of Caucasian like Gregory, made him look like the victim of a tanning-booth experiment gone awry. Thirty seconds later, he was passing the updates on to Stewart. "Sir, Argus One has reported further slowing of several of the inbound IRGC Ships, presumably, they are also slowing to board commercial vessels and perform searches. The rest are continuing to move in the general direction of our patrol path."

Ten minutes later, "Global Hawk" had confirmed that three more of the Boghammer boats which had stopped their advance towards the Enterprise CSG were engaged in searches of commercial trading vessels.

Admiral Stewart's position was very delicate. Things were tense with Iran, particularly with the bullshit accusation that the US Navy had sunk the Shaheed. He knew better than anyone that the accusation was bullshit, because if that had happened, he would have been the guy who gave the order to one of his Sea Wolf fast attack submarines, and no such order had been given. He also knew that a search like this was unprecedented in Iran's history, and guessed that whatever Iran was trying to do, it wouldn't include any favors for the US Navy. Which meant his best course was to make sure they didn't get whatever they were looking for, and that meant finding it first. "X-ray, do me a favor and grab Captain Collins immediately." Collins commanded the destroyer squadron attached to the Lincoln Carrier Strike Group.

A six-foot man with a weathered, ruddy face, blond hair streaked with gray, and the slight pot-belly not uncommon to overworked sailors approached the Dead Reckoning Tracer. "Admiral, you wanted to see me?"

"Captain, the Iranians are looking for something. I don't know what it is. I do know that I'd prefer to find it first. I want all ships in the destroyer screen to ramp up search and interdiction operations immediately. Get boarding parties out there, but keep a tight rein on them, and close track of what they are find. I know you technically don't control the Littoral Combat Ships attached to the Group for this patrol, but get hold of their skippers and tell them to get busy, too. Whatever is out there, we're gonna do our best to find it."

CHAPTER 44-WAR OF NERVES

A few hours after boarding the Mowj, now contemplating the pungent stink of the smuggling compartment he was hiding in, Joe, thought to himself, "Shit, it's *always* something."

Joe had felt their luck was holding when, two and a half hours after boarding, Captain Shirazi had started to grin and explained that they had made it out of the waters that Iran usually patrolled. The Captain declared that in five more minutes, as the Mowj entered the main shipping channel of the Gulf, he would stop running like a smuggler and would turn his running lights back on.

Two minutes after Shirazi hit the lights, Joe saw the shape of fast-moving boat making an unmistakable beeline for the Mowj. He switched his goggles over to infrared, and noticed several man-sized shapes aboard, all of whom were holding their arms in a position that suggested they carried rifles or automatic weapons.

Joe immediately scrambled down below into the hidden cargo compartments with the suddenly terrified Saeeds.

From within the padded compartment, Joe could hear loud squawks of noise outside. He guessed that someone was hailing the Mowj with a loudspeaker, but the sound was muffled by the acoustic padding in the compartment and the words were indistinct.

Joe's inner ear told him that the Mowj was slowing.

Joe was in one compartment with Mohammed, Fatameh, and the little girl, whose name Joe suddenly couldn't recall. Cynthia was in the other compartment with Mohsen and Lily; Joe was confident that Commander Saeed would not panic; he just hoped that Lily remained calm, too. Across from Joe, Fatameh was crooning to the girl and stroking her hair to keep her calm. Joe was glad that he had to look strong to give the others confidence. If he was alone, he might vomit from the level of adrenaline and anxiety suddenly coursing through his veins. As it was, he was thankful his duty required him to appear calm and collected, to keep the disease of panic from spreading among the Saeeds, an eventuality which could get them all killed.

Joe had never suffered from claustrophobia, but if there was a situation custom tailored to bring that particular anxiety on, this would have to be it. Yet for some reason, he didn't feel even a trace of it, and he wondered why, allowing his subconscious to chase that tangent as a distraction, as he had nothing better to dwell on at the moment. Suddenly it came to him: he didn't feel enclosed because the sensation that usually accompanied being enclosed in a small space was that of absolutely no air movement and air that rapidly became stale and stuffy, and that sensation was missing. He suddenly realized he could feel the faintest stirrings in the air and realized the compartment must have a separate, whisper-quiet, ventilation system. The realization was a relief in more ways than one. Not only did it mean they could stay in the compartment for hours at a time, if necessary, it also meant that, just as the small put perceptible stream of fresh air attenuated the risk of claustrophobia for him, it would probably do so for the others hiding in the compartment with him as well. Joe relaxed ever so slightly.

That calm feeling lasted for all of 23 seconds.

Trapped in the near pitch black, seeing only the dim outlines of Mohammed and his wife by the light of a tiny LED pocket flashlight Joe had had the foresight to bring, Joe could have sworn, right at the edge of audibility, he heard something that sounded like a large dog barking.

Soon, there was no doubt. A barking dog could clearly be heard, and it was getting closer.

Mohammed looked grimly worried, but then touched his pocket which held the L-pill Joe had given him, and gravely nodded his thanks to Joe. Joe felt for the location of his own L pill, and noted that just having it really did impart a sense of security. Five minutes later, they heard muffled thumps; footsteps on the hatch compartment above. The smuggling compartments were so tightly constructed that Joe was sure that none of the light from his tiny flashlight could be seen outside. Nevertheless, to be on the safe side, as soon as the thumps began, Joe extinguished the light. Everyone in the compartment immediately noticed the huge difference between *nearly* pitch black, and *actually* pitch black. It suddenly became clear to Mohammed how extended sensory deprivation could be considered a form of torture. Under these circumstances the absolute darkness was an oppressive weight.

While not particularly religious, Joe reflected as his heart raced that the saying, "There are no atheists in foxholes" probably applied equally well to those hiding from searches in concealed smuggling compartments. In the silence of his own mind, Joe started to pray, not least that the presence of a ventilation system meant their scents were being vented outside the ship, well away from the sensitive nose of the dog directly over their heads.

*   *   *

IRGC Navy Lieutenant Mumtaz was worried. He slipped away from his radio console to make a call to a friend; a friend who happened to be a senior Captain in the Iranian Navy. If word of his actions got out, he could be court-martialed for going outside the chain of command, particularly because he appealed to a rival service. Despite the personal risk, Mumtaz trusted the competence of Admiral Sayyari far more than the imbecilic Jafari, who was clearly out of his depth, and who, just as clearly, had been drinking heavily. Something bad was going to happen unless Jafari stopped this madness, this crazy emergency search, Mumtaz just knew it.

What he just heard coming out of speakers of the radios in the command center did nothing to make him feel any better.

"Iranian vessel, Iranian vessel, we are instructing you not to approach our boarding party."

*   *   *

Commander David Lewis, Captain of the USS Kidd, one of two Arleigh-Burke class destroyers attached to the Lincoln Strike Group, strained to see out the square windows lining the bridge of the Kidd what his radar told him was there: an approaching Iranian fastboat. His eyes couldn't pierce the gloom, but radar doesn't lie. Picking up the black plastic radiotelephone handset that looked like a bulky 1970s Ma-Bell phone, he keyed the microphone and warned off the approaching ship, striving to keep his voice calm, nonconfrontational, yet firm. This was not the first time he'd been in the situation; IRGC fastboats had been playing games with US ships transiting the Persian Gulf for decades. This was, however, the first time he'd been ordered to do crash priority interdiction and search mission in the middle of the damn night!

One of Kidd's boarding parties was out conducting a search, having been vectored by the Kidd's surface-contact radar towards a small costal trader flying a Libyan flag of convenience. Unfortunately, seemingly out of nowhere, an IRGC Boghammer was fast approaching the boarding party aboard the Libyan-flagged trader at 40 knots. Boghammers were very lightly armed, compared to a modern destroyer like the Kidd, but a Boghammer definitely had more speed and firepower than the exposed boarding-party sailors on one of Kidd's rubber boats.

While the Kidd could wipe that IRGC Boghammer off the map with a push of button, Captain Collins had been clear: no weapons release authority was granted, past a shot across the bow in the case of particularly provocative action, which is just where this situation seemed to be heading.

Lewis keyed the mike on the radiotelephone handset again.

*　　　*　　　*

"Iranian vessel, Iranian vessel, do not approach our boarding party. Request you maintain 1,000 meter distance." Lieutenant Jafari heard the English coming out of the speaker in the naval command center in Bandar Abbas, and cursed the interfering Americans. "What the devil are they doing?" He went over to the communications officer in contact with Junior Lieutenant Assidi, Commander of the Boghammer fastboat the arrogant Americans were warning off.

"Assidi, this is the command center. What can you see?"

"I am almost a kilometer distant. All I can see is a costal trader with one of the American's little rubber boats tied up. Through my night vision goggles, I can see the outline of a larger vessel, possibly an American destroyer, perhaps three kilometers away."

"What are the American's doing on the trader? Are they searching it? Putting anything on or taking anything or any people off? I must know!"

After a moment's hesitation, the reply came, "Command Center, I simply cannot see. We're too far back. I can see a few shapes moving about on deck, and somebody in the wheelhouse, but I have no idea what is going on. The range is too great, and even with night vision goggles, the darkness cloaks their actions. The rubber boat is the standard one the Americans use for their search parties. What would you like me to do?"

"Stand by, Assidi. Do nothing for the moment." This was the closest Lieutenant Jafari had ever been to the responsibilities of command, and he found it not at all to his liking. Emotionally exhausted with anxiety, still half drunk from his earlier binging, his stomach suddenly knotted with fear at what might happen if weapons were fired: his cousin had delegated authority of IRGC vessels to Jafari if needed for the Saeed investigation, but most definitely had NOT given Lieutenant Jafari the authority to get in a shooting match with the Navy of the Great Satan.

Still, desperation drove him. The only thing worse than inadvertently starting a shooting war would be failing to find the Saeeds. Every means of exiting Iran but the sea had been blockaded by General Jafari's troops. If Ziyaii had gotten out of Iran on a ship, as now seemed very likely, the Saeeds could be doing the same. "Assidi, I want you to continue towards that trader. Go slowly. Stay away from your gun mounts. Do nothing provocative. But I need you to get close enough to that trader to see what is going on, and if anyone comes off it besides Americans.

*   *   *

Commander Lewis, aboard the Kidd, did not like what he was seeing. What did these fuckers think they were doing? Did they think that by slowly inching closer to the boarding party, he was going to be faked out? He had men out there; he couldn't let that Boghammer get into firing range. His boarding crew would be easy pickings for the Boghammer.

He keyed the mike again. "Iranian vessel, immediately halt your advance towards our boarding party! This is your final warning. I say again, this is your final warning."

The fuckers weren't stopping. Shit. He called the Tactical Action Officer, Lieutenant David Rodgers, over to the Plot, the Kidd's own dead reckoning tracker.

"Dave, you see this sonofabitch here, just creeping towards our boarding party on that Libyan-flagged costal trader?"

"Yes, sir."

"They've disregarded instructions to hold their distance; they're at 750 meters from our party and closing. We need to persuade them that we are not joking around. Time to give the Phalanx a little workout. I want a shot across their bow they won't forget. Draw me a line halfway between their position and our boarding party. Can you do that?"

"Yes, Captain. The Phalanx can take out a target moving at more than 1500 mph, I'm sure we can manage to put the fear of God into a little speedboat chugging in at five knots. We won't leave a scratch on em, but they'll remember it, I guarantee."

"Good. Get it done, Mike. Keep a sharp eye out and no mistakes on this one."

"Aye-Aye, Sir."

Lewis went over to the radio with encrypted tactical link to the boarding party searching the costal trader. He keyed the mike and warned the officer leading the party, "Lieutenant, be advised, there's a Boghammer out there creeping up on you. He's ignored orders not to approach closer. We're putting a shot across his bow. Keep your head down."

"Aye-aye, Captain."

*   *   *

"Chief, the Captain wants you to draw a line in the water, so to speak, between our boarding party and that Boghammer. Can you do that?" In a world where everything was high tech and computer controlled precision, Chief Petty Officer Reginald Marshall had earned a reputation as an artist with a master's touch when it came to running the Kidd's weapons systems in manual mode. Nobody was a better shooter with the Phalanx than Marshall.

"Yes sir. You want a 5 second burst?"

The heart of the Phalanx was a 20 MM Vulcan cannon. Originally intended to take out incoming cruise missiles, Phalanx's role had been taken over by the Sea Ram anti-missile system. After an Al-Qaeda suicide crew crashed a small boat packed with explosives into the USS Cole, killing 17 sailors, the Navy realized that while the Phalanx Close-In Weapons System might no longer be "state of the art" when it came to cruise missile defense, it was just the ticket for engaging small surface contacts. Although not originally part of the Kidd's armament, a Phalanx system had been retrofitted onto the Kidd two years earlier, both to protect against small surface contacts and provide backup missile defense. With a rate of fire up to 4,500 rounds per minute, the 5 second burst the Chief suggested would put more than 350 slugs downrange.

"Sounds about right, Chief. Do it." Lieutenant Rodgers restrained his impulse to the tell Chief Marshall to "be careful." The Chief had forgotten more about the Kidd's weapon systems than Rodgers would ever know.

Carefully monitoring the distance between the two surface contacts, Chief Marshall moving the control pipper for the Phalanx gun into a position on his control screen dead center between the costal trader and the creeping Boghammer speedboat, grunted his satisfaction at the result, and depressed the trigger switch that manually fired the cannon.

*　　　*　　　*

As Cynthia, Mohsen, and Lily huddled in the stygian darkness in the other compartment, Lily tried to appreciate the irony of the situation, but failed. Her fear was too strong. Still, the irony *was* rich.

The Saeeds arrived safely aboard the Mowj, at least in part because she had helped Sima Bushehri *not* to commit suicide. When they jumped in the smuggling compartment, frantic at the unexpected arrival of a patrol boat, the first thing this Sam woman did, with her kind manner, her soft voice, and her excellent Persian, was offer Lily a pill that would help Lily commit suicide.

Lily took the pill and secreted it in the knot of her headscarf. She thought to herself, "It is one thing to kill yourself simply because you are sad. It is another to put an end to constant, ghastly suffering at the hands of torturers. Surely, if it comes to that, *Khoda* would be merciful enough to forgive me." The panting sound of her own breathing was harsh in here ears, at least it was, until that sound was blotted out by another. It came through the hull, a deep, vibrating, ripping sound, unlike anything she had ever heard. A moment before, sitting in the total darkness, she thought she could not be more afraid. She now knew she had been wrong.

Cynthia, of course, knew what that sound was, as she had taken part in Navy live-fire exercises in her former life. She whispered three words to the others, giving the ancient name for a Greek armored column. "It's a Phalanx."

*　　　*　　　*

Lieutenant Assidi should have known better, but he had only been in charge of his Boghammer for three months. Dressed in a faded green uniform, bright orange life-vest, with a lightly checked keffiyah scarf wrapped around his neck, he and his identically-dressed two man crew cut what he considered very dashing figures of Iranian manhood aboard their Boghammer fastboat, a craft which sported two high-power outboard engines surmounting an incongruously bright baby-blue fiberglass hull. In truth, Assidi's small-boat handling skills were excellent, and he had always displayed courage in accepting the various physical risks in small boat operations. But…he had never engaged in combat beyond war game simulations. He knew intellectually that the Great Satan had weapons of great precision, and that if they wanted him and his crew dead, the Boghammer would be swatted out of the water without a second thought.

This professional knowledge of his enemies' capabilities went right out the window when an unearthly vibrating shriek was heard and the water less than 200 meters from him erupted in a line in response to the impact of hundreds of armor-piercing tungsten slugs hitting the water at 3,600 feet per second, or roughly 2,500 mph. It seemed as if *Khoda* himself was drawing a fountaining line in the water, and warning him not to cross that line.

He threw the throttles on his boat to their maximum and immediately turned the boat 180 degrees from his previous heading, putting as much space between himself, the coastal trader, and the USS Kidd as possible. Unfortunately, his next action triggered an inexorable chain of action and response. When he keyed his radio's mike as his boat made its rapid reverse, panic was clearly audible in his voice, "Alarm, alarm, the American's are shooting at us with a giant cannon, they're shooting at us."

*   *   *

Hunched forward over his radio set in the command center lit by buzzing fluorescent lights, when Lieutenant Mumtaz heard Assidi's panicked exclamation, he immediately keyed his mike and said, iron in his voice, "Assidi, report! What happened? Are there any injuries or damage? Are you still taking fire?" The shaky Assidi, shouting above the noise of his speedboat's roaring motors, managed to convey the experience in about thirty seconds, by which point in time Mumtaz concluded the Americans had simply put a shot across Assidi's bow. Sitting safe in the command center, he had enough perspective to know that if they had wanted Assidi's boat gone, it would now be nothing but bobbing wreckage.

But by the time he reached that conclusion, correct as it was, it was too late.

*   *   *

The commander of the cruise missile battery detachment on the Iranian Island of Abu Musa, Lieutenant Commander Mohammed Ardeshir, had taken an immediate liking to Lieutenant Assidi when the junior lieutenant had been given command of a Boghammer boat stationed at the IRGC Naval base on Abu Musa. Ardeshir had taken the young Lieutenant under his wing, explained how to make the most out of the often dysfunctional bureaucracy that managed the IRGC, and used his connections to make sure Assidi had parts for his boat, bullets for the Boghammer's twin cannons, and rockets for its onboard missile launchers. He had started to think of the young man, inexperienced, perhaps, but earnest and hardworking nevertheless, as a second son.

When he heard Assidi's panicked cries, he switched the radar in his installation from passive search to active targeting mode. The Kidd was threatening his young friend.

*   *   *

The electronic warfare, or EW, aircraft known as Growler-Two was orbiting in a racetrack pattern fifteen miles from Abu Musa. The EW officer in the back seat of the E/A -18 Super Hornet, USMC Major Robert Allen, noticed immediately when Abu Musa's radar switched into attack mode. Indeed, he could hardly miss it, a pulsing point of light over the position representing Abu Musa appeared on the computer screen in front of Allen, and while simultaneous his radar gear generated a warbling warning tone to make damn sure the EW officer noticed attack radar was active in his neighborhood. Having been watching for just that thing, he reported over the radio to the Abe Lincoln, "Abu Musa's gone active, I'm gonna fry 'em." He used a joystick to position a targeting pipper on top of Abu Musa's location on the screen, then pushed a button that activated the Growler's powerful jammers. A huge volume of electromagnetic energy pulsed towards the missile battery on Abu Musa at close to light speed.

*   *   *

History is littered with the corpses of military officers who made snap decisions with inadequate information or imperfect understanding of the surrounding environment. Less than ten seconds after switching to active targeting mode, Commander Ardeshir's radios were nothing but hash, his radar displays were crawling with pulsing static. He knew immediately he was being jammed. Unfortunately, that jamming meant he did not hear the follow-on conversation between Mumtaz in the Command Center and Assidi in his Boghammer, explaining that the Boghammer was not under sustained fire, and that his boat and crew were completely intact. Ardeshir made the not-unreasonable but incorrect assumption that active jamming, often a prelude to an attack in and of itself, coming on the heels of Assidi's report that he was taking fire, meant the Americans were making a general attack.

Cruise missile warfare, due to its lightning speed, is a "use-em-or-lose em" proposition. If you wait to fire until you are already taking hits, you are dead. He approached the first of his battery's six Sunburn cruise missiles. The Russians called this missile the Moskit, or Mosquito. In truth, it was not insectoid at all in appearance; looking at its sharply pointed nose, dull gray paint, stubby wing surfaces, and molded ram-air intakes, one could not help but envision a Great White, the deadliest predator of the deep.

Commander Ardeshir's radar was now useless, and without the radar information to give his missile their initial "look" at the target, he could not automatically fire them. However, he did have the coordinates of the Kidd's last known position before the jamming started. The Sunburn missile had an active seeker head. Once it was out of the jamming zone, it would be able to acquire the target on its own. He just needed to get it pointed in the right general direction and launch it. He manually typed the GPS coordinates for the USS Kidd into his system, confirmed that the Sunburn missile accepted the coordinates, turned the firing key, and pressed the "Launch" button. He started feeding the same coordinate set into the next Sunburn missile.

*   *   *

Across every Combat Information Center in the Abraham Lincoln Carrier Strike Group, the same warning was shouted. "Vampire, Vampire, Vampire. We have a cruise missile launch signature from Abu Musa Island. "

Hearing that report, the Lincoln's CAG, "X-Ray" Gregory, did not wait for an order from Admiral Stewart. He had "weapons release' authority when any of the ships in the Lincoln CSG came under direct attack. He shouted across the CDC to the Air Control Officer, whose job it was to relay message to the Lincoln's air assets, "Tell Growler-Two to take that cruise missile battery out now!"

The HARM AGM-88D mounted on the wing pylons of the E/A-18 Growler currently jamming Abu Musa's radar is a devastating weapon. At least, it is in most circumstances. Aboard ship, the missiles are kept in "safe" mode with the insertion of a small pin to prevent firing. This pin is connected to a bright red flag, bright red so that the ground crew can easily see it and remove it prior to launching a Growler off the catapults of a super-carrier like the Abe Lincoln. Unfortunately, the "plane captain," the enlisted man in charge of Growler-Two when it was aboard the Enterprise, was in sick bay with a serious bout of flu when the crash launch orders came down to get the Growlers airborne ASAP. The plane captain's replacement was green and made a rookie mistake, missing the flags in his haste and exhaustion, and the rushed pilot didn't have time for a thorough pre-flight inspection. Given the safeguards built into the system, such a mistake *almost* never happens, but *almost never* is not the same as never. When Major Allen tried to drop the hammer on the cruise missile battery, he noted with disgust that he couldn't, because his missiles were in "safe" mode. He should have noticed the "safe" indicator earlier, but in the information overload environment of the modern jet fighter, he had simply overlooked it until that piece of information demanded his attention.

"Negative, negative, Lincoln, be advised, my weapons are safe. Say again, I cannot fire, my weapons are safe."

*   *   *

The speed with which a Sunburn cruise missile can engage a surface target was terrifying, particularly if you were the one being targeted. Even worse was the sense of helplessness: the Sunburn is simply too fast for human decision-makers to be in the loop. The missile that Commander Ardeshir had managed to get off had indeed acquired the USS Kidd after getting clear of the Growler's jamming. Now it was inbound on the USS Kidd, 40 miles from Abu Musa at the time of launch, at 1,900 mph. Aboard the CIC of the Kidd, the "battle stations" klaxon automatically began to hoot, but Captain Lewis silenced it after a few seconds, finding it an unneeded distraction. Simultaneous with the start of the alarm klaxon, the conventional overhead lighting aboard the CIC of the kid went off as "Battle stations" lights came on. The CIC was transformed from a relatively bright space into one illuminated only by the spectral red 'battle station" lights and the light of dozens of illuminated consoles. Lewis let the red lights stay on; they were better for the crew's night vision…not that such a tiny advantage could really matter at this point; with the exception of the electronic countermeasures crew in the CIC, who were actively employing chaff, decoys, and jamming to try to derail in the inbound missile, the rest of the crew in the CIC on the

Kidd could only sit back, pray, and let the automated cruise missile defenses of the Kidd do the fighting.

The automated systems had a tiny window to stop the "vampire". While actual time from launch to impact was 75 seconds, an eternity in combat, unfortunately the Sea Ram anti-cruise missile defense system aboard the Kidd could only engage an incoming cruise missile from five miles out. That left about 10 seconds from the time the 'vampire' came in range until the time it would impact the ship. If the missile's 700 lb high-explosive warhead hit near the USS Kidd, even in best case scenario, loses would be heavy. If the Sunburn popped up at the last second and successfully crashed down onto the deck of the Kidd, as it was designed to do, the Kidd would be the second destroyer to go to the floor of the Persian Gulf in less than ten days.

Twenty seconds before impact, from the eleven-missile magazine under the radome of the Sea Ram system, three blazing streaks shot forth, headed towards the inbound Sunburn. The crew of the Kidd couldn't know, but the Sunburn's stealthy design and final phase evasive maneuvers were giving the Sea Ram's attack radar fits. The first two missiles from the Sea Ram exploded in the buffeting wake of the Sunburn, tumbling it a bit, but leaving it unfazed. Fortunately, the tumbling did let the infrared seeker head in the third missile get a better look at the hot exhaust of the inbound missile. As designed, the Sea-Ram missile detonated directly in the path of the oncoming cruise missile. But it was too little, too late.

Damaged, but not destroyed, the cruise missile continued its rapid advance towards the Kidd.

*   *   *

A man does not rise to the position of Commander, Air Group, USS Abraham Lincoln, without the capacity to integrate a vast quantity of data and make snap decisions. Captain "X-ray" Gregory was about to prove that winning the plum assignment of CAG for the Lincoln Strike Group was no mistake. Not two seconds after receiving the report from Growler Two that his weapons were "safe" and unable to fire, Gregory was on the radio to the only other air asset he had in the region. Without having to look at orange air traffic radar screen, he knew just where his

"Hundred-Eyed Monster" was, orbiting ahead of the transiting Strike Group, approximately 25 miles from Abu Musa. He also knew its weapons load-out today included two AGM-88D HARM anti-radiation missiles.

"Argus-One, Growler-Two's weapons are 'safed.' The cruise missile battery on Abu Musa has fired on the Kidd. Take that battery out. I say again, you are 'weapons free,'" take that battery out."

Closely following the engagement aboard Argus-One, CPO Daniels responded immediately. "Roger, Lincoln, we will engage. Wait one."

Useless though it was because of Growler-Two's jamming, the radar battery at Abu Musa was still radiating high energy attack radar waves. The Tac-O, or tactical officer in charge of the Argus-One's weapons, Lieutenant Junior Grade Paul Oats, designated Abu Musa's radiating battery with his targeting pipper, which automatically loaded GPS data for the cruise missile battery into the HARM. When the missile's status changed to "ready to fire" on his computer screen, Oats quickly turned the launch key, and pressed the "Fire" button. Argus-One shuddered as the HARM missile dropped off the wing pylon and rocketed towards Abu Musa at 1,400 mph, following a trail of attack-radar energy like a bloodhound follows a scent. Earlier versions of the HARM might have put the nearby Growler-Two at risk, as it was also radiating a huge quantity of radar energy, which is what a HARM follows to its target, but the GPS back-up kept the missile on track and prevented fratricide with the Growler.

Daniels got back on the line to the Lincoln. "Missile away, Lincoln. Impact estimated in three-five seconds. Will advise."

*   *   *

Less than two minutes after going "active," Commander Ardeshir was still trying to get a second Sunburn, which had picked this moment to be balky, to accept the same GPS coordinates as the first one he had managed to launch in spite the Americans' jamming.

Human reaction time has finite limits, which is not always a bad thing. It was probably a mercy that from the time of the thunderous explosion until his body was pierced by 15 of the more than 12,000 tungsten fragments produced by the explosion of the HARM on top of his cruise missile battery, Ardeshir simply didn't have time to hear the roar and feel the impacts before his consciousness was snuffed out forever.

* * *

"Lincoln, Argus-One. Scratch one missile battery."

CHAPTER 45-BETTER TO BE LUCKY THAN GOOD

Battered by the Sea-Ram missiles though it was, the Sunburn continued towards its target, the USS Kid. Although the last missile had not stopped the "vampire," the damage inflicted did have one key effect: it had partially crippled one wing and abraded the radar-absorbing surfaces of the stealthy cruise missile. Suddenly, the attack radar of the Phalanx Close-In Weapons System had a clear lock on the inbound missile. For the second time that night, but this time in automated anti-ship-cruise missile defense mode, the 20 MM Vulcan cannon of the Phalanx roared to life. A mere two seconds from impact with the Kidd, three of the 200 rounds spat out by the Gatling gun scored hits on the Sunburn. The last sabot round to impact the Sunburn destroyed a wing, which caused it to nose over into the waves it was skimming above. The missile's impact fuse caused an immediate detonation. The shock wave from the explosion, only 200 meters from the Kidd, knocked several people off their feet and resulted in multiple contusions and at least one broken ankle among the Kidd's crew.

In the late 1970s, US shipyards were building Spruance-class destroyers to fill an order for the Shah of Iran. When the Shah fell, the mullahs cancelled the order and paid a major penalty to do so. The US Navy got the ships, to include the USS Kidd, DDG-993, for a song, and they became known within Navy circles as "the Ayatollahs' Gifts." That earlier USS Kidd, DDG-993 was decommissioned in 1998 after 18 faithful years of service to the US Navy. But the Navy cherishes tradition, and when a newer and more powerful Aegis destroyer, DDG-100, needed a name for its christening in 2007, the US Navy revived the name USS Kidd.

This bit of lore about their lore of their namesake was common knowledge to everyone aboard the CIC of the Kidd. Commander Lewis was not normally one for profanity. Even so, a few seconds after the detonation, relief evident in his voice, he said, "Fuck, people, that was a close one! That's one Ayatollahs' gift I can do without." This self-evident statement drew an explosive laugh from the crew that had to be experienced to be believed. Even the salty, unflappable Chief Marshall laughed until tears were squeezing out of his eyes.

CHAPTER 46-PICKING UP THE PIECES

Joe, never having served in the Navy, had no idea that the thrumming vibration he heard earlier came from the impact of Phalanx rounds 200 yards from the hold of the ship in which he was currently hiding. He did know that he had no idea what the hell was going on, and that is not a great thing if you're a professional intelligence officer by trade. He risked the LED light again for a brief second and was happy to see that Mohammed and his wife, though clearly afraid, were drawing strength from each other. Being a kilometer and a half from the Kidd when the Sunburn detonated, the overpressure "thump" of the explosion caused the hull of the Mowj to groan. Joe and Mohammed traded looks of alarm, but there was nothing they could do but sit tight, be quiet, and wait.

*   *   *

Admiral Sayyari stormed into the Naval Command Center two minutes after Abu Musa missile battery went blank on the center's radar screens. He found the center in an uproar. Spying the Admiral, Lieutenant Mumtaz waved him over frantically. Mumtaz quickly recapped the evolution of the situation: disregarded warnings, a shot across the bow, the Boghammer's retreat, unscathed, radar tracks that suggested one of Abu Musa's batteries fired a cruise missile at the USS Kidd, and finally, loss of contact with Abu Musa, likely due to a retaliatory attack from the Americans. Sayyari listed to Mumtaz' succinct recitation while his anger mounted to record heights. Meanwhile, Lieutenant Jafari, clearly in shock at the turn of events, sat at one of the radio consoles in a daze.

Stalking over to Jafari, Sayyari spat the words, "I don't know what game you have been playing at, but it is now over! Were you stupid enough to send a wave of boats towards the Americans in the middle of the night, unannounced, to ignore multiple warnings to stand off, and think you'd get no reaction?

There will be an investigation here…a real one, this time." A smile of ill-concealed shadenfruede crept onto the Admiral's face. "Whatever has been going on here, whatever plots you may have been scheming, they are over now. Soon it will be time for you to "face the music" as the Americans say. I hope you find the tune to your liking."

The Admiral waved his hand at the armed guard standing near the entrance.

With obvious relish, the Admiral said, "Guard, arrest this man, on my authority. He is charged with negligence, malfeasance, and use of the military assets of the Holy Regime to conduct unauthorized combat actions. Take him away."

Returning to the radio console that Jafari had occupied, Sayyari picked up the mike and said, "All IRGC vessels, All IRGC vessels, cease your search operations, return to base, and stand down until further notice."

* * *

After the longest twenty minutes of his life, the hatch to the compartment was thrown open with a clatter, to reveal the grinning face of Captain Shirazi. The sound of a small boat motoring away filtered down into the open hold; obviously whoever had searched the ship was departing. Shirazi said proudly in broken English, "I told you, Mr. Hank, is good boat, hiding places *very* well built! They even bring a smelling doggie, but no find nothing! Good thing no guns or bad stuff on board this trip, heh, heh! That they smell for sure."

Immensely relieved, Joe replied in Farsi, "Who stopped us?"

Shirazi laughed again, this time a full belly laugh, and continued in his broken English, "Who board my Mowj, Mr. Hank? *You.* Speedboat was launch from USA ship 'Kidd,' look for drug smuggler, terrorist, bad men taking guns from Iran to other places to make trouble. So they say. But my compartments too good for them, Ha!"

Joe and Mohammed couldn't help but burst into relieved laughter. When Mohammed translated the English for Fatameh, she joined them.

CHAPTER 47-A NEW DAY

Emotionally exhausted, reeking of the nasty bilge water which sloshed about in the smuggling compartments, the Saeeds, Joe, and Cynthia nevertheless crowded together on the deck of the Mowj to watch the sun dawning on a new day as Captain Shirazi deftly maneuvered his dhow up Dubai Creek, headed towards a mooring on the industrial waterfront. Despite, or perhaps because of, the suppressed fear of the previous night's events, all found themselves giddy with relief over their hair's-breadth escape.

Even before reaching the shore, Joe used his cell phone to call them two cabs, and then made another call to book two more rooms in the Novotel for the Saeeds to stay in while Joe was arranging flights to London. Finally, Joe called Henry Waterston.

The handshakes and embraces all the disembarking passengers gave to Captain Shirazi and his crew were heartfelt, to say the least. At last, Cynthia's mischievous curiosity finally overcame her and she asked Shirazi and the crewman with the "Baby on Board" T-shirts if they knew what their T-shirts said. They admitted they did not. When Cynthia explained to Shirazi that his T-shirt said "Kiss me, I'm Irish," Shirazi just grinned and shook his head. Not one to take things quite so lightly, the young crewman sporting the "Baby on Board" T-shirt colored with embarrassment and moved rapidly towards what Cynthia guessed was the crew quarters, probably to change shirts.

This reaction was particularly uproarious to Lily and Fatameh, who clung both to the ship's railing and each other to keep from falling to the deck in hysterical convulsions. There is really nothing funnier to an Iranian woman than a petulant Iranian man with a wounded sense of pride.

The Captain and crew, for their part, had no idea who they had just gotten out of Iran, but the events of the night gave them an indefinable sense that somehow they had struck a blow against

"The Holy Regime," which was fine by them. Between that sense of satisfaction, and the fat stack of money Joe passed him, Shirazi went home to his wife that morning grinning from ear to ear.

*   *   *

Three hours later, freshly showered and revived by copious quantities of coffee, Cynthia admitted the grinning Brit into Joe's hotel room, and ushered Henry to a plush couch where Joe was perched. All the gear Joe had borrowed from Waterston was on the coffee table before them. Holding up first the goggles, then the tin of L-pills, Joe said, "These came in handy, while these, thankfully, did not." Joe stood, picked up both, and then handed the borrowed night vision goggles and L-pills back to Henry with a theatrical bow.

"Do you have the visas ready, Henry?"

"Yes, of course, Joe. But a moment, man! Have you seen the news? Gunfire exchanged, a cruise missile launched at one of your ships, an Iranian battery blown up. Washington's in an uproar! Did you have anything to do with that?"

"Not a thing, Henry. Smooth sailing the whole way. Odd coincidence, though. We were lucky to have dodged it, I guess."

When Henry finally left, Cynthia finally let go the gales of laughter she had been suppressing at Joe's answer.

"Not a thing, Joe? Smooth sailing?" she repeated with a questioning note of irony.

"There's a phrase you need to remember from your Navy days, Cyn."

"Yah? What's that?"

"Don't ask, don't tell."

*   *   *

On their arrival in London, Joe was happy to see that the Saeeds didn't receive undue scrutiny from British customs. In fact, they sped through so quickly, Joe suspected that in addition to providing some short-term tourist visas for the Saeeds, Waterston had called ahead to make sure there were no problems. Joe figured by now, Henry had more than paid off the debt he owed Joe for

Herat. When the time came in a few weeks for the CIA to share the information obtained from the Saeeds with the British Secret Intelligence Service, Joe made a mental note to informally let the higher ups in SIS know the CIA was being so forthcoming only because of Waterston's help. That should help raise Waterston's stock…and make Henry that much more willing to help out next time Joe needed another favor.

After installing the Saeeds in a luxurious multi-roomed suite at London's posh Savoy, Joe inquired if the Savoy's concierge might be able to obtain a mini-DV camera for a short while. The concierge promptly located a nice Sony in the Savoy's lost and found room, and shortly thereafter, Mohammed was walking Joe and Cynthia through the videotape of the Fajr Project that Ali Hosseini had helpfully, but likely fatally, filmed.

Fifteen minutes later, Joe and Cynthia couldn't stop grinning.

Joe said to Cynthia, "If you relax here and keep our new friends company, I'll go write the cable."

CHAPTER 48-LEMONS INTO LEMONADE

With a sour expression on his face, the Director of the Central Intelligence Agency posed a question to the three men standing before his desk. "Can you explain to me why we just got a cable saying Mohammed and Mohsen Saeed are in London, ready to be debriefed?"

One of the men, Counter-Proliferation Division Chief of Operations Norman Bates, looked behind the Director, out the huge windows in the Directors 7th floor office. Surrounding CIA Hqs was a seeming ocean of trees with bright green foliage. After a moment spent appreciating that vegetation, he answered with a calculated blandness, "With all due respect, Mr. Director, I think the important part of the cable is that Joe Cerrato and Cynthia Marks have looked at Mohammed's video tape and judged it authentic. Cynthia is trained in recognizing nuclear technology, and she speaks fluent Farsi. If she thinks it's genuine, we have to seriously consider the possibility that it is. More to the point, Joe said that if we don't bring the Saeeds in, the SIS would be more than happy to, and they don't even *know* that we've bagged a nuclear physicist. The Brits think this is just about the Shaheed and the IRGC Navy. If the Saeeds go to the Brits and their info turns out to be genuine, its going be the 'Mitrokhin' debacle all over again, squared. We'll all be crucified in the press for having turned the Saeeds away."

As soon as Joe's miraculous cable had come in, Fred Sandler and Norman Bates had strategized the best way to spin it to "The Seventh Floor." The new Director was a political appointee with no intelligence experience. He was widely unpopular in the Agency for his consistent habit of bowing to the slightest political pressure. Fred and Norman had both quickly agreed that the Director would be more susceptible to an argument based on fear than rational discussion of the intelligence merits. They had therefore decided to emphasize the downside of what would happen to the Agency and the Director *personally* if he turned away the Saeeds and the Brits got them.

It worked.

Of course, the fact that Javid Ziyaii had just surfaced didn't hurt. Ziyaii released a video tape to Al-Jazeera in Dubai which included an audio recording of mines detonating on the Shaheed. The tape also featured a solemn-faced and obviously guilt-stricken Ziyaii explaining how he had been tricked into planting the mines, and footage of the smoldering corpses of six men. Ziyaii claimed they were Iranian Qods Force operatives who had been sent to Dubai to kill him, to cover up Ziyaii's knowledge of why the Shaheed really sank. Ziyaii even showed two of the charred Iranian diplomatic passports he had recovered from the bodies.

The Office of Naval Intelligence had quickly confirmed that Ziyaii's recording of the mines detonating matched the sound their sensors had recorded at approximately the time and place the Shaheed went down. Ziyaii's story matched Commander Saeed's account in all particulars, which made it very hard for the Director to continue to ignore the Saeeds.

The Director knew he was boxed in. "Pants Boy" and his sponsors were just going to have to suck it up. He said, "Get them on the next plane in. 'You know who' is going to be pissed. So, how do we make this 'into lemonade'?"

Fred Sandler, who had been waiting for this question or one like it, answered. "This doesn't *have* to lead to a major bombing campaign. This administration has trumpeted about the need for more international cooperation. So let's use the system. If Mohammed Saeed's info is true, we don't have to shove this down the world's throat. We can let someone else do that for us. We need to call Olaf Henrikson and…"

*　　　*　　　*

Sitting in a safe house in Northern Virginia with the Saeeds, everyone sat gazing at the TV screen with rapt attention. At the top of the hour, the news cycle started again with the lead story. "Sources in the US Navy are calling the confrontation with the Iranian Revolutionary Guard Corps Navy ships an act of 'unprovoked aggression.' They have reiterated that the US Navy had nothing to do with the loss of the Shaheed, and stated that any Iranian evidence to the contrary is patently false. Navy and State Department spokesmen have reiterated their call for an UN-led investigation to be granted access to the wreckage of the Shaheed, to determine the cause for the loss of the Iranian destroyer. The Iranian government, meanwhile, remains strangely silent about recent events, including the missile duel that left one Iranian cruise missile battery a smoking ruin. Sources say that internal turmoil in Iran appears to be…"

Cynthia clicked off the TV, and said in Farsi to the assembled Saeeds, "Mohsen, Mohammed, your debriefing begins tomorrow. As long as you are absolutely truthful, everything will go fine. Except on one point: Joe and I picked you up on a boat. We motored to Dubai. We weren't stopped, and we didn't hear any gunfire or explosions. Understand? People in the CIA and the US Navy may suspect we had some involvement in what happened, however, nobody but the people in this room and Joe *know* what really happened. We need to keep it that way. If we start talking about having been in the middle of that naval confrontation, the information your provide will become even more of a political 'football' then it already is. So, for your own sake, as well as mine and Joe's, as far as you're concerned, the entire trip went off without a hitch, it was 'smooth sailing' and you were surprised to later find out that there had been a confrontation. Got it?"

Smiling slyly, Mohsen said in theatrical tones, "As *Khoda* is my witness, it was nothing but 'smooth sailing."

Cynthia laughed and said, "Perfect, my friend, perfect."

*   *   *

After two full days of debriefing at the safe house in the horse country of northern Virginia, it was obvious to almost every analyst that spoke with him that Mohammed Saeed was a genuine defector, and that his video tape was an intelligence treasure trove. Office of Naval Intelligence analysts were having a similar field day with Commander Saeed; they gleefully told Joe that Mohsen provided more information on the IRGC Navy and Iranian Navy than any number of multi-million dollar spy satellites could have provided.

The lone fly in the ointment was Lorne Stevens, an intelligence analyst from the National Counter-Proliferation Center, who loudly maintained that Mohammed Saeed was bogus, despite the accumulating evidence to the contrary. Cynthia knew that Stevens had been strident in insisting in last year's National Intelligence Estimate that Iran's nuclear weapons program was moribund, but she suspected more that professional embarrassment was at issue.

Despite Stevens, Cynthia was enjoying herself immensely, ebullient at the detailed information Mohammed was providing, and reveling in the freedom of being away from the restrictive social mores of Dubai. Free to indulge her fashionista impulses, she was dressed to the nines in a white silk blouse and form-fitting pearl-gray cashmere skirt and jacket that was very professional, but nonetheless had half the analysts in the room drooling. During one of the breaks, CIA analyst Mark Barnes sidled up to Cynthia and whispered, "Stevens is an asshole. And a shoddy analyst, to boot. He's 'Pants Boy's' little 'mole' in this debriefing, sent in to make a last-ditch effort to derail it. But don't worry, everyone, even the contrarian jerkoffs from State's Bureau of Intelligence and Research, know Stevens is a jackass and a total lightweight."

Cynthia was presiding over the debriefing of Mohammed with a protectiveness reminiscent of a mama bear defending her young. She knew she had to take care of the Stevens problem, but bided her time until the moment was right. She waited until late afternoon, when Mohammed was out of the room on a tea break. Predictably, as soon as Mohammed was out the door, Stevens revived his objections to Mohammed's information. She held up her hands to cut off responses from the other analysts to Steven's gibberish. Although no physicist herself, she knew more than enough to systematically demolish Stevens' flimsy arguments in front of the group of nuclear weapons analysts, which she did, point by point.

Stevens' response to this humiliation was to leap to his feet, red faced and shouting, "You aren't an analyst and aren't *qualified* to comment on technical matters."

Cynthia's did not respond verbally, at least not at first. She surveyed the room quickly, and took its temperature. Everyone was looking at Stevens with an expression of somewhere between hate and disgust. Even dense as he was, Stevens had to be able to sense that the other analysts present considered him not so much a colleague as an interfering piece of shit that needed to be scraped off the bottom of their collective shoes. She quickly assessed what she could get away with, and decided that with the mood of this particular crowd, the answer was, "Almost anything."

She walked over to Stevens, who was shaking with impotent rage, and put a nerve pinch on the inside of his left elbow that left him on the ground and whimpering for mercy in the space of three seconds.

As Stevens writhed beneath her, she said, "It's time for you to shut up and leave. And when you get out of here, you can phone 'Pants Boy' and tell him to go fuck himself."

Given the litigious nature of American society, some might have been afraid to so blatantly kick Steven's ass, and in an official setting, too. Cynthia wasn't worried. She knew the more insecure a guy was, the less likely he was to admit that a woman kicked his ass, particularly a petite woman who looked more like a fashion model than a CIA field officer. Stevens radiated insecurity as pungent as bad halitosis, insecurity which Cynthia was quick to take advantage of.

Plus, she figured any investigator assigned to check out allegations of assault would take one look at doe-eyed 110 lb Cynthia, then look at Stevens, who outweighed her by 60 lbs, and immediately be skeptical. If the investigator questioned the other analysts present, Cynthia knew they would all back up Cynthia. Most, in fact, would probably root for Stevens to get fired for filing false charges.

Stevens staggered out of the room to the accompaniment of jeers and applause for Cynthia by analysts from WINPAC, the CIA's Weapons Intelligence, Proliferation and Arms Control Center.

Cynthia said to the assembled analysts, "You're welcome very much, and in case anyone asks, that never happened."

The balance of Mohammed's debriefing proceeded quite smoothly.

When Joe later heard what Cynthia had done, he laughed his ass off and bought her a case of beer as a reward. "That's my Honey-Bunny," he thought to himself.

CHAPTER 49-VIENNA

"Goooooooaaaaall!!!" Olaf, a rabid soccer fan in his off hours, couldn't help but shout the victorious refrain when he finally reached the privacy of his office in the Vienna International Center, headquarters of the International Atomic Energy Agency. Having been in his job as Director of the Department of Safeguards for almost a decade, Olaf Henrikson knew better than just about anyone how stormy the IAEA's relationship with the CIA had been. The IAEA's Department of Safeguards could perform inspections of known or suspected nuclear facilities, and collect and analyze open-source material, but that was *all* it could do. It had neither the mandate nor the funding to conduct independent intelligence operations, which left the IAEA dependant on intelligence "donations" about suspect facilities. The CIA had provided many such tip-offs over the years. Some of the information had been good and some, like their information on Saddam's WMD, not so good.

This time, Olaf thought, the CIA truly *had* scored.

Olaf knew the ins and outs of nuclear inspections; after running Safeguards for so long, he could practically smell when a country was trying to hide something about their nuclear activities. Of course, suspicion did not equal proof, if it did, Olaf would have declared Iran guilty of concealing a nuclear weapons program years ago. Still, there is a consistent pattern of activity in countries that are above-board about their nuclear affairs. Vociferous protestations of lily-white innocence aside, the canny Swede knew that Iran had never matched that pattern, and had always treated the IAEA's inquiries into Iran's nuclear activities with open hostility. That attitude told Henrikson, better than any mere evidence could, that the Iranian government was definitely hiding something. What the IAEA had been lacking was the concrete proof.

Until today.

Henrikson had sat through plenty of briefings from the CIA, but none nearly so compelling as the one he had just left. Olaf reflected that it probably helped that instead of giving him reams of "finished intelligence," the standard US practice, the CIA had just quietly smuggled Mohammed Saeed and his video to Vienna, played Mohammed's tape for Olaf, and then let Olaf question Mohammed in person. Mohammed simply knew too much to be a fake.

As he heard the details of the Fajr Project, Olaf felt chagrined. Clearly, the Iranian government, having been caught red handed repeatedly by the IAEA, had designed Fajr in a way that took into account the methodology of the IAEA's nuclear detectives. As a result, all the sampling, measuring, filming, and nuclear materials accounting that the IAEA had done in the last few years had not managed to detect even a whiff of Fajr.

Olaf admitted to a grudging admiration at the cleverness of the deception measures, particularly building a large covert enrichment facility directly below the medium-sized centrifuge cascade the IAEA already knew about and monitored. The smaller cascade had provided the perfect cover for movement of people and materials to the covert Fajr Project. Iran had tunneled directly under the facility the IAEA was already watching to create a space for Fajr.

When Mohammed Saeed explained how his team had gone to extraordinary lengths to cleverly conceal the spoil from the tunneling and hide power-consumption tell-tales which would have raised questions about the size of the Qom facility, Olaf could only muse that no matter how high the resolution of US spy satellite photos, they could not tell the US the truth about Iran when all the photos could see was what Iran *intentionally* showed the US.

Until now, satellite photos of equipment and people heading into the mountains near Qom had been attributed to the known enrichment facility, not the covert Fajr Project.

Olaf admitted his ego stung a bit at how he and his inspectors had been tricked, but none of that really mattered now. *Now* the Safeguards inspectors knew where to look and what to look for. Olaf knew with those clues, his boys would have no trouble unearthing Iran's secret bomb program. How the UN dealt with the information Olaf would uncover was not Olaf's problem, but he suspected at the very least the sanctions that Iran had endured to date would be upgraded to something resembling a complete embargo on all commerce with Iran, something that might economically strangle the theocratic regime. Even China and Russia would finally be forced to join in the sanctions.

Now it was time for a new move in the IAEA's chess match with Iran. Ten minutes from now, Olaf would dispatch a team of Department of Safeguards inspectors to Vienna's Schwechat Airport to board a jet for Tehran. Not only had they provided the information from Mohammed, the CIA had helpfully chartered the jet for the IAEA, gratis. They wanted Olaf to move on this as fast as he could, and he was more than willing to play ball; it was payback time.

Before that jet touched down in Iran, Olaf would make one phone call. He was eager to contact the Supreme Leader's office and say a team of Safeguards inspectors was headed to Qom to, "Confirm compelling new information the IAEA had just received that suggested the existence of a heretofore unknown nuclear weapons program designated the 'Fajr Project.' "

He suspected that as soon as he made the call, the area around the Qom facility would resemble an anthill that had been poked with a stick. The US had already agreed to provide continuous satellite coverage of the region around Qom for the next 72 hours. Olaf looked forward to seeing satellite photos of frantic Iranian efforts to hide all traces of the Fajr Project. He knew that the Iranian government would try to fall back on their old tactics of delay and denial, but now that Olaf had a real "smoking gun" to find, any Iranian attempts to bury the truth would ultimately prove useless.

It was a good day to be a nuclear detective.

CHAPTER 50-ENDGAME

The Gulfstream V that Hamid Ansari had chartered sat on the apron astride the tarmac at Imam Khomeini airport, awaiting departure. Except for the hushed, low-pitch rumble of the onboard Auxiliary Power Unit, the luxury jet was quiet. Shortly after the aircraft had started to taxi towards the take-off queue, Ansari had asked the pilot to taxi back off the runway and shut down the main engines. He wanted the aircraft's cabin as close to silent as possible, as he had one last thing to do before leaving Iran. It was a pleasure rather than a duty, but one that required a degree of quiet for Ansari to fully savor. As soon as it was done, he would tell the pilot to light-up the engines again and depart immediately.

On the way to the airport, he had noticed Basij buses, attempting to deliver demonstrators into the heart of Tehran. The Basij, the hard-line conservative student militia controlled by the IRGC, regularly bused in demonstrators when the Supreme Leader wanted a televised show of public support for the regime. The demonstrations were composed of Basij members, and supplemented by bored men who were not in the Basij, but who would take part in any demonstration, simply because they were unemployed and had nothing better to do. Five Basij buses passed Ansari's jet-black Range Rover as he headed for the airport; all were almost empty, instead of having men packed in like sardines, as they normally would. That told Ansari that not only were the bored and unemployed staying away, most members of the Basij itself were no-shows.

This was undoubtedly due to the release of Javid Ziyaii's video tape three days ago. Ziyaii came across as very believable. The demonstrations in support of Iran had stopped across the Muslim world. The photos of the charred corpses of the Qods Force team sent to kill Ziyaii were particularly gruesome. There had even been a few calls for investigation into Iranian abuse of diplomatic status by sending abroad Qods Force assassins posing as diplomats.

After Ziyaii's story broke, General Jafari had predictably announced that he had discovered that Captain Rahimi and certain "counter-revolutionary elements" in the IRGC had contrived to sink the Shaheed with mines and mislead Iran into thinking the US had done it. He predictably scapegoated Captain Rahimi. The strategy had worked, at first. The grumbling in the Muslim world slowed. After all, believable as he seemed, Ziyaii was a common sailor. Competing conspiracy theories soon filled the airwaves.

Still, once Ziyaii's tape had aired, Ansari had known all the details of the plot against the Shaheed would eventually surface. Right from the beginning, Ansari had told General Jafari the biggest liability of his plan was that the Shaheed would be sitting on the bottom of the Gulf for decades, with mine holes plain for anyone to see. The General had given blithe assurances that nobody would be able to approach the wreck. Yet Saeed had, and then slipped away to *Khoda* knows where, taking his brother, who knew all Iran's nuclear secrets, with him. All under Jafari's nose. Ansari had known in his gut they had not seen the last of the Saeeds.

Then came the phone call from the IAEA yesterday about Fajr. It had only confirmed Ansari's instinct that the theocratic regime in Iran, no matter who retained control of it, was headed for disaster. It was time to go. As soon as the withering phone call with the IAEA had ended, Ansari had hung up his phone, then immediately picked it back up to dial the number of the exclusive Swiss charter service he favored.

After he boarded the plane, Ansari had clicked on the large plasma screen TV mounted on the Gulfstream's forward bulkhead. Although he had known something like this would happen, *especially* after getting the call from the IAEA, which strongly suggested the Saeeds had escaped cleanly, Ansari was still shocked to see the elusive Commander Saeed on CNN, saying, "This plot originated in the Supreme Leader's office. As you can see from this letter, Captain Akhlagi was suspicious. I can attest, as does this letter that the false sonar readings that suggested torpedoes attack came from software installed at the order of the Supreme Leader…"

Watching the *very* credible Commander Saeed, Ansari was horrified at first, then thought, "What did it matter?" In fact, it gave him an idea too delicious to resist. He ordered the pilot to stop taxiing to the takeoff queue and shut down the plane's engines for a few minutes while he made a call. Ansari withdrew his encrypted cellphone and speed-dialed General Jafari's number one last time.

The General answered gruffly, "What do *you* want, Ansari?"

With malice that was all the more apparent because of the gloating in Ansari's voice, he said, "My *dear* General, it seems your plan is unraveling! First Ziyaii, who I believe your idiot cousin assured us was a naïve fool, managed to best six of your Qods Force commandos as if they were retarded children, and then publicized the fact. Now I'm watching Commander Saeed on CNN, who is even more convincing than Ziyaii, explain how you and your cousin are implicated, how Rahimi was really nothing more than a scapegoat. What*ever* will you do, General?"

Ever since General Jafari had informed Ansari that Ansari's proxy authority had evaporated, Jafari had felt free to loose his temper on Ansari at any excuse. Ansari tolerated that until all his money was safe in Lichtenstein and the private charter of the Gulfstream had been arranged. Ansari needed endure the General's tantrums no more.

When the General responded to Ansari's taunting with an inarticulate cry of rage, Ansari laughed out loud, ended the call, and switched off the cell-phone. *Khoda*, that had felt good!

Ansari reached for the intercom switch. "Pilot, you may resume preparations for takeoff."

Now that he thought about it, he might just give CNN a call himself.

CHAPTER 51-HOLLOW STRENGTH

The Islamic Revolution, which had erupted in Iran with the vigor of a virulent plague thirty-four years ago, had finally run its course.

If the bitterly proud but confused old man staring out the cavernous window in astonishment had ever consented to see a psychiatrist, he would have received a diagnosis of paranoia and aggressive behavior arising out of senile dementia. Now the old man would never learn that his certainty that the Council of Guardians had been plotting against him arose only from his brain's growing inability to synthesize several key proteins. It had never had any basis in fact.

It was too late, now. Like King Lear, the Supreme Leader's position had long protected him from his own folly. Also like Lear, he had eventually made mistakes of such magnitude that even his lofty position could not protect him.

The sweet taste of victory after his elimination of the meddlesome Guardians had turned to ashes in his mouth as the truth about the Shaheed became known. Of course, even had he not suffered from the disease, even had the old man remained perfectly healthy, still he would not have seen this fate coming. The Leader had been out of touch with the average Iranian so long that he did not realize that the public had not been demonstrating *for* the Supreme Leader, they were demonstrating *against* the loss of the Shaheed. Thus he could not comprehend how quickly the tide of opinion would shift when Commander Saeed, and even more damning, his own chief aide, Ansari, confirmed Ziyaii's allegations as the truth.

The old-man's long-standing practice of habitual denial meant that when the rioting on the streets of Tehran started, he refused to acknowledge it. When IRGC and Basij members started deserting in droves, he continued to pretend all was well. When General Jafari was found shot to death by outraged members of his own security detail, *still* the old man maintained his illusions. And when, today, his own palace in Central Tehran had a ringing emptiness that said his staff had not come to work and never would, the Leader ignored that, too.

After all, smoking *Teryaak,* as opium is known in Iran, could make many unpleasant realities seem to vanish.

It was thus a genuine shock when he looked out his window to see rioters pouring over the walls of his vast compound. The Leader had once been an eloquent man, but dazed as he was from days of heavy opium use, all he could think of was the phrase, "I have been betrayed!"

The Leader was not given to introspection; the idea that *he* had long ago betrayed his country by letting it ferment into a morass of corruption and pernicious zealotry never crossed his mind. Nevertheless, he was soon to join the infamous ranks of leaders such as the Romanian Ceausescu and the Italian Mussolini, dictators who had met their fate at the hands of their own outraged citizens.

For the US and other nations, it was the information about the nuclear weapons program that mattered the most. To the average Iranian, though, such weapons were an abstraction. They majority were simply sick of a life of economic despair and rampant corruption. They didn't care about nuclear bombs or sanctions, but about the price of wheat and rice, gasoline, and joblessness. As the tattered promises of the Revolution had became ever more threadbare, the Iranian "Street" had become a pile of tinder awaiting a match. Then had come the loss of the Shaheed. Their barely-suppressed fury was redoubled and redirected by the damning testimony from Javid Ziyaii, Commander Saeed, and Hamid Ansari.

Their outrage would no longer be contained.

There had been no vote, no referendum, nothing that could be suppressed or subverted by the ruling power elites, just a common decision, reached by millions of minds at once: such a betrayal of loyal Iranian sailors could not be tolerated; anyone who would hatch such a plot could no longer be allowed to wield power in Iran.

The old man's regime had once seemed as solid as a mighty oak, but that tree had long since rotted from the inside out. The Supreme Leader was about to learn that it held now only a hollow strength, one doomed to fail in the first real storm.

EPILOGUE - 2016

Joe had long since forgotten about the money he spent getting the Saeeds out of Iran. He had never been paid back, and assumed he never would be. Out of petty spite, the then-Director of the CIA had refused to reimburse Joe for the money he spent on the Saeeds. Joe had begun to look on the non-payment as a badge of honor of sorts.

Having met the Saeeds, Claire could hardly blame Joe for that attitude. They were good people, and for less than a twentieth of what a single cruise missile cost, her husband, Cynthia, and the Saeeds had set in motion events that helped topple one of the worst dictatorships in modern history; unquestionably a bargain.

Joe's money was no good when he went out with Iranian friends, or Iran Task Force colleagues, and he was not above basking in their gratitude a little. So in the grand scheme of things, what did the money matter?

But still, she was sick of driving a dowdy Camry! And half the money Joe spent was *hers*. Joe was an "our lives, our fortunes, our sacred honor" kind of guy, and she was glad he was. That's one of the reasons she married him. But, for God's sake, that was *their money*.

When a new Director was appointed last year, Joe assumed the new Director would be just as much of a political hack as the old one had been.

Claire, on the other hand, was a very patient woman. Like Cynthia, she also knew how to bide her time.

When the new Director appointed Fred Sandler as Deputy Director of Operations, she redoubled her efforts to get that money back.

When a check finally arrived for $49,000, which was just about what Joe spent on the Saeeds, plus five percent interest per annum, Claire was not surprised; she had called in a whole passel of favors to make it happen.

But she did have to ask Joe to explain the note that Sandler had enclosed, which said, "Joe, I finally managed to break the 'fence' around my pot of money. Sorry it took so long, buddy."

*　　　*　　　*

Mohsen and Mohammed often dreamed of going back.

Yes, they were happy in their new lives, and very happy that the Ayatollahs had finally lost their grip on power. They had many Iranian friends in the US, and more material comforts than they had ever had in Iran.

Still, it was not the same, could never be the same. This was a great land, but *not* their homeland. Once a month they asked Mr. Joe, whose real name they knew now, when it might be safe for them to return. The old government had been swept away, after all.

Joe's reply was always the same: it will be safe to go back when you can ask someone from Iran who Commander Mohsen Saeed is, and they don't immediately know the answer. Joe warned them repeatedly that the hardliners that had been swept from power still hungered, however unjustly, for the blood of the Saeeds. One additional unspoken reason that Joe was against the idea was that Joe knew if Mohsen returned to Iran, the Commander would probably be able to find out what happened to the crew of the Ababeel; he asked Joe on a regular basis if he had learned anything about Saboori and the others. Joe did know what happened, and also knew if Mohsen found out the fate his men had met, Mohsen would be wracked with guilt. Best to spare him that.

Joe gently suggested the Saeeds simply accept there was a cost to be paid for freeing Iran: life in exile in America. And it was not a *bad* life, the Saeeds admitted.

(Update, Jan 2012: this afterword was originally penned in early 2008, many months before the disputed Iranian Presidential elections of 2009. Having looked it over in light of the turmoil of those elections, I'm pleased to say my predictions in both the afterword and the indirect predictions in the novel seem to be holding up so far. Part of the afterword was used in an article that ran in August 2010 on "Foreign Policy.com" entitled "It worked on Saddam, Why Patience, not Bombs, is the best way to deal with Iran's nuclear ambitions.")

Afterword

One nice thing about being a *former* intelligence officer is that I am no longer required to apply the rigid objectivity which can rob the written word of useful context. Now I can say what *I* believe and why I believe it.

To the many people in the foreign affairs arena who have legitimate worries about the spreading influence of Iran in the Middle East, the following declaration may sound insane.

Nevertheless, I stick by it: the Islamic Republic of Iran is *dying.*

Of course, the date of the final demise is unpredictable, but the likelihood of a collapse is a virtual certainty. My gut feeling is that it will occur well before 2030, probably before 2020.

The CIA took a lot of flak for failing to predict the fall of the Soviet Union. In hindsight, it's easy to see how that mistake was made. When Gorbachev started his attempts at reform and increased openness, the now famous *glasnost* and *perestroika*, there was no serious alternative to the Communist Party. The Party and the KGB still had their hands on all the levers of power. How, then, did it collapse so quickly that the CIA didn't see it coming?

What few in the West truly appreciated in the late 1980s was how profound the level of disaffection with the Soviet system was, *even within the ranks of the apparatchiks who were at the top of it*. It was *not* a yearning for democracy that destroyed the Soviet

Union, just a longing to get out from under the yoke of a failed economic and social system.

Of course, one of the key ingredients of Soviet disaffection was the disastrous Soviet invasion of Afghanistan in 1979, which led to almost 15,000 dead Soviet soldiers and over 50,000 casualties from injury or disease. The Soviet Union might have staggered on for another decade or two if Afghanistan had not accelerated and deepened the spread of discontent within the Soviet Union. Nevertheless, the invasion of Afghanistan only hastened the process. The inefficiency and brutality of the Soviet system were the seeds of its own demise, and they were growing fast throughout the Brezhnev era in the late 70s. The Afghan conflict was simply fertilizer.

The Soviet Union is not a perfect equivalent for Iran. Iran is not fighting a war (currently) and the Iranian version of an "apparatchik" professes loyalty to a hard-line Shia theology instead of socialist ideology. Despite those differences, Iran is rapidly moving towards the same set of preconditions that existed before the Soviet Union collapsed.

More than 70% of Iranians alive today were born after the 1979 Islamic Revolution. They have little or no stake in seeing the current regime propped up. As the Soviets did, the current regime in Iran strives to isolate Iran from Western influences, and even more than the Soviets, the Islamic Republic is failing miserably at this goal. Many, many Iranians have friends and relatives in the US and elsewhere. These ex-pats relate that Muslims, while they may face some discrimination, are not actively persecuted in the West, nor is Islam suppressed in the US, the UK, or most other Western countries. At the same time, economic, educational, and other opportunities for success are far greater in the West.

Meanwhile, the Iranian economy is in shambles, not least due to the spectacular incompetence of Iranian President Mahmood Ahmadi-Nejad, who has managed to auger the economy straight into the ground despite record oil prices to prop up Iran's budget.

As if the current state of the Iranian economy weren't bad enough, the Iranian government, especially the Council of Guardians (featured prominently in Hollow Strength) consistently blocks economic and political reform by blocking all reform candidates for the parliament, the Majlis, and voiding any reform legislation.

Hard-line Shia clerics in the Supreme Leader's faction appear to be so bent on maintaining control and beating back *any* notion of reform that they have put Iran unmistakably on the path of revolution camp (it is worth pointing out there are many senior Ayatollahs who oppose the Supreme Leader, but they have been vigorously marginalized by the Supreme Leader's faction).

Discontent with the conservative faction that backs the Supreme Leader is widespread and growing.

The internet is proving to be a river of information too wide and deep to be dammed. The Iranian blogosphere is extremely lively, both inside Iran and abroad. This inadvertent "fifth column" asks questions that the Islamic Republic cannot answer: Why should the average Iranian put up with the iron fisted rule of the Ayatollahs? What does such rule offer to the Shia faithful that they cannot get more and better of elsewhere? And what are they giving up to get such "purity" as the Islamic Republic claims to offer?

The Soviet Union of the 1960s was full of hope as Khrushchev swept into power and denounced the abuses of Stalin. Khrushchev even managed to initiate some (unsuccessful) reform policies. Yet less than 30 years after this hopeful era, the Soviet Union collapsed under the weight of pervasive disaffection and apathy at every rank in government.

By way of contrast, Iran's "reformers," like former President Khatami, do not have one single major change to their credit, successful or otherwise.

As the majority of Iranians born after the Islamic Revolution slowly move into "middle management" over the next two decades, that same rot of deep disaffection that destroyed the Soviet Union will spread with accelerating speed throughout the public and private sectors of Iran. Tight as the Ayatollah's grip on power may be, the one thing they cannot halt or even slow are the demographic trends that undermine the base of the Islamic Republic every minute of every hour of every day.

Eventually, a turning point will be reached. Perhaps a critical mass of opinion will allow reformers to finally force their way into the Iranian government. In my view, by the time that happens, there will be such ill will among the long-suffering reformers that a violent backlash against the Ayatollahs is highly likely. The Ayatollahs, having shown absolutely no willingness to compromise when they were in power, will probably be on the receiving end of violent retaliation.

The other possibility I foresee is the one described in "Hollow Strength": a continued slow, silent erosion of public support for the Islamic Republic, which will finally collapse after a precipitating incident triggers a popular uprising that neither the IRGC nor other Iranian military or security services will be willing to oppose. In Hollow Strength, the precipitating incident was an assassination plot involving the loss of a ship and the Council of Guardians. In real life, any similar confluence of events, i.e. news of major malfeasance by the rulers of Iran, could easily serve as such a trigger-point.

If the Islamic Republic is doomed to eventually fail as I contend, what is the US's role in hastening the end of that harsh regime?

Nothing. We should do *nothing*.

I'm minded of a saying attributed to Napoleon Bonaparte:

"Never interrupt your enemy when he is making a mistake."

The forces undermining the Islamic Republic are powerful. Despite the anti-US demonstrations that still periodically show up on western media outlets, the reality is that the majority of Iranians are now pro-US and anti-ruling-Ayatollah.

The one and only thing that will give the Ayatollahs' regime a shot in the arm is a major military attack from the US or other powers. In fact, as the Ayatollahs' grip continues to weaken, it is not unreasonable to fear that Iran's leadership may engage in provocative action *designed* to lure the US into conflict, solely to rally public support and shore up the theocratic regime. In my view, even such a conflict would not save the Islamic Republic, but it might let it stumble on for another decade longer than it otherwise might have.

Of course, when I say we should do nothing, I refer to the fact that the US should avoid a major armed intervention unless *absolutely* necessary. And what would meet that threshold? If Iran acquires "The Bomb", would that be sufficient reason?

No, it would not.

I fail to see why US policy towards Iran should be significantly different than US policy towards the Soviet Union during the Cold War. Did we start bombing the Soviet Union because they acquired nuclear capability in 1949? Even though the Soviets regularly released propaganda broadsides against the US? Even though Soviets gave arms and money to anti-US proxies around the world, including direct and indirect support for leftist terrorist organizations? Even though they posed a far greater direct military and ideological threat than Iran ever could?

No, we did not.

Are we doing that with North Korea? Even though the North Koreans have "The Bomb" and have often used anti-US rhetoric that is even harsher than the Soviets?

No, we are not.

Nuclear capability does not imply *intent to use* the capability. Nor, as history has shown, has harsh anti-US (or anti-Israeli) rhetoric or even support for terrorist organizations been a reliable guide to deciphering such intent.

Yes, *if* Iran develops a bomb, and yes, *if* the US's intelligence community develops iron-clad information that Iran intends to use the bomb, or put it in the hands of some group that intends to use it, then that would be sufficient grounds for armed intervention. As long as we remain (foolishly) dependant on oil from the Persian Gulf region, any concerted Iranian effort to strangle the flow of the black fluid that is the lifeblood of the US economy might under extreme circumstances provide sufficient grounds for military conflict.

Excepting such dire scenarios, we need to *keep our Tomahawks in our pants*!

When I was a case officer for the CIA's Counter-Proliferation Division, or CPD, I worked to prevent "countries of concern" from building or expanding their WMD capability. Based on past experience and what I have learned subsequent to my time with Uncle Sam, I firmly believe that, despite Iran's public claims to the contrary, the Islamic Republic intends to develop nuclear weapons, and their nuclear centrifuge capability is being developed towards that end.

That is most definitely NOT a good thing...but neither is it the end of the world.

Looking back on our sworn enemies from WWII, we now see both Japan and Germany with vast technical prowess and large stocks of enriched uranium or plutonium. Both countries could become nuclear-weapons powers almost overnight, should they desire to do so. Those stocks are of some concern, yet few people lose much sleep worrying about that, and for good reason. Enemies thought they might once have been, they now walk a different path, and employ nuclear technology for peaceful ends. The *technology* is not the problem; the problem is the ideology of those that control it. An astute observer of Asia might reasonably have some apprehension about Japan deciding to join the nuclear club. In my view, that would likely come to pass only as a defensive response if nuclear disarmament talks with North Korea fail utterly, and a serious prospect of conflict with either North Korea or China loomed on the horizon.

The US can and should work to put as many obstacles into the path or Iranian nuclear development as possible, but not because there is any long-term hope of success. The idea that such technology can be permanently dammed-up is wishful thinking. The US endgame vis-à-vis Iran should simply be to delay and degrade any capability Iran does develop until the Islamic Republic collapses and a government that can use nuclear technology responsibly replaces it.

With both the Soviet Union and North Korea, the US strove to implement a policy of "Containment," which is nothing more or less than a quiet stranglehold on the economy, access to sensitive technology, and the influence of those countries.

There is no reason why such a policy cannot hold Iran at bay until it collapses of its own weight. Distasteful as it may be to some, multilateral cooperation can keep Iran's influence largely in check and keep the poison the Supreme Leader's and his cronies spew largely bottled up in Iran.

And proof that such an approach can work?

Many now forget that before Iraq turned into a giant vacuum that sucked US troops and money for almost a decade, Iraq had been a multilateral **success** story.

Before the 2003 invasion, the CIA knew the sanctions that kept Iraq and Saddam "in a box" were deeply flawed: my CPD and WINPAC colleagues tracked smuggled shipments of dual-use goods into Iraq; these were goods with potential military or WMD uses, things Iraq was not supposed to have.

Based on past experience with Saddam hiding his WMD, the CIA assessed, not unreasonably, that the dual use goods were being used for clandestine WMD programs: nobody was willing to give Saddam the benefit of the doubt. The CIA was wrong about that, but few have noticed the positive implications of what the Iraq Survey Group (ISG) did NOT find in Iraq during the hunt for Saddam's non-existent WMD.

The ISG was the post-invasion group of intelligence officers and weapons inspectors assigned to "Find the WMD"; I served in the ISG on two separate occasions. Despite the smuggled shipments of dual-use goods, the ISG definitely established that Saddam had felt he was under tremendous pressure from the combination of the US sanctions, UN sanctions, and UN weapons inspectors.

That Saddam had "intent to reconstitute" his previous WMD programs is undeniable, but neither is the fact that when the US invaded Iraq in 2003, *Iraq had no active nuclear, biological, or chemical WMD programs, and had not had them for years.*

Our successful stranglehold on Saddam's WMD development was accomplished by multilateral cooperation with many US allies, by working through the UN, and also by a judicious mix of unilateral US actions behind the scenes, which included intelligence operations to track and block shipments of dual use goods, as well as other intelligence operations aimed at impairing the growth of any WMD program that Saddam managed to cobble together. Sadly, the success of such operations has now been overshadowed by the erroneous judgments on the National Intelligence Estimate on Iraq, an estimate which was stripped of cautionary caveats in public debate, and then used to bludgeon US public opinion into supporting an attack on Saddam.

"Containment" worked on the Soviet Union, and it worked on Iraq...until the US blew it. It will work on Iran, assuming we are not so impatient to see the last of the Islamic Republic that we shoot ourselves in the foot by an armed intervention.

The most important thing the US can do to "put paid" to the rule of the Ayatollahs in Iran is to prepare for the day when the Ayatollahs are swept away by popular uprising, and be prepared to offer massive and immediate support for the establishment of a society that follows true democratic norms, even if some moderate elements of Islamic Sharia law are incorporated into Iranian institutions, as will likely be the case in a country that has been a theocracy for decades.

In fairness, I should say there was one other major mistake we made with Iraq, and one we must avoid replicating with Iran. While the US cranked the sanctions as tight as possible on Iraq and used our political leverage to get others to do the same, we overstepped in tightening them so indiscriminately that the greatest sufferers from the sanctions were not die-hard supporters of Saddam's regime, but rather the average Iraqi, with the upshot being tens of thousands of deaths of Iraqi children due to malnutrition and starvation.

In the case of Iran, I advocate that the US's Office of Foreign Asset Control, which administers US sanctions, undertake continual reviews and adjustments to insure we do not trigger the same sort of humanitarian crisis which sanctions contributed to in Iraq. At the same time, we cannot back off, but rather must continue to strive for finely tuned sanctions aimed at specific senior officials (and their bank accounts and assets) to insure that regime hardliners in the executive branch, the IRGC, the Guardian Council, the Majlis, and the Bonyads unmistakably feel the pinch.

In addition to looking back on the opening decade of the new millennium as a time when US policy became mired in Iraq, I have no doubt that history will one day judge the US harshly for letting Russia slip back into totalitarianism masquerading under an ever-thinner façade of democracy. US defense and intelligence resources have been so wrapped up in Iraq and other fronts in the "Global War on Terror" that the gains of 50+ years of the Cold War evaporated before our very eyes. While it is not certain that the US could have blocked the ascendancy of Vladimir Putin and his "forward to the past" policies that is turning Russia into a virtual dictatorship, one thing *is* certain: we barely tried, and one day will certainly pay the cost for that lapse.

History will doubly condemn the US if, through similar negligent inattention, the coming collapse of the Islamic Republic is not used as an opportunity to insure that the hard-line Ayatollahs, when they finally lose their grip on power, do not regain it.

Separating Truth from Fiction in Hollow Strength

Hollow Strength is a work of fiction, but like most "historical" fiction, it relies on large elements of truth to tell the tale. What is true? I strove to make as many of the details about Iran and Iranian society as true as I could.

There *is* a fierce rivalry for funding and manpower between the regular Iranian military, and the military forces of the Iranian Revolutionary Guard Corps.

There *are* persistent rumors that many senior Ayatollahs in Iran, to include the current Supreme Leader, use opium.

As of the writing of this book, Mohammed Ali Jafari was the Commanding General of the Iranian Revolutionary Guard Corps.

The two plane crashes I attributed to Jafari, one in 2006, another in 2007, did indeed take place, wiping out many senior IRGC officers. There have been persistent rumors that the plane crashes were the result of deliberate sabotage, not shoddy maintenance. I have no idea if the real General Jafari was really involved, but based on what my Iranian friends have told me of the man, it would not surprise me in the least.

Gholam Reza Aghazadeh is no longer head of the AEOI; he was replaced by Ali Akbar Salehi, who was in turn replaced by Fereydoon Abbasi-Davani in 2011. But Aghazadeh is the "devil I know," so I used him instead of the current head. The current head of the AEOI, Abbasi-Davani, has in fact been accused of personally participating in Iran's nuclear weapons programs, and he was reportedly the target of an assassination attempt in 2010. I do not know whether Mohammed Saeedi is still a deputy at the AEOI, but he was during Aghazadeh's tenure.

Admiral Sayyari is a real Iranian Admiral, but he probably doesn't have a nephew quite as stupid as the Qeshm police constable in the novel.

Bandar Abbas is the main naval and shipbuilding center for Iran. Iran does have a destroyer called the Jamaran, which was launched in 2007.

My Uncle Napoleon is a charming and whimsical novel about life in pre-Revolutionary Iran. It was so popular in Iran it became a sitcom....before being banned by the Ayatollahs. I highly recommend the book.

Sadly, a female Canadian photojournalist really was taken into Iranian custody in 2003 for taking photos of Evin prison. She died in custody and coroners subsequently found evidence of torture and rape. CIA officer William Buckley really was captured by Hezbollah in Lebanon; whether he endured torture in captivity in Evin prison remains a question of debate.

As of 2007, publicly available satellite imagery spotted tunneling in the mountains near Qom. In late 2009 the US accused Iran of building a covert enrichment facility there, which Iran subsequently confirmed. My novel is based on the premise that this known facility provides cover for the construction of a larger, covert facility unknown to the CIA or the IAEA.

Iran has developed and is working to deploy the IR-2 centrifuges referred to in the novel, as well as centrifuges even more advanced. One the main limiting factors so far has been Iran's inability to acquire the necessary parts and raw materials from foreign suppliers, and a lack of a supply of uranium to enrich that is not under the watchful eye of the IAEA's Department of Safeguards.

The Bonyad Mostazafan exists. It does **some** charitable work, but also runs hundreds of businesses and has been linked to nuclear smuggling, arms purchases, and a variety of other shady deals. As an economic entity within Iran, the Bonyad Mostazafan's revenues are second only to the Iranian Government's, and the government revenues are only larger because of oil income. A chunk of the Bonyad's profits do indeed serve as a giant slush fund for the Iranian Supreme Leader. The Bonyad wields enormous influence in Iran. I believe the US should devote far more resources to tracking the Bonyad's activity than it currently does.

As far as my (imperfect) research has been able to determine, the USS Kidd does not currently mount either the Phalanx or the Sea Ram anti-missile systems, although other Arleigh-Burke class destroyers do. But I happen to think those systems are pretty cool, so I put them on the Kidd. I have no idea if a Phalanx can actually depress sufficiently to engage small surface targets or if has ever been used manually for that purpose. The story about the US getting destroyers on the cheap after the 1979 revolution in Iran, the previous USS Kidd among them, is true, as was their nickname in the US Navy, "The Ayatollah's Gifts."

I did take one major liberty: as currently constituted; only six of members of the Council of Guardians are Ayatollahs, or senior Shia clerics. The other six are "jurists" of some sort. In the story I stated that all 12 were Ayatollahs.

Central to Hollow Strength is the point that political pressure was applied to the CIA to suppress information that was politically unpalatable. Do such things happen?

Sadly, in my experience, they do. I saw this first hand in CIA's Hqs reaction to information from a source that suggested Saddam had given up his WMD. This was a source with very high credibility, no reason to lie, and compelling reasons to be truthful. His information had always proved extremely accurate...yet when he supplied information suggesting the "aluminum tubes" Iraq had bought were not for nuclear centrifuge rotors, but rather for simple rockets, the source's credibility was called into question by CIA Hqs. (Turns out the tubes *were* for rockets, by the way.)

On a larger and more compelling scale, I note that the Economist reported that six analysts from the Directorate of Intelligence complained to the CIA Ombudsman that they felt they were being pressured by the Bush Administration to manipulate the intelligence on Iraq and Al-Qaeda to reach the conclusions the Administration wanted to hear. The Republic-controlled Senate Select Committee for Intelligence investigated these complaints, and found, to the surprise of few, that no undue influence was used, despite Vice President Cheney's regular and unprecedented trips to the CIA to "review the intelligence" with the analysts.

Cheney's trips were akin to an Army general looking over the shoulder of a company commander and asking the lowly captain, again, and again, and again, "Hey Captain...are you *sure* you want to do *this*?" The fact that no direct order to change the intelligence was given does not mean repeated questioning by a general would carry less weight, or that it would not get the General's point about what he wanted to hear across. Subtle and artfully applied pressure is still pressure.

In 2004, the then-head of the CIA's Weapons Intelligence, Arms Control Center (WINPAC) within the Directorate of Intelligence visited the CIA Station where I was posted to brief CIA officers who worked on WMD proliferation issues. After the briefing, I lingered in the room and got a chance to pose a question to the WINPAC chief directly. I asked him point-blank if his analysts felt the Bush Administration had pressured them to say what the Administration wanted to hear on Iraq's WMD. With no hesitation, the man said unambiguously, "Yes, they felt they were being pressured, and they reported it. In my opinion, they were definitely being pressured."

Lacking the subtlety of the pressure from the Vice President were the legendary temper tantrums of Administration official John Bolton. After a less-than-distinguished stint at the State Department, Bolton was appointed *acting* US Ambassador to the UN. Why only an *acting* appointment? A permanent appointment was blocked when his shenanigans as Undersecretary of State for Arms Control came to light in confirmation hearings. Bolton had tried to fire the chief bioweapons analyst in the State Department's Bureau of Intelligence and Research. The analyst's crime? He refused to reach the conclusions on Cuba's WMD that Bolton wanted to hear, for the simple reason that there was no real evidence to suggest that Cuba had an active bioweapons program.

Bolton's defense for this gross abuse of his authority boiled down to, "Well, I wasn't *successful* in getting the guy fired, so the fact that I abused my authority in making the attempt doesn't matter, right?" Bolton also pushed to have false information on Iraq's alleged purchase of uranium from Niger, claims which the CIA did not substantiate and had repeatedly warned the Bush Administration not to use, included in President Bush's 2003 State of the Union address. The CIA was later blamed for failing to keep this statement out of the speech, despite repeated attempts to block the Niger information from appearing in *any* speech by any Administration official.

I know more about the Bush Administration's failings because that Bush administration was in power during the majority of my time I served at the CIA. Lest the reader think that attempting to manipulate intelligence and ignore things you don't want to hear is strictly a Republican failing, I have to say it was probably during my very first week of employment at the CIA when an old hand in "Russia House" related a tale that shows such manipulations are not the sole province of any particular party.

During the Clinton Administration, the CIA delivered to Vice President Al Gore an intelligence report which related that a senior Russian official that Gore had met with repeatedly was lying to Gore on important issues.

Gore scrawled "Bullshit" on the report and sent it back to CIA.

Apparently the information on the lying official was one "Inconvenient Truth" that Gore was quite comfortable ignoring. History does not relate the former Vice President's reaction when events subsequently proved the CIA right on the matter, but I can say that to my knowledge, no apologies from Gore have been forthcoming to date.

About the Author

Art Keller is a former CIA case officer and freelance writer on intelligence and national security issues. He has been published in the New York Times, the Washington Post, The New York Daily News, Foreign Policy.com and The Sentinel, The Journal of the Army's Combating Terrorism Center. He lives in New Mexico, where he also owns and operates Keller Investigations.

11575273R00231

Made in the USA
Charleston, SC
06 March 2012